Praise  Delaney

MURDER BY SYLLABUB

"Ellen McKenzie is back to solve another mystery in *Murder By Syllabub*. This time she helps her Aunt Mary tackle a problem with a ghost in Colonial dress at an old plantation house in Virginia. The house belongs to Aunt Mary's friend, Mildred. They find the ghost may have been very much alive at one point, but it is now dead, thanks to a poisoned batch of syllabub Mildred made. Ellen doesn't like the sound of that and sets out to find the truth. Ellen is a sheer delight to read! I've enjoyed all five of author Kathleen Delaney's McKenzie mysteries, and look forward to many more!"
—Joyce Lavene, author, along with her husband Jim, of over 50 books

MURDER HALF-BAKED

5 Lips: "If you like cozy mysteries at all, you'll love this story; I know I did."
– Rose, Two Lips Reviews

4.5 out of 5 stars: "I love a good murder mystery and this one seems to have all the right ingredients .... *Murder Half-Baked* is a cracking good mystery, which you won't guess before it is time."
– Patrizia Murray, Manic Readers

"*Murder Half Baked* is an exciting and fun mystery that will keep the pages turning."
–Small Press Bookwatch/Midwest Book Review

"At the center of *Murder Half Baked*, itself a delightful mix of humor (wedding plans going astray) and crime (murder and arson), are Ellen and Dan, two people who seem ideally suited for each other and really make this mystery so enjoyable. The Grace House women, who are all suspects in the fire that burned down their residence, are a diverse group of characters, and interesting in their own way. Despite all the diversions that are presented to Ellen and Dan (and, by extension, to the reader), the storyline is easy to follow making this overall a fast, entertaining read."
—Mysterious Reviews

"From the first sentence to the last paragraph, I could not put this book down. This page-turning mystery kept my attention as the story played out with many of the pieces coming together in a surprising twist. With strong characters, great conversations and intriguing storylines, this is the best one yet in this charming series."
—Dru's Book Musings

"A fascinating mix of a harried woman trying to carry on with her business affairs, plan for a wedding with too much help from others, and assist her fiancé in solving a crime which may well involve someone Ellen knows. Delaney has a flair for turning mundane matters into intriguing background for a murder mystery."
–John A. Broussard, I Love a Mystery

AND MURDER FOR DESSERT

"Harvest Festival Dinner at the Silver Springs Winery

sounds ideal, and it is—until master chef Otto turns up dead before the sumptuous final course in Delaney's auspicious first outing in California wine country. Real estate broker Ellen McKenzie and her fiancé, chief of police Dan Dunham, are soon embroiled in the case. Ellen's niece Sabrina and Sabrina's new husband, Mark Tortelli, were counting on this splashy event to solidify their reputation as new managers of Silver Springs—especially since there's some question as to why they left their last job. The legendarily cantankerous Otto had numerous fans but even more foes, including Mark's father. Feuding shareholders and real estate developers further threaten the winery's tranquility, and Ellen must sift through all the drama to find the killer, while planning her wedding and solving family problems. Delaney's choice of setting, gossipy milieu and colorful (if somewhat predictable) suspects help to keep Ellen scrambling and move the action right along."
–Publishers Weekly

"Spotting the killer is easy, but congenial characters make Delaney's debut an enjoyable addition to the cozy scene."
– Kirkus Reviews

MURDER
BY
SYLLABUB

MURDER
BY
SYLLABUB

An Ellen McKenzie Mystery

KATHLEEN DELANEY

PRESS

Seattle, WA

CAMEL PRESS

Camel Press
PO Box 70515
Seattle, WA 98127

For more information go to: www.camelpress.com
delaney.camelpress.com

Cover design by Sabrina Sun
Cover Photo by Nancy Johnson

Murder by Syllabub
Copyright © 2013 by Kathleen Delaney

ISBN: 978-1-60381-957-2 (Trade Paper)
ISBN: 978-1-60381-958-9 (eBook)

Library of Congress Control Number: 2013940693

Printed in the United States of America

Acknowledgments

WHEN I GOT the idea for this book, I wasn't sure where to look for the information I knew I needed. I'd been to Colonial Williamsburg several times, so I called the general information number. The wonderful people on the other line made arrangements for me to meet with people in the kitchens, who told me about hearth cooking, and people in the barns, who told me about their rare breed program, and they all answered my many questions with patience and humor.

I'm not sure this book would have been written even then if it hadn't been for my wonderful agent, Dawn Dowdle, who keeps nudging me forward all the while with red pen in hand, never allowing a manuscript to get past her until it's as perfect as we can make it. Catherine Treadgold, my wonderful editor at Camel Press, takes it from there. With tact and grace, she points out the parts that don't make sense, where I get carried away with my own verbosity (like right now) and gets me back on track. It is a privilege to work with such talented and kind women.

And then there is my brother, and my first reader. He spends hours with me on the phone, discussing the plot, telling me what doesn't work, and in the end, telling me that whatever we are discussing and pruning is the best thing I've written to date.

Thank you, all.

For Mike and Mary, who were with me when
the idea for this book was born.

Chapter One

I WAS RUNNING late. Wednesday morning was our weekly real estate office meeting and attendance was required. And we were expected to be on time. So, of course, it was this morning my alarm decided not to function.

I stood at the sink, swallowing coffee and stuffing papers into my briefcase. My devoted husband Dan Dunham, chief of police of our little Central California town of Santa Louisa, sat at the kitchen table calmly spooning cornflakes into his mouth, watching me.

"I like that dress. It's the same one you wore the day you came back to town, isn't it?"

I nodded, put my cup in the sink and smiled. "You remembered."

Dan smiled back. The smile I loved so well was framed by a neatly trimmed salt and pepper mustache, and his blue eyes were sparkling. "I'm a policeman. I'm trained to notice things."

Maybe so, but the way he looked at me had nothing to do with police work. It was the reason I was drinking coffee with no cream or sugar—one of them, anyway. I counted calories for both of us. Once you left forty behind, pounds seemed to accumulate overnight. I wanted Dan to keep looking at me just as he was doing now. I wanted to enjoy my view of him as well. Which wasn't hard. Tall, light brown hair dusted with just enough gray to make him look distinguished, short, straight nose and a mouth made for smiling; he was a sight to make any woman smile back. Especially in his navy blue boxers.

I thought, briefly, of the difference between him and my not in the least lamented ex-husband, Dr. Brian McKenzie. Brian would never have remembered a dress I wore unless he had been complimented on his wife's good taste. Then he would have assured the compliment giver that he'd picked it out, implying I didn't have much taste. His idea of a compliment was to tell me the gray in my dark brown hair didn't show. Much. Or that the pants I thought fell so nicely over my still size ten hips bunched a bit around the waist and had I thought about going on a diet. I'd wondered, more than once, what he said to his many little "friends."

I snapped my briefcase shut, put my cup in the sink and, car keys in hand, started for the door.

"Oh, Susannah called," Dan said, maddeningly calm.

I skidded to a stop. "Is she all right?"

Susannah, my daughter from my first marriage, had decided to follow me up north and was now going to college only a couple of hours from our small town. I was, of course, delighted. I was even more delighted when she and Dan became good friends, but I worried. She was a grown woman—I knew that—but somehow, to me, she was still the little girl who had needed a lot of mothering. That she'd matured into a beautiful and self-sufficient woman was hard to accept. However, I felt blessed by her easy acceptance of her, and my, new life. Her father, who despised small towns and sneered at those who lived in them, seemed surprised she would choose to live in such a backwater instead of Newport Beach, in the huge house he still kept there, but if he was disappointed he got over it quickly. Or perhaps he didn't want her around when he brought home those little "friends."

Life here suited me fine. I'd grown up in this town with Dan next door. After high school we'd gone different directions— me to UCLA, where I met Brian, and Dan up north, where he became a policeman. Now we were both back, living in the house where I grew up and loving it. Susannah seemed equally happy with the arrangement, coming home frequently. I would have loved to think it was because she missed me but my washing machine and her boyfriend, Neil Bennington, were probably the main attractions. I didn't care what her reasons were, as long as she kept coming back.

"Is she visiting this weekend?"

"No. Midterm exams are starting and she won't be back up for a couple of weeks," Dan said. He put down his spoon and grinned. "Oh, I almost forgot. Could you put some money in her account? Seems she needs supplies." The grin got broader.

"I'll call her after my meeting," I said. Before I could exit, the door opened and my Aunt Mary burst in. She is one of my mother's four sisters, and the only one still residing in Santa Louisa. I'd practically lived at her house growing up and since I moved back to Santa Louisa, we'd grown even closer. She is a ball of energy for a woman in her seventies even if she is growing rounder every year thanks to her love of cooking.

"You'll never believe what happened," she said, breathless and holding onto the kitchen island for support.

I was too surprised to answer. I couldn't help but notice that Aunt Mary's white hair stuck out in little tufts as if she'd just climbed out of bed. Maybe she had. Those had to be pajama bottoms that hung below the cuffs of her sweatpants and the collar that curled crookedly over the top of her lipstick-red sweatshirt was surely her PJ top. Her feet were encased in lamb's wool lined moccasins and she wasn't wearing socks. My aunt Mary came up with some pretty bizarre outfits sometimes, but she'd never appeared with uncombed hair and in her nightclothes before. At least, I didn't think she had.

Dan also dropped his newspaper and stared, but he managed to recover more quickly than I did. Probably his police training. "What's happened? Is anyone hurt?"

"Not yet." She walked over to the hutch, took down a coffee mug and proceeded to fill it, leaving Dan and me to stare at each other. She pointed at the coffeemaker. "You'll need to make another pot, Ellen," she said.

She carried her mug over to the table, pulled out a chair and sank into it. "I'm going to Virginia."

Briefcase and office meeting forgotten, I carried my cup over to the table and took my regular seat, opposite Dan. "Say what?" Aunt Mary never went anywhere.

"My friend, Elizabeth Smithwood, is in some kind of trouble and I'm going to Virginia to help her."

Dan blinked then almost smiled. "In your pajamas?"

"Of course not. Whatever gave you—oh." She glanced at the cuff of her pajama top, which had slipped out from under her sweatshirt arm, but ignored it. "Elizabeth is going to send me an airplane ticket and wants my email address. I don't have one, but you do, don't you?"

Of course she didn't have an email address. She didn't have a computer. "Yes. We both do. But before I give it to you, will you please tell me what's going on?"

She poured cream into her coffee then ladled in sugar, taking her time as she stirred. It looked as if she was trying to figure out how to frame what she was about to tell us. "You remember my friend, Elizabeth, don't you? My old college roommate?"

Dan shook his head.

I did. I'd never actually met Elizabeth but had grown up on stories about her. Elizabeth, the activist. She'd gone on to get her PhD after she and Aunt Mary graduated. Aunt Mary came home to teach Home Economics in our local middle school and marry my uncle Samuel, a pillar of the community and president of Rotary Club. Elizabeth had gotten a job teaching history in a small college in Wisconsin and spent her summers saving old-growth redwoods, painting baby seals green so they couldn't be slaughtered for their pelts and registering voters in the south during the civil rights movement. Aunt Mary and Uncle Samuel had bailed her out of jail for that one. She'd lived with William Smithwood, a mathematics professor at the same college, for years without benefit of holy matrimony. Until last Christmas. They'd been married only a couple of weeks when he died, leaving her an old plantation in Virginia. What kind of trouble could she have gotten herself into now? I was pretty sure I was about to find out.

"Elizabeth says strange things have been happening at Smithwood ever since William died and now she thinks she has a ghost. He appears in Colonial dress, and last night he tried to kill her."

Dan's coffee cup hit the saucer but my eyes were glued on Aunt Mary.

Had I heard correctly? "Say again? A ghost? A colonial ghost? Where? What happened to make her think he-it tried to kill her?"

"He pushed a crate over and it just missed her."

"A crate. What crate? How could a ghost push a crate?"

I gave Dan my most disdainful look. There was no ghost. I had no idea what Elizabeth saw, but it wasn't a ghost. "Where was she when this happened?"

"I'm not sure. She wasn't very clear. She sounded scared, though. She said she needs someone she can trust and who has a clear head. So, I'm going."

I looked at the determined set of her chin and the steel in her eyes and knew there was no arguing. I turned toward Dan and raised my eyebrows.

He sighed. "Mary, I don't know what's going on out there, but it doesn't sound good. As a matter of fact, it sounds bizarre. Exactly what does Elizabeth want you to do? Capture a prowler? That's most likely who it is. Why doesn't she call the police?

They're a whole lot better equipped to handle something like this than two ladies in their seventies."

"I don't know. I only know she's scared and that's not one bit like Elizabeth. I couldn't go help her when William died, but I can go now, and I will. Now, can I have that email address?"

Aunt Mary had missed William's funeral because she was helping with Dan's and my wedding. We're both on our second marriages. His ended because his wife and two-year-old son were killed by a drunk driver, and mine, because my ex wanted different things from life, and at some point I had stopped being one of them. Dan and I saw eye to eye, and it was wonderful to be appreciated again. Guilt sat on my shoulders. I had no reason to heed it. After all, it wasn't my fault William had died right before my wedding day, but I knew that made her doubly determined to help Elizabeth now.

What should I do? Go with her, of course.

"You're not going out there alone."

She gave me a scornful look. "I don't need a babysitter, you know. I can take care of myself just fine."

"You never go anywhere. Suddenly you want to fly from California to Virginia all by yourself, changing planes I don't know how many times, so you can help your friend chase a ghost, who's probably a common burglar, out of her house? The whole thing is idiotic, but if you're determined, well, I'll go too."

"You'll do no such thing. You have a real estate business to run, a husband and a daughter to take care of and a cat to feed. You can't come."

I opened my mouth to say something, but Dan got there first. "Mary, Susannah is at the university studying for finals. At least, we hope she's studying. I managed to eat just fine before Ellen and I got married and the cat doesn't care who opens the cat food as long as it gets in his dish. As for the real estate, let's ask Ellen." He looked at me expectantly.

"I took care of Donna's business last summer while they went to Hawaii. She owes me. Besides, we won't be gone too long. I don't know what your friend saw, but it shouldn't take long to straighten it all out. You two can have a nice visit while I—" the look on her face said I'd better change pronouns and fast—"*we* work it all out. We'll be back here before you know it."

She gave a loud "humph," but I thought there was a little relief in her eyes.

"I'll email Elizabeth right now and we'll see what travel arrangements she had in mind."

"Better call the airlines yourself." Dan picked up his paper then put it right back down. "I'm not sure I like this. Maybe I'd better come along. It's not a good time, though. I'm hosting the California Sheriffs' conference next week. I could get Kent Walker from Sonoma County to sit in."

"No," Aunt Mary and I said in unison.

"I'm sure this will prove to be nothing, and you've been planning this conference for months." I smiled.

Aunt Mary didn't look so sure. "Elizabeth doesn't panic, but I can't imagine a ghost prowling around her hallways, and I've never heard of one tipping over crates. Ellen's right. It's bound to be someone playing a silly prank. We'll get it all cleared up in no time."

"Hmmm. All right, but if this turns out to be anything serious, I'll be on the next plane."

I got up, took the slip of paper she handed me with Elizabeth's email address and headed for the computer. "Let's see what she has in mind."

"She wants me to come Saturday."

"Saturday?" I wheeled around to stare at her.

"Saturday!" Dan almost spat out the word. "What's the damn rush?"

"She doesn't want to be there alone if the ghost comes back."

I thought Dan was going to fall out of his chair. "This is the most ridiculous ... Ellen, you tell her to call her local police right now."

Chapter Two

THE AIRPORT WAS small, even smaller than San Luis Obispo's, and filled with people, almost all in uniform. They seemed cheerful enough as they crowded around the luggage carousel. More cheerful than I felt. We'd caught the first flight out of San Luis Obispo, waited in L.A. an hour for our next flight to Philadelphia and almost missed our connection to Newport News. A light flashed and the conveyor belt started to move. Luggage came out of a chute and fell onto the moving belt. My eyes were glued on it. We'd made our connection. I wasn't sure our luggage had.

Aunt Mary paid no attention. She kept looking around the terminal. "Elizabeth's not here." She tugged at the hem of her cranberry wool jacket, trying to pull it down farther over her best—actually her only—pair of gray pants. She'd bought that jacket at St. Mark's fall rummage sale, definitely one of her better buys. She'd called me up after the event, riddled with guilt because as the organizer, she felt she shouldn't buy anything until the very end, after all the best items were gone. But the jacket was to her liking, her size and only two dollars. Did I think she should put it back for the next rummage sale?

No. So, she kept it and it looked nice.

"What if something happened and Elizabeth doesn't come? What will we do?"

Never forgive her. I wasn't about to say that aloud. "You have her cell number. We'll call if she doesn't appear soon. Is that your suitcase?"

Her suitcase came sliding down the chute, much to my relief. I'd advised her to tie a ribbon to the handle so she could find it easily. She had followed my suggestion, choosing a bright blue plaid ribbon. Before I could get there, she leaned forward and grabbed it, heaving it up and stepping backward. I could only watch as her heel landed on someone's foot.

"Oh. I'm so sorry." She turned to look into the face of the silent man who had sat beside her from Los Angeles to Philadelphia.

"No problem." He winced a little and stared down at the toe of his once immaculate black loafer. "That your bag?"

She nodded. He took hold of it and set it upright, facing away from him. "You might want to get a cart."

She looked over at me, a little lost. "It has those little wheels."

He nodded and looked toward me as well. "Yes. Are you with someone or is someone meeting you?"

Was he afraid he'd get stuck with the old girl? I started toward her but my own case slid down the ramp and I hurried forward to grab it. I turned just in time to catch her reply.

"My friend, Elizabeth Smithwood. I don't see her, but I'm sure she'll be here soon." She took another look around the terminal, which was emptying rapidly.

"Smithwood?" For a moment his expression lost its neutrality, but not long enough to be read. What had I seen, surprise, annoyance? Impatience, definitely.

"Yes. Do you know her?"

The man's eyes darted around the terminal then settled back on Aunt Mary. "I hope you enjoy your stay," he said. Suitcase trailing behind him, he headed for the terminal door, paused and headed for a side door. A sign above it proclaimed, "Rental Cars."

"Friendly sort." I parked my suitcase next to hers and gave the place a once-over. I was beginning to feel concerned. The terminal was almost empty. The fading light said it was getting late and so did my growling stomach. What would we do if Elizabeth didn't show up?

A tall, angular-looking woman rushed into the building, clutching a straw hat onto her head. A long gray braid hung down her back and a full denim skirt swirled around her legs, which were covered with bright red stockings. Her face had a sculptured look—high cheekbones, straight, strong nose, large gray eyes that seemed to take in the whole room, and a very determined chin. Elizabeth.

She came toward Aunt Mary at a gallop. "Mary."

Aunt Mary beamed. "We made it." She gave Elizabeth a hug then held her at arm's length. "You look great."

She didn't look great to me. Elizabeth was too thin. There were bruise-like smudges under her eyes and hollows under her cheekbones. The rigidity in the way she held herself screamed tension. Elizabeth smiled at Aunt Mary, though, and shook her head slightly. "If it was only so." She enveloped her in another hug, almost lifting her off her feet. "Oh, I'm so glad you're here. Both of you." She turned to me and grinned. "Did you have a good trip? Where's your luggage? Is that it? You didn't bring much. Oh, well. We can always go shopping."

"We can also wash," Aunt Mary said. "I assume you have a washing machine?"

Elizabeth nodded and laughed. "Mary, you never change. Of course I do, but if my sister-in-law has anything to say about it, you'll go shopping. Come on. The car's right outside so we won't have to walk. No. I'll get that."

Elizabeth, towing Aunt Mary by one arm and her suitcase by the other, headed for the terminal door. I trailed behind. A silver blue Toyota Prius waited in the loading zone.

A tall black man in a police uniform stood beside it. "Miss Elizabeth, if you don't quit parking like this, you're going to get a ticket." His voice had the soft accents of a native Virginian.

"I know, Noah, but I was late and I had to rush. What are you doing here anyway?" Pulling open the back door, she shoved Mary forward and added, "This is Mary McGill, my oldest friend. We went to college together." She picked up Mary's suitcase and tried to shove it through the opening. "This is her niece, Ellen McKenzie. Dunham. I almost forgot. She got married right about the time William died." She gestured at me as her introduction ground to a halt.

Noah sighed. "I know. Get in and pop the trunk."

Aunt Mary and I were equally surprised when Elizabeth meekly did as she was told.

Noah took Aunt Mary's suitcase, then mine, and heaved them in. He reached for my carry-on bag. "You want this in here or in the backseat?"

"Back there is fine." Who was this man who was obviously so well acquainted with Elizabeth and shouldn't—if his uniform was any clue—be handling luggage. He shouldn't even be here, in Newport News. His arm patch clearly read "Williamsburg Police Department" and the stripes, "sergeant."

He held out his hand to Aunt Mary who, though confused, extended hers. He took it and helped her into the car. "Glad you're here safe and sound. Ever since she heard you were coming, Miss Elizabeth has been fretting something would happen to you. Only thing that got her through was knowing you'd be with her." He grinned at me and opened the back door. I climbed in. He smiled, closed my door and poked his head in Aunt Mary's open window. "Fasten your seat belts, all of you, and get out of here. Chief Brewley's coming in on the next plane and I've got to meet him."

"Thanks, Noah," Elizabeth called out. "See you at home later. Tell your mama to come by. I've made syllabub."

She pulled out into traffic, barely missing a hotel bus. Tires screeched and a horn blasted. I looked back. Noah stood on the curb, hands on hips, watching us drive away.

Chapter Three

ELIZABETH DROVE DOWN a dark country road, nervously peering over the steering wheel. She talked almost nonstop during the drive, providing a somewhat abbreviated history of the last few months—William's and her retirement from the college, their return to Smithwood, William's stroke and their hasty marriage right before his death. None of this was news to Aunt Mary and little of it to me. It was the mysterious and frightening events that had prompted Elizabeth's plea for help we wanted to know about.

"I saw him a couple of days before I called. It must have been after midnight, not too long after I'd put down my book and turned off the light. The dog started to growl so I got up to investigate. It never occurred to me someone might actually be in the house. I opened my door and there he was. Looking for all the world like a Colonial gentleman with his pigtail and tri-corner hat. He turned when he heard the door but didn't seem surprised, at least not until the dog charged out. That's when he turned and headed back down the stairs."

"What did you do?" I leaned over the back of Aunt Mary's seat as much as my seat belt would allow.

"Nothing, at first. I was so startled I couldn't think what to do. Finally, I put the upstairs light on and went downstairs. Nothing. No one around. No open doors. No sign anyone had been there. I decided I'd had a bad and very real dream and went back upstairs. It wasn't until a couple of days later I went down into the cellar. Petal, my dog, was with me then too. Good thing. It was her growling that made me stop just in time for that crate to miss me."

"You must have been terrified." An understatement. I would have been paralyzed with fear.

"I was. I followed the dog up the stairs and out of the cellar. I pushed a table in front of the cellar door, grabbed the poker and ran upstairs."

"Then what happened?"

"Not one damn thing. I sat on the bed for over an hour, trying to listen. Finally I went back downstairs. The table hadn't been moved. I finally got up enough courage to open the door. The cellar light was still on. The remains of the crate lay there but nothing else. I checked to make sure all the doors were locked, even the outside cellar door. They were. I didn't know what to do. I thought maybe I was going crazy, but the crate had fallen and I thought I'd seen someone, just a glimpse. Only, I wasn't sure."

"So you called me." Aunt Mary's statement wasn't quite a question, but not quite a statement either.

"Isn't that what I always do? Whoops. Almost missed it." Without slowing down, she turned into a dark drive. Large iron gates, attached to brick pillars topped with a design I couldn't make out, stood open. Huge old trees lined both sides of the gravel road, bending gracefully toward each other, creating a tunnel of fresh spring leaves. On one side, shadowy animals stood behind white fences, silently watching us pass and then taking off to race us to the house. Horses. White, almost silver in the moonlight. A row of small houses was tucked behind the trees on the other side of the road.

"What are those little houses?"

Elizabeth's drama was temporarily eclipsed by the unexpected sight of the cluster of houses.

Elizabeth decelerated and hit a rut. Aunt Mary lurched forward, held in place only by her seat belt.

"Sorry." Elizabeth glanced at Aunt Mary and slowed down a bit more. "You all right? We're doing a lot to the old place but haven't gotten around to fixing the road yet." Coming almost to a stop, she twisted in her seat to look at the cabins. "It's the original slave cabins. Most slave cabins were wood, but those are made of brick. Smithwood had a kiln, a quarry—whatever you call those places where you make bricks—and they used the chipped or broken ones to build the cabins. They came out looking a little lopsided but were a lot warmer than the wood ones and didn't burn down. We're in the process of restoring them."

"Oh." I felt faintly embarrassed.

"My goodness." Aunt Mary sounded as uncomfortable as I felt. There were no slave cabins in California. At least none I knew of. However, there were plenty of migrant workers' cabins. I doubted there was much difference.

"Slavery was a part of colonial life, just like outhouses, detached kitchens and well water drawn by hand." Elizabeth didn't sound as if she approved of any of it.

Slave cabins. Lots of them. People had lived in them, but how? "They're so tiny. They look like dollhouses."

"They're tiny, all right. I imagine they were smoky, as well. Not the most comfortable accommodations on the plantation."

"Oh." I couldn't think of anything else to say. Instead, I looked out the window at the horses. "I didn't know you had horses. My daughter, Susannah, likes horses."

"They're Noah's. He's working with Colonial Williamsburg to keep the breed alive."

"Are they all white?"

Elizabeth smiled. "They're called American Creams and, yes, they're all white. Well, cream."

Aunt Mary didn't seem interested in horses. "Is Noah a Longo?"

Elizabeth stopped the car, evidently to give us a better look at the white faces peering intently over the fence. "Yes. Noah and his mother are the only ones who still live here. Their house is way over a hundred years old. They raise horses, chickens and sheep. All rare breeds. I get fresh eggs and none of the work."

I wondered who the Longos were, why and where they lived on the property and how Aunt Mary knew about them. Before I could ask, Elizabeth flicked on her brights. "There. That's Smithwood."

"Oh! It's beautiful." Aunt Mary leaned forward.

Horses forgotten, I craned my neck to see over her shoulder. It was beautiful.

Elizabeth nodded. She rested her arms on the steering wheel, a smile in her voice. "I love to look at it like this, in the moonlight, or with just the car lights on it. You can't see the old age marks until you get a lot closer."

"If that house is suffering the deterioration of old age, I hope it treats me as gently." Aunt Mary seemed mesmerized by the beautiful Georgian mansion, red brick softened by the lights, white pillars and shutters gleaming.

"It's huge!" It was as elegant as a movie set in the moonlight. At any minute I expected a woman in a hoop skirt to come out onto the covered front porch.

"It's actually three separate houses linked together by brick passageways. The third story of the main house, the one with the dormers, is attic storage. I think the house slaves used to sleep up there, but now it's full of boxes, trunks and old furniture. The second floor is bedrooms for the family. The first floor has the dining room, sitting rooms and big hall. I'll show you tomorrow. The other houses are smaller."

"Why would anyone want three houses right next to each

other?" I'd dealt with properties that had small guesthouses before, but nothing like this.

Elizabeth started the car and we crept closer. Now I could make out the passageways. They weren't very long, but they were tall, in keeping with the proportions of the houses, with openings like windows without the glass.

Elizabeth gave a snort of laughter. "They're guest wings. Back then, travelers expected to stay at the plantations. Roads were bad, travel was slow, and inns infrequent. Guests just showed up. They stayed, sometimes for days or weeks. They used those covered passageways to get to and from the main house, mainly for meals."

For meals. People you didn't know came to stay with you for days, ate at your table, used your beds and then just left? I thought of all the estate properties I'd seen in my relatively brief real estate career, both in Southern California and Santa Louisa. Not one had facilities like that. Not one had an owner who would have considered such a thing.

"The house on the west side is mine. William and I renovated it last year when we moved in. Actually, Cora Lee did a lot of it before we came back to live here full-time." Elizabeth took a long breath and let it out slowly. "We'd barely finished when he had his stroke."

Aunt Mary gave what sounded like a small sob. "Elizabeth, I'm so sorry. I should have been here for you."

Elizabeth reached over and squeezed her hand. "And done what? You were involved with Ellen's wedding and all your charities. We were busy winding things up at the college, moving down here and getting the house ready. Then William had his first stroke and decided we needed to get married. I'd never given marriage a thought, but he insisted. We got married in our house." She pointed to the west wing and sighed.

"Why not the main house?" That was really none of my business but curiosity got the better of me.

Luckily, Elizabeth didn't seem to mind. "Why didn't we get

"Only more so." Elizabeth waved her hand in the air, pointing at the slave quarters, the big house and the fenced pasture where several horses stood, as if transfixed by her enthusiasm. "The people who work in the historic district are actors. They go home and change clothes. My students will live in the main house exactly as they would if they were living in the eighteenth century. They'll each have a role, a job. They'll sleep in beds with ropes for springs and straw for mattresses. They'll warm themselves with fireplace heat and wash up with pitchers and basins and use slop jars for … other things. We'll take field trips to the historic district to see events reenacted then come back and talk about them as if they had just happened, assess their effect on people's lives. It's going to be wonderful."

A light went on over the porch on the west wing. A small figure appeared on the top step, looking down the driveway.

"That'll be Cora Lee. We better get on up there." Elizabeth let out the clutch with a jerk and the car moved forward. "The first time I came here with William, I fell in love. It's so beautiful, and the history! I'd been teaching American history for years, but in this place it came alive for me as never before. I want to instill that feeling in other history teachers." She slowed down as the driveway split to make a circle with the houses at its top. "I'll take you into Colonial Williamsburg. It isn't far. We'll go to the House of Burgess and stand in the same hall where Patrick Henry gave his famous 'Give me liberty or give me death' speech. It's enough to make a shiver go up your spine." She stopped behind a bright red BMW. "Yep. Cora Lee's back."

Elizabeth was out of the car, tugging at the suitcases, before I could untangle my seat belt. I was glad to get out. I was tired, rumpled and hungry. I had no idea who Cora Lee was but hoped she'd started dinner. It was after eight (dinnertime in California) and neither Aunt Mary nor I had eaten since we grabbed a quick bite in between planes in L.A. That seemed a long time ago. Aunt Mary climbed out of the front seat slowly. She seemed to be feeling much the same. She stopped, rested her hand on the open door and looked at the houses. So did I.

The main house was dark, as was the one on the east side, but the west wing was ablaze with light. The fresh white paint on the shutters and the trim around the windows gleamed against the soft red of the brick walls. A small woman stood on the porch. She was impeccably dressed in pale blue slacks and a matching cardigan over a white silk blouse. Her silver hair, not a strand out of place, glistened in the porch light. She leaned on a cane of burnished wood with a silver handle as Elizabeth dragged the last suitcase out of the trunk. She didn't look like someone who'd get dinner.

"What on earth took you so long? I've been just worried to death. I figured, even if they lost their luggage, y'all'd be here an hour ago."

"Mary, this is Cora Lee Wittingham, William's sister. Cora Lee, this is Mary McGill and her niece, Ellen McKenzie. Dunham. Sorry, Ellen. I keep forgetting."

I smiled and nodded. Didn't want to tell her I was having the same problem. I'd been McKenzie much longer than I'd been Dunham, but I liked being Dunham a whole lot better.

Elizabeth continued, "I took Mary and Ellen on a little tour since there was some daylight left."

"Unless you've taken to picking up perfect strangers, I assumed that's who they were." Cora Lee came down the stairs, using her cane on every step, and slipped her arm through Aunt Mary's. "Elizabeth's talked about you so much over the years, I feel I already know you. How was your flight? I see you made your connections. I'm sure Elizabeth meant well, driving you around and all, and, goodness knows, there's a lot to see around here, but not tonight. You must be exhausted." She stopped, beamed at Mary and looked over her shoulder at me. "Anyway, you're here now, and they didn't lose your bags." She nodded at the bag Elizabeth wrestled to the base of the stairs. "Seems to me every time I get near an airplane nowadays, they lose something of mine." She steered Aunt Mary toward a shallow set of stairs with a handrail, leading to the front porch. Letting go of Aunt Mary's arm, she set her cane on the first step and started to climb. She held her head high and her shoulders straight but it took her awhile.

It didn't take Aunt Mary as long, but she held onto the railing. At the top of the steps, she paused to rest and look around. Elizabeth was right behind them. I tried to take Aunt Mary's suitcase away from her, but she waved me off. She puffed a little as she manhandled it up the stairs. I waited until I was certain all three were safely up before I started to roll mine upwards. Thank goodness for whoever equipped luggage with little wheels.

On the porch everyone stopped to catch their breath.

"Damn. I don't do that as easily as I used to." Elizabeth leaned heavily on the handle of the suitcase, took off her hat and wiped her brow with her arm. "I think I need a drink."

"I'm sure you both do. So do I." Cora Lee frowned at Mary and me. "You do drink, don't you? Just a little wine, of course."

Aunt Mary looked as though she thought a glass of wine sounded like heaven but only nodded.

I put in a hearty, "I'd love one."

Cora Lee smiled. "Dinner's all ready. You two can wash up and then we'll all sit down and have a nice chat."

"Of course dinner's ready. I made it before I left. Wanted Mary to know I learned something in all these years. Did you put it in the oven?" Elizabeth's expression was somewhere between amusement and exasperation.

"No, but I put together the salad." Cora Lee smiled at them both and turned toward the door.

Hoping that whatever needed to go in the oven wouldn't take too long, I looked back to see where Aunt Mary was. She'd paused to gaze down the driveway. The tunnel of trees was fast disappearing in the gathering darkness. The moon lit up the circular drive in front of the houses, illuminating two horses whose heads hung over the bordering fence. One gave a soft nicker as if in greeting, then they both turned and walked away. She took another step and looked over at the dark main house. Steep, shallow stairs led to a veranda that stretched over half the front of the house. You could just make out the old paint peeling off the large round pillars, showing wood underneath. The doorway, high and solid, was almost invisible in the shadows cast by the tall, blank windows on each side. The stained glass window on top barely showed any color and even the weathered white paint on the casing was barely visible. Elizabeth was right. Old age had settled down around this wonderful old house in a less than graceful way. It didn't look gloomy as much as grumpy.

I was beginning to feel that way myself. "Come on." I turned away again to go through the door Elizabeth held open.

Something flickered. I caught it out of the corner of my eyes. Then it was gone.

"What was that light?"

"I don't know." Aunt Mary walked to the end of the porch for a better look. It had come from the tall windows beside the front door of the main house, but it wasn't there now. She peered at the windows. So did I.

"Did you see that?"

"I'm not sure. Look. There it is again. Oh, it's gone."

She took another step, but she'd reached the end of the porch. Besides, there was no longer anything to see.

"What?" Elizabeth left the door and came up beside us. "What is it?"

Aunt Mary pointed at the front door and the windows that flanked it. Not a flicker of light showed behind them.

"Was it a light?" Elizabeth moved down several steps and stared intently at the other house.

"I don't know. It was just a flicker. Will you please come up here?"

"Like a candle?"

"I don't know. Maybe it was the moon."

"No. It's not that high. It was something else. Or somebody. There's been someone carrying a candle around over there before. Remember? I told you about it. I finally decided it was my ghost."

Elizabeth had told Aunt Mary about the ghost, told us a little more in the car but I didn't think she'd said anything about it being in the main house. I was sure the figure Elizabeth saw in her upstairs hallway was no ghost but a prowler and that the crate had been hoisted over the stair rail. If she'd seen a candle in the main house before, someone alive was carrying it. It seemed reasonable to conclude the same person was in there now. A thought in no way reassuring.

"I thought you said that house was empty."

"It's supposed to be. No one's lived there since, well, for ages."

Cora Lee appeared beside me, also peering at the dark windows of the main building, and I gave a little start. "Why? Is someone over there? How do you know?"

"I thought I saw a flicker. Aunt Mary saw it, also."

"This is too much," Elizabeth said. "I'm going to have a look, and when I catch whoever is doing this, they won't be happy." She started up the steps toward the porch where Aunt Mary, Cora Lee, and I stood. "The key to that house is in my purse."

"What do you mean, 'too much'? You've seen a light over there before? We've got an intruder and you haven't told me?" Cora Lee appeared to be more incensed that she'd been kept in the dark than frightened by the thought of an intruder.

"You were in Atlanta, remember? I haven't had time to tell you anything." Elizabeth brushed by Cora Lee and headed for the door, every step full of purpose. "Besides, when I went to check, no one was there." She paused, eyes flashing. "Someone had been. Warm candle wax pooled on the dining room buffet. If they think they can scare me with all this ghost stuff, they've got another think coming." She started through the doorway, her skirt swirling around her legs.

"What ghost? We don't have ghosts at Smithwood," Cora

Lee called after her. "As for my being gone, you've heard of the telephone, I suppose?"

Elizabeth hesitated, as if she'd blurted out more than she wanted to say. She hadn't told Cora Lee. Why? This wasn't the time for speculation.

"Someone's been prowling around," Elizabeth finally said. "I saw a light over there a couple of weeks ago."

"What did you do?" Was the tremor in Cora Lee's voice purely due to fear, or was there excitement and a little thrill mixed in?

"I called Noah. We went through the house. No one was there. Someone had been, though. It was about a week later I thought I saw someone in the upstairs hall and then again in the cellar." Elizabeth eyed Cora Lee with no trace of humor. "Whoever, or whatever, was there tipped the crate over."

"The one that almost hit you? But you said …" Cora Lee's lips tightened as her sentence broke off. So did the hand that rested on her cane. "Go get that key."

I almost felt sorry for whoever was in there. Elizabeth had clearly had enough, and Cora Lee just as clearly planned on providing backup. However, considering what Elizabeth had told us on the drive out here, this didn't seem safe.

"You two aren't going in there alone. That's no ghost over there and it wasn't a ghost who pushed over that crate. We either call the police or we all go."

Aunt Mary gave a little gasp just as I realized what I'd said. There might be safety in numbers, but I didn't think it applied to us. What I meant was, we needed the police. I was the only one who thought so.

"Elizabeth, if whoever's in there is the same person that pushed over the crate, we could be asking for trouble. Let's think about this." Aunt Mary glanced over at me.

I nodded my approval.

"Ellen and Mary are right. We're all going." Cora Lee straightened her back and brandished her cane.

I blinked. That wasn't at all what I'd said. Was it? It wasn't what I'd meant.

"I can't imagine who would have the gall to prowl around my mother's house." Core Lee was building up a good case of righteous anger. "Well, they're not getting away with it. Candle wax on my mother's buffet! Why, that buffet is over two hundred years old. Candle wax could take the finish right off." Indignation that the buffet might be damaged seemed to have banished Cora Lee's fear and, in my opinion, her good sense. She gave her cane an experimental swing. "This might not be enough. I don't suppose one of you has a gun?"

"A gun!" The idea seemed to catch Elizabeth off guard. "Of course not. I don't want to shoot anyone. I just want whoever is doing this to get out of my house. Now. "

I didn't approve of guns and I was pretty sure Aunt Mary didn't either. At least, I didn't approve of every Tom, Dick or Henrietta carrying one in his or her pocket or pocketbook. However, Cora Lee had a point. Whoever was creeping around in the dark, leaving candle wax and scaring the bejesus out of everybody, needed scaring. Unless, of course, someone really had meant to do Elizabeth some damage. No, there had to be a logical explanation for what had happened. Just because I couldn't think of one right now didn't mean it didn't exist. We wouldn't shoot whoever was in there. Just give them a good scare. However, since none of us seemed to have one, I'd better come up with plan B. "My cellphone's in my purse. I think we should call the police."

"It'll take too long. We have to go. Wait. There's something I've got to do first. Don't any of you move." Elizabeth pushed open the door to her house and disappeared. Before I had time to be surprised, she was back.

"What on earth were you doing?" Cora Lee sounded equally surprised and definitely annoyed.

"I wanted to see if the passageway door into my house was locked. It wasn't, but it is now. He's trapped. Let's go and, for heaven's sake, be quiet. No point in advertising we're on our way."

Trapping a prowler didn't appeal to me. From the look on Aunt Mary's face, she shared my feelings but it seemed that was what we were about to do. As for announcing our intentions, we couldn't have done it more loudly if we'd had a brass band.

Elizabeth led the way, her braid bobbing up and down on her back and her denim skirt swaying forcefully as she marched down the steps. Cora Lee followed, cane tapping on each step as she descended. They didn't look very threatening. Neither did we. Aunt Mary had her tote bag, but there was nothing in it but her wallet and her, by now, useless airline ticket. I think she had a paperback mystery novel as well, but that wasn't going to strike terror into the heart of even the most timid prowler. I had my cellphone. I glanced at it as I dropped it into my bag. It only had one bar and it needed charging. We weren't well armed. Sending up a silent prayer that the prowler wasn't either, I hurried after them.

One flickering candle wasn't something to get scared about. However, ghosts in the hallway and crates tipped over onto stairways were. If someone really was trying to harm Elizabeth, or even just scare her to death, barging in armed with nothing but a fancy cane and a practically useless cellphone didn't seem prudent.

At the base of the steps of the main house, we stopped. The moon only lit the bottom half, so that shadows obscured the entire porch. Everyone stared at the barely visible, closed front door.

"Are you sure we shouldn't call the police and let them handle it?" Aunt Mary offered in a small voice. No light, no handrail and a possibly dangerous prowler. It was clear she didn't think this was a good idea. I couldn't have agreed more.

"And let whoever this little bastard is get away?"

"Language, language, Elizabeth," Cora Lee almost purred.

I suddenly realized Cora Lee was having a great time, as if

this were a wonderful adventure. It didn't feel that way to me. Did she know something we didn't? I immediately dismissed that thought. It was probably nerves, and that I understood.

Elizabeth ignored Cora Lee's criticism. "It'll take them too long to get out here. No, let's go find out who we're dealing with."

"How about Noah? You said he lives here. Can we call him?" Leave it to Aunt Mary to be sensible. Why hadn't I thought of that?

Maybe Cora Lee was reconsidering barging in on who knew what. "That's a good idea. Let's do it."

"He's not home yet and I'm not waiting. Besides, I've faced down bigger threats than some wimpy candle carrier." Elizabeth forged forward up the porch stairs. Cora Lee nodded. She planted her cane on the first step and followed.

Aunt Mary looked up the stairs, then at me. Both the other women were already up, and Elizabeth was trying to fit the key in the heavy front door. Cora Lee leaned on her cane, watching.

I took a deep breath, put my foot firmly on the first step, paused and turned to her. "Stay down here. If something happens, run. Do you have the cellphone I got you?"

She nodded.

"Do you remember how to use it?

I got a scornful look.

"If something happens, call nine-one-one. After you run away." I turned back and started up the stairs, grateful for the moonlight that made the climb, if not less treacherous, at least visible. Footsteps sounded behind me. Aunt Mary. I paused, sighed and kept going. At least I'd tried.

Elizabeth still fumbled with the heavy key, trying to fit it into the lock. "Blast." She tried the latch, but it was firmly locked. The door didn't respond to rattling, either. She tried the key again. "I don't suppose either of you has a flashlight." Frustration was ripe in her voice as she bent down closer to the door.

Aunt Mary opened her tote bag purse, fished around and found the small flashlight she always carried. She flashed it on the keyhole.

Elizabeth glanced up. "That part of your girl scout training?"

"Came in handy, didn't it?"

Elizabeth laughed and the key went in. The door opened with a loud creak. Cora Lee gave a little gasp and clutched Aunt Mary's arm.

"What, what!" Aunt Mary clutched Cora Lee right back. "Do you see something?"

"No." She dropped her arm.

"What are you two doing?" Elizabeth pushed the door open a little more. "You coming or not?"

Aunt Mary gulped.

So did I.

Cora Lee straightened and clutched her cane a little tighter. "Right behind you," she whispered loudly.

We crept through the doorway into a pitch-black hallway. The only light was the dim beam of the moon that stopped at the porch.

"What's that smell?" Cora Lee's whisper broke the silence like a shout.

"Shhh. You'll scare him away. Listen."

We did. Cora Lee clutched Aunt Mary again with her left arm, swinging the cane with her right. The gleam of the silver handle shone in the tiny sliver of light from the open door. Elizabeth stood a little in front of us, a barely discernible shadow, turning her head one way and then the other.

"Ouch! Cora Lee, will you watch what you're doing? You darn near broke my ankle."

I could just make out Elizabeth standing on one leg like a crane in a skirt. I smothered the nervous laugh that almost escaped and my hand that held the cellphone shook a little. I couldn't seem to make it stop. I let it drop into the open mouth of my drawstring bag. If I dropped it on the floor in this cavernous darkness, I'd never find it again.

"What is that smell? It's horrible."

I had no idea but Cora Lee was right.

Aunt Mary sniffed the air. "It smells like someone lost their cookies."

"Or worse." Elizabeth gave a little cough. "Ugh. Where's it coming from?"

The rancid smell was strong but there was something else, something faint but familiar. I gingerly sniffed the air, trying to identify the other smell. Candle wax. A freshly blown out candle. Unmistakable. I sniffed again. The horrible odor almost covered it up, but it was there. I quit sniffing and stirred. We couldn't stay huddled in this room, hallway, whatever it was, all night. I whispered at Aunt Mary, "Where's your flashlight?" She fished around in her bag, finally pulled it out and flicked it on. The beam traveled but illuminated nothing more threatening than closed doors.

"Do the lights work in this house?" I asked in a loud whisper. Why, I had no idea. If anyone was here, they knew we were also. "If so, will someone please turn them on?"

Cora Lee moved toward the wall. "Flash that light over … no, more … there."

Lights appeared. Aunt Mary blinked and tensed, ready to run. Or hide. Only, no one jumped out waving a pistol or brandishing a knife. Nothing happened, and there was no sound. She relaxed a little. So did I. I shook out my shoulders and looked around. The room where we stood was actually a wide hallway that ran the length of the house. In the middle was a round table with a badly tarnished empty silver bowl on it. Two straight-backed chairs sat against the walls on each side of the hallway, one with a small table beside it. A huge chandelier hung over the table, but that wasn't the source of the light. Small sconces glowed on the wall areas between two closed doors. There were double doors at the very end. "What's behind those doors?"

"The river." Cora Lee crept down the hallway, cane tapping, slowly examining each closed door, pausing before one. It was slightly ajar.

"They open on the river side. In the summer, both sets of doors would be left open to let a cross breeze cool the house." Elizabeth tiptoed closer to Cora Lee. "Can you see anything?"

"Not a thing, but I think the smell is coming from in there." She gestured at the partially opened door.

Elizabeth pinched her nose and coughed. Her voice sounded gravelly as she tried to see around Cora Lee. "Ugh. That's foul."

Cora Lee held her cane over her shoulder, as if it were a baseball bat. "Don't just stand there. Push it open all the way."

Elizabeth pushed. The smell rushed out to fill the hallway.

"Oh. I'm going to be sick."

"Cora Lee, don't you dare! I'll never forgive you." Elizabeth peered into the room. The light from the great hall only cast more shadows. "Someone's drawn the curtains. Damn. Where's the light switch? Mary, where's that flashlight?"

"The switch is there, by your left hand."

Elizabeth stepped into the room and felt along the wall. Aunt Mary squeezed in behind her, flashing her light around. The house felt empty, but someone had been here. Was he hiding in some other part of the house, waiting for us to leave so he could make his escape? Phew. Cora Lee was right. The smell was overpowering. So overpowering I forgot for a minute to be afraid. Aunt Mary flashed her light on the dark oak floor, then along the walls, but all it illuminated was wood wainscoting topped with red and gold flocked wallpaper. Her light lingered on it a second. Hideous. The light traveled on. An elegant Oriental rug lay inside the door. A long dining room table above another, larger rug was located farther in the room. Carved chairs with ball feet sat around the table. Heavy draperies covered what was probably a window on the far wall. Nothing that could be the source of the smell. I took another sniff and instantly covered my mouth with my hand. We had to find out what it was and get rid of it. Quickly.

Lights came on. The crystal chandelier above the dining room table blazed, pouring light into every corner of the room. Elizabeth rounded the table, stopped abruptly, and gasped. She was seemingly transfixed by something on the floor behind the table. Aunt Mary moved around and stopped just as abruptly as she, too, stared at the floor by the buffet. "Oh, dear God in heaven." She gagged and almost dropped the flashlight. "It's George Washington."

Cora Lee pushed in between them. "What's the matter with you two?" There was a sharp intake of breath as she skidded to a stop. She didn't say anything for a moment and when she did, her words were almost inaudible. "No, it's not. It's Montgomery Eslick."

I rounded the table from the other end, confused. What lay there halted me just as quickly. My gasp was loud in the silent room. A man lay on the Oriental rug, body bent backward as if in agony. It wasn't just any man. For one brief moment, I thought Aunt Mary had been right—it was George Washington. Of course it wasn't, but this man was dressed in dark-blue knee pants tied just below the knees. Rumpled white hose showed above black buckled shoes. The blue jacket had long, wide skirts, now half wrapped around the corpse. A ruffled white fissure, only partly visible, was white at the throat, the ruffles stained yellow. Yellow stained the Oriental carpet under the head of the man as well. A small crystal glass lay beside his hand, its pale yellow contents mixed with what had once been the contents of his stomach. A blue tri-corner hat lay half under the table.

No one spoke for a moment. I don't think any of us could.

Finally, Elizabeth said, "It's the ghost. Only, it's not. It really is Monty. What's he doing here?"

"I have no idea." Cora Lee stared at the body, then at an array of small tapered glasses on the buffet. "Looks like he was having a party that didn't turn out so well." She took a step closer.

"What are you talking about?" Elizabeth looked around the room, then back at the body. "Why would Monty have a party in the dining room? Cora Lee, what are you doing?"

"Making sure this time he's dead. If this is who you saw in our upstairs hallway, he was no ghost. At least, he wasn't then."

"You're making sure by poking him with your cane?"

"How else am I going to find out?"

"If he was faking it, he wouldn't be lying in all that." Elizabeth shuddered and took a step back. "He's dead all right."

"Hmm." Cora Lee pulled her cane back and leaned on it, still staring at the body. "I guess you're right."

I didn't realize I'd stopped breathing. The need to take a deep breath suddenly became strong. I gave in, to my immediate dismay. Knowing what the stench was somehow made it worse. Much worse. So did the realization of what must have happened. "Not much of a party with only two people."

"How do you know there was someone else?"

"Elizabeth, we're here because we saw a light through the front windows, a light that shouldn't have been there. This person," I gestured at the dead man, "is very dead, and has been for more than a few minutes, so someone else had to have been present. Unless, of course, you think he swallowed something lethal, walked around with a candle until he started to feel bad, blew it out and came in here to die."

"A very unlikely scenario. I see a glass but no candle." Cora Lee's voice was amazingly matter of fact.

From where I stood, only the back of the dead man's head was visible. His white wig, its hair tied neatly back with a dark blue ribbon, had slipped to one side, covering one ear and obscuring his face. If he had appeared in my hallway, I'd have been just as terrified as Elizabeth evidently had been. Only, he wasn't in the hallway. He was in the dining room of what was supposed to be an empty house, with one small glass from a set lying on the floor beside him. I looked a little closer. It appeared to have contained some liquid, yellow and sticky, that had not agreed with him.

Aunt Mary looked a little white. I hoped she wasn't going to faint. Cora Lee didn't look much better. Her hand shook as she leaned on her cane.

"Are you all right?" Should I pull out one, or two, or maybe three, of the chairs? Vague thoughts of crime scenes and much less vague thoughts of interfering with the scene stopped me.

"Of course." Cora Lee stood straighter, visibly trying to stop the trembling.

"We've got to get the police." Aunt Mary fumbled in her tote bag for her cellphone, dropping it back in before getting it all the way out. Luckily, it hadn't landed on the floor. "Drat. Ellen, do you have yours?"

"Let me call." Elizabeth's voice had a distinct tremor, but she still had enough control to take charge. She reached for my phone, and I handed it over. "I can describe better where we are. Then I think we should try to reach Noah."

"Call Noah first." Cora Lee quit leaning on her cane. She glanced at the other two, then me, walked to the doorway and looked into the hall. "You locked the passageway door to your house, didn't you, Elizabeth? I can see the front doors and also the back ones from here, and about the only other way out of this house is through my father's conservatory. You don't suppose whoever was here with Monty hasn't left yet?"

Elizabeth's hand seemed to freeze in place as she started to punch the buttons on my phone. "The conservatory door's locked with a padlock."

"How about the cellar? Could someone get out that way?" I looked around, wondering where the steps might be.

"The only inside cellar steps are in my house and the only outside door is padlocked. I think we'd better leave. I can make those calls from the other house."

"Wait." Cora Lee hurried back into the room, avoided the

corpse, and stopped at the buffet to stare at the little glasses. "I thought so. Why, those are my mother's. The original Smithwood Syllabub glasses." She took a step closer to the buffet, but Elizabeth grabbed her arm.

"Those glasses aren't going anywhere, but we are. Right now." She let go of Cora Lee and crept over to the door. She peeked around it toward the back doors then took a step into the wide hallway. "Seems to be all clear. Cora Lee, you go first. You have the cane."

I thought Cora Lee might balk, but after a second, she nodded, raised her cane up over her head, ready to strike, and bolted for the hallway, out the front door and onto the porch. Elizabeth, clutching my cellphone, was right behind her. Aunt Mary paused for a second, glanced at me and hurried after them. I looked quickly around the room, at the beautiful but dusty buffet, at the glasses on it and finally at the corpse and shuddered. There were details here I would need to remember later. I wasn't married to a policeman for nothing. I took another deep breath, swallowed the gag it produced and headed for the front door. Elizabeth was waiting for me. "Follow Cora Lee," she said. "Get inside my house and close the door but don't lock it. Not yet."

"What are you going to do?" Aunt Mary sounded breathless. Actually, she sounded scared. So was I. "Elizabeth, this is no time for heroics. Let's go."

"Oh, I'm coming. I want to make sure this door locks. It's supposed to lock when it shuts, but I don't trust it. I don't know how that person thinks he's going to get out, but it's not going to be this way."

I opened my mouth to say something but couldn't think what it might be. Aunt Mary pointed her light at the steps and Cora Lee started down, her cane lightly touching each step. Elizabeth gave the door one final tug and followed Aunt Mary, who was taking the stairs faster than I'd seen her do in years. I wasn't far behind.

Chapter Four

THE FOUR OF us sat in Elizabeth's house, in the large room she called the gathering room, and waited. We had immediately checked the doors to make sure we were locked in and whoever was out there was locked out. Only then had Elizabeth phoned 9-1-1. Then she called Noah. He arrived first.

The tall young man who walked through the door had been transformed from the handsome, immaculate man I'd met at the airport. Noah had been in the barn when he got the call, feeding horses and mucking out stalls, and he looked it. His jeans were dirty, and his flannel shirt hung open over a sweaty blue T-shirt that clung to his well muscled shoulders and arms with a tenacity that would have inspired envy in the heart of any red-blooded male contender in a wet T-shirt contest. His black boots were manure-stained, as were his jeans that fit tightly over slim hips. He looked and smelled like a horse handler ending his day.

"Sorry. I was just finishing up." He was a little breathless and it was obvious his mind was no longer on horses. "Tell me again. Monty's dead? In the dining room next door?"

He didn't act like a policeman, either. More like someone

who couldn't quite believe what he was hearing. Something I understood. I was also having a hard time believing any of this and I'd seen the body.

"What was he doing there?"

"Getting himself killed, evidently," Cora Lee answered.

"I doubt that was his reason for coming." The look Noah gave Cora Lee was not one of admiration. "I'll try again. Monty wouldn't have come out here, especially dressed as a colonial gentleman, unless he had a darn good reason. What was that?"

"I have no idea." Elizabeth leaned back and rubbed her eyes as if they pained her.

Cora Lee didn't seem to be bothered by eye trouble. Hers were open wide and staring at Noah, somehow challenging him. "None of us knew he was here. We didn't know anyone was here. Mary saw a light in the window by the door and we went over to investigate. There he was, dead as a skunk, right on Mother's Aubusson carpet. And he'd thrown up on it!"

That seemed to be the final affront. How dare he desecrate her mother's carpet? Maybe it was shock that made her act so callous, but I was beginning to suspect not. She'd been worried about wax on the buffet. She was indignant at the thought that Monty and whoever else had been with him had used her mother's glasses. She certainly had an attachment to her mother's possessions. Or, was it to the possessions of Smithwood? That was, I supposed, understandable. She'd grown up here. This had been her home. That brought another thought. Why hadn't Cora Lee inherited Smithwood? Or at least some portion of it. Women hadn't been allowed to inherit in years past, but certainly that no longer held true.

Noah brought my attention back to the problem at hand. He took a deep breath and let it out slowly. "Monty's dead on the carpet. We have that established. You know because you saw a light and went over to investigate and there was Monty. Did any of you ever stop to think that whoever was over there might not have wanted to be found? Anyone sneaking around someone else's house in the middle of the night has to be considered dangerous. Why didn't you call the police?" No one answered him. He sighed deeply and ran his hand through his short-cropped hair. "I don't suppose any of you have any idea how he died?"

"He was poisoned." I hadn't said much up till now, but it was time to put a stop to Cora Lee's little side trips and get down to business.

"What makes you think that?" Noah's head snapped around. I had his attention now.

"He's all twisted like he died in agony, and he threw up. He'd been drinking something yellow and sticky looking, and I think he still had the glass in his hand when he fell. It didn't break. Whatever was in it was fast-acting. It looked as if he just keeled right over."

"That's right. Ellen's right. He dropped like a stone." Cora Lee's voice was low and theatrical.

Elizabeth's lips twitched with what might have been the beginnings of a smile.

Aunt Mary wasn't as generous. I knew that look of disapproval well. I'd had occasion to cause it growing up. Evidently, she too had her reservations about Cora Lee.

"Like a stone," Noah repeated and shook his head. "Then you called nine-one-one and me?"

"We didn't call anyone until we left that house and came over here," Elizabeth said.

"We left *fast*." Cora Lee put a little stress on the word "fast."

"Why?" There was concern in his voice along with more than a little alarm. "Did you think someone was still in there?"

"Oh, yes." Cora Lee tapped her cane on the floor a couple times as if to emphasize that point.

"Whoever was with Monty had to still be in the house, hidden somewhere." A shiver of fear ran through me more intense than I had felt when I looked at Monty's body, or even after we had run back to Elizabeth's house. The stupidity of going over there, just the four of us, was suddenly overwhelming.

Noah's expression hardened and his voice settled down into police deadpan. "Why did you think someone was still there? Was there a noise? Did you see something?"

"It wasn't that." Elizabeth leaned forward. There was a tightness in her voice that hadn't been there before. "Whoever it was couldn't have gotten out."

Surprise passed over Noah's face, followed quickly by disbelief. "Go on."

"You need a key to get into that house. The latches engage when the doors close and you need a key to get out."

She paused. Noah nodded as if he knew that.

"Mary saw that candle just a few minutes before we went over. No one came out the front door, and if someone went out the big doors that overlook the river, we would have seen him. We didn't. The conservatory doors are also locked. I have the key. I locked the passageway door leading to this house before we went over. That person had to still be inside, and I think he's there right now."

Noah didn't say anything for a minute, but his eyes widened and the muscles around his mouth tightened. "I'd better get up with the lieutenant. We'll need the S.W.A.T. team." He patted his pockets for his cellphone but came up empty. Elizabeth handed him mine. He appeared a little surprised but accepted it.

Before he could dial, sirens split the air.

"I'd better get out there and tell them we might have a murderer trapped." He dropped the phone on the table, pushed back his chair and was halfway to the door in almost one motion. He stopped and turned back. "Elizabeth, I'll need your keys."

Reluctantly, she reached into her skirt pocket and handed them to him.

Noah tossed them in his hand, as if assessing their weight, or what they might unlock. "Stay here, all of you."

Whatever else he might have added was drowned out by the howling of a dog.

"Oh, dear God. It's Petal. How could I have forgotten?" Elizabeth rushed to the French doors that opened on the side of the house that overlooked the river. She yanked at the door. It didn't move. "Damn. I forget. What did that locksmith say to do?"

Another siren blast split the air. Two dogs howled. Noah appeared beside Elizabeth, his mouth set in a straight line. "That's Max. I can't leave him out there. He'll get in the way. What locksmith? What did he do?"

"Put on a new lock and put in some kind of rod. There." She pulled up a lever. A rod slipped out of a hole in the floor and the door obligingly opened. Two dogs charged through. The large one skidded to a stop in front of Noah and tried to jump into his arms. Not an easy task considering its size. A Golden Retriever. The little one ignored everyone in the room and ran for the wing-backed chair that sat beside the fireplace, jumped in, buried its nose under a pillow and started to shake. Elizabeth scooped it in her arms, crooning. The sirens got louder; the dog shook harder.

"You four wait here. Don't move. Don't come outside. Don't do anything. Someone will come to you as soon as possible." He looked thoughtfully at Elizabeth's keys and started for the door, the large dog on his heels. He paused. "Max, sit." The dog sat, but he looked expectant, ears cocked, tongue lolling to one side. Noah sighed. "Can Max stay here?"

"Of course." Elizabeth had the little dog clutched tight against her and she made no move to put it down. Max let Noah go out the door that led into the main hall before he followed.

"Max, get back. Will one of you please come get this dog?"

Tires crunched on gravel, strange voices issued orders, car doors slammed and impatience was giving way to anger in Noah's voice.

"Cora Lee, go get that dog. I'll get the door." Aunt Mary

hurried toward the French doors, got them closed and managed to drop the rod into its hole. Max reluctantly came back into the room, but as soon as Cora Lee let go of his collar, he ran for the doors. He pawed as if expecting them to open. They didn't. He turned toward us and whined. We didn't respond. Max turned back to the doors. He sat down and stared through them, mumbling dog curses under his breath.

"What are they doing?" Cora Lee peered at the windows beside the front door. "Damn. I knew you shouldn't have hung those blasted curtains on those windows. I can't see a thing."

"They were your idea." Holding the trembling little dog seemed to help Elizabeth. Her voice was crisp. The fear that had been evident when she told Noah she thought the prowler was trapped had dissipated. Of course, having the circle driveway filled with police cars was reassuring.

"What's got Max so enthralled?" Aunt Mary walked over to the French doors to stand beside the dog, who was staring intently into the dark yard. "They have the house surrounded." Surprise filled her voice. "There's a man in a black jacket doing that silly looking crouch run. He's got a rifle! Good grief. Surely they don't plan on shooting someone."

"Only if someone tries to shoot them first." The same fear I felt when Dan was on a call ran through me. I crossed my fingers, hard, hoping that the only thing our prowler was armed with was poison.

"Where? Who's shooting who?" Elizabeth pushed up against the doors for a better look. Max gave a small yelp. "Sorry." She gave him an absentminded pat on the head. Max wound his tail around his front feet and kept looking.

"I hope those idiots don't do something stupid like shoot through a door or break a window," Cora Lee said. "The glass in some of those windows is original." She pushed in beside Aunt Mary.

Max was in danger of getting edged out again, but he held his ground. I didn't even bother. There was no more room in front of the doors. I'd settle for a description of the action.

"Where's the S.W.A.T. team guy?"

"He went toward the back of the house. It's so dark, you can't see anything."

"For heaven's sake, Cora Lee, you almost knocked me over." Elizabeth edged to the side of the doors. Suddenly, lights went on. "Where are those lights coming from?"

"It looks like someone pulled the curtains back. I think that's the dining room, but it's hard to tell from here." Straining to see more, Cora Lee had her hand up by her face, which was almost pressed against the window. "Look. The upstairs windows have lights. They must be up there looking for the prowler." There was no mistaking the excitement in her voice.

"What are those men doing?" Aunt Mary held her ground at the doors, pressed almost as tight against them as Cora Lee.

"Don't know, but they're not going to find anything in those planters. There's nothing in them but weeds. Uh-oh. That man better watch where he's walking. The ground slopes down the hill pretty fast right there."

I listened to their blow-by-blow with great interest, wondering what would happen when they found the prowler. So far the voices outside hadn't risen above a murmur and there hadn't been a single gunshot.

"I don't think they've found anyone." Cora Lee turned to leave the doors and almost tripped over Max. He yelped. "Damn that dog. He's always in the way."

Elizabeth stood in front of the doors, the small dog still in her arms, shaking her head slightly. "That's not possible. We know someone was over there. Where did he go?"

"I don't know." Aunt Mary inched closer to the door. I stood right behind her. We said nothing as we watched the searchers' bobbing flashlights. House lights blazed, lighting up the yard, making them unnecessary.

"Are you sure there are no other doors? No other way out of there?"

"There is one other way."

"Where?" Elizabeth wheeled around to stare at Cora Lee. "I don't know of any other way. Oh."

Cora Lee's tight little smile said *I told you so.*

"Right. The other passageway door."

I felt a little like Alice, minus the white rabbit, of course. "What other passageway?"

"The one from the main house to the east house. It's the twin of this one, at least it used to be until we remodeled." Elizabeth's face and voice were both thoughtful. "Why I didn't think of that before, I can't imagine." She stopped and frowned. "No. That wouldn't do him any good."

"What do you mean?" Aunt Mary turned away from the doors to look around the room, as if trying to locate the door to the passageway from this house to the main house. The one Elizabeth had locked. She looked puzzled, as if she'd forgotten there was another house, the twin of this one. So had I. Was Cora Lee saying that whoever was in the main house with Monty could have gotten out that way?

"It means he could have gone through the east wing passageway to the staircase." Cora Lee sounded triumphant, as if she'd solved the mystery.

"Gone through the house? Which house? What staircase? "

"The main house. We know he was there, whoever poisoned Monty. What we don't know is how he got out. The passageway between the main house and the east house has a staircase in the middle. It was put there so the servants could come up from the kitchen and the laundry below. If he left that way, all he'd have to do is go down the stairs and he'd be gone."

Cora Lee sounded proud of herself. I didn't think she'd solved anything. That might be how the prowler—murderer—escaped, but a whole lot of other questions remained unanswered. Like, who was "he"? Why did he kill Monty, and what were they doing in Elizabeth's dining room? The biggest question of all, at least in my mind, was who was Monty?

"Good theory, but there's one thing wrong with it." Elizabeth put both hands on the table and leaned forward, with the tiniest trace of a smile.

Cora Lee raised one carefully plucked eyebrow and uttered a quizzical, "Oh?"

"The door that leads into that passageway from the main house is locked. So is the door leading into the east house. Our prowler may have tried to get into the passageway from the main house but, unless he has a key, he didn't."

"How do you know that?" Cora Lee sounded indignant. A perfectly good theory shot down before she ever got it off the ground.

"William and I locked both doors. We were exploring both houses not too long before he had his stroke, trying to decide what we wanted to do, and he locked the doors as we left. I remember specifically because we both laughed. We had no idea who we were locking out, but William said it was an old habit." She paused and a single tear rolled down her cheek.

Aunt Mary reached over and patted her hand.

Elizabeth smiled at her and brushed the tear away. "Anyway, he locked them, and since I have the only key I know about, they're still locked."

"So, how did the intruder get in? Or out?" I was getting more confused by the moment. Ghosts in the upstairs hall, dead men in the dining room, people coming and going through locked doors. None of this made sense.

"I don't know." Elizabeth's brow furrowed into a scowl. "I don't know how Monty got in, or why he came, and I don't know how the other person got out."

"Well, dear ..." Cora Lee shifted slightly in her chair and frowned. The frown was replaced quickly by a sly smile. "I think one thing is certain. What he drank was syllabub. What was in it, and who put it there, I don't know, but I'm sure that's what it was."

Elizabeth turned white. Now what?

Aunt Mary was quickly at her side. "Elizabeth, I think you need to sit down."

"Yes. Maybe I do. This has been quite a shock." Elizabeth left the French doors and headed for a square table that sat in the middle of the room. She pulled out a chair and sank onto it. "You really think it was syllabub in that glass?"

"I'd bet real money on it." Cora Lee bypassed the table and went directly to an elegant buffet that sat against the same wall that held the French doors. A wine rack and a set of delicate crystal balloon wineglasses sat on top. She opened a drawer, fumbled around for a minute and pulled out a corkscrew. It took only a minute to open the bottle she selected and pour a generous amount of wine into four glasses. She picked up two and headed for the table. "Mary? Ellen?" She nodded her head at the other glasses as she settled into another chair and lifted hers.

Aunt Mary picked up the other two glasses, nodded at me, and joined them at the table. So did I. There was nothing to see outside, anyway. I took a sip. Nice. I tried another then set the glass down. "I have a few questions." I was getting tired of Wonderland.

"So do I." Aunt Mary's tone left no doubt she expected answers.

"Such as?" Cora Lee swirled her wine. The corners of her mouth curved with the tiniest of smiles.

"Such as, what is syllabub?"

Elizabeth and Cora Lee looked at each other, then at me as if I'd just come from outer space. Or California.

"It's a drink, a sweet dessert drink. The colonials loved it."

"So does Elizabeth." Much to my surprise, the smile Cora Lee gave Elizabeth spoke of fondness, but it immediately gave way to one of the sarcastic little digs Cora Lee seemed to favor. "We gave her one the first time she came here and told her how it was made. Just as soon as she figured out she didn't have to catch the cow, she decided she loved it."

Wonderland was back. "Catch what cow?" Aunt Mary and I looked at each other in complete bewilderment.

"Cora Lee, will you stop it?" Elizabeth didn't sound irritated so much as tired. She set her glass down, barely touched, and turned to Mary. "It's a dessert drink composed of lemon juice, white wine and cream. You can also thicken it and eat it with a tiny spoon. It's said that when the colonials made it, they milked the cow directly into the wine and lemon juice to make it frothy. I'm not in the least sure if that's true; now it's made with whipped cream. It's really good."

There was something familiar about the word, syllabub. Of course. "Didn't you say something about it to Noah? Right as we left the airport?"

Any trace of amusement disappeared from Elizabeth's face. "I did. I always make it when we have company. I love it, and it seems so fitting to have a colonial drink in this colonial house. I made a bowl of it and it's in the refrigerator right now."

"In this kitchen?"

Elizabeth nodded.

The "oh" that Aunt Mary let out was long and slow. Mine was quieter. The implications were just beginning to sink in when the front door opened. Noah was back. He walked over to the table. Max's head popped up and he bounded over. Noah pushed him out of the way, pulled a chair from against the wall over to the table and sat down.

"There's no one in the house. We've looked everywhere, including the attic." He paused, studied Elizabeth's face and then stared intently at Cora Lee. "However, someone's been in there."

"How do you know that?" There should have been surprise in Cora Lee's voice. There wasn't.

"A couple of the upstairs chests of drawers look as if they've been searched. Drawers not quite put back, a closet door standing open. If someone didn't know the house, they'd never notice, but no one around here would ever leave a drawer open."

"I knew it!" Elizabeth sat a little straighter. There was a steely look in her eyes and her jaw clenched. "Didn't I tell you? I didn't imagine that damned ghost, or the person who tipped that crate almost on top of me. Someone's been all over this place."

Noah got very still. "What ghost? What crate? Just exactly what has been going on around here you haven't bothered to tell me?"

Elizabeth squirmed. She dropped her eyes down to her glass, picked it up and swirled it a little, buying time. For what? Framing the words so her story made sense? It was pretty bizarre, or had been until we found the murdered man. After she finished, Noah threw himself back in his chair and stared at her. "Why didn't you tell me?"

"I did. The first time it happened, only no one was there. When the ghost appeared in the hallway, it seemed impossible. There was no way he could get in, and no way out." Her voice was faint, her eyes still on the wine she swirled in her glass. "I was beginning to think I was losing my mind."

"So you called Mary. What did you think she could do?" He let his eyes rest on Aunt Mary. Up until now, she had simply been Elizabeth's old lady friend, come to visit. Now, he was wondering … what?

"Make me sane again. That's what she always does." I was glad to hear a little tartness back in Elizabeth's voice. However, her reasons for calling Aunt Mary didn't cover why she hadn't told Noah or Cora Lee what was going on. I needed to get Elizabeth alone with Aunt Mary, and soon. There were a whole lot of questions floating around and not nearly enough answers.

"Did you know about this before you came?"

Aunt Mary's face flushed. It wasn't embarrassment. I knew the signs. It was anger. She'd done nothing but come visit a friend, one who recently lost her husband. Hardly a crime. If

Elizabeth happened to mention she needed help with other things, well, that was between the two of them. And, of course, me.

"Elizabeth needed some company from an old friend. It hasn't been all that long since William died. I was glad to come."

Noah stared at her for a moment then transferred his attention back to Elizabeth. "Did it ever occur to you that whoever was roaming around upstairs was dangerous? That's what the police are for. To protect you. I want to protect you too. I can't believe all this."

Cora Lee said, "If it's any consolation, Noah, she didn't tell me, either."

The opening of the front door kept Noah from answering.

"Noah? They're ready. Lieutenant wants you."

"Thanks. Be right there." He glared at Elizabeth and pushed his chair back. "I've got to get out there. They're ready to remove the body, and they'll be taking the rug and the glass Monty drank from as well. That's what I came to tell you. The fingerprint people are going over everything, so you won't be able to go in there for a while. They're going to need all of your prints as well. I'll let you know." He held onto the back of the chair for a moment then shook his head in disbelief. "I'll be back, and I want to know about this ghost you saw and especially about the crate." It was clear he meant to have answers.

I wanted to sit in on that conversation. A few answers would be welcome.

"What's all this about taking the carpet?" Cora Lee sat rigid in her chair, hands clasped around her cane, the very picture of a displeased Victorian Grande dame.

"It's going to the lab. The stuff on the carpet is what was in the glass and in Monty's stomach."

Cora Lee's knuckles turned white as she tightened her grasp on the cane. "They can't do that."

"Can't do what?"

"Take the rug. That's a real Aubusson and it's old."

"Oh, for heaven's sake, Cora Lee. They'll give it back. Won't they, Noah?" Elizabeth scowled at Cora Lee before she turned toward Noah.

"They can't have it." Cora Lee wasn't acting rational.

"They have to take it. They need to find out what the poison was and, since the entire contents of the man's stomach are on it, they don't have much choice."

Cora Lee looked at me as if my sentence had been replete with four letter words. "That's disgusting."

I wasn't sure if she meant the contents of Monty's stomach or murder was disgusting. If she meant murder, she was right. As for the rug, it was evidence. Didn't the woman watch *CSI*? Everyone else in the western hemisphere did.

"Mrs. Dunham's right."

"It's Ellen."

Noah paused for a moment then smiled. "Ellen." He turned back to Cora Lee. "They have to test what's on the rug. See what was in the drink, then match that against what's in Monty's stomach."

Cora Lee looked even whiter, if that was possible.

"Anyway, we'll get it back to you as soon as we can. Tell you what. I'll make sure it goes to Heritage Cleaners. They're the ones who do the historic district work, so they know about old rugs. All right?" Noah leaned down toward Cora Lee and rested his hand on top of hers. "It's going to be fine. Really."

Noah was, in my opinion, a little too conciliatory to Cora Lee. It wasn't going to be fine. Not one bit. Oh, the rug might be. As for the rest of it, someone had murdered that man, Monty, who everyone seemed to know but no one seemed to mourn. That wasn't fine.

Noah gave Cora Lee's hand another squeeze. "I've got to go. You all stay here. I'll be back."

No one said anything. Cora Lee's eyes burned holes in

Elizabeth, who was seemingly lost in thought and didn't notice. Aunt Mary seemed to be fading fast. I could hardly blame her. I felt much the same. The few sips I'd taken of the wine hit my empty stomach with a bang and I was thinking about a bath and bed. It had been a confusing and, frankly, exhausting day. We'd both had a lot to do before we climbed onto our first plane earlier, much earlier, this morning. We'd changed planes three times—in itself nerve-racking—before arriving in Newport News where Elizabeth regaled us with impossible to believe stories of ghosts and attempted murder. Then came real murder. I glanced at my watch. It was only six on the west coast. Dan should be home by now. I needed to call him. He'd have a fit if I told him we had found a body and would want to take the first plane east. I couldn't see how that would help, at least not right now. However, I'd promised to call to let him know we'd arrived in one piece, and I could hardly keep this from him. Besides, I wanted to talk it over. I needed a little time to figure this one out. I raised my glass and took what I hoped was a restorative drink.

"Elizabeth." Aunt Mary twisted in her chair a little so she could see her friend better. "Didn't you tell me the person you saw upstairs was dressed in a period costume?"

Elizabeth nodded. She looked as if she knew what was coming next.

"Was he dressed like the dead man next door?"

Elizabeth nodded again. "Before you ask the next question, yes, I think it might have been Monty. I didn't get a good look. I was shocked to see someone standing there and the dog was barking and growling, the light was bad, but even then, I thought it might be him. Only, why would Monty be in my upstairs hallway?"

"What was he doing?" Cora Lee sounded apprehensive and this time her voice didn't contain any of her barbs.

"Standing outside one of the bedroom doors. The one Ellen's going to use. I think he was about to go in, but when he saw me, he turned. It was dark, so all I got was an impression. He was about Monty's build, wore a tri-corner hat, and his hair was tied with a ribbon in back.

"The dead man, Monty. He had on a wig, didn't he?" I remembered hair over one eye.

Elizabeth nodded. "Then Petal ran out, barking hysterically. Whoever it was kicked out at her. She ran back into the room and he headed for the stairs and just sort of disappeared."

Cora Lee wasn't easily put off. "Do you think it was him in the cellar?"

Elizabeth sighed deeply and picked up her glass. She held it up, examined it, and set it back down. "I don't know. That happened so fast. I turned on the light at the top of the stairs and was halfway down when, out of the corner of my eye, I saw movement. I guess Petal also saw it because she started to bark then turned tail and ran back up the stairs, right through my legs. I was so startled I stopped. That's when I heard the crate creak. It was dark on that side of the stairs, but there seemed to be a figure in colonial dress. I couldn't be sure. When that crate fell, well, I turned and ran back up the stairs almost as fast as the dog."

"Then what happened?" Aunt Mary tensed up again. This whole thing was too much. She picked up her glass and sipped.

"Nothing. I pulled a table in front of the cellar door, grabbed the poker and ran upstairs after the dog. Then I sat on the side of the bed and waited. Petal was hiding under it."

"For heaven's sake, Elizabeth, why didn't you wait by the cellar door and smack whoever came up?" Cora Lee bounced her cane a little on the floor, as if to show that she would have acted a lot more forcefully.

I wondered. According to Aunt Mary, Elizabeth had been in a lot of tough situations in her life, but this time she'd been caught off guard. Of course, getting older probably didn't help, although I doubted she'd thank me for saying so. I would have taken the poker and locked myself in the bedroom as well.

"How long did you wait?"

Elizabeth sighed. "Must have been an hour or so. Nothing happened, so I decided whoever was in there was long gone. Only, I couldn't figure out how. Finally I opened the door and, holding the poker up and, feeling like an idiot, I went downstairs. The table was still up against the cellar door."

"He went out the outside cellar door. Must have." Cora Lee sounded positive, but there was a question in her voice.

Elizabeth shook her head. "It's padlocked. Was then. Still is. I went around the side of the house and looked."

"There must be another way." Aunt Mary nodded with certainty.

Elizabeth and Cora Lee shook their heads.

"Only two ways in or out," Elizabeth said. "One is through that door over there." She pointed to a door on the opposite side of the fireplace from where we sat, one that blended into the paneling that covered the wall so well it was easy to miss. "Or through the outside door. I have no idea how whoever was down there got in or out."

We all looked at each other, saying nothing, trying to come up with a logical answer. There didn't seem to be one.

Finally, Aunt Mary took another sip of her wine and placed the glass back directly in front of her. She let her fingers run down the slender stem for a second and then raised her head. "I've got one question I think you two can answer."

"What's that?" Elizabeth sounded a little guarded.

"Just who exactly is, or was, Monty?"

Chapter Five

MONTY'S IDENTITY REMAINED a mystery, at least for the moment. The front door opened and Noah appeared in the doorway of the gathering room.

He walked over to the table where the four of us sat, pulled over a ladder-backed chair that was against the wall, and sat down. "Monty's gone and so is the rug," he told Cora Lee. "Lieutenant McMann will be in soon to ask you all some questions."

Cora Lee bristled. "Leo? Leo McMann? You mean to tell me with all the police in that department of yours, we get Leo McMann?"

Noah's expression hardened. "*Lieutenant*"—there was a definite emphasis—"McMann is head of our homicide squad, as you well know. Please try not to bait him. It will make life easier for all of us."

"Humph."

I hoped Cora Lee confined herself to that remark. Policemen liked straight answers with no barbs thrown in. That could do nothing but cause us problems and we already had plenty. The thought of the syllabub sitting in Elizabeth's refrigerator, and the possibility that syllabub was what was in Monty's glass, made me nervous. Which raised another possibility. The syllabub glass had been beside Monty's outstretched hand. There were matching glasses on the buffet. I tried to remember. Maybe I was wrong, but I didn't think so. "Where was the other glass?"

Noah looked at me as if he'd only now noticed I was there. "What?"

"The other glass. Monty drank something and died. Someone was with him. Monty didn't get himself a glass of syllabub, poison it and drink it all by himself. At least, I don't think so. Only, I didn't see another sticky glass. Only those clean ones on the buffet."

Noah's expression started to change. A small smile formed and once again he ran his hand over his hair. "You're right. There wasn't one."

I turned to Cora Lee. "How many glasses did your mother have?"

The answer was prompt and emphatic. "Eight."

The gleam in Aunt Mary's eye told me she'd caught on to what I was thinking. Her question to Noah was sharp and to the point. "Did you count them?"

"There are seven. Six on the buffet and one beside Monty. That's the one the crime scene guys took away."

"They took that *and* the rug? Those glasses are two hundred years old! They belong in a museum, not banging around in some lab somewhere. If that glass gets broken, it will be on your head, Noah Long."

This time Noah didn't even acknowledge Cora Lee. "Eight. One's missing. Isn't that interesting?"

"Someone took one away." Elizabeth pushed her wineglass to the side and stared at Noah. "Why? Why would they do that?"

"I don't know." Noah looked around. "I don't suppose you have any coffee made?"

Aunt Mary started to push back her chair then stopped. The room where we sat was long, the table almost in the middle.

One end of the room—the end, I thought, that faced the river—had a floor to ceiling fireplace and paneled walls on each side. The wingback chair that contained the small dog, Petal, and a rocking chair sat on each side of it. The buffet was on the inside wall. The opposite end of the room was a kitchen as elegant as any I'd seen in magazines, nothing like the one in my old house or Aunt Mary's. She'd taken stock of it and I knew her fingers were itching to explore its huge gas range, the copper hood, the stainless steel French door refrigerator, but not now. Especially not the refrigerator. That was where I kept my coffee and so did Aunt Mary. I had no idea where Elizabeth kept hers, but I knew where the syllabub was. We didn't need to open that door.

"I'll do it." Elizabeth headed for the kitchen end of the room.

I held my breath. She opened a cupboard and took out the coffee tin and filters. I let my breath out with a sigh but caught it again as I looked at Noah's face. What was he thinking? He looked from Elizabeth to Cora Lee with a speculative gaze. Was it the glasses? Cora Lee had made no secret they were old and belonged to Smithwood. Or was it what had been in one of them? I didn't like that thought at all. It wasn't hard to figure out what Cora Lee was thinking. Her expression had been mulish ever since she heard that Lt. McMann—whoever he might be—would be coming in to ask questions. That she had no use for him was obvious, but why?

I guessed we'd find out eventually. "Noah, do you know what Monty was drinking? It was something yellow, thick and a little sticky looking."

Cora Lee's head jerked up, Lt. McMann forgotten. Elizabeth stiffened. She'd been taking cups from the cupboard but now seemed barely able to put the cup she was holding on the counter before she froze, waiting for Noah's answer.

Noah seemed conscious of the reaction my question set off. He turned slightly so as to see Elizabeth at the sink. It was impossible to miss Cora Lee. Her eyes bored holes in him.

However, it was me he addressed.

"It looked, and smelled, like syllabub. Do you know what that is?" He included Aunt Mary in his question.

We both nodded.

He smiled slightly. "We'll know for sure after the lab guys get through with it."

"Syllabub? Impossible." Cora Lee almost snorted in her zeal to prove Noah wrong. "Where would Monty have gotten that?"

"An excellent question. If it proves that's what he drank, it's a question we'll have to answer. Along with all the other questions, such as what else was in the drink and who gave it to him."

"And why."

The look Noah gave Aunt Mary was speculative. "Yes. And why." He turned around in his chair and said directly to Elizabeth, "Did Monty still have a key?"

Elizabeth's hand shook slightly as she poured the coffee. "I have no idea." She picked up one cup only, walked back to the table and set it in front of Noah. She didn't offer any to the rest of us. Instead, she sat and picked up her wineglass. "Is there any wine left, Cora Lee? If so, I think I'd like some."

Cora Lee rose and brought the bottle back to the table. She poured a little in Elizabeth's glass then finished it off between herself and Aunt Mary. I still had an almost full glass, a situation I planned on correcting soon.

"He didn't have a key. I took it."

The Wonderland feeling was back. Why would Cora Lee take Monty's key? Why did he have one? Who on earth was he, anyway?

"Are you sure?" Noah didn't look convinced. He shoveled sugar into his coffee and stirred, not noticing when it sloshed.

Aunt Mary's fingers actually twitched with an almost overwhelming need to mop up the small pool. She removed her hands from the table and folded them in her lap. I almost laughed, but refrained.

"It wouldn't matter if I hadn't." Cora Lee smiled. "I didn't trust Monty not to have another one. I got Colonial Lock and Key to come out and change the locks on all the outside doors on all three houses, oh, a couple of years ago. I made sure they kept the old colonial style keys. Those blasted things are heavy, too."

The cat that ate the canary. The expression on Cora Lee's face had to be where that old expression came from. Only, why would she do that and why was she so pleased?"

"Why would Monty have a key?" Leave it to Aunt Mary to get right to the point.

"Because his mamma died."

I looked at Aunt Mary. She looked at me, and I shrugged.

She narrowed her eyebrows and her nostrils flared a little, a sure sign her patience was wearing thin. "What does Monty's mother have to do with anything? Who was he, anyway?"

"Oh, dear. You don't know, do you?" Cora Lee clicked her tongue and smiled. "Why, honey, his mamma was my brother William's first wife, the one who lived here while William lived with Elizabeth at that college in Wisconsin where they taught whatever it was they taught. Monty and William didn't get on one little bit. Actually, William couldn't stand to be around him." She paused for a moment, as if reliving the events of long ago. Finally she sighed and went on. "That was a marriage that should never have happened. It was a disaster from the moment they said, 'I do.' "

She looked at Elizabeth and smiled. Elizabeth smiled back. Clearly, Cora Lee approved of William's second wife.

"That's why, after she died and I found out Monty was fixing to move in here with his wife and kids, I had to do something. William would have had that stroke a whole lot earlier if he thought Monty was living in his house. So, I dropped into Mr. Monty's law office one day, collected the key and told him the only way he'd ever move into Smithwood again would be over my dead body. Or his." The old sarcastic smile was back on

Cora Lee's face. "Mr. Montgomery Eslick was pretty unhappy with me, but there wasn't a thing he could do. It was a nice day for me. I don't think Monty enjoyed it nearly as much, and I'll bet he enjoyed it even less when he went home and told that little social climbing wife of his."

Cora Lee's southern accent had gotten thicker as the story went on, but I had no problem understanding her.

"So Monty was William's stepson? He used to live here?" Aunt Mary looked from Cora Lee to Elizabeth.

"All the time he was in high school and during all the holidays while he went to college. He was a disgusting teenager and didn't improve with age. Happiest day of my life was when I picked up that key." Cora Lee beamed.

Aunt Mary looked stunned. Evidently, Elizabeth had never mentioned a stepson. I wondered if she'd mentioned a wife. That Elizabeth and William lived together without benefit of wedlock she'd known for years and accepted without batting an eyelash. But that William still had a wife in the background? She glanced over at Elizabeth.

Elizabeth's eyes were fixed on her wineglass. "I guess I should have told you. It just, somehow, never came up."

It never came up? Aunt Mary's face showed she was having trouble with that one. It was, of course, none of her business. If Elizabeth chose not to mention them, well, she didn't have to. But I also could tell Aunt Mary was hurt. Elizabeth never did anything in a conventional way. Aunt Mary expected that. Living with William in one state while his wife and stepchild resided in his ancestral home in another wouldn't have surprised her. She would have worried about it, but she would never have thought less of Elizabeth or even questioned her about it, I was sure. All this did answer one question, however. We now knew who Monty was. Now for the other questions …

"Okay, Monty lived here, grew up here and at one time had a key. If he wasn't supposed to be here now, and didn't have a new key, how was he getting in and out? Why was he here?"

I paused, waiting for someone to comment, add something, guess. No one said a thing. "Who would want Monty dead, and why was he killed here, in the old Smithwood mansion, on your dining room rug?"

Everyone was silent, even Cora Lee.

Chapter Six

I WAS AWAKE. I didn't want to be. Every nerve in my body told me I was tired, to go back to sleep, but I needed to use the bathroom. I opened my eyes halfway then snapped them wide open. There was a plaid ceiling over my bed I'd never seen before. I moved my arm, looking for Dan. He'd explain why, only he wasn't there. I lay still for a moment, trying not to panic, to remember where I was. My eyes moved without moving my head, which seemed a good idea. My head didn't feel like moving. Plaid curtains. No, green and cream plaid bed hangings. I was in a poster bed, the hangings held back with cream velvet tassels, the canopy draped down over the sides of the fabric top. How had I gotten here and where was Dan?

Of course. I took a deep breath and my hands relaxed their tight grip on the sheet. I was in Elizabeth's guest room. One of her guest rooms. Aunt Mary was next door. I let out the air I hadn't realized I held in, pushed back the matching plaid quilt and slid out from under the cream eyelet trimmed sheets. I needed the bathroom, now.

My slippers were beside the bed, my robe draped over the end of it. Had I left them there? It didn't seem likely. I didn't do that at home when I was at my best. I hadn't been at my best last night. The overwhelmingly horrible memory of the murder scene came rushing back and erased any recollection of doing small, mundane things like unpacking a robe or setting out slippers. Slipping into both, I headed toward the half-opened door on the wall opposite the bed. I sank down on the white porcelain toilet with relief and looked around.

My small sundries case sat on a glass shelf above a freestanding sink. I'd been more efficient than I thought. It had been very late when we were finally allowed to go to bed. Noah told us it would be a long night and advised us to switch to coffee after our first glass of wine. Somehow the anxiety of having a murder investigation in full swing and the increasingly pointed questions Lt. McMann addressed to both Elizabeth and Cora Lee made dinner an unrealized goal. He'd finished off the coffee, and Cora Lee had opened another bottle of wine. Another pot had been brewed, which Noah finished off. At least, I thought he had. I rummaged through my sundries case, looking for the Tylenol.

A glass sat on a lovely small chest that held towels and washcloths. I filled it and downed two of the pills. I probably wouldn't have had that last glass of wine if Lt. McMann hadn't been so rude. He'd refused to acknowledge my existence or Aunt Mary's for over an hour, even though she was the one who had seen the light. We hadn't known the victim but we'd been there, we'd seen the body and probably had something to contribute. Rude. The man had been rude to all of us, Noah included. Dan was incensed when I told him. I swallowed the pills and thought about that phone call. He'd been prepared to drop everything and head east. It took me a while to convince him neither Aunt Mary nor I was in danger. Besides, from the little I'd seen of McMann, I was certain he wouldn't want the chief of police from a small town in California horning in on his case. Elizabeth was probably safer without that extra strain. What I did tell him was that I missed him, and I did. I promised to call him often—a promise I intended to keep—and that I would try not to "stick my nose in where it didn't belong." His words. I wasn't so sure about that one.

While I waited for the pills to numb my headache, my eyes wandered. Bathrooms didn't look like this in the eighteenth century, I was sure. Did they even have bathrooms back then? I didn't think so. Chamber pots. That's what they used. I sent up a small "thank you" for modern facilities, especially for the soaking tub with its handheld showerhead and delicately embroidered shower curtain. I looked closer. All kinds of flowers, interspersed with small, brightly colored birds, appeared on a crisp white background. Charming. The bathroom walls were painted a soft yellow. The door, all of the trim around the window, and the high baseboards were white. So were the towels and the fluffy bath rug. The bird prints that hung above the chest were obviously old. So was the wood-framed mirror above the sink. A delightful blending of new and old. How did Elizabeth pull it off? According to Aunt Mary, she hadn't been interested in decorating, cooking or anything domestic when they were in college. Causes were what held her interest, what aroused her passion. Causes and history. However, someone had put quite a little history into doing both the bathroom and bedroom.

I washed my face. That felt better. Teeth next. My mouth felt, and tasted, like cotton wool. Old cotton wool. Were my eyes bloodshot? Of course not. If they looked a little tired, well, it had been quite a day. All those questions the police asked. Over and over. They hadn't found the syllabub. No one asked to look in the refrigerator and none of us suggested it. I fluffed my hair out a little. Not too bad. Should I shower? I yawned. Coffee then shower.

I walked back into the bedroom. What time was it? I hadn't heard movement. No doors opening. No footsteps. I needed coffee. There wasn't a pot or a hot plate up here, at least not in this room. There was the canopy bed and a small table beside it. A secretary sat on the wall opposite the door, its top down, displaying little cubbyholes for letters, envelopes and things. An armless Windsor chair sat in front of it. A highboy took up the space between the two windows. It looked old. I walked over for a better look. I'd seen pictures of highboys like this. Were those drawer pulls original? They didn't look like any I'd seen at Lowe's. I pulled on one. The drawer slid open easily. What was it you were supposed to look for to see if it was old? No nails. I examined the corners. There weren't any. Was this piece a true antique? I stood back to take a better look. The bottom had three deep drawers. The top half seemed only to rest on the bottom. It was narrower, with three drawers across the bottom; two small ones on top and another narrow one in-between. The top was flat with a charming trim that reminded me of the crown molding around Elizabeth's ceiling downstairs. I reached up and let my fingers trace the lines. How beautifully it was made. I'd put my clothes in it right after breakfast.

I pulled back the drapes that covered one of the windows. The sun trying to invade the room now flooded it, leaving no doubt the morning was advancing quickly. A beautiful morning it was. The pasture I'd only glimpsed last night showed green and crisp. White fences outlined it and followed its slope halfway down to the river. There was a copse of trees just outside the fence line, and below them lay the wide river, peacefully meandering toward the ocean. Who owned the land on the other side? It was covered in trees up to the ridgeline— no house in sight and no fence. A doe appeared through the trees, stopped and stared at the house. Could she see me? Of course she couldn't. The doe appeared satisfied with whatever she saw because she put her head down and started to nibble.

How lovely it would have been to wake up every day and gaze out at this view. How peaceful life must have been in the eighteenth century. Peaceful, perhaps, but they didn't have bathrooms or coffeemakers. The circle driveway was directly below my window. Scraggly flower beds encased in untrimmed

too large for her, and had green and purple reindeer prancing all over it. Her slippers were bright green moccasins. Purple pajama bottoms showed under the hem of her robe. At least she matched.

"What?" She paused and gave me "the look."

"Nothing. I need coffee, that's all."

"So do I." She headed for the stairs, and I followed. Should I laugh? I didn't. Her ensemble was undoubtedly made up of rummage sale items. I'd seen her in worse and at least she was warm.

The staircase had a beautifully carved, dark-wood banister I hadn't noticed last night. The treads were bare and almost noiseless under our slippered feet. Noiseless but slippery. Aunt Mary put the handrail to good use as she descended.

No one was in the gathering room but the small dog, waiting impatiently at the French doors. She barked once and got up, intent on going outside.

Aunt Mary walked over. "Does this one only work with a key? Good. A dead bolt." She turned the bolt, pulled up the rod and pushed open the door. The dog shot out, gone before I could blink. I joined her and together we watched the dog bound down the hill and disappear on the other side of the barn.

"What kind of dog did Elizabeth say she was? She looks like a greyhound, but smaller."

"She's beautiful. I like that blue-gray color and the white paws and circle of white around her neck. I think greyhounds are bigger. She's a little dog. Maybe she's a Whippet."

"No. Elizabeth mentioned some country. Italian Greyhound, that's what she called her."

"I've never heard of them." Aunt Mary's face had an anxious expression. "Do you think we should go after her?"

"She'll come back when she's was ready. She lives here. Let's make coffee."

"What's that noise?"

The gardener, or whoever he was, had moved closer to the house. The din from his weed whacker felt like a dentist's drill in my head. I shut the door. "It's the gardener, I guess. Noisy, isn't he?"

Aunt Mary dismissed the gardener and turned back into the room. "I didn't pay much attention to this room last night. The shock of finding the body, Noah's questions then that rude Lieutenant McMann practically badgering everybody. When he finally left, Cora Lee poured us another glass."

"Or two. I lost count."

Aunt Mary smiled. "She did keep topping off the glasses. It certainly was more than I'm used to."

"Especially on an empty stomach. I'm starved but I need coffee first."

Aunt Mary nodded and headed for the kitchen area. The coffeepot sat on a granite counter just waiting to be filled. Aunt Mary looked like she planned on obliging it. Elizabeth had put the coffee away in the refrigerator before we all went to bed. I walked over and opened the door. There it was. The bowl of syllabub looked up at me from the confines of a delicate etched glass punch bowl. It seemed innocent enough. Was it really laced with poison? If so, it could have wiped out most of the Smithwood household before Monty even got a taste. I doubted the murderer had that in mind. More likely the poison had been meant only for Monty. If the murderer filled both glasses, what could be easier than adding a little something to Monty's? Why would someone do that? More importantly, who had done it? That thought didn't do a thing to settle my stomach. A covered casserole sat next to the syllabub, the one we never managed to get into the oven last night. The sight of it made my stomach turn over. I reached for the coffee and closed the door.

Aunt Mary was searching through cupboards, muttering to herself, while she looked for the filters. "Isn't there any food in this house? I know she's got filters. I saw them last night." There were plates, cups and saucers, serving dishes, baking dishes, finally cupboards with food and, right in front, filters. She took the coffee from me, filled the pot, turned it on and leaned back against the counter.

The coffee started to swirl its aroma around the room and I let my gaze follow it. The kitchen part, where we stood, looked a lot like the kitchens they advertised in the home magazines I thumbed through while waiting in the dentist's office. A Wolf stove with a stainless steel hood over it, a French-door refrigerator, ice and water in the door and a stainless steel dishwasher with more control buttons than most airplanes. The sink sat under a small bay window that looked out on a kitchen garden. I walked over for a better view. I'd been thinking of replacing my vintage sink, the same one I'd done dishes in as a girl. This sink was made of some material new to me but I liked it. Two separate sides, one deep enough for the largest stockpot, the other, shallow and efficient, had the open mouth of a garbage disposal. That surprised me. Didn't Elizabeth compost? A white crockery pot sat on the drain board, beside the sink. Curious, I reached over and flipped open the lid. Phew. She composted. I snapped the lid closed.

A large butcher-block island took up the middle of the room. A pot rack hung above it, the array of cooking utensils impressive. Deep drawers held more pots, lids and baking dishes. Whoever designed this kitchen was a cook. Elizabeth? Didn't seem likely. I shut the drawer.

Aunt Mary stood right behind me. "This kitchen is a dream come true."

I nodded. "I thought you said Elizabeth wasn't interested in cooking."

"She never was before. Food, yes, cooking, not in the least. Someone is, though." She continued the tour of inspection, raising the concealed vent in the island, testing the simmer burner, attempting to reach the pots on the rack.

While she drooled over the kitchen, I walked down to

inspect the rest of the room. The ceiling was high, with deep crown molding; the baseboards were also high and both were painted white. The rest of the room was a soft robin's egg blue that deepened as the color extended into the paneled dining end of the room. The wood was painted. I sighed. No one would paint that beautiful wood now. Was that the way they did things in the eighteenth century? A question for Elizabeth.

The end of the room we had occupied last night was a combined sitting and dining area and determinately old. The table was square and seated four comfortably, six with a little squeezing. It sat on a beautiful Oriental rug that was almost threadbare in places. For much of the evening, Aunt Mary had used the little rocker by the fireplace. I'd barely given it a glance, but now I observed that it was wider, higher than any I'd ever seen; it was also shallower, with a hearth that extended well into the room. Why? Something that must be a table was pushed up against the wall behind the rocker. The round top was tipped so it sat horizontal with the base, which was pushed up against the wall.

"What's that?" I walked over for a closer look.

Aunt Mary joined me. "A colonial table. I've seen them in magazines. There wasn't much room in lots of houses, so they made tables with the top on a hinge so they could sort of fold it up when they didn't need it, like that one." The joint showed where the top folded upright. What a wonderful idea. There when you needed it but out of the way when you didn't. Very practical.

My gaze wandered over the rest of the room. Old pictures featuring women in long full skirts hung on the walls, and heavy draperies, which we'd forgotten to let down from their ties last night, flanked the tall French doors Aunt Mary had opened earlier to let Petal out.

It wasn't until I turned to go back into the kitchen, anxious to see if the coffee was ready, that I noticed the small door on the other side of the fireplace. The door to the cellar. I moved in closer. Wrought-iron hinges held the door in place. A wrought-iron latch held it closed. I reached out and pushed the thumb latch down. The door opened, revealing nothing but a black hole.

"Come look at this."

Aunt Mary hurried over to stand behind me and stare down into nothingness. All you could see was the top couple of steps. "Should we try and find a light?"

I didn't even have to think about it. "No." I reached for the door. "We're not going down there, at least not without Elizabeth." I closed the door again and examined the latch. No lock that I could see.

"Oh, that smells good."

I wheeled around so fast I almost tripped. "Elizabeth. You're up. How do you feel?"

"Like I need coffee. I came down to start it, but I see you beat me to it. Thank goodness. I'd probably kill for a cup if I had to."

An unfortunate phrase under the circumstances. Elizabeth pulled down three large mugs from one of the cabinets. Bright blue, red and yellow flowers, a bee and dancing butterflies showed gaily against white porcelain. Filled with hot, black coffee, they were a lovely way to start what was going to be, I was certain, a difficult day.

"Have you seen Petal? Cream and sugar or black? I see you found the cellar door. Have you gone down?"

"Black. Petal just went outside. She seemed anxious. And no, we haven't. We thought we'd wait for you."

Elizabeth nodded and poured coffee into the mugs. She set two on the island and motioned to them. The other she carried to the table, where she pulled out a chair. Aunt Mary headed for the island and reached for her mug. Steam rose from it. She sighed but picked it up anyway, holding it gingerly as she walked to the table. I picked up mine and joined her. A little cream would cool them right off.

Elizabeth picked up hers, stared at the steam and set it back down. "Thanks for letting the dog out. She's not the most patient thing in the world. She'll hold it just so long. Then if you don't let her out … well."

Aunt Mary frowned. She liked dogs, although I didn't remember her ever having one. Maybe because she didn't like puddles. "Elizabeth, we've got to talk."

Elizabeth pushed back her chair and started to rise to her feet. She acted as if she hadn't heard. "Don't know why I'm sitting here. That dog will be along shortly and will want in."

"Never mind the dog. Please sit back down. You called us out to help you, and we want to, but there's too much going on here we don't understand. You need to tell us about Monty and what syllabub has to do with all of this."

Elizabeth sighed and rubbed her eyes. "I'd better give you some background." She paused again, put her hand on top of her coffee mug, as if to warm it, but quickly removed it. Without looking up, she began.

"Things have been hard lately. I haven't been sleeping very well. I keep waking up in the middle of the night and then I can't seem to go back to sleep."

Aunt Mary nodded. The first year or so after Uncle Samuel died had been hard. I'd stayed with her for a week or so after the funeral, but I knew it had taken her a while to even begin to adjust. She nodded at Elizabeth. "Thinking. Yes, I remember."

Elizabeth almost smiled. "There's been a lot to think about lately." The smile disappeared and she gave a choking sort of sigh. "About Monty. His mother wanted William to adopt him. Legally. Monty wanted that too. He wanted to be a Smithwood, wanted to live here, wanted to own it. That was the last thing William wanted. He wanted a divorce."

She paused again, seemingly lost in a past only she could see. We waited a minute before Aunt Mary gently prodded her. "Go on."

Elizabeth started a little, as if she'd forgotten our presence. "Oh. Yes. William was a gentle man. Controversy made him sick to his stomach." Her smile was full of fondness. "I used to keep Maalox handy at all times."

I could almost see Elizabeth shake herself to try to stop remembering these details, at least about William. She took a healthy gulp of coffee.

"Anyway, William was offered the mathematics chair at Westover. He was delighted. His wife refused to go. William was even more delighted. He told her she could stay on, which was exactly what she wanted, and so could Monty. His one stipulation was that Cora Lee would manage the plantation and all the money." Elizabeth's smile was mirthless. "She wasn't pleased, but she didn't have any choice, and staying here was important to her. She stayed for over twenty years."

Aunt Mary blinked. "Twenty years?" She put down the coffee. "Then what happened?"

"She died. Monty had long since moved out. He was married and had a law office in town. That's when William and I started to come back—summers, Christmas, that kind of thing. I loved it here and when I got the idea for my project, he agreed. After we retired, we moved here. We'd only been here a couple of months when he had the stroke."

I sipped my coffee. It was still too hot, but I needed the caffeine to clear my head if I was going to piece any of this together. I opened my mouth to ask Elizabeth a question.

Aunt Mary got there first. She began with what had obviously been nagging at her. "Why didn't you tell me about his wife? It wouldn't have bothered me, you know."

The sigh Elizabeth heaved was deep and long. "I know, but it bothered me." Her brow furrowed and her eyes stayed on the contents of her mug. "Not being married to William didn't, but the fact he had a wife did." She almost smiled. "Don't ask me why. I was the original nonconformist. It shouldn't have, but it did." She paused, turning her mug around slowly, watching the coffee sway back and forth. "We only came here once when she was alive. It wasn't a pleasant experience."

We both waited for Elizabeth to gather herself. Was she going to go on? I tried to imagine not being married to Dan, or him with his first wife, who died in a fiery car crash. I couldn't. Our lives together seemed so right, so intertwined. I sure hadn't felt like that when I was married to Brian. Living without his constant put-downs had proved to be easy.

I couldn't begin to imagine the sense of loss Elizabeth was feeling and didn't want to try. Aunt Mary could. It must be very much like what she felt when she lost Uncle Samuel. Their lives had been the opposite of unconventional. He owned the most successful insurance office in Santa Louisa, which wasn't saying much, considering the size of the town. They had a secure and happy, although somewhat uneventful, life, but it suited them. They'd been happy.

Marriage wasn't what I needed to dwell on. Murder was. "So, you and William came back here to retire?"

Elizabeth nodded. "We'd already remodeled this house but hadn't touched the main house or the east house. Those we planned to take back to the eighteenth century. This one, well, neither of us was willing to give up electric lights or modern bathrooms."

Aunt Mary nodded. "Get to the part about Monty."

Elizabeth stirred her coffee, staring down into it, watching it swirl. It seemed physically painful to talk about him. "When he found out William left everything to me and nothing to him, he had a fit. A real major one." She shuddered slightly. "I've never seen anyone like that before. Even the captain of that whaling boat we rammed wasn't that bad." She paused. "Of course, he didn't speak English, so maybe he was and I just didn't know it."

"Elizabeth, try to stick to Monty. What did he say?"

"That if I didn't sign Smithwood over to him, he'd take me to court and claim William's will was invalid due to diminished capacity. That I married him when he wasn't capable of making a decision." Her eyes filled with tears and she stopped.

Aunt Mary waited and I took my cue from her. She knew Elizabeth. Elizabeth wiped the tears away with the edge of the tablecloth and smiled. "I told the little bastard to get lost."

Aunt Mary exploded in laughter but immediately turned serious. "Did he? Have diminished capacity, I mean. You never said anything about his mind, just that he had trouble with his left side."

"That was all that was wrong. Until the second stroke. The one that killed him." The smile faded and the worried frown reappeared. "Monty knew all that. He said he'd tie up the estate so tight I'd never get my school up and running before I ran out of money or out of life, whichever came first. In the end he was going to own Smithwood."

There was no laughter left in Aunt Mary when Elizabeth finished that statement. "Could he have?"

"He could have, and he would have. The Smithwoods have a ton of money, but even they don't have enough to withstand years in court. Monty had the advantage of not having to hire an attorney. We would have needed one. He could have bled us dry."

Cora Lee drifted into the kitchen, clutching a flimsy dressing gown around her. Satin mules tapped on the floor as she headed for the coffee. "I smelled this all the way upstairs. It's the only thing that could have gotten me out of bed. That and Calvin's weed whacker. Does he have to make that much noise?" She filled a pretty china cup with coffee, set it on a matching saucer and carried it to the table, cane hung over her arm.

I held my breath as I watched. The cane swung. Cora Lee's slipper heels were high and her dressing gown kept slipping down over one shoulder. A perfect recipe for a crash, but she made it. The cup and saucer was set on the table, the cane was propped beside the chair and the dressing gown was yanked back into place before Cora Lee got herself seated. Taking a small sip of her coffee, she said, "Monty was despicable as a child and he didn't get better with age. He got what he deserved. Now, we're going to have to decide what to do with that bowl of syllabub before the police come back. Leo McMann would like nothing better than to find some reason to put you in jail." She paused, and her smile was rather self-satisfied under the circumstances. "Dear Leo would love to put any or all of us in jail." She straightened a little and the smile got a little larger. "However, I look just awful in orange and it would make Elizabeth look downright peaked. So, let's dump that stuff down the drain."

"No!"

"We can't!" Aunt Mary and I blurted out in unison.

"Why not?" How Cora Lee managed to look so innocent while she proposed destroying evidence, or what might be evidence, I didn't know, but I wasn't about to let it happen.

"Cora Lee, sometimes you get the worst ideas of any human being I've ever known."

I jerked around, almost knocking over my coffee at the sound of this new voice. I hadn't heard the French doors open, but there stood a tall, black woman holding a covered dish. The two dogs at her side were gazing up at her with hope in their eyes.

"Don't even think about it," she said as she advanced into the room. "That Leo isn't going to arrest Elizabeth. Syllabub or no syllabub, there's not a shred of evidence against her. Why would there be? She didn't kill that little weasel. I brought baked oatmeal. None of you would have eaten a bite otherwise. Did you know Calvin's here? One of you had better get out there pretty soon or he'll whack down every living plant we've got left. I'd do it, but that man won't listen to me."

Who was this woman who so obviously knew every inch of the kitchen? Tall and slender, she showed her age only by the fine lines around her upper lip and eyes and the parchment thin brown skin on her hands. Her black hair was cut short, framing an elegantly shaped skull and showing off huge brown eyes and high cheekbones. She gave off an air of confidence and competency as she opened the oven door, unwrapped the casserole dish, slid it in, and set the dial that operated the oven and the timer.

I felt Aunt Mary's desire to get up and watch the woman work. Cooking on a Wolf stove had been a lifelong dream and she was clearly determined to find an opportunity during our visit.

"Mildred, you really didn't need to bring breakfast." Elizabeth's voice faded to a whisper under the glare of the black woman.

"If I hadn't, would you have eaten? Cora Lee would eat a half piece of toast if she thought of it and maybe a couple of bites of yogurt, and you'd just have another cup of coffee." She headed for the refrigerator and reached for the door. "You wouldn't even get juice …" She stopped and stared at the bottom shelf. "I thought so."

Mildred. Noah's mother. Had to be. Aunt Mary pushed her chair back and walked to the refrigerator. I followed. Layers of yellow liquid and whipped cream were visible through the clear glass.

"Is that it?" Aunt Mary pointed to it.

"That's it."

"It's pretty with those layers. Only, it doesn't look disturbed."

Elizabeth was right behind us. "It looks just like it did when I put it in there."

Cora Lee hadn't moved. "It would. The lemon wine stuff sinks to the bottom again after you dip some out and you'd never be able to tell any was taken."

I bent down to get a better look. "So looking at what's in this bowl doesn't prove anything one way or another?"

"It proves you people weren't very upfront with us poor police last night."

I jumped back, almost banging my head on the refrigerator door.

Noah stood in the middle of the kitchen. "I smelled baked

oatmeal and I'm starved. Calvin's here. I thought he was supposed to spade up the garden and get it ready for planting." He walked over to the refrigerator, looked in the open the door and sighed. "We're going to have to tell the lieutenant, you know."

"I don't see why." The mulish look was back on Cora Lee's face.

Why was she so set on not letting Lt. McMann know about the syllabub? Because she thought it would incriminate Elizabeth?

"Cora Lee, we have no choice. Besides, they're not going to find anything in that bowl that shouldn't be there. I doubt whoever killed Monty wanted to wipe out the whole Smithfield family. That's what would have happened if he, or she, poisoned the whole bowl." The impatience in Noah's voice was becoming more evident with each sentence.

"The syllabub in Monty's glass was poisoned. It had to be." Cora Lee's eyes narrowed to slits and I watched her jaw tighten.

"That's probably true, but it doesn't mean it's in the bowl. It was probably put in his glass." Leave it to Aunt Mary to be practical.

Cora Lee leaned forward. "Maybe the syllabub in his glass didn't come from that bowl."

Everyone in the kitchen looked at her. No one said a word.

She shrugged. "Guess I'm stretching it on that one."

Noah closed the refrigerator door and turned to face us. Max came to sit beside him. We were about to get a lecture. Noah had the same look on his face Dan got when he thought either Susannah or I was about to get mixed up in something he wasn't going to like.

"Lieutenant McMann will be here shortly. He's got some more questions, especially for Elizabeth. The crime scene people will probably need to take your fingerprints."

"I won't be here." Elizabeth walked back toward the now

empty coffeepot and proceeded to rinse it out. "Another pot, everyone?"

The timer rang. Mildred headed for the stove. "Oatmeal's done. Cora Lee, you get the bowls. Noah, step away from that refrigerator. We need milk, and I think a little orange juice would be nice. Mary, glasses are in the cupboard there."

Noah didn't get to start his lecture until everyone was at the table, toast had been served and coffee cups refilled.

"You're going to have to face the fact there aren't a lot of options here. Monty was found dead in a locked house, having drunk, we think, syllabub, a drink that isn't readily available, and there absolutely wasn't any in that old house. There was, however, a whole bowlful of said drink in the refrigerator in this house."

"We get the picture," Mildred said

Noah glanced at his mother but picked up the pace. "That doesn't leave a lot of wiggle room. Lieutenant McMann has no choice but to suspect someone who has free access to this refrigerator. That means every one of us in this room." He stopped and looked at Aunt Mary and me. "Not you two, but the rest of us, and particularly you, Elizabeth." All spoons went down into bowls and three pairs of eyes stared at him. "It's no secret Monty was giving you a hard time."

"This is absolutely ridiculous." Cora Lee's cheeks were flushed. Eyes narrowed, she pushed her bowl away and glared at Noah.

"Don't get mad at me." Noah leaned forward a little, as if to emphasize his point. "It's hard to get in and out of locked houses unless you have the key. Currently the only keys we know of are Elizabeth's and, I assume, Cora Lee's. Mom and I have a set as well, given to us by Cora Lee after she had the locks changed. Narrows the field somewhat, doesn't it? None of us liked Monty, but it was Elizabeth he was harassing. McMann knows that, and he's going to worry it for all it's worth." He reached over and put his hand on Elizabeth's arm. "I'm not trying to scare you, or any of you, just warn you it's not going to be too much fun around here for a while. McMann's going to be here soon." He paused, which gave additional weight to his next words. "They found something in Monty's glass. They're not sure what it is yet, but it's something that doesn't belong there. The autopsy will be performed this morning and the docs are going to look for poison." He sighed, sat back and ran his hand over his short-cropped hair. "Somehow, I think the ghost you claim was prowling around here is going to be a hard sell." He stopped again and looked at his mother, who sat rigid, lips tightly pursed, then at Cora Lee, who was still flushed with anger, and finally at Elizabeth. "We have a witness who says Monty was putting a lot of pressure on you to sell him Smithwood at a discounted price. It that true?"

It wasn't hard to tell Elizabeth would rather be boiled in oil than talk about it, but she didn't have much choice. "You think I killed him so he'd go away and stop bothering me? Your snitch has it wrong. Monty didn't want to *buy* Smithwood. He wanted me to *give* it to him. He said I could take a little of the cash, or some stock, but he wanted the plantation and everything on it. He wanted me out. If I didn't do as he wanted, he'd take me to court and tie everything up until I either ran out of money defending myself or ran out of life. Whichever came first. That was how he put it."

Noah didn't say anything for a moment. Neither did anyone else. Aunt Mary caught her breath. What Elizabeth said made her motive to permanently remove Monty seem more than plausible. Elizabeth shouldn't be talking about this. The police weren't dumb. It would take them no time at all to realize Elizabeth could have presented Monty with that glass before she left. I had a quick vision of Elizabeth flying into the airport waiting room, late. Then, according to Aunt Mary, she was always late. I didn't think Elizabeth could murder anyone. She saved things—trees, whales, salmon, streams—and if she decided to get rid of Monty, it wouldn't have been with poison.

The police might not see it that way. Cora Lee. She was here. Could she have offered Monty that drink? Why? She didn't own Smithwood. Why didn't she? Had she already gotten her inheritance? Then there were the Longos. What motive could they have? It all came back to Elizabeth. Wait! Someone else had been there. The person with the candle. That wasn't Elizabeth. Only, the police would only have my word, Aunt Mary's and Cora Lee's that we saw a light. I looked over at Cora Lee, then at Mildred. From the expressions on their faces, I knew they were thinking the same thing.

Noah stared at Elizabeth. "So, it's true. Monty really did think he'd end up with Smithwood." He sighed and looked at his mother. Something passed between them, some communication I couldn't follow. I glanced around but no one else seemed to have noticed.

"Monty was a fool. He'd never have gotten Smithwood." Cora Lee looked up from mashing her oatmeal to glare at Noah and his mother. "Not while I had breath in my body."

I almost choked on my oatmeal. Did Cora Lee realize what she'd said? Evidently not. She went on mashing. There were a lot of things going on around here I hadn't begun to understand, but first I had to get Elizabeth to shut up. Also Cora Lee. I didn't know if that last statement made her a suspect as well, but it made it clear there was no love lost between her and Monty. Anger still blazed in those pale blue eyes. It showed in the pile of crumbs she'd made of a piece of toast. Cora Lee. She was here when we arrived and had been for some time. She'd made salad. She could easily have found time to invite Monty to share a glass of syllabub with her. It seemed likely she would have removed her glass, not so much to protect herself as to protect the glass. She wouldn't want any heavy-handed policeman dropping Smithwood treasures.

"Lieutenant McMann will be back out this morning. You might want to think about getting an attorney."

Elizabeth turned white. "Why do I need an attorney? I didn't kill the little creep. If I'd known he was even on the property, I'd have taken him by the scruff of the neck and pitched his rear end off." She paused for a breath and glared at Noah. "As for Lieutenant McMann, he didn't tell me he was coming back. I have an appointment and I intend to keep it. If he wants to talk to me, let him call and we'll arrange a convenient time."

Elizabeth's jaw snapped shut. Her gray eyes lost their soft expression and took on the hardness of agates. I glanced over at Aunt Mary, who sighed and shrugged. She'd seen that look before. Lt. McMann just might not get his interview.

"Did anyone else know you made syllabub, Elizabeth?"

"What?" My question took her by surprise. It seemed to have startled the rest of them also.

"What do you mean?" Cora Lee set her cup down with a little too much force. "Why would that matter? Oh."

"Exactly. Noah said we would all be under suspicion because we knew about the syllabub. That seems a rather narrow view. Usually you need a little more reason to suspect someone of murder, but still, someone else had to know that bowl was there."

"A narrow view." Noah looked like he might start laughing. "I've never heard it put quite so delicately, but you've got a point."

"Humph. Leo McMann would be more than ready to throw us all in jail with less evidence than that."

I almost asked Cora Lee what all the enmity was between Lt. McMann and the Smithwoods but first, I needed an answer to another question. "Elizabeth, who else knew you made syllabub?"

She appeared to think back. "I met Hattie in the grocery store. She commented on the lemons and the cream."

"That's not much help," Cora Lee snapped. "Who else did you tell?"

Elizabeth sighed. "Monty knew."

"Monty!" Cora Lee stiffened. "How would he know?"

"I told him." Elizabeth's voice was mild but her eyes flashed. I doubted the conversation had been a pleasant one.

"He called to ask if I'd thought over his offer. Offer! I told him I couldn't talk, I was leaving to go to the airport to pick up a friend, and besides, I'd already given him my answer."

"When did you tell him about the syllabub?" Mildred seemed puzzled, as well she might. It didn't sound like a conversation about a dessert drink.

"I didn't. He brought it up. Asked if I'd made some, like I always did for company. Told me to save him a glass. I told him to get lost and hung up."

There was silence around the table, broken only by Petal's whine. Elizabeth absent-mindedly handed her a piece of toast. She immediately took it to the safety of the wingback chair and growled at Max as she devoured it.

Mildred was the first to break the silence. "Whoever was with Monty didn't have to know about the syllabub. Monty could have, and probably did, fill both glasses."

"I think they knew."

We all turned to stare at Aunt Mary. "Why do you say that?

"Whoever it was brought the poison with them. He or she had to know there was going to be an opportunity to use it. I'll bet Monty told them, said something like they'd have a glass while they talked over whatever it was they were meeting about."

"Which means, it could have been anybody with Monty." Cora Lee sounded a little hopeful.

I hated to dash her hopes. "Even if that's true, it doesn't get us any closer to knowing who wanted Monty dead, or why. It doesn't tell us why here, in your old house, or how they got in and out."

Noah nodded. "All questions that need answers."

"Leo won't look for them. He'll just assume it was Elizabeth, or one of us, and that'll be the end of it." The bitterness was deep in Mildred's voice, deeper even than in Cora Lee's.

"Mom." It didn't sound, from the resigned tone of Noah's voice, as if this was a new sentiment for Mildred.

"Don't you *Mom* me. The police department, the whole town, will be better off when you pass that test and can move into his job."

Noah opened his mouth as if in protest, or to chastise his mother, but she paid no attention. "As for all of you, the police will be here shortly and if you don't want to get caught in your night clothes, I think you better get yourselves upstairs and into something decent."

Aunt Mary ran her hands down the front of her flannel robe, the one with the antelope galloping around it. If "decent" meant being covered, she was as decent as you could get. Still, a shower and real clothes would be better. Those antelope were distracting. I glanced at Cora Lee. Maybe she should go first. That dressing gown wasn't decent. Elizabeth seemed almost dressed in blue plaid pajamas, but maybe it wasn't the thing she'd choose to wear to confront Lt. McMann. "That's a great idea. Why don't you go first, Cora Lee?"

"Good idea." Elizabeth pushed back her chair. "Mary, Ellen and I will help Mildred get this kitchen cleared and then we'll be up. We have an appointment in the Historic District at ten."

We did? First I'd heard of it. I glanced over at Aunt Mary. She seemed equally puzzled.

"You'll have to cancel it. McMann will want you here." Noah sounded decisive.

"So he can ask more questions?" Cora Lee stood and picked up her cane. "He can ask all he wants, but he won't get any answers. We don't have any left."

"His questions will have to wait." Elizabeth dropped her comment into the conversation casually. "I'm taking Mary and Ellen over to the Payton Randolph house in the Historic area this morning. Hattie Culpepper is working there today, and she's going to help me learn about hearth cooking."

"Learn about what?" Aunt Mary gaped at Elizabeth.

"You're going to introduce these two to Hattie? Why would you do a thing like that to friends?" Cora Lee looked like she'd just sucked a lemon.

"Hattie's not so bad. Just sort of obsessed." Mildred didn't look any more enthusiastic than Cora Lee, who snorted.

"Obsessed with being a Culpepper. She doesn't have a drop of Culpepper blood, as if it mattered anyway."

Mildred waved away Cora Lee's assessment of Hattie, whoever she was. "Elizabeth, this time I agree with Noah. I'm afraid you aren't going anywhere. Lieutenant McMann's going to have a bunch of new questions as soon as he hears about that syllabub. I don't think he'll take it kindly if you aren't here to answer them."

Elizabeth looked from Noah to Mildred to Cora Lee, and finally to us. There was a set to her chin that didn't bode well for Lt. McMann's questions. "I told everything I know last night. I made an appointment and I'm keeping it. Hattie may be a pain in the rear, but she knows about colonial kitchens and I need her. So, you tell Lieutenant McMann he can question me when I get back. Right now, I'm going outside to talk to Calvin. Then I'm going upstairs and take a shower. When I come down, Mary, Ellen and I are going to Colonial Williamsburg."

She picked up her half-full cereal dish and carried it to the sink, washed it out and put it on the counter. "I think there are clean towels in your bathrooms."

Mildred leaned over and picked up Cora Lee's dish. "You finished with this?" She got up, walked over to the sink, and set the dish in it. It was Elizabeth who had her attention. "Now, listen. If the police want to talk to you, they get to talk to you. Nothin' makes a policeman madder than to have someone skip out on him. I know. I had a father who was a policeman and have another one in the house right now. Go get your shower. Cora Lee, Ellen and Mary are going up now also. They'll head over to see Hattie. They can take notes. When they come back, we'll all go down in the old kitchen here and see what's left."

She looked thoughtful. "I don't think anybody's been in that kitchen for donkey's years. Probably nothing down there but dead mice and spiders."

"Let's hope they're dead." Cora Lee gave a genteel little shudder. Her robe slipped off her shoulder again. She yanked it back.

"I think learning about hearth cooking sounds interesting. I've heard women baked pies and cakes in fireplaces. I can't imagine how. But, Elizabeth, I think you should stay here. I'll stay with you. Maybe Ellen could go meet this Hattie."

I stared at Aunt Mary, appalled. She might be interested in cooking in a fireplace, but I wasn't. Besides, if anyone was equipped to talk to the police, it was me. I was married to one.

"I'm going to stay here. I've already called for someone to take over my Sunday school class. I don't have to go anywhere." Mildred's tone left no room for doubt. "I've known Leo McMann for years. He's always been difficult and he hasn't improved with age. I'll just stay and remind him that suspicion isn't the same as proof."

Cora Lee sighed heavily. "I don't suppose there's any way I can get out of this one."

"No, there's not." Elizabeth's face was rigid. "I want to get started on that project and I need some help. Hattie's an expert. So, for God's sake, try to be nice for a change. You don't have to talk to her. Just introduce Mary and Ellen and go stand in the yard or something."

"If that woman makes one crack about JD and pork bellies, I swear, I'll brain her with her precious brass pot."

"Your JD made a fortune on those pork bellies. Her husband ended up in jail for embezzlement. You're a Smithwood by blood. She's a Culpepper by marriage. Every time she looks at you, she sees all the things she's always wanted and never got. Be nice."

"Being a Smithwood didn't get me much and JD's made me pay for every dollar. If she's envious of me, she's an even bigger fool than I thought." Cora Lee pushed her coffee away so hard the cup swayed in the saucer.

That statement shocked me all the way to my toes. It wasn't the words as much as the bitterness and anger in Cora Lee's tone. That didn't last long. Her sarcastic little smile was immediately pasted back in place. "I'll take them over there, and I'll try to be nice. But Elizabeth, you'll owe me."

"Go on now." Mildred made shooing gestures with her hands. "Get ready. You, too, Elizabeth. You can talk to Calvin when you're dressed. Seeing you in your pajamas is a treat he doesn't need." She grinned.

Elizabeth looked at herself, nodded and turned toward the stairs.

Mildred turned to face Noah. "If you haven't gathered the eggs yet, you'd best do it before you leave to go into town. I won't have time once McMann and all of his troops arrive. I'm not leaving Elizabeth alone with that man." She gathered the last dish off the table and went toward the dishwasher.

Noah smiled, whistled for Max and headed for the French doors, Petal right on their heels. Cora Lee grumbled under her breath but started toward the stairs. Elizabeth pushed back her chair and followed. Aunt Mary walked over to join Mildred. "Can I help?"

"There's not much to do. Go get ready. Elizabeth won't settle down until she knows you're on your way. She's decided the kitchen is the next thing we're going to tackle and she'll say all the wrong things to McMann if she's worried about it. I'll make sure she doesn't say too much."

Aunt Mary turned to go then paused. "Are you coming up, Ellen?"

"In a minute. We can't all shower at once, so I'll just help Mildred. Then I'll be up."

She looked undecided but finally nodded and headed for the hallway.

"She's a woman who's used to getting in and getting things

done, isn't she?" Mildred paused in the act of rinsing a dish to smile at me. It didn't last long. "This doesn't look good. Elizabeth's no murderer, but she hated Monty and didn't care who knew it." She scraped the oatmeal out of another dish and ran water over it. "The thought that someone came in here, helped themselves to syllabub, poisoned it and then fed it to Monty is enough to make my skin crawl."

I took the rinsed dish from her and reached for the door of the dishwasher, ready to pull it open.

"Better wait until you have all finished your showers." Mildred leaned back against the drain board, as if she needed it to prop her up. "Do you think he'll be back?"

I set the dish on the drain board along with the other rinsed dishes. "You mean the murderer?"

Mildred nodded.

I'd wondered the same thing. "I think it was Monty prowling around upstairs, looking for something. Why he was dressed like that, I can't imagine, but I don't think he found whatever it was he was looking for. The only reason I can think of for both Monty and whoever slipped him the poison to be here is they were looking for the same thing. I don't think they found it. So, yes, I think whoever it is will be back."

Mildred nodded. "I think so, too. That crate was no accident." She paused before going on, her voice filled with apprehension. "You know, McMann isn't going to buy the mysterious prowler story. He's going to take the easy way out. Elizabeth fed Monty the poison before she left for the airport and we're protecting her." She sighed deeply and turned to the dishwasher. "Might as well load this. Can you hand me that bowl?"

She opened the door, pulled out the top rack and froze. "How did that get in here?"

"What's the matter? Oh no."

We stood, frozen, staring at the immaculately clean crystal glass, sitting on the top rack in solitary splendor.

"That's one of the old syllabub glasses." Mildred turned

around to look at the glasses on the hutch and returned her gaze to the dishwasher. She pulled the rack out all the way but the dishwasher was empty, except for the one glass.

I'd had a close enough look at the glass next to Monty to know this was from the same set. "It's the missing syllabub glass."

"Missing?" Mildred's hand went out to touch it, but she quickly withdrew. "Where are the others? Cora Lee and I packed these away years ago. There were eight of them. How did this one get in here?"

"Noah didn't tell you?"

"That boy only tells me what he wants me to know. What was it he should have told me?"

"The set of these glasses were on the sideboard in the dining room where Monty was killed. Six of them. One was beside Monty with the remains of a sticky drink in it. That made seven. One was missing. The one the murderer used."

We stared at each other then back into the dishwasher. "That's got to be the missing one, right there." Mildred took a better look. "It's clean. Someone's trying to frame Elizabeth."

"Yes." What Mildred said made sense. To me, at least. What would the police think? "How did it get in there? What do we do now?"

Chapter Seven

"THIS IS AS close as we can get."

Cora Lee pulled her car into a small parking lot in back of a row of houses. Deep backyards were sprinkled with low picket fences and little outbuildings.

"What are those?" Aunt Mary walked over to one fence and peered into the backyard. Neat rows of vegetables, set out somewhat optimistically in the early spring weather, were freshly planted in recently weeded beds. There were flowers, too new to tell what kind, around the perimeter or interspersed between the rows. Roses climbed on the fences, their leaves fresh and green. The tiny buds just showed a hint of pink.

"It's a vegetable garden."

"I can see that." Aunt Mary didn't bother to soften her tone. Evidently Cora Lee's sarcastic little barbs were getting old. "I meant the buildings. Like that one." She pointed to one at the end of the property.

Cora Lee grinned. "Life in Colonial Williamsburg was pretty smelly. Those building were the 'necessaries.'"

"The what? Oh." The white building was small but pretty, painted white with vents close up by the roof. "That was an outhouse?" I looked at the main house then back down the yard. Quite a hike. "They came all the way out here?"

Cora Lee's eyes narrowed as she laughed. "They used chamber pots, and the lady of the house was rarely the one emptying them. The colonists put all the smelly things at the end of their lots. Small barns for animals, outhouses, garbage. Discouraged people from lurking around in alleyways."

We followed Cora Lee up the side street, looking into the backyards as we went.

"This garden is huge." Aunt Mary stopped again and walked over to a picket fence. "What is all that stuff? I recognize some of it. That, for instance. What's that?"

Cora Lee stopped next to the fence. "Potatoes. Just starting to sprout. That pile of dead looking brush is a compost pile. Come on. We've still got to cross the square and it's getting late."

Aunt Mary didn't move. She loved gardens. I could tell she wanted to get into this one, wander around and sit on the bench under a tree whose leaves were the palest of green. I would have loved to join her. I hadn't had one minute to tell her about the syllabub glass. The sight of it shook me more than I wanted to admit. I'd helped Mildred stuff all the breakfast dishes into the dishwasher and close it quickly. "Let's not mention this to anyone At least, until we figure out what to do."

Mildred had immediately agreed. "Someone's trying to frame Elizabeth." Her mouth had formed a straight line and worry, or possibly anger, creased her forehead.

I nodded. "We're going to have to find out who, and fast." I didn't think anyone would go near the dishwasher. Not Elizabeth, and the rest of us were leaving.

Still, I'd worried all the way to the Historic district, barely listening to Cora Lee's chatter. Mildred was right. Someone was trying to frame Elizabeth. I wondered when it had been placed there. It wasn't running when we got home. We hadn't opened the thing last night. The only "dirty" dishes had been wineglasses. A smile tugged at my mouth. There certainly had been wineglasses. This morning we'd had coffee, then Mildred's oatmeal, so the dishwasher hadn't been opened since we'd arrived. I wondered how long Monty had been dead when we found him. He'd looked gray. Horrible. Rigid? I didn't know. I tried to remember his hand, his fingers, but I couldn't. It was cold in that house. He could have been dead long enough for the murderer to go back into Elizabeth's house, rinse out the glass and put it into the dishwasher. What was it Noah said? Someone searched upstairs. Had the murderer hung around after Monty died, going through things upstairs, looking for whatever it was he wanted to find? Only, how had he gotten out? He'd still been there when we arrived. The candle proved that.

"Oh, how charming." The small building that had caught Aunt Mary's attention was white, two stories, with green shutters open to let light and air into glassless windows. A tall chimney ran up one side of the building and a thin stream of smoke made its way out of the chimney pot. A Dutch door was closed against the midday sun. "I always wanted a Dutch door."

Cora Lee came back to get her.

"What is this, anyway?"

"A kitchen. Will you come on? Hattie is difficult enough at the best of times, but if we're late, she'll out and out grumble the whole time and we'll never learn anything."

"The kitchen? Way out here? Why isn't it in the house?" Aunt Mary stood, transfixed, looking from the small house to the large house at the front of the long lot.

"Kitchens were hot and smelly from the constant fire, and they sometimes burned the house down. Will you come on?"

Aunt Mary let herself be dragged out onto the main street, but there she stopped again. "Look at that." A man dressed in brown knee britches, his voluminous white shirt tucked into the wide leather belt that held them up, walked alongside a wooden cart slowly pulled by two large cattle with horns. "What are they?"

"Oxen. There were a lot of them back then. Mary, you can look at this later. The Payton Randolph house is right across the square." Cora Lee pointed to a two-story reddish house across from a large park; one with no tennis courts or children's play equipment. Instead, it was flanked by a round brick building with a heavy wooden door, fences made of crisscrossed pointed stakes and paths covered with crushed white something.

"Ouch. Are these pebbles?"

"Oyster shells. The colonists used them for all kinds of things. After they ate all the oysters, of course. The Indians showed them how. The Indians helped the settlers a lot and their only reward was smallpox and starvation."

"What?" I stopped and stared at Cora Lee. "What are you talking about?"

Cora Lee sighed. "Never mind."

I decided Cora Lee had more sides to her personality than a Rubik's Cube and was just as hard to figure out.

We crossed the street and walked around the side of a large house. A woman—dressed in a colonial full-skirted blue dress that ended just above the ankle, white stockings and a white apron—sat on a chair while she talked to several people seated on benches. She looked up and smiled broadly.

"Why, Cora Lee, you're a sight for sore eyes. Haven't seen you since William's funeral. You doing okay? We were all so sad when he passed. I tried to speak to you, but there were so many people. Is Elizabeth doing all right?"

"It's been hard, but she's making it. I thought I'd stay on for a while, help out with things."

The woman smiled, a knowing kind of smile. "Well, honey, I think that's a good idea. You both could do with a little family right now." She kept her eyes on Cora Lee as if trying to gauge her expression. "I hear your granddaughter's graduating next month. Stanford, isn't it? I expect you're going out to California for it."

"I'm planning on it."

Startled, I glanced at Cora Lee. There hadn't been any mention of a granddaughter. Why? Not everyone graduated from Stanford. Most never got in. Cora Lee should be crowing. She wasn't. Of course, we'd had a few distractions since we arrived.

"CJ is going to be there?" There was a hint of sympathy in the woman's voice.

Cora Lee nodded.

"Hmm. Well, I hear Elizabeth's going ahead with the project, so you tell her to call me. Sounds like fun."

"That's real sweet of you, Amy. I appreciate it. Is Hattie back in the kitchen? I'm supposed to ask her a bunch of questions. Elizabeth can't make it."

"I heard about Monty getting himself killed out at your place. I expect Leo McMann's handling the investigation. Poor Elizabeth." She stood, smoothed down her skirt and walked over to the waiting group. "Good day, all." She started her pre-tour lecture.

Cora Lee took Mary's arm and pulled her forward a little. "We go this way."

"What's that cap she has on?" I'd had seen pictures of them and wondered. "They look pretty useless."

"It's a mob cap. People back then wore wigs and in order for them to fit and not make your head sweat, they shaved their heads. Women wore those caps when they didn't want to wear a wig. It was better than going around baldheaded. Can you imagine shaving all your hair off so you could wear a scratchy old wig? There weren't any showers back then. Washing your hair would have been a real challenge, so maybe it made sense. Through this gate."

"Shaved heads?"

Cora Lee nodded absently. "Both men and women. Pretty stupid custom, if you ask me."

I thought about long heavy hair and no showers. Maybe not that stupid. Aunt Mary and I followed Cora Lee into a fenced yard, which held a cluster of small buildings.

"What are those?"

"Smokehouse, dovecote, woodshed, dairy—watch your step. The kitchen is over here."

A long shed-looking building sat on the left side of the yard. There were several open doors, all with shallow wooden steps leading up to them. Each door had a sign on it. I walked closer. The far one said "Laundry." It contained nothing but several large tubs, a fireplace and a long table. A black iron sat on the table.

"That iron looks heavy. How do you suppose they heated it?" Aunt Mary spoke from right behind me.

"Ben Franklin hadn't invented electricity yet. The fireplace?"

"Surely not." There was horror in her voice.

"Over here." Cora Lee peeked out of a doorway two doors down. The sign said "Kitchen."

The doorway in the middle was marked "Scullery." I wanted to look into that one. I'd read about sculleries but had never seen one. I wasn't going to now, either. Cora Lee disappeared into the kitchen and the murmur of voices was clear. Aunt Mary climbed the stairs and stepped inside. I followed.

I wasn't sure what I expected, but not this. The early spring day was pleasantly warm, but in this small room, it was hot. A fireplace took up almost one side of the room. The fire was small but appeared to have been going for some time. Coals burned red and the smell of smoke hung in the air. The windows on the opposite wall were open; under them was a shelf piled with bowls, copper pots, ceramic platters, mugs and a mortar and pestle. The shelves at the back of the room held platters filled with food. Aunt Mary was already down there examining the contents. The spinach salad, topped with finely chopped hardboiled eggs, looked a lot like the one she served. The tarts didn't. The crust was thicker, but it didn't look tough. It was brown and flaky. A plate was heaped high with fluffy biscuits. Platters held meats; bowls were full of puddings. Where had all this food come from? There was nothing in the room but a wooden table in the middle of the floor and a rather sour-looking woman standing by the fireplace, tongs in hand, watching us with an expression of equal parts amusement and disdain.

"Guess you've never seen an eighteenth-century kitchen before."

Hattie. The small, round woman had piercing blue eyes and faded yellow hair twisted into sausage roll curls that stuck out from under her not very clean mob cap. She wore a full-sleeved white blouse that came down over her light blue skirt, held in place around her waist with a wide belt. Over it was a faded blue plaid apron, pinned to her blouse at the top and tied at the waist. She picked up a corner of the apron and wiped greasy hands as she continued to study us. There was nothing welcoming about her arrogant smile. There was nothing welcoming about Hattie. I knew I wasn't being very charitable, but her attitude made that easy. Besides, the color of hair dye she used was all wrong. It made her look like a stuck-up canary.

"You must be Mary McGill, Elizabeth's friend."

There was a lack of enthusiasm in that statement that didn't bode well for a future relationship. Aunt Mary nodded and smiled. A speculative kind of smile.

"Where's Elizabeth?" Hattie turned her back on us and leaned into the fireplace. She dipped a rough-looking brush into a pot, took the end of her apron and moved back a plank that was propped in front of the open fire. A large fish was tied on it. A whole fish. Head, tail, fins, and all. Hattie dabbed some clear liquid on it and then turned the board back toward the fire.

Aunt Mary sniffed. "Butter?"

Hattie nodded with what might have been approval. "Yep. That's what a cook back then would have used, butter being plentiful and all. Of course, so was fresh lard."

"Lard?" Ever since Uncle Samuel dropped dead of a heart attack, Aunt Mary had been vigilant about cholesterol. She was an excellent cook and she knew it. So did all of Santa Louisa. Only now, she served more vegetables, fruit and salads. Muffins, potatoes, steamed puddings and lemon meringue pie were no more. She still believed firmly in butter, though. So had Julia Child, who lived to a ripe old age. But lard? She didn't seem too sure about that.

"See those crusts over there?" Hattie pointed to the shelves that held the finished platters of food. "Made with lard. Not that grease you buy in tins, but good fresh lard made from a recently butchered pig. I should know. I made it. Want to see?" She walked over to a barrel and removed the lid. A pungent smell crept into the room and mixed with the smell of fish and smoke.

Aunt Mary looked in. I peeked over her shoulder. Cora Lee didn't bother to move. The lard had a congealed look but wasn't artificially white like the shortenings I used.

Hattie took a small bowl and scooped some out. "I'm fixing to make what passed for French toast in colonial America. Bread dried out pretty fast back then, so this was one way they used it up. Come over here."

Aunt Mary edged over beside the table. She'd made French toast for years, and she, too, made it with leftover bread. I'd eaten lots of it. "What are you dipping it in?"

French toast was made, at least in Aunt Mary's kitchen and now in mine, by dipping the stale bread in a beaten egg and milk mixture then frying it in butter on a hot griddle. There was no milk on the table in front of Hattie.

"White wine."

"Are you really?"

"Umuh." Hattie cut the loaf into thick slices. She dipped one slice in a shallow bowl of white wine, barely dampening it before she fished it out and dipped it into a beaten egg. A trivet straddled a small pile of hot coals on the brick floor in front of the fireplace. Hattie set an iron skillet on it, dropped lard into it, waited until it sizzled and put in the bread. The smell made my mouth water.

Hattie smiled. "Nothing like fresh lard."

Cora Lee walked over and glanced into the frying pan. "The wine doesn't hurt. Hattie, Elizabeth sent us for the list of stuff she's going to need for her kitchen."

"Where is Elizabeth, anyway?"

Cora Lee gritted her teeth. The taut lines around her mouth told how much she didn't want to answer that question, but she didn't have much choice, short, of course, of telling Hattie to mind her own business. "She had to stay home this morning."

"Because of poor Monty?"

"How did you know about that?"

"Why, it's all over the TV. Prominent attorney found dead in the old Smithwood mansion. They said three elderly ladies found him." Hattie smiled. "Didn't mention the young one. The news media's having a wonderful time." Smile gone, Hattie sighed. "Poor Monty. I expect the police are asking Elizabeth all kinds of questions." She paused and turned over the beautifully browned piece of bread. "There. Doesn't that smell lovely? Do the police know who did it?"

Cora Lee stood behind Hattie, rigid, hands clasped into fists at her sides, probably to keep from putting them around Hattie's throat. She was going to have nail marks on her palms. Was it really all over the TV? I hoped not. The last thing we needed were TV trucks, reporters sticking microphones in our faces and newspaper people running around with cameras and little notebooks. Tension clawed at my stomach. What if one of the reporters found out about that syllabub glass? Impossible, but my stomach knotted.

"Hattie, take the damn French toast off the fire and tell me what we need to have to stock the kitchen." I wasn't the only victim of too much tension. Cora Lee sounded as if she'd snap any minute.

It was obvious Hattie knew it, too. Evidenced by the tiny smile on her lips as she slipped another piece of bread into the frying pan.

"I never could figure out why Elizabeth wants to do this. So much money to get that old plantation put back into authentic condition, and for what? Several of the old plantations around here give tours and all that, but they're sure not getting rich. Colonial Williamsburg couldn't even make Carter's Grove pay for itself. Why does she think Smithwood will?" Hattie gave the pan a little shake.

"Smithwood won't have tours. William would never have agreed to busloads of strangers trooping through our house." Cora Lee sounded as if she was talking through clenched teeth.

"Then what's she going to do?" Hattie left the toast to slather more butter on the fish.

"It's going to be a cross between a school and a living history museum, but for students only."

Hattie looked blank. The French toast sizzled. Aunt Mary glanced at it but did nothing. It needed turning but, from what I'd seen of Hattie, Aunt Mary's help wouldn't be appreciated.

Cora Lee took a deep breath and spoke more slowly, enunciating her words as if Hattie wouldn't quite get them if she didn't. The subtle insult wasn't lost on Hattie, who flushed an unbecoming red.

"Elizabeth is a history major, has her PhD. She thinks people find history boring because it's taught that way. She wants to make early American history come alive for the teachers so they'll make it come alive for the kids. She's going to have them step back in time." Cora Lee cocked her head to one side and smiled brightly. "Isn't that a good idea?"

"No." Hattie's eyes narrowed. "Won't work."

"Yes, it will." Cora Lee walked closer to the fireplace. She gestured at the frying pan setting on the trivet and at the fish tied to its board, both giving off wonderful aromas. "She's going to take the plantation back to the eighteenth century. The main house will be restored as accurately as possible, so will the east wing. The students will cook, just like you're doing here."

Cora Lee glanced at the fish, shuddered a little, walked back over to the table and reached out to touch a blue and white bowl of eggs. "I suppose you took these this morning from some poor unsuspecting chicken's nest?"

"That's not how I'd put it, but yes." Hattie also looked at the bowl, her face devoid of expression.

"The milk in that pitcher, that came from a cow?"

"Milk usually does."

"Today, most people think it comes from a store. Did you milk the poor thing, or did someone else?"

"Someone else did. That's yesterday's milking. So's the cream I just put in that." She gestured toward a tall slopping barrel with a wood top and a long handle sticking out of it. "The dairy woman poured the milk into those round pans and let it sit all night, so the cream could rise. She skimmed it off for me this morning. I'll make butter as soon as the bread's finished."

"Really?" Aunt Mary walked over to the barrel. "My great aunt had one of these."

Hattie stared at her with what was almost a sneer. "So you know how to churn?"

"No. I was little. I just remember her sitting on the porch, turning the paddle."

"Go ahead. Try it. Grab that handle and start moving it around in a circle. I could use the help."

Aunt Mary didn't look one bit happy with Hattie's tone of voice, but I could tell she was curious. She grabbed the handle and started moving it. "This isn't hard at all."

"Wait until it starts to turn. You can put out more effort than that. Let's get it churned before tomorrow some time."

Aunt Mary stopped churning. "I'll stop by the store on our way home. Their butter's already churned."

Hattie's face got red and she started to say something but apparently thought better of it.

Cora Lee laughed. "You just proved my point. Or rather, Elizabeth's. People want to see how things were done and they want to see if they can do it. Not everyone, of course, but lots of people. If you hadn't been so rude to Mary, you just might have gotten your butter churned."

I was disgusted with both of them, and judging from Aunt Mary's frown, so was she. Hattie was both rude and arrogant and Cora Lee's needling only egged her on. Elizabeth needed this very disagreeable person to help her and the chances of that happening were disappearing fast.

Aunt Mary glared at Cora Lee, which amused me, then returned to churn. "I'll try again. Hattie, but I didn't tolerate sarcasm from my seventh graders and don't intend to start now."

Hattie looked taken aback. Cora Lee seemed ready to explode with laughter. Aunt Mary gave her best disapproving look.

"You know, Hattie," Cora Lee said, "Elizabeth not only wants to talk to you about a list of utensils and things, but possibly acting as an instructor. She'll need someone with your kind of expertise." Cora Lee could change tactics faster than a chameleon changed color.

"I'll bet you anything not one of them has the slightest idea of how to do any of this. Since we don't want to starve Elizabeth's students, or let them burn the place down, Elizabeth thought she'd ask you. It won't interfere with your other job and it'll pay a lot better."

Hattie glared at her. "I'm already an instructor. I teach classes at home. I only work here when they need an expert to fill in. It's not easy to find a descendent of one of the founding families, especially one who's kept all the old traditions alive like I have."

"Of course," Cora Lee murmured. "First families like the Culpeppers. Right?"

"We can trace the history of the Culpeppers back to the beginnings of Williamsburg. There's even a town named in their honor. I brought my Payton up to be proud of his heritage."

"Yes. We know." Cora Lee had that sucking-on-a-lemon look again. "By the way, didn't I hear Payton was having a little trouble? Something about his lobbying funds? Seems people are getting pretty picky lately, what with all those lobbyists caught paying bribes, not using their clients' money the way they're supposed to. It'd be a shame if Payton got himself in trouble."

Cora Lee had really done it this time.

Hattie caught her breath and turned an alarming shade of red. Aunt Mary stopped churning and watched. How would Cora Lee get herself out of this one?

"My Payton never did anything dishonest in his life. That's a vicious rumor."

"I'm sure you're right." Cora Lee ducked her head to hide her smile. "DC can be a pretty tough town, rumors always flying every which way. Do think about helping Elizabeth. You'd also be keeping the names and the traditions of all the first families alive."

Cora Lee had obviously been the chairwoman of one too many committees. The chairwoman's main job wasn't to organize, although that came in handy, but to talk people into doing things they didn't really want to do by making them feel only they could do the job. Cora Lee had just made Hattie feel she'd be letting the Culpeppers down if she didn't help Elizabeth. Her southern accent had gotten thicker with every layer of flattery and family pride she'd poured on. Masterful.

Aunt Mary caught Cora Lee's eye and nodded, just a little. A flicker of a smile flashed across Cora Lee's lips and just as quickly disappeared.

Hattie stared at Cora Lee for a moment, hands on hips, cooking fork in one hand and sticking out to the side. Her nose, curved a bit like a beak, and the curls sticking out from under her cap gave her the look of an angry canary. "What else does Elizabeth want me to do?"

"I have no idea."

"These teachers, or whoever she's planning on training. She's going all the way with them? They're going to sleep on rope beds and feather mattresses? Heat the house from the fireplace, wear the same clothes they did then? These folks won't be going home at night and taking off their costumes? They'll work in the garden and keep a chamber pot by the bed at night? Read by candlelight? Everything will be the same?" She paused and let her hand with the cooking fork drop down by her side. Her voice changed as well. A slight calculating note crept in. "Elizabeth's going to bring out all the old stuff? China, silver, all that stuff, and use it? She's not goin' to sell it all off?"

Cora Lee solemnly shook her head. "No. She wouldn't even if the school idea doesn't work out. Elizabeth's a historian. She respects Smithwood's historical importance, and that includes everything there."

Cora Lee hadn't mentioned founding families, just general historical importance.

"You sure about that?"

"Far as I know. That's the idea of the school, of course, to preserve everything, to recreate the eighteenth century. She'll need someone to help put it all together. That's where you come in. You being an expert on the eighteenth century and a Culpepper and all."

Hattie didn't say anything but she chewed her lip for a moment. "She's going to pay?"

"You always pay for expert advice."

Cora Lee didn't look as if she thought much of Hattie's expert advice, but Hattie didn't seem to notice. She'd clearly registered the praise part. I felt embarrassed by Cora Lee's insincere flattery but also by Hattie's need to take it, no matter how falsely given. I didn't like the way this conversation was turning out.

Aunt Mary went back to turning the paddle, but her task looked as if it was getting more arduous by the minute. She turned slower and slower. She pushed a little harder. Beads of perspiration popped out on her forehead, but she kept churning.

"I could teach those people a lot. About cooking, sure, but about life around here in those days and also about the families. The important families. That'd be a valuable thing, wouldn't it?"

"Very valuable." It was obvious to me that Cora Lee didn't believe a word she said.

"How can you tell when this stuff is butter?" Aunt Mary quit paddling and wiped her brow with the back of her hand. The paddle barely turned and the stuff in the barrel no longer smelled like cream. It smelled like butter.

Hattie returned to the twenty-first century with a jerk. "Oh, I should have been watching. You don't want it to get too hard. Move over."

Aunt Mary seemed glad to relinquish her place at the churn. I thought it would have been nice of Hattie to thank her, but I wasn't surprised. My brief time with Hattie led me to suspect that she rarely bothered with politeness. Unless, of course, you were a descendant of one of the founding families. Aunt Mary rolled her shoulders and watched Hattie take the lid off the churn and peer inside.

Her little sausage curls bobbed as she leaned over the barrel and her cap slid sideways. She didn't seem to notice. "This is almost too stiff. Mary, help me lift this thing. We'll pour the whey off into that shallow pan. There, that one on the table. Yes. Careful. Now we'll scoop the butter out and put it into a firkin."

"What's a firkin?"

"Drat. I forgot to bring it over. Wait just a minute."

Hattie hurried toward the door and scrambled down the steep stairs without bothering with the railing. I turned to look at Cora Lee, thinking this was a good time to go, but she had taken a seat in the rocking chair beside the table.

She watched Aunt Mary's annoyance with mild amusement. "Told you, didn't I?"

Before she could answer, the doorway filled with a small barrel, Hattie hidden behind it.

"Oh, let me help you." Early childhood training in politeness rather than concern for Hattie sent me toward the door.

"No, no. Get out of the way. This thing ain't heavy. It's empty." Hattie set the barrel down on the table, next to the butter churn. "I scoured this out last night getting it ready for the butter. Now, if we were really in the eighteenth century, we'd wash the butter, get the curds off. Then we'd cover this with a brine of some sort, salt water you know, put the cover on it and put it down in the cellar to keep cool. We could get months out of it that way."

Months? Without it going rancid?

Aunt Mary shuddered. "All that salt. It couldn't have been good for them."

The corners of Hattie's mouth twitched. "Kept stuff from spoiling. If it went rancid, you could melt what you needed and let it simmer then dip a toasted crust of bread in it. That'd take the bad taste out. I'll leave the firkin here, open, so the folks who come through on the tour can see it. They'll be along soon. After Amy finishes showing them the house."

Aunt Mary had a smaller version of the butter paddle in her hand, scooping the butter into the firkin. "Is that how they did it back then?"

"Yeah. They layered it just like that. Now sprinkle a little salt over it. More. The best families sometimes made little individual patties. They had special molds with the family crest in the bottom. Like little Jell-O molds. They put those on the table when they had company, which was most of the time. It's all in those cookbooks up there. They tell you exactly how they made everything, including the lard. Did you know that when you brine meat to preserve it for winter, you have enough salt in the water to keep an egg afloat?"

I didn't think Julia Child had covered that particular subject and doubted it was a piece of information I'd need in the near future. Hattie pointed toward a shelf, so Aunt Mary reached up and indicated various books until Hattie nodded her approval. She took down a small paperback, *The American Frugal Housewife*. A woman in period dress graced the cover.

Hattie reached over, took the book and put it back on the shelf. "Go on over to the Colonial Williamsburg Visitor's Center. They have a really good bookstore."

Cora Lee observed all this with a carefully blank expression, but it was evident she wanted no part of churning butter, planking fish or making French toast over coals, with wine or any other way. She looked at her watch. "What do you want me to tell Elizabeth? Do you have any kind of list I can take her?"

Hattie set the firkin on the table and wiped her hands on her apron. It looked as if she did that a lot. "I have to take this churn into the scullery and clean it, take the butter to the dairy, and get food ready for the next tour so people can see how it was done. Some of this has to go to the Governor's Palace. Besides, I won't know what she needs until I see what's there." She paused a moment then nodded. "She really wants to use that old kitchen?"

Cora Lee opened her eyes wide with surprise. "Of course. What else would she use?"

"Hmm. Tell her I'll come out as soon as I can. Day after

tomorrow? Unless, of course, this business with Monty blows everything to smithereens."

Cora Lee gave her a disgusted look, leaving no doubt she thought this entire visit had been a waste of her time. "How about the other stuff, helping her with the main house? I can do some of it, and will. I'm good at decorating, but I don't know a thing about chamber pots and rope mattresses, and I don't want to. Do you want to work on that also?"

"Maybe. What's she done so far?"

"Mostly outside stuff. William had that stroke before they could get anything done but their house. Noah's worked on the outbuildings and he's started on one of the slave cabins, but he's got his precious rare breeds and he's studying for his lieutenant's test, plus he has a full-time job. Noah's busy."

"Noah. I heard he's taking the test for lieutenant. That won't set well with McMann, now will it? I expect Noah'll need the extra pay since he's getting married."

Exasperated, Cora Lee shook her head. "Hattie, that's not why he's taking the test. Noah's got a career." She sighed and shook her head. "I'm sure they can use the extra money. Anyway, he's only going to be able to pitch in a little. Calvin's supposed to start the garden, but we're going to need lots more help."

"Calvin! Calvin Campbell? What's he doing back out there?"

"William planned on hiring him as soon as he got out of jail. Elizabeth wanted to honor William's wishes. Besides, no one knows more about eighteenth century gardens than he does."

Hattie didn't say anything for a moment but her pursed lips and rigid stance expressed strong disapproved. "I'm going to have to have Elizabeth out to my house in Yorktown. She needs to see a real Colonial garden."

Cora Lee sighed. "Tomatoes, spinach, yams, none of them have changed much."

"It's the herbs she needs to see. They used things most people have forgotten about."

Cora Lee glanced again at her watch. "Well, maybe she will. We have to go. I'll have Elizabeth call you."

A cellphone rang. I fumbled in my tote bag but it was Cora Lee's. She pulled it out and read the screen. Her mouth got tight and she flipped it open immediately.

"Mildred. What's wrong? Oh. Oh, no. They can't. They found what? Where's Noah?" She listened a minute. Her face got white and her mouth more pinched. "All right. We're on our way."

Something was burning. The arid smell finally made its way through the growing tension that came from Cora Lee's one-sided conversation. I wheeled around. Smoke rose from the cast iron frying pan. The toast was on fire, smoke and small tongues of flames reaching for the ceiling. Hattie, who'd been listening intently, swiveled about and, with a corner of her apron, grabbed the frying pan off the little fire.

"Dad gum it." She shook the pan a little and flung the offending piece into the main fire then walked back over to the table and set the frying pan down on another trivet to cool.

"What's wrong? Is it Elizabeth?"

Cora Lee didn't seem to hear. She trembled slightly as she shoved the phone back into her pants pocket. I wasn't sure she even noticed the toast burning.

"Mildred says Lieutenant McMann just read Elizabeth her rights and is going to take her down to the police station. They're charging her with Monty's murder." Cora Lee paused, and the breath she took in seemed labored. "Ellen, she said to tell you they found the syllabub glass."

Chapter Eight

A small cluster of cars and people huddled around the closed front gates of the plantation. One was a white van, antenna on top, call letters from a local TV station on its side. A heavily made-up, very shapely young woman stood beside it, watching a skinny young man in jeans and a sweatshirt with a Washington Redskins logo try to mount a camera on a tripod. The small SUV next to them had a Newport News Press logo on the front door with two men in the front seat. The press had arrived.

"Thank goodness." I stared at them.

"You've got to be kidding. What's good about them?" Cora Lee stopped the car and narrowed her eyes.

"Just wait. If Fox or CNN thinks this is important, we're in for an avalanche of reporters, and they're not shy about sticking those things in your face."

"What things?"

"Microphones. Cameras. Their faces."

Cora Lee edged the car through the few reporters up to the gate and stared at the chain that held it closed. "Who put that there? Ellen, would you mind?"

I did mind. I was tired, confused and upset at the thought Elizabeth might actually go to jail. How had they found that blasted glass? Who had? I didn't want Aunt Mary to brave the reporters so I opened the passenger side door and swung my legs out. They were around me before I could stand up.

"Who are you?" A middle-aged man in a rumpled-looking sports jacket got there first, notepad and pen ready.

"Are they going to arrest Mrs. Smithwood?" The voluptuous young reporter blocked my way with a microphone. The cameraman stood right behind her, camera raised to his eye, ready in case I said anything interesting.

"Leo McMann went in there a while ago. Then we saw Payton Culpepper. What's happening? Is Culpepper going to defend her?" Another one of the reporters tried to block my way to the gate. I skewered him with my eyes and pushed my way through to stand in front of it. The press formed a half circle around my back and continued to bombard me with questions, which I ignored. The gate wasn't locked, just secured with a chain held in place with a snap, which had no intention of giving up its job easily. I muttered a word not usually in my vocabulary and pushed on the thumb latch again.

"Do they know what killed him yet?" Why was the cameraman asking questions?

"Do you think there really is a ghost involved?" Surely the female reporter wasn't serious.

The latch came loose. I slipped off the chain, pushed the gate open and waved Cora Lee forward. I held the gate open only enough for her to get the car through.

"Hey. That's Mrs. Wittingham. CJ Wittingham's wife. She used to be a Smithwood. Hey, Mrs. Wittingham, is it true you and CJ are estranged? Did he have one too many floozies?" The reporter tried to slip through the gate, obviously prepared to chase after the car.

"You can't come in here." I stood just inside the gate and started to push it closed.

The man tried to slip through anyway.

"I told you. You can't come through."

The reporter didn't even glance at me. He pushed at the gate and managed to get halfway in.

I told everyone later he must have been off balance or I never would have been able to catch him mid-stride like that. I hadn't realized he was caught on the gate. He certainly made a fuss. It wasn't my fault his leg was still inside while the rest of him was out. I quit pushing so he could pull his leg out. As for the tear in his pants, well, I told him not to come in.

"Ouch. Damn. Oh, pain." He leaned against the gate pillar holding his leg. "You've broken it."

"Oh, I don't think so." I checked to make sure he really was out and we were safely in before I slipped the chain back on. This time the snap was more than ready to do its job. "Don't even think of opening this gate. The police are here and I wouldn't hesitate to have them remove you for trespassing." I deliberately raised my voice so everyone heard. "When Mrs. Smithwood is ready to make a statement, she'll call a press conference and include all of you. In the meantime, do not enter this property. And, young man, you might try Neosporin on that leg. I've found it's good for all kinds of things."

I turned back toward the car.

He muttered, "Not if the damn thing's broken."

I smiled broadly as I slid into the backseat. "Ready."

The car didn't move.

"What's the matter? If we don't get going, those blasted reporters will scale the gate to get at us."

"Where did you learn to handle the press that way?" Cora Lee looked torn between amusement and awe.

"I've had a couple of run-ins with them over the years." I settled myself as the car started to move forward. "Isn't Payton Culpepper Hattie's son?"

"He is, and he's one of DC's famous lobbyists. He and Monty were friends when they were in high school. He hung around here all the time, but that was years ago. Why?"

"That newspaper man said he entered through the gate a short time ago. He asked if he's going to defend Elizabeth."

"Payton?" Cora Lee slammed on the brakes and twisted in her seat to stare at me. "Are you sure he said Payton Culpepper?"

"Yes. I'm positive. If he's a lobbyist—I guess a lot of them are attorneys." I didn't know much about lobbyists. To the best of my knowledge, I'd never met one, but I didn't think they did criminal law. Not that Elizabeth was a criminal, but she might need an attorney. A criminal attorney. My fists tightened.

Cora Lee continued to stare at me. "I can't imagine why Payton would be here. Unless Hattie called him. That can't be right. She wouldn't call and he wouldn't come." She started the car, moving a little faster than the uneven road allowed. "We need to see what's going on."

Not much. A small knot of people stood on the front porch of the west house. Elizabeth was among them and she wasn't wearing handcuffs. Mildred stood beside her and Noah behind them both. Lt. McMann, a bald man with a bulbous nose and florid cheeks, stood more or less in the middle. His pants, easily visible under his unbuttoned sports jacket, sat a little below his stomach in a manner I thought most unbecoming for a policeman. At least he was talking, not yelling as he had last night. A tall man in a beautifully cut charcoal gray suit, almost blindingly white shirt and maroon stripped tie stood on Elizabeth's other side. Payton Culpepper? We crept closer and came to a stop behind two police cars. One was marked Crime Scene Investigations. The other was identifiable only because of the uniformed officer sitting in the driver's seat.

A young man dressed in khakis and a polo shirt came out the front door carrying a large carton with a small brown paper bag on top. He walked carefully, putting one foot deliberately in front of the other as if worried he might spill its contents. He nodded to the group on the stairs, said something to Lt. McMann and started carefully down the stairs. Everyone was watching him. The attorney turned full face toward me.

I gasped. "Aunt Mary, look. That man."

I heard a quick intake of breath as she leaned on the dashboard to stare at the man. "That's him. I know it's him."

"What's the matter?" Cora Lee twisted the other way. The young man walked toward the car. "That's the crime scene man. Look, he's putting a box in the back of that SUV. I'll bet that's the syllabub." Her expression changed. "You don't think that's our punch bowl, do you? He wouldn't. Would he? That punch bowl is over two hundred years old. He has no business touching it. If he breaks it—what do they think they're doing?"

I wasn't looking at the crime scene man or his SUV. Instead, I stared at the attorney. "That man, the one standing by Elizabeth. Is that Payton Culpepper?"

"That's him."

"That's the man we flew in with yesterday."

Cora Lee had her door open and was struggling to unhook her seat belt, but she stopped, twisted again to look at Aunt Mary, then back at me. "Flew in where?"

"From L.A. to Philadelphia. He sat next to Aunt Mary. We changed planes there and flew to Newport News. So did he."

Cora Lee paused, the door half opened. "He did? I thought he and Hattie had—I wonder why he came here. Never mind. I'm going to rescue my punch bowl."

She edged out of the car, slammed the door and, jamming her cane into the ground with every step, started toward the Crime Scene vehicle. I climbed the stairs behind Aunt Mary to join the group standing on the porch watching them.

"Where's Cora Lee going?" Elizabeth said, as she watched Cora Lee tap her cane forcefully on the closed window of the SUV.

"To rescue your punch bowl." Aunt Mary nodded at Payton Culpepper.

He nodded back. "We meet again."

"Yes."

There wasn't time to say anything more because both Lt. McMann and Elizabeth started down the stairs.

"Cora Lee, it's all right. He doesn't have the bowl." Elizabeth was in the lead, almost to the car. "I gave him a glass jar."

"Cora Lee, you're interfering with police procedures." Lt. McMann edged past Elizabeth and grabbed Cora Lee's arm. "You're going to break that window."

"Leo McMann, take your hands off me at once." The look she gave him would have blistered paint. "Is there some reason you're accosting me?"

Lt. McMann's face reddened, but he took his hand off her arm. "Cora Lee, you've been a pain in the ass ever since I met you. We didn't take your damn punch bowl. Mrs. Smithwood explained about its 'historic value' and, frankly, I'd rather face a python than have one of you women after me if we broke it. We got fingerprints off it and put the contents in a glass jar. That all right with you?"

Cora Lee dropped her cane from the car window and brushed at her sleeve, as if to brush off his touch. The insult apparently wasn't lost on Lt. McMann. His already florid face turned beet red.

"Leo, you are the rudest man alive. You've been practicing rudeness since you were a kid and I had to babysit you." She turned back toward the house but paused. "Or did you learn it in police school. If so, you passed with flying colors."

With that, she walked to the stairs, leaning on her cane with each step, followed by an obviously unhappy Elizabeth.

I watched Cora Lee's impertinence with foreboding. Provoking the police was, in my opinion, never a good idea. It was especially dumb right now, with so much at stake. I looked over at Aunt Mary. She looked equally grim.

Cora Lee reached the top of the stairs, paused and addressed Elizabeth. "Just what is going on? Mildred called and scared us near half to death. Hello, Payton." She nodded to him. "The way she sounded, I thought you were halfway to the electric chair."

Elizabeth sighed. "You do have a way with words, don't you?" She sighed again. "If Payton hadn't shown up, that might have been the case."

Cora Lee turned to Payton. "Why? What did you do?"

"I'm glad to see you, too." He gave her a small bow.

"Oh, stop that. How did you keep Leo from arresting Elizabeth?"

Icicles dripped from every word of Payton's answer. "I merely pointed out that he didn't have enough evidence."

"What he actually said was, Leo couldn't make spaghetti stick to the wall with the evidence he had and he didn't have a warrant. If he arrested me, Payton would make sure all hell broke loose."

Elizabeth was clearly furious but trying not to let it show. With Lt. McMann? My eyes shifted behind Elizabeth to where Noah stood beside his mother. He hadn't said a word but he seemed equally as angry. Mildred just looked miserable.

Payton Culpepper didn't seem to notice. He pushed back the sleeve of his immaculate white shirt to reveal a beautiful gold watch, which I thought he exhibited a little too long. "I'm booked on the last flight out to DC and have to leave now if I'm going to make it." He turned to address Lt. McMann, who had followed Cora Lee up the stairs. "Leo, I'm glad you're being sensible about this. We both know your evidence is insufficient to arrest Mrs. Smithwood. I'd hate to see you embarrass yourself by trying. If you have more questions, her attorney will be happy to accompany her." He took Elizabeth's hand. "Elizabeth, Harrison Silverstein will call you tomorrow, or his secretary will. He's the best criminal attorney in the state of Virginia. I'll call him and fill him in. You don't have to do a thing." He scanned our little group, nodded once to Noah and let his eyes rest on Aunt Mary. They narrowed in an expression of … what—speculation, recognition, suspicion? A difficult man to read. In an instant he had regained the air he had presented in the airport, one of calm command. This man knew he was in charge.

A car slowly drove around the circle toward the steps. "I'll be in touch." He walked down the stairs, ignoring the remaining police car, and waited until the driver had the rear door open. If he looked back, no one on the stairs knew it.

"Do all limousines have black windows?" Aunt Mary watched the car navigate the bumpy road. Santa Louisa didn't have many stretch limos, only ones used for wine tasting tours. They didn't need black windows.

"Lots do. People around DC like their privacy." Mildred's voice was flat.

"Harrison Silverstein." Lt. Mann muttered another word under his breath I couldn't quite catch but I thought it started with an "s." He, too, watched the car until the trees hid it from sight. No one had trouble hearing what he said this time. "Arrogant bastard."

"Really, Leo." Cora Lee's lips were pursed.

"You think he isn't?"

Cora Lee's lips parted in a twisted smile. "Evidently, he's an effective one."

If a loud growl had come out of Lt. McMann's mouth, I wouldn't have been surprised. His eyes narrowed to slits and the broken capillaries in his cheeks made them glow bright red. He'd better not have a stroke. My only first aid training had been in Girl Scouts.

"Longo." Lt. McMann didn't bother to look at Noah. "Why are you standing around? Aren't you supposed to be working?"

"I'm off the clock. Have been for an hour or so."

"Then go home."

"I *am* home. That house down the road is mine. Those horses behind that fence, they're mine also."

As if on cue, two white heads appeared over the pasture fence. One nickered softly. Lt. McMann stared at the horses, then at Noah. "Yeah. Now, how could I forget a thing like that?"

There was something in that statement I didn't understand. Something calculated. His eyes flickered over Mildred, who flinched, then shifted back to Noah, who stood, rigid and unmoving. Cora Lee opened her mouth but shut it before Elizabeth could land the kick she so plainly aimed at her ankle. That Payton Culpepper inflamed everyone, Lt. McMann included, was obvious. There was more to it than his patronizing attitude, but what?

Lt. McMann turned toward Elizabeth. "Contrary to what the famous Mr. Culpepper thinks, we aren't finished. Just as soon as we check that glass for fingerprints and other substances, we'll talk again. Tomorrow. Please have your *attorney*—" there was no escaping the stress on the word "attorney"—"contact us to set up an appointment." His voice oozed sarcasm. He glared at all of us before starting down the stairs toward the only remaining car.

"Goodbye, Leo." Cora Lee's voice was almost cheery as she waved.

Lt. McMann turned back toward her and almost lost his footing on the stairs. "You know, I'm up for early retirement. I didn't think I was ready but, Cora Lee, I've changed my mind."

She smiled and waved as Lt. McMann climbed into the passenger seat of the unmarked police car. The door slammed and the engine started immediately. The car moved forward slowly then quickly picked up speed.

"I wonder what he said to that poor driver to make him move so fast." Cora Lee's smile was gone, her tone thoughtful as she stared after it.

"Whatever it was, I'll bet that young man didn't like it." Aunt Mary, hands on hips, watched the car disappear down the drive.

Elizabeth had also watched the car but had said nothing up to now. She shuddered slightly. "The only good thing is that I'm not in it. At least, not yet."

"Thanks to Payton Culpepper?" There was a question implied in Cora Lee's voice.

"Yes, thanks to him. But no thanks to you, Cora Lee. Leo hates us enough without your goading him."

"Elizabeth, honey, I just can't help myself. Leo was a horrible child. He was ugly to my daddy when he worked here, which was why he got thrown off the place, and he's downright hateful as a policeman. Just look at how he treats Noah."

Lt. McMann worked at Smithwood? He was fired? When? Was that the source of all this animosity? He treated them all, Noah especially, with disdain, and he acted as if Mildred didn't exist. Did the roots of his animosity go that far back?

"Elizabeth's right. It's just going to make him more determined to find enough evidence to arrest her, and Payton didn't help much." Noah looked furious but also worried. "We would have been fine if it hadn't been for that glass."

The glass. "What happened? How did Lieutenant McMann find out about it?"

Mildred sighed. She shook her head. "It all happened so fast. I couldn't stop her."

Aunt Mary looked worried as well, but she also looked tired. "Let's go inside where we can sit down. Then you can tell us about this glass."

"What glass?" Cora Lee was staying put until she got an answer, and Aunt Mary needed to sit down.

I sighed. "Mildred and I found the missing syllabub glass in the dishwasher this morning. Someone, undoubtedly the murderer, put it in there. I want to know how Lieutenant McMann found it. Then we're going to try and figure out what happened and what we do now."

It was Mildred who went inside first. After a moment, everyone else followed, except Noah.

"Aren't you coming?" I held back a little, waiting for him. "We need you."

"So do the animals." He was already down the steps,

pausing only to answer me. It seemed as if he was going to say something more. I waited. "I don't think there's anything to find on that glass. Neither does McMann. If he did, Elizabeth would be on her way to a jail cell. No. Whoever put it in the dishwasher made sure it was clean. By charging in here and throwing his weight around, Culpepper just made McMann more determined. If there's even a trace of poison in that syllabub, well, Elizabeth could be in real trouble."

Noah headed for the barn, his back rigid. His long stride, fueled by anger, covered even more ground. He disappeared around the corner of the barn.

I was about to follow the others, but a flicker of movement stopped me. Someone stood at the end of the east house, watching. He turned and disappeared around the corner, I supposed down the hill toward the river. It was Calvin. No one else on the plantation had long gray hair pulled back and tied with a ribbon. What was he doing up here? Listening? Why? Who was this Calvin, anyway? Why had he been in jail and why was William so determined to give him a job after he got out? I followed the rest of them into the house, deep in thought and eager to consult Dan.

Chapter Nine

THE CLOCK ON the wall struck six. I looked out the French doors at the sunlight that hadn't faded. The sky was still blue, the leaves on the trees dappled with light, the flowers that edged the side of Elizabeth's garden showed no sign of closing their petals and settling in for the night. The clock must be wrong. Only, it wasn't. Daylight savings accounted for the brightness, but where had the day gone?

My stomach growled. No one else seemed to be thinking of food, not even Aunt Mary, which amazed me. Elizabeth was seated at the table where she had sat last night. She told us how Lt. McMann had questioned her, badgered her, actually. She had risen to help herself to more coffee, more to get away from Lt. McMann's face staring into hers than the need for it. Examining the remains in the pot, she'd decided she'd had enough and opened the dishwasher to put in her cup. That's when she saw the crystal glass and gasped.

"McMann was on her like a cat on a crippled mouse. I tried to get there before she opened that door, but I was too late." Mildred looked at me almost apologetically. "Why we left it there, I don't know. We should have hidden it."

"Quit tearing yourself up," Cora Lee said. "If you had hidden it, and the police found out, you'd have made things worse. None of this is your fault."

I was amazed to see Cora Lee actually trying to give comfort. She reached over and patted Mildred's hand before quickly withdrawing hers. Afraid someone would see her and think she was weak? I thought again of Rubik's Cubes. Pushed one way you got one pattern, pushed another square and you got something totally different. Cora Lee was like that. Only Rubik's Cubes didn't offer caustic little remarks. What had happened to make her so angry?

Elizabeth's long braid had fallen forward over her shoulder. She threw it back and raised her head. "It's one thing to choose to put yourself in danger because you're fighting for a cause you believe in. Trust me, chaining yourself to an old growth tree when you've got furious loggers bearing down on you with skip loaders is pretty scary. It's nothing like as scary as having someone think you're a murderer."

"Murderess."

"Thanks, Cora Lee." Elizabeth didn't bother to turn her head. "That made me feel better."

"No one thinks you're a murderess, and there's no evidence, either. Quit worrying." Cora Lee's tone contained its usual nip of sarcasm, but this time there was also a seriousness that surprised me.

"How do you figure that?" Mildred sat up straighter.

Aunt Mary nodded slowly. "I think she's right. Whoever put that glass there couldn't take the chance his or her fingerprints might be on it, so they'd already washed it. They only put it there to throw suspicion on Elizabeth."

"It seems to have worked." Elizabeth blinked back tears. The muscles around her mouth tightened.

"I'm not so sure," Aunt Mary said. "If Lieutenant McMann thought he had something, he'd have you in a cell right now. As for the syllabub, I don't think there's anything in there, either."

Cora Lee smiled. "Mary's right. Not unless whoever's doing this wanted to wipe out the whole household."

There it ended. Elizabeth dropped her head again, apparently lost in thought. Cora Lee fiddled with her cane and stared at Mildred, who absentmindedly rolled a napkin into a cylinder, unrolled it and rolled it up again.

The French doors rattled, followed by a deep bark.

The start went through my whole body. Evidently I'd been so absorbed in my own thoughts, I hadn't noticed the dog. I pulled up the bar and let Max in. Petal appeared out of nowhere, greeted him with licks on his nose then sat down in front and stared intently at the humans. Max joined her. Was it time for them to be fed? No one paid them any heed.

"Where do you keep the dog food?"

"I'll do it." Mildred pushed back her chair and headed for what looked like a broom closet. The dogs followed her, tails wagging vigorously.

She ladled food into bowls.

My stomach growled again. "Aren't any of you hungry? Has anyone eaten since Mildred's oatmeal this morning? We need food." At least, I did.

"We also need alcohol." Cora Lee picked a bottle from the wine rack and pulled open a drawer in the chest on which it sat. "Where's the foil cutter? I had it last night. Never mind."

She examined the corkscrew, used it to remove the foil then stabbed the cork with it. Without asking, she took four balloon glasses off the buffet, poured a little in each glass and started handing them around.

"First things first." Aunt Mary set her glass down on the old highboy. "Ellen's right. Elizabeth, is that lasagna still in the fridge?"

Mildred nodded.

"Good. I'll slip that into the oven. We're going to have to eat dinner."

Elizabeth looked as if the concept of dinner was foreign and didn't give a tinker's damn if she never figured it out.

Cora Lee grimaced and shook her head. "I'm not one bit hungry."

"Be that as it may, we have to eat. I imagine the salad is still there and I think I saw bread. I'll butter some of that later."

Mildred started to laugh.

Aunt Mary looked startled then joined in. "Once a Home Ec teacher, is that it?"

"Yes. Always a Home Ec teacher. Or a mother. We just can't seem to shake that need to feed people. Go ahead. Do you know how to turn on the oven?"

"Yes. No. I'm not sure. Is it this thing here?"

"You got it. You want me to help?"

I doubted Aunt Mary did, but Mildred needed something to do with her hands. Something that made her feel useful. Mildred's day had probably left her feeling quite useless. Aunt Mary must have realized it, because she smiled. "Please."

Mildred picked up the edge of the foil on the lasagna. "Just checking to make sure there's no plastic wrap under here. I didn't check one time."

Mary laughed again, this time with genuine mirth. "I made that same mistake. I believe we went out to dinner that night."

Mildred took a bowl from the refrigerator, peeled back the plastic wrap and shook her head. "Cora Lee, you dressed this salad last night. It's mush now. I'll make a fresh one."

"It's going to be a while. Make it later. Let's sit down."

Aunt Mary picked up the glass of wine Cora Lee had poured for her, made a face, and set it down. "I'm going to make tea. Want some?"

Mildred immediately headed for a cupboard, brought down two mugs and, from another cupboard, a box of green tea bags. "Wine later. Maybe."

Maybe. After last night, I wasn't so sure. Aunt Mary filled the kettle and she and Mildred pulled out chairs and joined us around the table.

The room was very still. Cora Lee reached for her wine and took a sip. She set it down carefully. "Damn. I just knew Payton would screw everything up."

"He did a good job, too." Mildred stared at her glass for a moment before pushing it away.

Elizabeth's glass was half gone. "How can I get rid of him? He thinks he's so blasted smart but all he's going to do is land me in jail."

Aunt Mary folded her hands, rested them on the table and leaned forward a little. "Will someone please tell me what's going on around here? Why was Mr. Culpepper here? Did he just show up or did someone call him?"

No one answered.

Aunt Mary sighed. "There has to be a reason. Elizabeth, I take it you didn't call him."

Elizabeth almost smiled. "It would never have entered my mind."

"Cora Lee? Mildred? Did either of you? No. I didn't think so. Then, why?"

The other three looked at each other.

"I have no idea." Elizabeth shrugged. "He just arrived. Climbed out of his limousine and said he was here to represent me. He demanded Leo tell him everything. Leo bristled like a cornered porcupine. Come to think of it, Leo hadn't said a word about arresting me until Payton got here." Her expression grew speculative, as if she, too, was trying to figure out what happened.

"You're right." The same look passed over Mildred's face. "How did he even know Leo was here?"

"Good questions." Cora Lee took another sip of her wine and smiled a little at Aunt Mary. "Helps me to think. I thought he'd gone back to DC." She took another sip and furrowed her brow. Probably to look as if she was thinking. "I guess Hattie might have told him."

"Told him what?" Aunt Mary got up as the teakettle began to

scream. She took it off the fire, pouring a little into the bottom of the teapot Mildred had set on the countertop. Then she swirled it, filled it and put in two tea bags. "Hattie didn't know Lieutenant McMann was out here or Elizabeth was in danger of arrest any sooner than we did. He moved awfully fast to get here ahead of us."

Mildred leaned forward on her arms, spreading her hands out on the table. "Not if he was at Hattie's house in Yorktown. It's about twenty minutes closer to Smithfield than Colonial Williamsburg. If he was there and Hattie called him, the timing fits."

"Only, why?" I waited for an answer. None came.

Finally Elizabeth spoke. "I don't know, but I wish he hadn't. Leo was dogged before, and I knew if he found one thing that seemed like real evidence, he'd go after me. Now he thinks he's got something."

Aunt Mary took two mugs of tea to the table, put one in front of Mildred and set the other in front of her empty chair. Finally she said, "You're not saying Lieutenant McMann might manufacture evidence?"

"He might not go that far, but he hates us." Cora Lee took another sip of her wine and glanced over at Mildred. "All of us."

"Why?"

"Another kind, enduring thing my father did." Cora Lee didn't try to hide the bitterness in her voice or her eyes. "Leo worked here his senior year in high school. Several of the local kids did. We still grew tobacco then and they hired on for the harvest. We used to have drying sheds down by the river, and a dock. Farmers from nearby plantations came to use it to ship their tobacco to the big auction houses." She stopped and examined Mildred's face, as if wondering if she should go on. Mildred didn't move. Cora Lee shrugged slightly. "There was a mix-up about some tobacco bales. One farmer, a relative of McMann's, got credit for too many, and someone else got shortchanged. My father blamed Leo. Actually got the police out here." She stopped again, and the look on her face was a combination of embarrassment and anguish. "Leo had nothing to do with it. It was a paperwork mistake, pure and simple, but my father still thought he was guilty. Not only did he fire him, but he blocked a college scholarship Leo was up for. Leo's never forgiven him, or any of us."

"That's not the only reason he doesn't like Noah." There was no emotion in Mildred's voice or on her face. Just a simple statement of fact.

"Why?"

"You heard what he said about retiring. It took Leo a long time to make lieutenant. I've never been sure how he managed it. He's not very good at the job. If he can hang on a little longer, he'll get more retirement. Only, the city council has put pressure on Captain Brewley to make Leo quit." Mildred paused, brought the mug of tea up to her lips, took a cautious sip, made a face and put it back down on the coaster Aunt Mary supplied. "If Noah passes this next exam, he'll be qualified for Leo's job."

Cora Lee eyed her empty glass as if trying to decide if she needed a refill. She pushed it away. "Losing his job would not make Leo happy, but to lose it to Noah … well … that wouldn't sit well. His hatred of Smithwood and everyone connected with it includes the Longos. Add that Noah is …" She didn't finish her sentence but she didn't have to. What she meant was only too clear. Noah was black. Lieutenant McMann was white.

Aunt Mary set her tea back down. Her hand shook. That simple statement had the power to send shockwaves through both of us. Why, I didn't know. We weren't exempt from prejudice in Santa Louisa. Several black families had moved in and been accepted without a ripple. The Hispanic families, however, had a harder time. The Sanchez family, who lived a few houses down from me, was the victim of a picket campaign. They were accused of being in the country illegally, which was nonsense. Mr. Sanchez was the local bank manager; his family had been there for generations. So had his wife's. She was an emergency room nurse at Trinities Hospital. Their three children all got good grades and were on half the sports teams in town. That hadn't made any difference to the protestors. Justice might be blind, but so was hate.

"That business about Harrison Silverstein. It made me furious." Elizabeth's eyes narrowed and she looked around the room as if hoping to find someone, or something, to smack. "The way Payton acted, you'd have thought I wasn't capable of making a decision harder than what color socks to buy." She paused and took a sip of her wine.

"Choosing the right socks can make or break an outfit."

Elizabeth glared at Cora Lee, who smiled and smoothed out her fine old linen napkin. "Well, I'm not using his blasted lawyer. I don't care if he is the best in the state. I'm going to call Aaron Glass. Now. Tonight. I know he won't be there, but I'll leave a message. I am not going to let Payton bully me."

Elizabeth couldn't have gotten everyone's attention quicker if she fired a shot across the room. Mildred choked a little on her tea before setting her mug down. Aunt Mary gaped.

Cora Lee burst into laughter. "Someone I know just got her mojo back."

"Cora Lee, hush up." Mildred reached over and took one of Elizabeth's hands. "That glass doesn't have a fingerprint on it, and there's no poison in the syllabub, either. I'm positive of it. Whoever's doing all this isn't that dumb. It's the key. McMann's going to pin everything on the key. You'd better tell that to Aaron."

"What key?" Cora Lee stared at Mildred's serious face with the same trepidation I felt.

"The one they couldn't find."

"Oh, Lord." Aunt Mary realized what Mildred meant almost before the words were out of her mouth. "The key Monty didn't have."

Mildred nodded. "McMann's decided there are only two ways Monty could have gotten in that house. One is someone opened the door and invited him in. The other is Monty had a key and let himself in. Noah says there were keys in his pocket, but none that fit these houses."

"So, according to the lieutenant, that leaves only one option. Elizabeth let him in and fed him poison. Logic was never Leo's strong point."

"Unfortunately, this time he's got logic on his side." I wished I could swallow every word, but it was a fact they had to face. "Monty had to get in somehow and, without a key, Leo could logically surmise someone let him in. Maybe that was true. The murderer let him in, and that has to be someone with a key. Someone who lives here."

"There's nothing to prove she did." Cora Lee's small mouth was set in a straight line, her eyes narrowed.

"There's nothing to prove she didn't, either." Mildred's voice was filled with worry and something else. Bitterness. "McMann's going to do everything in his power to make sure she at least goes to trial, just as he's going to do everything he can to make sure Noah never gets on the homicide squad."

All eyes turned toward Elizabeth, whose face was white and pinched. Her hands shook a little as she pushed back her chair and headed for the phone. "Then Aaron had better think of a way to stop him from doing either of those things."

Chapter Ten

I PICKED MY way down the gravel road, muttering a little under my breath. The dogs left the house with me but bounded on ahead, evidently undeterred by the gravel.

I paused for a moment and looked out over the pasture, down toward the river, admiring the view. The lasagna wouldn't be ready for about an hour and there was nothing for me to do in the house. Aunt Mary and Mildred were talking about recipes, Elizabeth was listening but with only half an ear and Cora Lee … I wasn't sure what she was doing, other than sitting, staring and drinking wine. It seemed a perfect time to call Dan. Only, he wasn't there. Lena, our new weekend dispatcher, told me old man Hartzog had gone missing and everyone was out looking for him. Old man Hartzog went missing on a regular basis. They usually found him walking down the dry riverbed. So, if I couldn't talk to Dan, I thought I'd look at the barn. Maybe talk to Noah about horses or chickens. Or possibly ghosts. I stopped abruptly. Were those sheep?

"Hi. What are you doing down here?" Noah walked up to the fence, a full pail in each hand. Several white wooly animals waited, not very patiently, in front of a metal trough. They greeted Noah's approach with loud baaahs.

"Are those sheep?" I walked over closer.

"Leicester Longwools."

"What?"

Noah laughed. He poured the contents of the pails into the feeder and set them on the ground. The sheep buried their faces in the grain. The noisy baaahs were replaced by the sounds of munching.

"Leicester Longwools. They were bred in England in the eighteenth century for their long fine wool. Some ended up over here. George Washington evidently had some. At least he mentioned them in his farm correspondence. They would have died out if Colonial Williamsburg hadn't worked to keep the breed going."

"What are they doing here?"

"The historic area has a space problem, so some of us with acreage help out."

He reached over the fence and scratched the ears of one of the ewes. She picked her head up, grain dripping from her mouth, let him scratch her ear for a moment and then dropped her head back into the feeder.

"That one's Beulah. She's going to lamb in another couple of weeks. Last year she wouldn't let the lamb get near her. We had to put her up against the wall and force her to let it nurse. One nursing and she was fine. I hope she doesn't do that again."

"Does that happen often?"

"Sometimes, especially first timers. I'll bet you came to see the horses. They're in the other pasture."

Noah walked back toward the barn. I followed. The barn was old. The boards were weathered, the paint a dusty light gray. Tall doors stood open, sagging on their iron hinges, showing an aisle wide enough for fenced off pens on each side. There was a small room halfway down the barn aisle, a concrete pad directly across from it. A rolled up black hose was attached to a water spigot beside the pad. Noah might be interested in restoring old breeds but he evidently had no interest in dealing with old barns that didn't feature running water or electricity.

The dirt barn aisle was newly raked, the small pens bedded with fresh straw. No cobwebs hung from the ceiling and no layers of dust clung to the windows. I'd been in houses that weren't as clean. Hay bales were stacked along one end opposite the pens. A large gray cat lay stretched out along one bale, about halfway up the stack. It surveyed all that went on, much like a lion overseeing his domain. Petal sat on the ground looking up at him.

"Isn't that cat afraid the dogs will attack?"

Noah laughed. "Not a chance. Lucifer's taught Petal that barn cats don't run. They whack." He paused before a large burlap sack. "Hold on just one minute." He measured grain into the pails he'd used to feed the sheep.

"What's this?" I dipped my hand into the sack. I recognized oats. I sniffed the mixture. "Molasses and oranges?"

"Three of our mares are pregnant and they need the vitamins and minerals in this mix." Noah headed toward the open doors at the far end of the barn. Two red calves in a pen complained loudly as we passed. "I'll be back. Just keep your shirts on."

I was so busy looking at the calves I almost tripped over a very red chicken. "Oh." The chicken said something that didn't sound like a compliment. "Where did that come from?"

"They roam, eat grubs and worms, pick through the manure, eat up the grain we spill and lay eggs in the hay. Mom's made nests along the back of the barn and they use them. Helps keep us from getting a rotten egg."

He smiled. Had he made a joke?

"Are they always that grumpy?"

"Chickens are born grumpy." Noah nodded toward the hen pecking around the feed sack. "She's a Red Dorking. The colonials considered them general purpose foul. They laid your breakfast egg in the morning and graced your dinner table that night."

I stopped and looked at the chicken with different eyes. "That's awful. The poor things."

"It beats the life of a commercial chicken. These roam free, have baby chicks, peck around comfortably for their food and have nice warm hay to nest in at night. When it's their time to go, well, death is quick and painless. Commercial chickens don't get any of that."

He picked up his pails and left the barn, me on his heels. Max gave up trying to play with the calves and came with us. Petal left the cat to join the parade. I glanced back at the Red Dorking. She looked plump and healthy. It made me think of the last whole chicken I'd bought, heavy in the breast but puny in the legs and thighs, its skin an unattractive yellow. Did chickens get jaundice?

Three white heads hung over the pasture fence.

"Hi, guys. Glad to see me?" Noah emptied his pails into three separate red plastic feeders. The horses immediately buried their faces. He laughed, put his buckets on the ground and leaned on the fence to watch them. "Beautiful, aren't they?"

They were. Creamy white coats, large heads with beautiful brown eyes, muscled shoulders, straight legs and big hoofs.

"Their feet look like dinner plates."

Noah nodded. "Try picking one. If they don't like what you're doing, they lean on you."

In my world, picking meant taking fruit off a tree or roses off a bush. "What?"

Noah smiled a little, reached into his back pocket and produced an L-shaped tool. It looked a little like a screwdriver with its top bent over.

"What's that?"

"A hoof pick. Hoofs have grooves on each side of a V-shaped pad called a frog. They get stuff packed in those grooves— mud, rocks—and can go lame. We use this to clean it out."

I looked from the hoof pick to the closest horse. Any picking I did would be apricots.

"I suppose the colonists used these horses for a lot of different things?"

"Yep. Horses pulled a plow or buggy, or took a young lady side saddle to visit friends. The breed is American Cream but they called them 'iron horses.' "

"If they were so versatile, why did they almost die out?" One of the horses lifted her head and blew. I glared at it and wiped off the front of my top. She looked back impassively and returned her head to the feeder.

"Time, mostly. Cars, tractors, trains came. Horses like these weren't needed and almost disappeared. These guys are part of the Foundation's breeding program, but the historic area doesn't have enough room."

"Like the chickens and the sheep?"

Noah nodded. "Horses need pastures, so I take some of the mares and the foals. They have their babies in the barn and stay here until the foals are weaned. Felicity, she's my fiancée, loves this program and helps me. When we get married, it'll be easier."

Until their first child appeared. As interesting as all this was, it wasn't what I wanted to talk about.

"See that house down the road there?" Noah said.

I could just make it out. A two-story house, painted white, with blue shutters on the only window I could see.

"That's ours. Longos built it soon after the civil war. It's changed some since then." He stared down the hill, seemingly lost in thought.

Content to watch the horses, I waited.

Finally he took a deep breath. "We've been on this land as long as the Smithwoods, and we're as tied to it as when we were slaves." His hand went out to stroke the nose of one of the horses. Uninterested in the conversation, she dropped her head back into the feeder.

I was interested and confused. The bitterness in Noah's voice was deep. "I don't understand."

"No. Of course not." Another one of the horses lifted its head and blew. Oats and foam splattered on Noah's shirt. He brushed at it then rubbed the horse's forehead. "This is Molly. She seems to think stuff like that's funny." He dropped his hand and turned toward me. "Do you want to see some of the rest of the place?"

"Oh, yes." There was plenty of time. The lasagna wouldn't be ready for another forty minutes or so; then it had to sit before we could cut it, and Dan wouldn't be available for who knew how long. "What's that place over there, with the cone-shaped roof?"

"That's the dovecote. Lots of the colonists raised them. That white building is the dairy. See the slats up there by the roof? It helps keep it cool, and if you look close you can see where a stream ran under it. They put a crock of butter or a jar of milk in the stream to keep it fresh longer. Stream's dried up now."

I walked beside Noah, listening, looking at all the different buildings and marveling at their uses. The smokehouse still had the heavy rafters with large hooks for hanging meat; the blacksmith shop still had a forge and anvil. Was Elizabeth going to use all this again?

I stopped in front of a large iron roller machine. "What's this?"

"A sorghum crusher."

"What is sorghum?"

"It's a plant with long stems, like sugar cane. They crush it between those rollers then cook it down. It comes out like molasses. The slaves got a certain ration of it. They'd use it in cooking and pour it over corn meal mush. It was a staple." Noah stopped and stared at the roller for a moment. "Would you like to see one of the slave cabins? They're just over there, across the road."

"Yes." They'd looked cute last night, but I bet they didn't look cute if you had to live in one. Noah turned toward the road and I started to follow.

"Watch where you step."

"Oh." I almost stepped in newly turned over earth. A large patch of black clods, just perfect for tripping a person, started right by the road and stretched back toward the barn.

"I didn't see that."

"The light's fading, that's why. Calvin started it today, but it's not near ready for planting."

"Calvin." I stared at the plowed-up piece of earth. The borders were as exact as if laid out with a ruler. The furrows were sprinkled with what seemed to be a mixture of straw and manure, waiting to be spaded in. "Ah, have you known him long?"

Noah gave a mirthless little laugh and took my elbow. "Are you asking me why we hired someone fresh out of jail?"

Heat warmed my cheeks. Had I really sounded that suspicious? I hadn't meant to, but Calvin was another loose end. There had to be a reason William wanted to hire him. I nodded. "I guess I am."

Noah stopped. He dropped my arm as we stepped onto the more level road and ran his arm across his brow. A faint aroma of horse floated toward me.

"Calvin did all of our gardening here for years. He had a great business, did lots of the old plantations and the large estate houses around here. He's a graduate horticulturist, holds a master's degree in history and consults with the Colonial Williamsburg people on eighteenth-century gardens. At least, he did. William and Elizabeth were talking to him about her project before they moved here. He'd already made some drawings of how the grounds should look and what would have grown in the kitchen garden before he went to jail."

"What happened to him?"

"He'd been drinking more and more, and one day he made two mistakes. First, he decided he was fine to drive home. He rammed into a car, the mayor's wife's car. The second mistake was, he hired Monty as his attorney. Might not have gone to jail if he'd gotten someone else."

The mayor's wife's car. I was grinning. It wasn't funny. The mayor most certainly hadn't been amused. "Why was hiring Monty a mistake?"

"Calvin, Monty, Payton Culpepper, they're all about the same age. They all knew each other, went to high school together. Calvin thought Monty would look out for him. Turned out, Monty was more interested in getting in good with the mayor and didn't put up much of a defense. Calvin got a year in jail and lost his business. Monty got to have lunch with the mayor. William and Elizabeth vowed they'd hire Calvin back when he got out. That's one vow Elizabeth's kept."

There was more bitterness in that last statement than I wanted to hear. Monty Eslick seemed to have left unhappiness in his wake wherever he went. Noah turned up the road we'd used last night, with me close behind and Max right on our heels. I looked back to see if Petal had joined us, but she was nowhere to be seen. Should I call her? No. She knew her way around here better than I did. We left the road and entered a pathway that led to the row of small houses. The brick was the same as that of the big houses, but there the resemblance ended. The mortar that held the bricks in place oozed out between them, not smooth and almost invisible as in the other houses. There was no glass in these windows; the wooden shutters hanging on iron hinges were the only barriers against the weather. The wind must have whipped vigorously through them in the winter. The stoop was just wide enough for one chair and high enough for a dog to lie under, or a chicken or maybe a small child. The door was solid and the hinges large and crudely hammered. The only lock was a bar that could be dropped into slots on the outside.

"Come on in." Noah pushed the door open. "I've done some restoration on this one. Tried to make it as much like it was in 1750 as I could." He stepped in and gave me a hand up. The cabin was one room with a fireplace on the far wall. The firebox simply ended on the packed earth floor. There was a mantel of sorts, at least a place to put things or hang utensils. Well-worn wooden planks covered most of the floor and a faded cotton braided rug lay over part of it. There was a log ladder in one corner. A loft covered almost half of the cabin, thinly covered with straw. I looked over at Noah.

He nodded. "Beds for the kids. The parents, or the old folks who could no longer climb, slept down here. You had a bedstead, if you were lucky, with ropes for springs, but instead of what the white folks used, these black folks had the leavings from the corncribs or straw. Anything the animals couldn't eat. If you had hay fever, you were in for a bad time."

I wondered if that was supposed to be another joke. There wasn't much room. By the time you got some kind of table in here, benches probably, maybe a chair, a bed, cooking pots and cupboards to hold plates, where did the people go?

I walked over to one window. Another cabin was only a few feet away. I turned back to the fireplace. Smaller than the one at the Payton Randolph kitchen or the one in Elizabeth's gathering room, but then, so was the room it serviced. Dare I ask Noah some of the questions that sprang to mind? He'd given me an opening up by the barn. If he didn't want to say anything more, he didn't have to.

"Would your family have lived in one of these?" The question came out more tentatively than I would have liked.

Noah smiled. At my discomfort? "Oh, yes. At least, up until after the Civil War. Which cabin, I don't know, but our family, at least some of it, has been on Smithwood since the mid eighteenth century."

"What did you mean, you're tied to Smithwood."

All traces of a smile faded. Noah walked over to the front door. His voice was muffled, almost as if talking to himself as much as to me. "I don't know what to do about it. William was going to take care of it, but now he's dead."

"Noah, I've never been very good at guessing games, so why don't you just tell me what's going on? You never know. Maybe I can help."

He shrugged. It wasn't hard to interpret. He didn't think there was any chance I could help.

Noah turned and leaned up against the doorjamb. He surveyed the room, paused at the fireplace and moved on to the loft. Finally, his eyes returned to me. "There's a chair on the porch. Let's go out there."

He motioned for me to take the chair and lowered himself down on the porch beside me, his back up against one of the pillars that held up the porch roof.

His voice was low and devoid of emotion. "The Longos came over from Portugal before the Revolutionary War. The family was educated. They worked as accountants, estate managers, craftsmen, that kind of thing, but were still slaves. The Smithwoods bought the whole family."

That simple statement made me flinch. The idea that someone could buy a person, let alone a whole family made me feel a little faint. Now, however, wasn't the time. Noah had to go on, but I couldn't suppress the disgust that ran through me.

"We were lucky. The Smithwoods used the skills we had and let us pass those on to our children. For the most part, anyway." He took a deep breath and let it out slowly.

"Right after the Civil War, Mr. James Smithwood made a deal with my great-great-grandfather. He'd give him that piece of land and several acres to do with as he wanted." Noah waved in the general direction of his house. "Only, it wasn't a gift. In return, my granddaddy had to stay here, on Smithwood, and run the estate."

It had once been against the law to teach a slave to read or write. A Negro recently freed, but with no formal education or place to go, would trust the word of a man of his own race over that of a white man. If a Longo ran the estate, he could get people to work here, lure them with the possibility of betterment, a school. Old Mr. Smithwood had made a shrewd bargain, one that benefited both of them, at least for a while.

It was as if Noah read my thoughts. His eyes reflected two hundred years of oppression, although his lips attempted a smile. "The story goes that this was the most popular place to work for years. A Longo has lived here ever since."

"A Longo still manages the plantation?"

Noah shook his head. "There hasn't been any plantation to manage since the last tobacco was harvested years ago. No, we stay because we have no choice. We don't officially own the land our house is on. We don't have a deed to the house, either. Legally, we're squatters. William was going to do something about that. Only, he died."

Noah looked deathly serious. Thumping his chest, he declared, "I'm the last one. Everyone else has moved on. If I do the same, then all the years, all the work, not to mention the money, we've invested in our little corner of Smithwood, will be gone. It will belong to whoever owns the plantation."

I didn't know what to say. There was passion in Noah's voice, and despair. I was surprised he'd risked revealing his innermost feelings but no, maybe I wasn't. He had to talk to someone, and so far, I presented no threat.

"This subject must have come up before. Did anyone talk to William's father?"

"Hanford Smithwood died when I was little. He was a mean old buzzard. I'm told my father brought it up with him several times, but he laughed. It served his purpose to keep things just as they were."

"You mean he could have kicked you off?"

"There's nothing in writing to back our claim. Oh, we could take it to court. We might even win. That costs money." It would also cost a friendship. I wondered how much that weighed on Noah. It would certainly matter to Mildred.

Noah looked down the hill toward the fenced pasture. One

of the horses raised its head, evidently finished with its grain, and walked off. Its coat glowed silver in the fading light. The other two followed. The cat came out of the barn, paused to make sure the coast was clear, then walked sedately over to the fence, jumped on it and preceded to sharpen its claws. Petal walked out of the barn, glanced at the cat and trotted down the fence line. A more peaceful, pastoral picture I couldn't imagine.

"I like it here. I like my animals. I don't want to leave. I don't want to be kicked out, either. This is my home, always has been. Felicity and I want a family. We'd like to raise our children here, but not if we can lose it all at any time. " He suddenly grinned. "No deed, but no mortgage, either. That's the only good thing."

"Won't Elizabeth help?"

"William was going to. I thought Elizabeth would follow through, but she hasn't."

I had an almost overwhelming need for another cup of tea. It had been an exhausting day in lots of ways, and Noah's narrative wasn't perking me up. What a terrible problem. Noah left me with more questions. Now didn't seem to be the time to ask them, but one question came to mind that needed an answer. No, two. "Noah, if Elizabeth went to jail, who would have control of the property? Cora Lee?"

"No. Well, yes. She's had control for years. It's not hers, though, and never will be. She can't inherit and neither can her children."

I'd suspected something like that. Only, why? I filed that question away for further investigation. "Monty thought he could get Smithwood away from Elizabeth. If he had succeeded, what would he have done?"

"You mean, would he have made trouble? You bet. He wanted to sell off the whole plantation, at least what's left of it, to developers. We would have been out, and without a dime. He told me so."

Noah turned to look at me, repressed anger flaming in his

eyes. "And, no, I didn't have a showdown with him. If I had, I would have beaten him to a pulp. Sneaky stuff, like poison, wouldn't be my style."

I nodded. I could see Noah holding Monty by the neck while he flattened his nose. Poison? No.

His mouth twisted into one of those tight little smiles. "Turns out Monty lied about his chances of getting Smithwood. He told me he'd already made a deal with Elizabeth. It was just a matter of time. I should have known. Monty always lied." He pushed away from the pillars, stretched and reached down for the pails. "I can hear those calves bellowing. Better get in there and feed them. They're off to a new home tomorrow. Wouldn't want Guy to think I neglected them."

I stood and stretched as well. Darkness had descended fast. The pasture lay in deep shadows. So did the steep road back up to the house. I swallowed a sigh and squared my shoulders. There was a little light. I'd go slow and be just fine. "Come up for dinner when you're through. Elizabeth's having a fit about that lawyer Payton Culpepper chose for her, and we need to calm her. She left a message for William's attorney, Aaron Glass. Do you know him?"

"Oh, yes. Best thing she could have done. He's a fine man."

I had one more question for Noah before he disappeared. "Why did Payton Culpepper show up here? Elizabeth didn't call him. No one in the family seems to like him. What was he doing here?"

Noah paused and his expression changed. The anger he had been trying to suppress was back. "Culpepper never does anything that doesn't benefit him. I have no idea why he showed up, but I'm sure he had something in mind. He hasn't been out here since he and Monty were in high school." He hesitated. "No, I guess the last time was right after Monty's mother died. Anyway, tell Elizabeth to make sure Glass understands it's urgent. Something's going on with Payton. Rumors are beginning to surface that aren't pleasant. What that has to do with us, I have no idea, but Elizabeth needs to stay away from him and that whole firm." He headed for the barn. "There's a yard light at the front of the barn. I'll turn it on for you. It won't reach all the way over here, but it'll help. Tell Mom I'll leave it on for her, too."

"Aren't you coming up for dinner?"

"No." He didn't turn, just tossed the word over his shoulder. "I'm meeting Felicity. We've got a lot to talk about."

"Wait."

Noah stopped and turned around, his patience clearly exhausted. "Yes?"

"How long had Monty been dead when we found him?"

"No more than a couple of hours, maybe less. The autopsy should tell us." He cocked his head and narrowed his eyes. I knew that speculative look. I'd seen it on my husband the policeman in his official capacity. "Why?"

"Just wondered." I waited for him to say something more, but instead he disappeared into the barn. Almost immediately the yard light went on. I started up the main road toward the house. The hill was steeper than I thought. I should have followed Noah back toward the barn where I could see where I was walking. What was that? Something by my legs, touching me. I quelled the scream that welled up just in time. It was Petal, touching me with her nose, urging me on. I took a deep breath to try to slow my racing heart. I wasn't used to all this farm stuff. At home we had cement sidewalks and streetlights.

I stood in front of the French doors for a second. Petal was at my feet, looking up expectantly. "In a minute." Noah and Felicity weren't the only ones who had a lot to talk about. I didn't want to be gasping for breath when I went in. Besides, I needed time to think. Noah's revelation had been disturbing. Had he believed Monty? Had Mildred? She had keys and she certainly knew her way around all the houses. How would I feel if someone tried to take my home away from me? Terrified, furious. Enough to commit murder? I didn't want to believe that either Mildred or Noah was capable of murder, but the loss of their home would be devastating. Did they believe the only way to protect it was through Monty's death? If so, what about the ghostly prowler? I reached for the door handle. I liked Mildred but couldn't let that influence me. Someone had committed murder. It wasn't Elizabeth. I had to figure out the real culprit. Another thought occurred to me. Everyone talked about Noah and his mother. No one mentioned his father. Why? I started to push the latch down but abruptly stopped. What was that? Movement. Down the hill toward the barn. Nothing. Only, there had been something. Just a flash, but something. Noah? No. He was whistling inside the barn. Was Calvin still here? Surely he'd finished for the day. A horse nickered. Of course, just one of the horses. I opened the door, Petal bounded through it, followed by Max. Where had he come from? The barn? I turned to look down the hill, but all was quiet. I followed them into the room.

Chapter Eleven

"IT'S DRY. IT shouldn't be. I used a whole jar of sauce." Disgusted, Elizabeth picked at the lasagna. "No matter how hard I try, nothing I make comes out very good. Next time I'll buy the frozen stuff."

Aunt Mary, whose lasagna never comes out dry, smiled at Elizabeth and took a mouthful of salad. "It's fine. I have a great recipe for basic tomato sauce. I'll send it to you."

Mildred tore off a piece of bread and took a bite. Cora Lee rolled hers up into a buttery little ball and dropped it on her plate.

I laid down my fork and took a sip of the wine. The lasagna was much more palatable with a few extra swigs of red wine. "I wish I knew if they'd done the autopsy yet."

"I don't see why you're so hung up on that. We know he was poisoned. What more is there?" Cora Lee abandoned her bread in favor of her wineglass.

"When."

"When what?" Elizabeth set her fork down as well and pushed her half-eaten lasagna aside.

"When he died." I hoped my relief didn't show as I pushed

mine aside also. "You aren't paying attention. Noah thought Monty had been dead about two hours when we found him. Cora Lee said she'd been back about an hour before we got here. That means whoever killed him stuck around for at least that long. That person didn't leave until we saw the light and started over there. That person was in the house, with Monty dead on the floor, the whole time Cora Lee was making salad and doing whatever else."

"Unpacking, putting my things away." Cora Lee turned white and set her glass down on the table with visibly shaking hands. "My God. That passageway door was unlocked. That person could have come over here at any time. I think I'm going to pass out."

"No, you're not. Have another sip of wine." Elizabeth followed her own advice. "Why? Why would anyone stay around with someone right next door who might discover them at any minute?" There was no more color in her face than in Cora Lee's.

"They were looking for something." Mildred was shaken, but I thought she was holding together better than the other two. "That's the only reason I can think of. Whoever it was spent that time searching the house. Then, when he heard Cora Lee, he stayed quiet. Maybe he thought she'd leave again or something. When everyone else turned up, he left."

I nodded. "At some point, almost certainly before Cora Lee arrived, he, or she, came over here and put the glass in the dishwasher. It's the only explanation that makes sense. Only, where did he or she go?"

Cora Lee's skin got even whiter, if possible. "I have no idea. What does Noah think?"

"I didn't ask him." I pushed back my chair, picked up my plate and started for the sink. "We talked about the animals."

Mildred stood also. She picked up Elizabeth's plate as well as her own. "Don't bother. I've got them." She addressed this to Cora Lee, who hadn't shown any sign she planned on making an effort. She smiled as Aunt Mary cleared everything else off the table. "He does love those animals. Always has, even when he was a little boy. But then, I'm pretty fond of my hens." She scraped lasagna into the sink as Aunt Mary emptied the salad bowl. It looked as if none of us had had much of an appetite after all.

"Is that all you talked about? Smelly sheep?" It was obvious Cora Lee didn't share Noah's fondness for farm animals.

"No." I turned to face them. "We talked about deeds and where he and Felicity are going to live."

Mildred's face froze. She just stood there, her hand on the tap, plate in the sink, incapable of movement.

Cora Lee clutched her cane, her mouth making a soft "oh."

"Oh, my God. The deed. I forgot all about it." Elizabeth's hands flew to her mouth, her eyes round. "How could I? I promised William I wouldn't. Oh, Mildred. I'm so sorry. Aaron is doing something. He had it figured out." She looked at Mildred's face and gasped. "You knew we were going to. Did you think I'd changed my mind?" She was on her feet, enveloping Mildred in a huge hug. "Oh, honey. You're one of my best friends. You're not going anywhere. You can't. Neither can Noah." She pushed Mildred away a little and studied her face. "Unless you want to." Her eyes welled up with tears. "You don't want to, do you?"

Mildred's eyes were just as damp. She reached out and hugged Elizabeth then turned her brightest smile on her. "Of course not. We knew you hadn't forgotten."

Only, what showed through the tears was fear. Mildred had thought they were going to lose their home. She thought Monty somehow made a deal with Elizabeth, or that his threats worked and he was going to own Smithwood. She might not have been absolutely positive, but she'd been scared. Noah also thought they would lose the tentative hold they had on their piece of Smithwood. Only, he wasn't scared. He was angry. Damn! It couldn't be true. Neither of these good people could have committed murder. But I knew almost anyone could if pushed hard enough. Had Monty pushed them over that very thin line?

"That's taken care of, then." Mildred turned back to the sink. Water ran, and so did the garbage disposal.

Mildred reached around Mary, took the dishtowel down off the peg and wiped her hands. Her hands shook a little as she hung it back up, and the lines around her mouth had deepened. "I'd best be going. Thank you for dinner and, Elizabeth, honey, thank you for telling me. It's good to know things are in progress. Let us know when Aaron calls back, will you? I'm going to be worried sick until I know he's taking care of you."

"Aaron's going to take care of everything." Cora Lee leaned on her cane, watching the little drama unfold. The raw anger in her eyes was new to me. The mocking, sarcastic Cora Lee was gone. This woman looked tired, sad and undeniably angry. "Go talk to Noah. You'll get your deed. Aaron and Elizabeth will take care of it. Don't you dare move, and don't you let Noah." Her voice changed and so did the look in her eyes. "After all, it's time we had little ones running around here again."

Mildred paused, took a quick intake of breath and smiled. Tight, uncertain, but still a smile. "There's nothing I'd love better than grandbabies but, Cora Lee, let's get through the wedding first." She opened the French doors and started out. Max was right behind her, Petal behind him. "Keep an eye on this door. Petal will be back as soon as she does her nightly." The door closed and she was gone.

Elizabeth handed me my glass of wine and poured herself another half-glass. She listed the bottle in the air and gave Cora Lee a questioning look.

"Of course." Cora Lee held out her glass. "I'd love to know what that rat Monty told them. Mildred actually thought he'd end up with Smithwood."

"So did Noah." Aunt Mary's voice was soft, thoughtful. "William, Elizabeth, Cora Lee, you've all been their friends.

Monty must have been pretty convincing to destroy that trust."

Exactly what I was thinking. Only, what had Monty done, or said, that resulted in his death?

"What was that?" Elizabeth's head jerked up. Barking. Shrill, frantic barking. "Petal. Where is she? She sounds hysterical." She started to push back her chair.

Deeper, more menacing barking joined in. "That's Max." Cora Lee said. "They're not up here. They must be down by the barn. Something's going on." She steadied herself with her cane and started toward the French doors.

The barking intensified. It became frantic. There was one loud yelp followed by a scream, then silence. Cora Lee stopped. Her whole body stiffened as she looked from the door back at us. "What was that?"

"Mildred." Elizabeth headed toward the door almost at a run, Cora Lee right behind her.

"Wait." Aunt Mary headed for the door as well. "You can't go down there. We don't know what's happening."

"That was Mildred. Something's wrong." Cora Lee paused only long enough to yell back. "Bring that cellphone. Bring the flashlight, too. Hurry."

My heart pounded so hard it was difficult to breathe. There could be no doubt something bad had happened. My purse was where? On the highboy. I grabbed it, fished around and finally came up with my cell. The flashlight? Aunt Mary already had it. She headed for the door and stepped through. I was at her heels. "At least there wasn't a gunshot."

"Are we supposed to be grateful for small favors?" She started down the steep incline as fast as the gravel would allow.

Chapter Twelve

WE HURRIED DOWN the road, only, where was the yard light? The moon was bright enough to show a bundle of some kind crumpled by the barn door. Not Mildred. Please, God, not Mildred. The only sounds were Aunt Mary's footsteps ahead of me and a car engine. A car engine? I came to an abrupt halt and listened. No mistake. That was a car. Where was it? Lights. There should be lights, but I couldn't see any. An engine engaged and tires crunched, faint but definite. Could it be Noah? There were no lights down by his house, either, and the moon was bright enough to reflect on a car, if one was there. Nothing. No movement. No reflection off metal. No sound.

"Ellen, hurry."

The bundle was Mildred. Elizabeth knelt by her crumpled figure in front of the barn. Max was poised over her, whining softly. Cora Lee stood beside him.

"Do you have your phone?" Elizabeth's face was white in the moonlight. Or maybe it was shock that gave it that pale, ghostly look. "Good. Give it to me. We need an ambulance. It looks like someone hit her good with something. There's blood all over the side of her head."

"How bad is it?"

"I don't know. Nine-one-one?" Elizabeth moved toward the barn while she made her call.

"We should try to stop the bleeding." Aunt Mary knelt beside Mildred's body and picked up her hand, feeling for her pulse. "She's got one. That's about all I can tell."

"That's more than I could do." Cora Lee was literally wringing her hands. "I think Noah keeps a first aid kit in the barn." She was gone.

Lights went on. Cora Lee might not know where Noah kept the first aid kit, but she found the light switch. Blood still seeped from the side of Mildred's head and from her ear. I saw a gash, but barely. Too much blood and bloody hair. "Should you try to push her hair back?"

"I don't know." Aunt Mary looked back toward the door of the barn. "Where's Cora Lee? The blood's more oozing than rushing. I think that's a good sign." She laid her hand on Mildred's chest. "A breath. Shallow, but still, her chest's moving." Max edged as close to her as he could, watching Aunt Mary's every move. He nudged her hand with his nose, as if to say, *Do something*. She reached over and touched him on the ears. "I'm trying, Max. I just don't know what else to do."

"How is she?" Elizabeth knelt down beside Aunt Mary. "The ambulance is on its way, but it'll take a few minutes. They said if the bleeding is real bad to try to put a compress on to stop it. I don't know what to use."

"Cora Lee went into the barn to find a first aid kit." I started toward the barn. At least it was something to do. I met her coming out, holding a white box with a red cross on top.

"Give it to Aunt Mary." I continued on into the barn. Something was lying on the dirt not too far from the grain sacks. I walked closer. A spade. The kind with the sharp sides and the pointed end. Noah would never leave a spade in the dirt. He wouldn't leave one with blood on the blade either. I stared at it then back at Mildred, lying also on the dirt. I'd found the weapon.

I walked back out to where Mildred lay but said nothing. Aunt Mary took out a big gauze square. She tore a package open and held the pad against Mildred's wound. It immediately filled with blood. She pushed down a little. More blood filled the pad. The flow slowed under her fingers. "Press firmly. I read that somewhere. It seems to be working."

"Is she going to be all right?" Cora Lee's knuckles were white as she clutched her cane. So was her face.

"I don't know." Mary's fingers pushed down a little more firmly. The gauze wasn't going to absorb much more blood.

"Should you try and put on another one?" I was already holding a new pad.

"The blood flow seems to have stopped. At least it's down to a trickle. I'd better keep doing what I'm doing until someone who can really help gets here."

I wasn't so sure the blood stopping was a good thing. How did we find out if her heart was still beating? The only way I could think of was to put my ear on her chest. Somehow that didn't seem like a good idea.

"Who could have done such a thing?" Elizabeth clutched the phone while she watched Aunt Mary hold the gauze in place. "If I ever get my hands on whoever it is that's terrorizing us, I'll … I think I'd better call Noah. Hope he doesn't have his cell turned off."

"Right now I'm not so interested in *who* it is as *where* he is." Cora Lee kept looking around as if she expected someone to jump out of the barn and attack at any minute.

"Whoever it was left."

Cora Lee snapped around to stare at me. Elizabeth, who'd started to enter Noah's number on my phone, stopped. "How do you know that?"

"I heard a car drive away."

"A car?" Elizabeth looked around as if she expected one to drive up any minute. "What car?"

"I don't know. It sounded as if it was behind the barn, but it couldn't have been. We'd have seen it."

"Are you sure?" Cora Lee asked.

"Quite sure."

Aunt Mary adjusted the bandage a little. That ambulance had better hurry up. Mildred's breathing sounded raspy and I didn't think that was a good sign.

"There aren't any other roads." Cora Lee leaned heavily on her cane, glancing back and forth from the barn to Mildred. "The road through the main gate goes by our houses and down to this barn and the other outbuildings. There's a driveway off the highway that leads to Noah and Mildred's house, but it ends there." Barn forgotten, her eyes were fixed on Mildred and Aunt Mary's hand. A shudder ran through her, strong enough so that her cane shook. "This has got to stop. Mildred. Why would anyone want to hurt her? I can't believe all this. First Elizabeth and that crate, then Monty dead in our dining room. Now this."

I thought Cora Lee was going to burst into tears. She better not. I couldn't handle a case of hysterics right now. Where was Elizabeth? She seemed to have taken root as she, too, stared at Mildred, hopelessness and despair written on her face. Mary reached into the first aid kit and took out another gauze square. "One of you needs to open this for me. Hurry. This one's not going to absorb much more blood."

I tried to hand her the one I held but she shook her head. I got it. Maybe doing something would shake some life back into Elizabeth and keep Cora Lee from dissolving into mush. It was Elizabeth who tore the paper off the square and handed it to Aunt Mary.

"Are you going to take the other one off?"

"No. I'm afraid to. I'll just slip this one on top. The bleeding's slowed down a lot, but I don't like the way she's breathing. I hope that ambulance hurries."

A shrill ambulance siren split the silence. Help had arrived, and it was coming in through the main gate.

Chapter Thirteen

Aunt Mary and I sat in the hospital waiting room staring uncomprehendingly at the television screen mounted in the corner. Elizabeth had gone in search of coffee and I had no idea where Cora Lee was.

Mildred had already been admitted when we finally got there. Noah had turned off his cell but Elizabeth found him and his fiancée, Felicity, eating dinner at the second place she tried. Felicity was on staff but had the night off. She, evidently, put herself back on. Noah paused only long enough to ask about the dogs. When we assured him they were locked in Elizabeth's house, he nodded and disappeared down the hall.

Aunt Mary sighed deeply. "I feel out of my depth and I don't like it. If we were in Santa Louisa, I'd know exactly what was going on because I'd be acquainted with almost everyone in the hospital. Here, we only know Elizabeth. And Cora Lee, of course."

I wasn't at all sure we knew Cora Lee. I couldn't quite figure her out. One minute she seemed devoted to Elizabeth, the next resentful and angry. She acted as if Smithwood was hers and seemed to have no plans to return to her life in Atlanta.

Only, Noah had said she couldn't inherit and neither could her children. Why? I thought again about Monty. He wanted Smithwood, but only in order to turn it over to a developer. Was the thought of condos replacing her childhood home so upsetting to Cora Lee that she'd resorted to murder? She might not own it, but there was no doubt she loved Smithwood and everything in it. Did she, too, think Monty would get his talons into the estate and destroy it? Sell off all the old family treasures? The time fit. Maybe it was Cora Lee who'd entertained Monty in the dining room, gone back over to Elizabeth's house—leaving Monty dead on the rug—calmly washed out the glass and put it in the dishwasher, then turned on the TV and waited. Only, Cora Lee hadn't been the one holding the candle we'd seen, and Cora Lee hadn't attacked Mildred or driven the mysterious car I'd heard. I sighed and glanced at the TV. Fox news. I never watched that channel. The sound was so low you couldn't hear a thing, but I watched for a minute. There was no sign Fox had picked up another attempted murder at the Smithwood place. I hoped it stayed that way.

Elizabeth sank into the chair beside Aunt Mary and handed each of us a white paper cup with what looked and smelled like hot mud.

"Sorry. It was all I could find." She peered into her cup, took a tentative sip and shuddered.

Aunt Mary looked into hers and set it on the floor beside her. I held mine. It was warm and for some reason my hands were cold.

"Has anyone come out?"

"No. No one. I think she'll be all right." I thought about the wound and the spade I'd seen and hoped I was right.

"Unless it cracked her skull." Elizabeth's mouth was set in a straight line and her eyes seemed suspiciously wet. "Oh, shit." A man turned the corner at the end of the hall, striding purposefully toward us. "Just what we need."

Aunt Mary peered down the corridor. She didn't have her

glasses on and didn't seem too sure until he got closer. She stiffened. "McMann. We could have done without him."

Lt. McMann stopped abruptly. He loomed over us, scowling down like an irate principal about to berate naughty third graders.

He'd picked the wrong ones. Elizabeth had faced down lumberjacks with chainsaws, and Aunt Mary had spent years with seventh graders whose only mission in life was to make adults miserable. Lt. McMann didn't stand a chance. We stared back at him.

He took one step back and his face softened. "How is Mrs. Longo?"

The ice in Elizabeth's voice practically clinked. "We don't know yet, but Mary thinks she's going to be all right."

Lt. McMann didn't need words to let us know he didn't think Aunt Mary could diagnose a common cold, but he seemed bent on being polite. At least, for now. "Mind if I sit?"

Nobody objected so he pulled up a chair and sat facing us.

"Want to tell me what happened?"

Aunt Mary and Elizabeth looked at each other, then at me. That seemed like a reasonable thing for a policeman to ask. I nodded. Elizabeth started.

"We finished dinner and Mildred headed home. She had school early tomorrow." She glanced over at Aunt Mary. "It is still Sunday, isn't it?"

"Barely." She nodded for her to go on.

"Max went with her."

"Who's Max?" The lieutenant lifted his head and his eyes narrowed. Now we're getting somewhere, he seemed to say.

"Noah's Golden Retriever."

"Oh." Interest died. "Go on."

"We were talking when we heard Petal barking, a frantic kind of bark, and then Max barked and we heard a scream." She stopped, as if there wasn't any more to say.

Lt. McMann didn't agree. "Then what did you do?"

"We ran out, of course. Ellen brought her cellphone."

"Cora Lee brought her cane."

"The same things you brought when you found Monty."

Aunt Mary nodded.

Lt. McMann sighed. "Where's Cora Lee now?"

"I don't know." Elizabeth looked around. "Do you know, Mary?"

"She went down that corridor after we got here. She didn't say where she was going. I didn't ask."

"Of course not." The corner of Lt. McMann's left eye twitched. "So you ran down to the barn. Then what?"

"Mildred was lying in front of the barn door. Max stood over her."

"Go on."

"I took Ellen's phone and called nine-one-one."

"Anything else?" The lieutenant seemed to be gritting his teeth. We were making him work for every detail. Pleasant as it might be to make his life difficult, I wanted this investigation to move right along. One man dead, one woman attacked. Where was it going to end? I didn't have much confidence in McMann's ability, or his desire, to get to the bottom of this. However, he was all we had. "The barn lights were off when we got there."

Lt. McMann blinked. "Don't you usually turn them off at night?"

I studied him. He had actually asked a polite question and was waiting for an answer. "I went down to the barn earlier, to talk to Noah. He turned them on for me when I went back up to the house and said he'd leave them on for his mother."

"So you think they were turned off by someone else down there, the same someone who hit Mrs. Longo alongside the head. Is that what you're telling me?"

It was Aunt Mary who finally answered. "It would seem that way, wouldn't it?"

Lt. McMann's neck started to redden and blotches crept

up his cheeks. Embarrassment? More likely temper. He was proving to be a most disagreeable man. "Ladies, it'd help if I didn't have to drag every syllable out of you. Mrs. Longo is your friend. Don't you want to help find who did this?"

He was right. He might be a disagreeable person and I might not like him or even trust him very much, but he was the police.

I sighed. "Cora Lee went into the barn and turned on the lights. She found the first aid kit Noah keeps down there and Aunt Mary put a compress on Mildred's wound to stop the bleeding until the emergency people got there." I paused. "There was a spade lying in the dirt beside the grain sacks. It had blood on it."

McMann didn't say anything, just stared at me. Finally, he gave one nod. "We found it. Did you see anything? Hear anything? See any signs of where whoever did this went?"

Once more Aunt Mary and Elizabeth exchanged looks. Aunt Mary turned toward me. "Tell him."

"Tell me what?"

He wasn't going to believe this. "I heard a car."

"A car."

"It sounded as if it was behind the barn, only there's no road there."

"Did you see it?" There was an odd expression on Lt. McMann's face. Surprise seemed to change to thoughtfulness. Not disbelief.

"No. I heard the engine start and then it drove off."

Lt. McMann turned toward Elizabeth. "Did you hear it, too?"

Elizabeth shook her head. "I was in front of the barn, so the sound wouldn't have been as loud. Besides, I was so upset about Mildred, I'm not sure it would have registered."

He transferred his gaze to Aunt Mary.

"No, I was too busy trying to see if Mildred was still alive."

McMann let that slide right off and turned back to me. "So, you're the only one who heard this car?"

I bit my tongue and nodded. He didn't believe me. I barely believed myself.

"No one drove up the road by the Longos' house or by the barn?"

"No. Really, Lieutenant, if someone drove by, we'd have mentioned it." Elizabeth's eyes snapped and she held her empty coffee cup as if she'd like to strangle it. Even Lt. McMann might have realized she'd had enough, but evidently he didn't.

"Only if it suited you." The time for politeness had come and gone. "You're sure?" He turned back to me.

"Yes, I'm sure. I have no idea where the car was, or where it went, but it's hard to mistake a car engine. This one was close by." Politeness had left the building.

He nodded and got to his feet. "Thanks, ladies. You've been a big help. Where's Longo?"

"In with his mother, I guess." Elizabeth got up. "I'll walk down to the nurse's station and see if I can find out anything. Are you two coming?"

It certainly beat staying with Lt. McMann. Besides, I wanted to know about Mildred. I also wanted to know what Cora Lee was up to. "Right behind you."

I stood there waiting to see if Aunt Mary needed help. She'd been sitting for some time. I should have known better. Elizabeth was already at the door. Aunt Mary hesitated for only a second before she followed, nodding politely to Lt. McMann as she passed. He turned and, without another word, stomped off in the opposite direction.

Elizabeth glared at his retreating back. "I wonder what he thinks now. He has to know I wasn't the one who attacked Mildred. Do you think he still suspects me of poisoning Monty?"

"I have no idea what he thinks." Aunt Mary sounded as disgusted as Elizabeth. This time some of her disgust was reserved for me. "Why didn't you tell us about the bloody spade?"

"Too busy worrying about Mildred. Then I forgot about it until just now."

"Humph. I thought he'd be more surprised about the car."

"This whole thing is bizarre," Elizabeth said. "Maybe he's just confused. I know I am." She looked around. "Where's the nurse's station?"

"I think it's around this corner." Aunt Mary led the way. "I doubt they'll tell us much."

"Let's try," Elizabeth said. "If I don't find out something soon, I'll explode." We started down the corridor again. "I hope Mildred's going to be all right."

"So do I." Aunt Mary stopped and put her hand on her friend's arm. "Elizabeth, none of us can go on this way. Mildred easily could have been killed, and even if she's all right, that doesn't mean this is over. I don't trust that Lieutenant McMann one bit. We're going to have to do something."

Emotions rolled across Elizabeth's face faster than I could read them. "Noah …"

"Noah's plate was full to overflowing before Mildred was attacked. We can't count on him, at least not for a while."

"That's not what I mean. I don't know what to think." She took Aunt Mary by the arm. "When I called and asked you to come out here, I said I needed someone I could trust."

Aunt Mary nodded.

"I needed you because I thought Noah was somehow making a deal with Monty." That came out with a rush. Her face twisted in anguish and her eyes glistened with unshed tears. She dropped Aunt Mary's arm and brushed them away.

"What made you think so?" I asked. I already had a pretty good idea but needed to make sure.

"I saw Monty down at his house the morning after I encountered the ghost in the upstairs hallway. I'd started down to tell Noah and ask him what I should do. There was Monty, standing outside with him, talking intently." Elizabeth looked at her clasped hands. "I didn't know what to do, or what to think. It was the next day the crate almost fell on me."

"You thought Noah was somehow involved."

Elizabeth nodded. "I couldn't see how, or even why, but that crate scared me more than the time we got rammed by the barbarian who was trying to harpoon a baby gray whale. I felt betrayed and scared. Oh, what a mistake I made! How can I make it up to him?"

I let Aunt Mary comfort her. I was trying to figure out time frames. "That must have been the day Monty came to tell Noah he was getting Smithwood and would be moving him and his mother out."

"Monty told him that? And Noah believed him. That's my fault. What a jewel that man was. If this wasn't so serious, I'd be tempted to thank whoever slipped him that doctored syllabub."

Whoever it was had to be familiar with the house and grounds. Knew how to get in and out. The movement outside earlier. Someone had been down by the barn. I'd thought it might be Calvin. He had a truck and had worked at Smithwood for a long time. That he hated Monty was a given. But why would Calvin attack Mildred? I thought about ponytails. Was it Calvin prowling the halls? Why? This was getting me nowhere.

"The first thing we're going to do is see how Mildred's doing. Then we're going to find Cora Lee and go down in that cellar and examine every square inch of it, until we know how this person is getting in and out. Then we're going to set a trap for them." My determination to find out who the prowler was and how he was getting in and out of the house was based partly on wanting to help Elizabeth.

The other part was curiosity. The attack on Mildred had turned that into anger. What was Monty up to in the dining room, dressed in colonial clothes? Who was the ghost and why was he-she-it roaming around upstairs? He had to be searching for something, but what? Where had the syllabub glasses come from? Cora Lee seemed surprised when she saw them. Calvin. Had he returned to Smithwood for some reason other than a gardening opportunity? Then there was Lt. McMann. He fit in somewhere and it wasn't as a policeman. There were too many people involved in this tangled mess and they all had a motive to want Monty dead. There had to be an answer here somewhere and I was determined to find it.

All of that must have shown in my face. Elizabeth paused to study me, and then nodded. She looked as if she was torn between amusement, excitement and disbelief.

"What sort of a trap?" Aunt Mary looked dubious.

"I don't know yet, but I'll think of something. Right now, let's find out about Mildred."

Chapter Fourteen

WE'D STAYED AT the hospital until late. When we finally arrived home all any of us had wanted was a shower, a cup of tea and bed. We laced the tea with a little something to help us sleep. It was even better for jagged nerves.

We were all up early, even Cora Lee. Elizabeth on the phone to the hospital before she'd poured her first cup of coffee. Mildred was doing well and, no, she couldn't come to the phone and the nurse couldn't release details.

"Damn it all to hell!" Elizabeth exclaimed after hanging up the phone. "How do they expect you to know anything if they won't tell you anything?"

"Ask Noah." I stood at the French doors, looking out at the garden and toward the barn. Petal ran that way, barking her fool head off at, it turned out, Max. Did dogs get embarrassed when they realized they were barking at the wrong people? Or other dogs? Noah appeared, pushing a full wheelbarrow. He tossed hay into the feeders on the fence and pushed the wheelbarrow toward the pasture behind the barn. "He's feeding. If I run down there, I can probably catch him before he leaves." I put my coffee on the table. My thin slippers looked inadequate for a gravel driveway, but they would have to do. I headed for the door.

"Call him on his cell." Aunt Mary set her coffee cup back on her saucer and leaned back a little. "No point in running up and down that hill."

Elizabeth reached for my cell again and tapped in the numbers. "How is she?" Elizabeth didn't bother with niceties like "Good morning." "That's wonderful. Yes, I'll bet she does. What time? Why don't you come up here for dinner? Of course, Felicity, too. Call me when you get her home. Of course, Max can stay. I'll talk to you later."

One-sided conversations could be frustrating but they could also tell you a lot. I could see Aunt Mary already planning a dinner menu.

"She's coming home today?" Cora Lee leaned forward on her cane a little, eyes bright, a real smile on her face for the first time that morning.

"She's going to be a bit shaky for a couple of days, but she's fine. He's bringing her home this afternoon. They'll be happy to come for dinner. Felicity will be with them. He wants Max to spend the day up here. I don't suppose any of you mind."

Cora Lee paled a little at that. "I don't mind about Max. I'm not much of a cook, though, and neither are you. I suppose we can get Chinese takeout."

"I'll take care of it." Aunt Mary was an excellent cook. Ask anyone in Santa Louisa. "Nothing too heavy. She's probably not going to be hungry, but Noah will be. We'll need to go to the store."

Aunt Mary was probably right. I added, "Before we do that, we need to go down in that cellar. We need to find out how whoever has been prowling around here is getting in and out. If we find something, we'll tell Noah at dinner."

Elizabeth balked. "I've only been in that cellar twice," she said. "The first time was with William, right before he … The second time I almost got killed. Going down there isn't on my bucket list."

Cora Lee wasn't any more agreeable. "I was scared to death of that cellar when I was a child and have never seen any reason to change my mind. You three go and let me know what you find."

It took both Aunt Mary and me to finally persuade them. Or, maybe it was the attack on Mildred. After Aunt Mary pointed out that our "ghost" might succeed in killing someone the next time, they finally agreed. Elizabeth was silent and white faced; Cora Lee complained with every step.

I led the way, turning on every light switch I found. Cora Lee was right behind me, with Elizabeth following. Aunt Mary brought up the rear. Cora Lee perked up when the lights I'd managed to turn on showed the cellar was surprisingly free of spiders and completely free of ghosts. However, she paled when the packing crate came into view. "Dear God in heaven. Is that what almost hit you?"

Elizabeth made it halfway down the stairs before she stopped and gasped. I turned to see if she was all right. Her eyes were fixed on the debris on the cellar floor. Her breath came fast and shallow and her fingers clasped the stair rail so tightly her knuckles were white. "That's it. If it hadn't been for Petal, I'd have been almost to the bottom, right under that crate when it fell."

Aunt Mary edged past Elizabeth to get a better look. A pile of crates was stacked up by the stairs, but they were different than the one that had fallen. They were larger, made of sturdy wood and each had what appeared to be a content list taped to the side. The one that fell wasn't as big, and it seemed to have been made of soft wood, pine maybe. It had been filled with pots. Iron pots and frying pans. Kettles and trivets, little iron trivets with cute little iron feet that would fit neatly into a skull. The fall split the crate open and its contents were scattered over the stairs and floor at the base of the stairs. Aunt Mary picked up a saucepan. "This thing is heavy. Where did it all come from?"

Cora Lee joined Aunt Mary. She leaned on her cane while she surveyed the wreckage. "I think that stuff all came from the old kitchen. I remember playing there as a kid before Mother dragged me out. Told me the black widows would get me. I haven't been in it since." She reached out with her cane to turn over a trivet. "I don't know who packed that."

Elizabeth edged by Aunt Mary to look at the lists taped to the sides of the large crates stacked by the stairs. "Duke of Gloucester table setting for twenty-four?" The expression on her face was almost reverent. "That's not original?"

Cora Lee sighed. "As far as I know, it is. There's sterling silver in there, also a setting for twenty-four. There are lots of extra pieces, as well. Mother hated it."

Elizabeth looked stricken. "She what?"

Cora Lee sighed again. "Mother liked Danish modern. It was my father who loved all this." She waved at the stacked crates. "It went along with his image of being a Smithwood." She walked around to the other side of the crates, leaned on her cane and stared at them as if what they really contained were memories. "I came back after he died. Mother wanted to move out, and she wasn't wasting any time. She wanted to have a garage sale. Can you imagine? A garage sale." She sighed again. "CJ didn't turn out to be good for anything but making money but I learned a lot about really nice things while I was spending it." She turned and walked over to the pile of crates and tapped one of them with her cane. "Mildred helped me. We brought in professionals and had everything that was valuable packed away and moved down here. That old kitchen stuff wasn't part of it." She shivered. "I wasn't about to fight off black widows for a lot of old kitchen junk."

Elizabeth squatted down to take a better look at an iron kettle, more than heavy enough to do some real damage. "I don't think this is junk."

Cora Lee dismissed that with a sniff. "That alcove down

there," she pointed to one of the alcoves at the far end of the cellar, "is full of furniture. One of those boxes contains portraits of original Smithwoods. Pretty ugly bunch, but we kept their pictures. These crates," she pointed with her cane toward the pile, "contain just household stuff. Linens, crystal, silver, beautiful old things."

"But you didn't pack that crate?" Aunt Mary pointed to the box that had fallen.

"No. I've never seen that one before."

"It was on top. I'm sure of that." Elizabeth got up off the steamer trunk where she squatted and walked over to investigate the shattered crate. "I saw it move. Petal started barking and ran back up the stairs, right through my legs. I turned and followed. That's when I saw the figure. It had on a cape and I think it was tall."

"Or standing on a stepstool."

"A stepstool. What gave you that idea?"

"The one beside the crates."

A stool stood close beside the bottom crate, almost hidden. It would have been easy for someone standing on it to maneuver the top crate just enough so it could be tipped off the top. The rough edges of the crate, the heavy pots inside it, and the force created when it fell were almost guaranteed to do real damage. Possibly permanent damage.

Elizabeth turned white. I could hardly blame her. She'd had a narrow escape.

"All right." Aunt Mary looked around. "We know how the crate fell. I'd like to know how it got up there."

She turned toward Cora Lee, who shook her head. "I've no idea."

"How about that one?" I pointed to a crate identical to the ones stacked by the stairs, but this one sat on the cellar floor, pushed back in the corner, its top not quite back in place.

"That's one of ours. Only, that's not where it should be." Cora Lee walked over to look at the crate. "I wasn't down here when the movers stored all these, but I told them to put them all together. Evidently they didn't get any further than the stairs. This one's been moved."

Aunt Mary walked over to stand next to her. They both stared at the crate. "It's been opened. Oh." Aunt Mary reached out to push the lid back further. "Look at this piece of embroidery. It's lovely."

It didn't look lovely to me. It looked old and faded. Something with teeth had been chewing on it and it smelled of mice.

Elizabeth knelt down beside the crate, peering at the inventory list taped to the side. "Look." She straightened up and motioned for all of us to come look. "See? Right here. Eight crystal syllabub glasses." She rocked back on her heels, looked up at us a little ashen faced, then leaned forward to check the list again.

"They're not in there anymore." Cora Lee tapped the side of the crate with her cane, then withdrew it to lean on it. "I wonder what else they took."

"I wonder who took it," said Aunt Mary.

I knew what she was implying. It was a safe bet whoever took the glasses also murdered Monty. Only, how did the murderer know where to find the glasses? Or, had Monty pulled them out? A larger question loomed. How did we find out who the murderer was? I looked around the cellar as if something would somehow jump up and provide an answer. All I saw was an old steamer trunk, pushed back behind the crates. It was what hung out of the trunk that caught my attention. "There."

Everyone turned toward me. "What?"

I pointed. "That trunk. There's something hanging out of it."

"So there is." Cora Lee glanced over at it, showing no interest whatsoever. "So what? It's just another old quilt or something."

"That old quilt confirms it. Someone's gone through that trunk. Whoever's been prowling around this house is looking for something." Aunt Mary walked over and looked down at the quilt, hands on her hips. She turned and once more surveyed the cellar. "Now all we have to do is find how they're getting in."

"And out." Cora Lee's voice was soft as she, too, examined the cellar.

So did I.

I was sure that, as soon as we started to look, we'd find a door, perhaps hidden behind the empty wine racks, or in back of the grain barrels. The staircase we'd descended was along the far wall of the cellar. There was nothing next to it except a light switch and some electric cables. Opposite the last step was the outside door Elizabeth had spoken of—the one padlocked on the outside. The stacks of crates were piled three to four high along the open part of the staircase, the step stool against the pile closest to the last step. The cellar wasn't very wide but it had three alcoves along both sides, and the far wall was covered with floor to ceiling cupboards. It was time to start looking.

I went down into the cellar, peering into each alcove as I passed it, the others following close behind. We examined the wall, looking for a crack that might mean a door, pushing into the alcoves and running fingers across walls that might yield to pressure. Nothing. Most of the alcoves were filled with things too good to toss, yet not good enough to bring upstairs. I paused in front of the one used as a wine cellar. A single bottle lay on one of the racks. Cora Lee suggested we bring it upstairs to see if it was still good. Elizabeth and Aunt Mary vetoed that suggestion. This would be the most logical alcove to hold a hidden door. Its back wall was plaster; the wine racks that remained were screwed into it with large bolts but there was no evidence of a door. Another alcove contained old trunks, boxes of books, records from the 70s, all layered in dust. None of it had been moved in years. Another held a couple of empty barrels. The remaining three spilled over with bicycles, ski equipment, fishing poles, a set of golf clubs hopelessly out of date ... Nowhere did we see an indication of a way in or out, let alone a way through it all. I stopped at the end of the cellar and studied the cabinets. One was spacious and tall enough to nearly touch the ceiling; no shelves. The door opened easily to disclose absolutely nothing. The cupboards next to it were equally bare except for a small mouse corpse on a middle shelf. I closed the door.

"I don't know where else to look." We were missing something. No ghost pushed over that crate; no ghost drove the car I heard. Someone was getting in and out of here, and like so many riddles, the answer would probably turn out to be incredibly simple.

"What time is it?" Elizabeth wiped her sweaty forehead and glanced at her wrist—at the watch that wasn't there. "I've an appointment with Mr. Glass at one. He's making a special effort to fit me in because of all this. I can't be late." She headed for the stairs. "We'll have to come back later." She stopped at the bottom of the staircase and looked at the pile of packing crates. "I want to bring that old inventory list down here and check it against the contents of these crates. I can't wait to get the dust covers off the furniture and see what we've got. The upholstery is probably beyond salvaging but the wood pieces should be fine."

Cora Lee joined her, leaning on her cane a little. "I've got to go into town, and Mary and Ellen need to make a trip to the grocery store. At least, if we're going to eat tonight. Mary, have you made a list or anything?"

Aunt Mary hadn't. She'd had no opportunity to take stock of what was in the refrigerator, let alone the freezer, and the only thing we'd found in the cupboards was the sugar jar. Maybe she shouldn't have volunteered. Only, I knew she'd always wanted to cook on a stove like the Wolf that sat in the kitchen. Now was her chance. We'd go to the grocery if she had to call a cab. I followed her down the cellar toward the stairs.

"I haven't made a list, but I will. Do we have time for a shower?"

Cora Lee peered at her delicate silver watch. "Elizabeth

needs to leave in about thirty minutes. We have a little more time."

I followed them up the stairs, thinking how tired they all looked. But then, what they'd been through the last two days would make anyone tired. Aunt Mary didn't usually show her age, but today, it told with every step she climbed. A long, hot shower before we headed for the store was what she needed. It was what we all needed.

The red light on the answering machine blinked. Elizabeth looked at it, turned away, then turned back, walked across the room and reached out to press the button. "Damn thing. It's probably Lieutenant McMann telling me he's on his way back out to arrest me."

It was Hattie. "Elizabeth, I wondered if you and Mary would like to drop by my house in Yorktown this afternoon. I can show you my kitchen and go over the things you're going to need. We can talk about the part you want me to play in your little school." She paused. "If you can't make it, maybe Mary can. She seemed so interested. I'd love to show her more and, of course, give her a cup of nice eighteenth-century tea." Another longer pause. "Well, let me know."

Elizabeth and Aunt Mary looked at each other. Cora Lee stared at the answering machine. "I see she didn't mention me." Her sarcastic smile was back. "Piece of luck for me, wasn't it?" She headed for the door leading into the hall but stopped. "Are you going?"

"I can't." Elizabeth looked imploringly at Aunt Mary. "Would you mind?"

"Why, no." She didn't mind a bit, I could tell. Hattie was not very likable but she *was* interesting, and hearth cooking was fascinating. She wanted to know more about it. "Ellen will go with me, won't you?" She raised an eyebrow in my direction.

I sighed and nodded. Actually, I didn't mind, either. I wanted to know more about Payton Culpepper. Who better to tell me than Payton's mother? I didn't see how he fit into any of this, but Noah said Payton was in some kind of legal trouble. My curiosity was piqued.

"How are we going to get there?"

"I can't take you but I can pick you up. Cora Lee?"

"Sure." Cora Lee cocked her head and nodded. "You can go shopping after Elizabeth collects you."

"All right." Elizabeth looked at Cora Lee appraisingly. "Where are you going?"

"I have some errands. You shouldn't be with Mr. Glass longer than an hour or so."

"I shouldn't think so. What kind of errands?"

"Just errands. Take your shower first, Elizabeth. You have to leave soon. Mary, here's Hattie's number. Why don't you give her a call and tell her you'll be there about two." Cora Lee went through the door into the center hall. We heard the tap of her cane helping her climb the stairs.

Elizabeth didn't say anything, just listened, an unfathomable expression on her face. When the footsteps died away, she sighed. "I won't be long in the shower."

She, too, went into the hallway. Her steps on the stairs were almost as laborious as Cora Lee's.

Aunt Mary looked at the phone, then at me. "I guess I'd better call Hattie."

"While you do that, I'll step outside and call Dan." I hoped I could reach him. If there was ever a time I needed to talk to him, it was now. A dog whined at the French doors. I opened the doors for Petal and waited while Max got himself up from under the table, stretched and followed her out.

I stepped through the doors, slid them closed them softly, and took out my cell.

Chapter Fifteen

YORKTOWN APPEARED AS a small cluster of houses clinging tightly to the side of the hill that overlooked the bay. Boats dotted the gently swaying water, and seagulls squawked overhead as they circled, looking for a handout. Right in the middle, moving slowly, was a huge naval ship. I knew nothing about naval vessels but thought I could make out the shape of men moving around the deck. I watched for a minute, hoping it wasn't on its way to someplace where it would get shot at.

Cora Lee slowed in order to turn down a narrow lane that seemed to dead end at the water.

"See that house over there?" She pointed to a rather ordinary looking house on the left. It had a plaque on the lawn that I couldn't make out.

"That's where Cornwallis surrendered to George Washington. Right there is where the Revolutionary War ended and the United States of America became official. I've often wondered why it's not a bigger tourist attraction. Not nearly as many people visit it as the Jamestown fort."

She pulled up in front of a small white board house with green shutters and front door. The roof was peaked and covered with heavy shake and a dormer window on each side. Smoke rose lazily from a brick chimney that seemed to take up one side of the house; the back extended out in what was obviously an add-on that ruined the symmetry of the cottage. Someone had wanted more space. People today weren't willing to pile on top of each other as in the eighteenth century.

A picket fence encircled the large yard and a climbing rose—the first spring flowers just beginning to show through green buds—wound through the slats. There were several outbuildings. I was pretty sure the one with the cone-shaped roof was a dovecote, although it probably doubled as a home for chickens. A small barn sat behind it and, at the very back of the lot, the "necessary" was half hidden by a large tree. A vegetable and herb garden, ready for planting, was located between the dovecote and the bricked backyard of the house. A hedge, white blooms just starting, edged one side of the garden.

"What's that?" Aunt Mary unbuckled her seat belt, opened her door, and stood. "It seems familiar, but I can't place it."

"Don't touch that hedge." Cora Lee rolled down the passenger window. "That's English Yew. It's poisonous. Elizabeth should be here in an hour or so. I probably won't be back until six, or around there."

The window rolled back up and the car started to move. Cora Lee wasn't coming in. She made a U-turn at the end of the street and passed us by without a wave. She turned the corner.

"She seems uptight this morning."

I nodded. She was tense, even more than usual. I wondered why, but was distracted by Aunt Mary staring at the house. Except for the smoke, there was no movement.

"Do you suppose she's home?"

I shrugged. If she wasn't, we had a long walk back. Aunt Mary opened the small gate, pausing to look at the iron chain on it. A heavy ball was attached to its end. She pushed the gate open, waited for me to start down the brick path and turned to push the gate shut. She didn't have to. As soon as she let go, the gate shut itself.

"Will you look at that? It acts like a spring, only better. I could use one of those on my back gate. That thing has never closed right." She came up the path, pausing occasionally to look at a plant or a tree. Some species she seemed to recognize. Others she examined more closely, like the yew hedge.

"I've heard about this for years," Aunt Mary said. "It's pretty. I wonder if it's poisonous in the same way Oleanders are. They're all over California and they never seem to cause any trouble."

I only cared about what was *in* the house, like Hattie. If she wasn't there, I was going to be seriously plucked. "Come on. You can look at that later."

The board door had no window, but it did have a heavy iron knocker. I raised it and let it fall. It responded with a loud clang. The door opened almost immediately and there stood Hattie, dressed like an eighteenth-century housewife. Didn't the woman have any modern clothes?

"Your timing's good. I just finished a class in hearth cooking." She stood aside and motioned us into a surprising room.

There was no hallway as in the Smithwood home. You stepped directly into a large, comfortable eighteenth-century room. Well-worn wood planked floor, recessed paned glass windows, beamed ceiling and one wall taken up with a fireplace. A high-backed rocker sat close beside it, an upholstered wing chair on the other side, a small table in easy reach. Ladder-backed chairs with rush seats were pulled up to the square table that sat in the middle of the room, a beautiful Windsor chair at the head. None of them looked particularly old. I'd seen more than one living room furnished in similar fashion. It was the rest of the room that looked as if we'd stepped back in time. An open-shelved cupboard sat against one wall. A large wooden tub stood on a bench beside it, along with a lantern and a large salt-glazed jug. A dresser stood against the other wall, serving dishes and platters stacked on top. The fireplace was the center of activity in the room, but it wasn't like the one in Elizabeth's gathering room. Hers seemed designed mainly for heat. This one, like the one in the Payton Randolph kitchen, was meant for cooking. Herbs hung from the rafters and pots dangled from an iron bar attached to the bricks with massive black nails. The wooden mantle held a couple of pewter candlesticks and one very lovely, and heavy-looking, brass one. Long-handled ladles hung from a hook on the side. Tall andirons on the floor close beside the fireplace were filled with logs, and a metal tub sat beside them on a tripod. An iron bar could swing over the fire or back over the hearth, which extended into the room. A small fire burned in the fireplace and coals had been pulled out onto the hearth. A trivet was perched atop the fire with a cast iron saucepan on top. I couldn't see what was in it and didn't care. What had my attention and certainly Aunt Mary's hung just inside the fireplace.

"What is that?"

"A chicken, of course."

She turned to face Hattie. "I know it's a chicken. Believe it or not, I've seen one before. I've never cooked one tied up like that and not with a crust on it."

Hattie's arrogant smile was back. "That bird is stuffed. It's pretty hard to cook a stuffed bird on a spit without all the stuffing falling out. The colonials trussed it up and hung it over the fire, basted it with a water and salt mixture, and let the drippings fall into a pan, like that one over the trivet. They dumped butter into the drippings, dusted the bird with flour then basted it with the drippings. Made that crust you see. You can serve it with boiled onions or cranberry sauce."

"Cranberry sauce." Aunt Mary walked a little closer to the fireplace and peered at the steam coming out of the breast. The crust was a lovely brown and smelled wonderful. "What did they stuff it with?"

"Different things. Mashed potato mixed with herbs, sometimes."

Was this a joke? "Is that what's in there?"

"No. We used bread we made in class. Yesterday's, so it would be good and dry."

"Of course," Aunt Mary muttered.

"We mixed it with eggs, fresh thyme, marjoram and some white wine."

I thought back to the French toast. They used a lot of wine in the eighteenth century. They must have made that, too. They certainly hadn't gotten it at the supermarket.

"This one's ready to come off." Hattie picked a pewter platter off the mantle and laid it down on the hearth. She pulled a pair of heavy shears out of her pocket and cut the twine holding the bird onto the hook. It plunked down on the platter. She moved the saucepan over to the side of the hearth and—using the side of her apron, of course—picked up the platter and set it on the table. Putting her hands on her hips, she leaned back on her heels, a satisfied smile on her face. "Looks good, don't it?"

Aunt Mary stared at the bird then walked over and peered into the pot. "I use dry bread and an egg in my stuffing, but not butter. I keep stock going as well, but haven't tried wine."

I could hardly wait to try her next chicken.

"Do you know what Elizabeth has in that old kitchen?" Hattie asked. "She's going to need some frying pans, sauce pans like that one, trivets for putting them on and, of course, a large kettle to hang over the fire. Does she have any of those things?" She dropped her apron but ran her hands down the front of it.

Aunt Mary was standing stock-still. I knew she was thinking about the contents of the broken crate. So was I. "We haven't been down to the kitchen, but I think she can lay her hands on some of those things."

"Hmm. I've got a cake in the oven. I'll give you a piece just as soon as it's cool. Tea?" Hattie didn't wait for an answer. She took off the top of the barrel and ladled water out of it into a large iron teakettle she placed on another trivet. Scooping some coals onto the bricks with a poker, she set the trivet and kettle on top. "It won't take long to get that water hot. The teapot is over here, on this sideboard."

She crossed the room to the cupboard with the open shelves on top. Welsh cupboards, that's what they were called. The ones I'd seen were open under the shelves. This one had two drawers and a closed cupboard underneath.

A collection of pewter plates and platters filled one shelf. Pewter tankards sat on another, along with several pottery mugs and a pestle and mortar. Aunt Mary walked closer. "Oh, I've always wanted one of those."

I consigned that item to my virtual Christmas list.

The bottom shelf was cluttered with an assortment of things. A large, white soup tureen sat in the middle; shallow white bowls were piled next to it. Crystal wineglasses and a few heavy syllabub glasses were placed in a neat row on the other side. The glass was thick, with little bubbles in it. Not quite like the Smithwood glasses.

"You have some beautiful pieces. Are they all old?"

"I like to keep everything authentic." Hattie opened the top of an earthenware jar and scooped tea into a china teapot. Her back was to us and she paid us no heed while she talked. "These things are Culpepper family icons. My late husband, Jerome, didn't have much from his side of the family, but I've kept what there was." She filled a tea caddy and dropped it into the pot then turned to face us, resting one hand on the sideboard. "It was his cousins who had the plantation and the town and all the land, but Jerome's people were important, too." She paused for a moment, as if making sure we understood that. I wondered how many times she'd reworked Jerome's family tree, trying to make his ancestors, and consequently Payton's, seem more important. I suspected she reshaped that tree a lot.

Hattie stood up straight and directly addressed Aunt Mary. "You're a widow, too, aren't you? Did you keep a lot of your husband's family things?" She turned back to the teapot, lifted the lid, glanced inside and placed the lid back on. She seemed more focused on getting an answer than on the tea as she leaned back against the hutch, clutching the teapot to her bosom.

"There wasn't much to keep. Samuel wanted his mother's lace tablecloth and the cut glass celery dish. His sisters took the rest."

"I've tried to keep what Jerome had for Payton but for some reason, he doesn't seem too interested." Hattie set the teapot down on the hutch, put the top back on the tea jar and pushed it to the back of the sideboard. "Do you take cream?"

Aunt Mary shook her head.

Hattie nodded. "It seems young people nowadays aren't as interested in their ancestry as we are." There was a sad smile on her face. "You think that's so?"

Our family had lived in Santa Louisa for four generations. None of us thought that had any special significance. As for possessions, my grandparents never had much. When they died, my mother and my aunts each took something to remember them and their childhood. The rest they gave away. That wasn't what Hattie meant, however, and I didn't think Aunt Mary knew how to respond. She didn't have to.

"How's Mildred? Are they letting her out of the hospital? Such a terrible thing to happen. I was shocked when I heard."

"How did you hear? Was it on the news?" I groaned. That was all we needed, another round with the press.

"Police scanner. One of my hearth-cooking students has one. She told us. Oh, the cake." Hattie stepped over to the fireplace and, again using the end of her apron, removed a wooden door that blocked a hole in the fireplace wall. Aunt Mary and I watched, fascinated, as Hattie removed a cake pan, carried it to the sideboard and placed it on a trivet. The smell of fresh cinnamon cake filled the air.

"The cake recipes in the old cookbooks call for so much flour and sugar, it's hard to cut down. One calls for eighteen eggs. Can you imagine? When they baked back then, they baked. Of course, they had a lot of people to feed. Nowadays, we think five or six is a bunch. I wanted to show you how to bake a cake in a fireplace oven and what it tastes like."

The cake was beautiful. Light brown, high in the middle, perfectly done. Aunt Mary examined it with a practiced eye. "How do you know when it's finished? And how do you regulate the heat?"

Hattie's self-satisfied smile, so familiar from our visit to the Payton Randolph house, was back. "You bank the coals and, when you think the oven is hot enough, you sprinkle flour on the bottom of it. If it burns, it's too hot. Then you stick your hand in. If you can hold it there until you count to twenty, you need more coals. Recipes usually tell you how long, but that's for a bigger cake. It's experience as much as anything. I've been doing hearth cooking since I was twelve. My mother taught me and her mother taught her. After you've made about a hundred of these, you just know." Hattie paused to put the hot cake on a trivet. She touched the top, much the way Aunt Mary did, to test a cake was done. She looked thoughtful, and then her lips twitched in what might be a smile. "Come to one of my classes. You'd learn a lot."

"You don't cook like this all the time, do you?" I waved my hand around the kitchen, thinking about the Wolf stove in Elizabeth's house.

"Of course I don't." Hattie gestured toward a closed door on the back wall. "That new addition is modern, but it's important to keep the old ways alive. Colonial Williamsburg does. So do I."

Hattie seemed more interested in keeping the Culpepper family name alive. I wondered if she'd ever read the Constitution or even knew who Patrick Henry was. However, she turned out great food.

"Do they know who attacked her?" she asked me.

"What? Oh." I was still on cake, Mildred temporarily forgotten. "I don't think so," I said.

"What happened?" Hattie picked up the kettle, poured a little water into a cup and tested it with her finger. It must have been hot enough because she winced and poured a very small amount in the bottom of the teapot, swirled it around until the bottom of the pot was hot, then carefully poured it full. "Just off the boil. That makes the best tea. We'll let that steep, allow the cake to cool a bit and have a nice chat. Pull up that chair. That's right."

I thought Hattie was going to show us around the kitchen, explain what the barrels contained, tell us about the strings of herbs hanging from the rafters and go into what furnishings they needed for the kitchen and how to use them. Evidently Aunt Mary did, too, because the look she gave me said she didn't want to chat. However, we all sat waiting for the tea to steep, like old friends.

Hattie settled herself deeper into her chair. "Now, tell me. What happened last night?"

"I really don't know." Aunt Mary's words were slow, measured. Hattie clearly intended that we settle in for a good gossip. Aunt Mary didn't gossip. "Mildred stayed to have dinner with us then walked home. She got as far as the barn when someone attacked her."

"Do the police know who?"

"If they do, they haven't told me."

"No. They wouldn't, would they?" Hattie paused. "I suppose Leo McMann is conducting the investigation?"

"He turned up at the hospital last night, but I didn't see him this morning." I didn't add we'd been down in the cellar almost all morning.

"Payton knows Leo McMann real well. Leo's a lot older, but Payton did some criminal law before he moved over to DC. That's when they got to be friends." As if rethinking that last statement, she added, "Not personal friends exactly, the age difference and all, but Leo, he's always looked up to Payton."

Aunt Mary made a little choking sound. I tried not to laugh. I'd only seen Payton Culpepper and Lt. McMann together once, but their exchange had been short on admiration and respect. Animosity and contempt was more like it.

"When Payton heard about Monty, and that Elizabeth was a suspect, well, he was upset. He called Leo to see what was going on, but Leo wouldn't tell him a thing. Said he could only talk to Elizabeth's attorney, so for him to call back when that happened. Payton wanted to help Elizabeth, felt he owed it to Monty." She paused, as if to emphasize her point. "They were best friends, you know."

"No, I didn't." All Cora Lee had said was that they went to school together. I was missing something. How did Payton and Monty being friends years ago translate into him wanting to protect Elizabeth? Or did Hattie have it wrong? Was it something else Payton was after?

Hattie, however, wasn't letting up on her story. "Payton practically grew up there, and Virginia and I were almost as close as sisters. Such a shock, the way she died."

I wondered if Aunt Mary was as confused as I was. The cast of characters around here was growing and no one was providing a playbill. "Was Virginia William's first wife?"

Hattie seemed surprised I hadn't known that. "She was, and Monty's mother. If what Monty and Payton suspect is so, she was his only wife."

"What?" Aunt Mary couldn't have sounded more indignant. "They don't believe Elizabeth and William got married?"

"They think they went through a ceremony. They just don't think it was legal."

"Why not?" The strands of this conversation were as tangled as a knitting basket full of yarn after the kitten got through with it.

"William's stroke, of course. Poor man couldn't walk, could hardly talk. Needed everything done for him. That's when he changed his will and that's when he married Elizabeth. Up 'til then, Cora Lee managed everything, and since she can't inherit, everyone thought the estate would go to Monty. It should have. Then to have him die like that, well, it's a good thing Payton's looking into it all."

"Looking into what? Monty's death? I don't understand."

"Why, he's taking care of Elizabeth. Monty would have wanted him to. He got her an attorney."

"Why?"

Aunt Mary's question was a good one. Why, indeed, would Monty care about Elizabeth? He'd been trying to rob her blind for months.

"Payton's not a trial lawyer," Hattie said, as if that explained everything.

"I know that," Aunt Mary snapped.

Frustration was getting the better of her. She needed to back off a little so I quickly got in the next question. "I thought Monty was going after Smithwood. Was Payton helping him?"

"Payton wasn't going to sue Elizabeth over the title to the plantation or anything like that. He likes her. He was just helping Monty. You know, Monty had rights, too."

Maybe so, but I didn't think they included Smithwood and I still had no idea why Payton injected himself into Elizabeth's dilemma. It was plain Hattie didn't either. Time to change the subject. "Are you planning on helping Elizabeth set up the school?"

"Do you think Elizabeth poisoned Monty?" Hattie asked.

So much for subject changing.

"Elizabeth didn't kill anyone." The tone in Aunt Mary's voice plainly said the subject was closed.

Hattie studied Aunt Mary for a moment, speculation in her eyes, then smiled that tiny smile. Walking over to the sideboard, she lifted the top off the teapot, placed a tiny strainer over one delicate china cup and poured. Nodding her approval, she filled two cups. She placed each on a saucer, then cut two slices of the cake, which she laid on small bone china plates of another pattern. She carried the cake to the table and set a plate in front of each of us. "I'll get your tea and bring a fork and napkin."

"Let me help you." I was already out of my chair. I didn't want any tea and wasn't sure I could swallow cake, but my offer got the subject changed, and changed it would stay. "Is this the right drawer?" I indicated the top drawer in the hutch. At Hattie's nod, I slid it open. It contained an assortment of silver pieces, no two alike, all lying in divided slots lined with purple velvet. In spite of my irritation, I was impressed. The pieces were heavy, with intricate patterns, but the most impressive thing was how well they were cared for. Sterling silver wasn't easy to keep. There wasn't one speck of tarnish on any of these. I picked up the top three forks and spoons. "Are these the ones you want to use?"

Though surprised and none too pleased, Hattie nodded.

"Napkins? Are they in here?" Aunt Mary stood beside me, looking into the drawer. Our eyes met. She nodded toward the drawer slightly as if to indicate approval. Hattie was busy with the cake so Aunt Mary pulled the other drawer open. No napkins. It contained a small bone china serving dish, a silver sugar bowl and sugar tongs, a silver gravy boat, and several beautiful sterling silver serving spoons—elaborately engraved, all beautiful, and all in different patterns. In the corner, nestled on a bed of what looked like silk, was a blue and white china bowl. That was all we saw before the drawer closed.

"That drawer is for things I don't use much. The napkins and tablecloths are in the chest over there." Hattie marched over to the chest on the other side of the room, the one that stood high off the floor and had closed doors across the front. "This is the linen press." She opened the doors. Linens were carefully laid out on shelves inside the cabinet, ready to be used. She selected three almond-colored napkins, heavy with embroidery, and returned to the table. She placed one beside Aunt Mary's plate, then mine and waited pointedly for us to return.

"You have beautiful things, all that silver and crystal," Aunt Mary said.

Hattie laughed, a little bell-like peal with absolutely no mirth. "Some of those things are priceless. Jerome's family things, you know. I'd die if one got broken, so I leave them in those drawers."

Aunt Mary nodded. "One can't be too careful." She paused and took another bite. "Delicious."

Hattie played with her fork, her eyes never leaving it. "Payton was wondering when Monty's body would be released. He's trying to make the funeral arrangements and needs to set a date."

"Didn't Monty have any family? You said his mother died."

"Yes, several years ago. Poor Virginia. She fell down the cellar stairs and broke her neck."

Aunt Mary choked on her tea. She held her napkin up to her mouth, coughing into it while she tried to get her breath. Hattie frowned. I wasn't sure if it was the coughing or because now she'd have to wash and iron the napkin.

Finally Aunt Mary could breathe again. "The Smithwood cellar stairs?"

"Yeah. That's where she lived. Not in the small house, of course. Cora Lee stayed in it when she came. Virginia lived in the big house. William had long since abandoned her to move in with Elizabeth, but Virginia stayed on. She loved Smithwood, you know. Just loved it. You would a' thought it was *her* ancestral home. Such a tragedy."

"What was she doing in that house if she lived in the big one?"

"Don't know. Except it's the only way to get to the cellar without going outside."

Hattie knew Smithwood.

"Ah, did Monty live there also?" That seemed safe and I really wanted to know.

"Oh, no. He'd moved out long since. He was still married to Melanie when his mother died, but they were getting ready to separate. He never told her, and that's a blessing. Virginia, she'd a' been devastated if she'd known. Melanie came from another one of the old families, you know."

That seemed to be a priority. I wondered if Payton was married. If so, Hattie had probably examined his wife's pedigree before she gave her blessing. By those standards, Monty wasn't much of a catch. Or, had Melanie, whoever she was, thought Smithwood came along with the deal and got tired of waiting? Now, *there* was an interesting idea.

"He thought about moving back out there after his mother died, him being alone, and it seemed a natural thing to do since he was sure he'd inherit the place. He could see to the management of it all, and he wouldn't have to get an apartment, either. Only, William wouldn't let him. Said Cora Lee managed it just fine. So Monty stayed in town. Closer to his law office, I guess."

He hadn't considered moving out there while his mother was alive. Or had Melanie refused to live with Virginia? I wondered what had caused her to fall. The stairs were fairly well lit. It was the floor of the cellar that was so dark, at least until you got down there and turned on the downstairs lights. I pushed back my cake plate. "This is wonderful, Hattie. I'm sure Elizabeth will want you to teach the students cake making. She should be here any time now. She'll probably have a lot of questions." I hoped not too many. It was already after two and we still had to go to the market.

"Perhaps we could look at the garden while we wait?" Aunt Mary pushed her empty cake plate away and started to stand. "I noticed how lovely it was as I came in. I want to ask you about a few of the plants."

Hattie didn't move. "Is Elizabeth really going to use Calvin Campbell to plant and care for her garden? Not that he don't—doesn't—know about gardens, but he's not reliable. Never was.

That's what my Payton says. He ought to know. They all went to school together." She paused. "He hated Monty, you know."

She pushed back her chair and gathered up her plate and cup to take to the sink.

Aunt Mary piled mine on hers and followed. "I don't know what Elizabeth is going to do. Why don't you ask her when she comes?"

Hattie got to the sink before Aunt Mary. "I'll take those. Everything in this room gets taken care of as if we were in the eighteenth century. I'll put them on the hutch and heat some more water and get them washed up later. The basin for washing them is over there"—she waved in the direction of a ceramic basin that sat on the bench—"and I keep the soap in that little crock."

"Soap." Aunt Mary walked over to the crock, lifted the lid and looked in. "You make your own soap?"

"Well, just for the things in here, and for what we do in the classes. I have a small kitchen in the new part of the house. I've got a bathroom, electric lights and a TV, too." She laughed a little self-consciously.

I thought it was the smartest statement Hattie had made all day. It was wonderful to know how our ancestors lived, and I thought it important for everyone to know how our country came into being. I'd always enjoyed the few history classes I'd taken, and the little I'd seen of Colonial Williamsburg had left me wanting to see more. However, reading about history— or even visiting reenactments of history—was one thing. No shower and no hot water crossed my limit line. I picked up my purse and followed them out into the garden.

Chapter Sixteen

"That was the best spinach salad I've ever eaten." Noah pushed his chair back a little and smiled. His mother looked at him. "Next to yours, Mom, of course."

Mildred started to shake her head but stopped. She put her hand up to the large white bandage that covered the left side of her head instead. "Mary's is better. You'll tell me how to make it?"

"It couldn't be easier. However, it's politically incorrect. I make the dressing with hot bacon fat."

"No wonder he liked it."

"Umhm. Very good." Elizabeth sounded as if she wasn't quite sure what she was claiming was good and the two bites missing from her plate didn't do much to validate her opinion. "I wonder where Cora Lee is? She didn't say in her message, did she?" Elizabeth knew she hadn't. She'd listened to it twice. "What's she doing in Richmond? I didn't know she had friends there."

Noah shifted in his chair. He opened his mouth as if to speak but closed it again. He glanced at Mildred, who stared down at her barely touched piece of chicken. Finally, he seemed to make up his mind. "She's got an attorney in Richmond."

Elizabeth almost dropped her fork. "An attorney. Is she finally going to divorce C.J.? I thought they had that all worked out."

"I don't think she's seeing a divorce attorney."

"Oh." This time the fork dropped and Elizabeth's hand flew up to her mouth. "It's about the will, isn't?" She took a deep breath and let it out slowly. "I guess I can't blame her. After all, Smithwood should, by all rights, be hers."

"I don't know," Noah said. "I don't know why she's seeing him."

Aunt Mary laid down her fork. "You know, I'm a little tired of you people speaking in code. Elizabeth, you asked me out here to help you, but so far I haven't been much help, largely because I have no idea what's going on." She turned to Noah. "Who is Cora Lee seeing and how do you know?" To Elizabeth, she said, "Whose will? What are you talking about?"

Noah pushed his plate away and glanced again at his mother. Her eyes didn't meet his. Noah sighed. "I guess we've been a little remiss."

"You might say that." Aunt Mary picked up her wineglass and settled back in her chair, as if waiting to hear a good story.

"One of our officers—a good friend of mine—was over in Richmond this afternoon, giving a deposition. He came into the station as I was leaving. He told me." Noah spoke slowly, as if his words were a minefield he was trying to pick his way through. "He knows Cora Lee. He knows her story. So, when he saw her going into Alan Baedeker's office, he asked me what was going on."

Aunt Mary said, "I don't know her story. I don't know who Alan Baedeker is or why Cora Lee would go to see him." Her tone left no room for discussion. Someone needed to enlighten her, now.

"Cora Lee's father disinherited her when she was nineteen or so." Elizabeth stabbed at her chicken with her fork as if it had personally insulted her.

I watched for a moment, waiting for her to go on, but she didn't. "All right," I said. "Why?"

"She got married, that's why." Mildred put her fork down and reached over to cover Elizabeth's hand with hers. "Elizabeth, you had nothing to do with it. Nobody knew you then. You weren't the one who threw Cora Lee out and you weren't the one who got her pregnant. So, quit feeling guilty."

I didn't know why I was so shocked. The scenario described by Mildred had played out many times, in many families, over the centuries. "I gather she married C.J.?"

Mildred nodded. "The old man hated C.J. and when he found out Cora Lee was not only pregnant, but married to him, he threw her out. Then he drew up a new will saying she could never inherit nor could any of her issue. Issue. That meant his grandchildren."

Some things were coming clear. Elizabeth's tolerance of Cora Lee and all her little barbs, for instance.

Aunt Mary looked from Mildred to Elizabeth. "I wondered why you hadn't told her to take a hike long ago. Guilt makes us do strange things. Mildred's right, though. You shouldn't feel any. What was so awful about this C.J., anyway?"

Mildred sighed and shook her head at Elizabeth, who appeared suddenly tongue-tied. "I'll tell them." She turned to face Aunt Mary and me. "Charles John Wittingham's family didn't come from Virginia. They came from New England originally and settled in Atlanta after the war. The important war, the one that counted. They were carpetbaggers. As far as Mr. Smithwood was concerned, they still were and always would be."

I made a face. "Are you telling me the only thing he had against that boy was he wasn't from Virginia?" I'd heard about this kind of thing, had read books where family was everything. Wasn't *Romeo and Juliet* the same story? The Hatfields and the

McCoys? But the Civil War had been over for a hundred and fifty years or more. As for the Revolutionary War, well, there'd been even more time for families to shift and change. "Family history doesn't seem enough to count someone as worthless."

"Hattie doesn't think so," Mildred continued, "but there was something else that old Mr. Smithwood could never forgive." She sighed again, reached up to touch the bandage on her head and winced. Dark circles had begun to form under her eyes and her mouth looked pinched and tired, but I needed her to finish.

I didn't think we'd get much out of Elizabeth. "Go on."

"C.J. got rich. Very rich. It seems he had the Midas touch. Started out making a fortune in pork bellies, or something like that, and didn't look back. Mr. Smithwood never forgave him." She gave Elizabeth a sad little smile. "I think he wanted Cora Lee to come crawling back broke, begging for her father's forgiveness. It didn't work out that way."

"And now?" Clearly, somewhere along the line the marriage had fallen apart. What happened wasn't any of our business, unless Cora Lee had it in mind to get her share of Smithwood back.

Elizabeth lifted her head, her eyes troubled. "She has two children, both grown, of course, and five grandchildren. One of her granddaughters is going to graduate from Stanford next month. Her kids have never been here. Neither have her grandkids. I'm not sure they care, but she does. She loves this place, and I know she thinks they got cheated."

"Old Mr. Smithwood is dead. So is Mrs. Smithwood. Why didn't William just change the will or give her part of the estate?" It seemed an obvious solution to a not very difficult problem.

"Mr. Smithwood held a deep grudge." Mildred kept patting Elizabeth's hand in a gesture I thought was meant to be comforting, but the bitterness in her voice wasn't. William's father hadn't treated Mildred and her family any better and

Elizabeth hadn't followed through on changing that situation. At least, not yet. "He had the will sewed up tighter than a tick clinging to a dog in summer." Mildred's face got tight and she squeezed Elizabeth's hand, making her flinch. "He wasn't a forgiving man. Neither is Cora Lee. C.J. started to cheat on her just as soon as his first million was in the bank. She would have left him flat, but she refused to give her father the satisfaction. The day he died she came back and started to help her mother. When William needed someone to manage the plantation while he taught, she jumped at the chance."

"You think she's seeing the attorney because now that William's also dead, she thinks Smithwood should be hers?" I asked. I couldn't believe it. Cora Lee had an acid tongue and a wicked sense of humor—if you could call her little barbs humor—but I thought she was genuinely fond of Elizabeth. Maybe she was fonder of Smithwood. Only, to go to an attorney behind Elizabeth's back to get the will set aside didn't make sense. "She'd have to get two wills set aside, wouldn't she?"

Elizabeth seemed confused. "Two wills?"

"Think about it. If her father cut her off and William got everything, and he left it all to you, she'd have to get both of them changed."

Noah had been silent. Now he sat up and shook his head. "I don't think so. If she could prove she had been wrongly cut out of her share by Smithwood, then William would have only his share to leave to Elizabeth."

"Would Cora Lee know that?"

"Oh, yes. Marriage to C.J. taught her a lot of things."

Mildred looked up for the first time. She put her hand up to her head again and touched the white bandage covering the stitches in her scalp, which also covered the hair that had been cut away. It was a different pain that bothered her. "Elizabeth."

Elizabeth turned to her expectantly.

"Have you made a will?"

Elizabeth was stunned. The implication was only too clear. "No."

"If something happens to you, what happens to Smithwood?"

There was probably more than one reason Mildred asked that question, but one stood out. If the Longos' house wasn't deeded over to them, they could be out on the street. I'd never been in a room this quiet, with people waiting for an answer they all knew already.

"I don't know." Elizabeth appeared to shrink in front of our eyes. "One more thing to ask Aaron Glass." She pushed her plate away as if the very sight of it made her sick. "The lawyer Cora Lee went to see, does he do divorce?"

Noah watched Elizabeth, as if he expected her to break down. She wouldn't, even if her straws collapsed. I was sure of that. "No," Noah said. "He specializes in estate law. Wills, deeds, that kind of thing."

The silence descended once again, settling down around us like a fog.

Aunt Mary broke it. "She could very well be setting up her own will. She's at the age where you need to think about that kind of thing. Cora Lee will have plenty to leave. Maybe it's as simple as that."

Noah brightened, looked around the table at each of them, almost imploring them to believe that theory.

Still, no one spoke. We all sat, lost in thought, not one of us wanting to believe the possible implications.

Finally Aunt Mary said, "Even if she is looking into her father's will, that doesn't mean she wants to contest it. It certainly doesn't mean she murdered someone. Besides, she wasn't the one who attacked Mildred." What was left unsaid was that Cora Lee had opportunity for everything else that had happened.

All eyes dropped back to the table. No one said a word.

Chapter Seventeen

THE FRONT DOOR opened.

"Anybody here?" A female voice echoed down the hallway.

Both dogs were on their feet, barking at the top of their lungs, running toward the doorway.

A slim brown woman in hospital scrubs, hair cropped short, brown eyes rimmed with fatigue, walked into the room. Noah was on his feet in an instant, gathering her in his arms, planting a soft kiss on her cheek. The dogs both danced around her, demanding her attention. She kissed Noah and bent down to rub Max's ears. She tried to do the same for Petal, but the little dog kept jumping away, barking and whining. "You'll have to stop that if you want a scratch, you silly thing."

Petal didn't take the hint. She kept on jumping and barking. Elizabeth got up and caught the little dog. "You're an idiot. Now stop that." Petal immediately settled down. Felicity, for it could be no one else, reached toward her and rubbed her ears. Petal whimpered with pleasure and licked the woman's hand.

Felicity grinned. "I'm sorry I'm so late. There was a wreck

on the Colonial Parkway and they needed another nurse in the ER. Did you get my message?"

"We did." Mildred pushed her chair back and started to her feet. "We saved you dinner. Balsamic Chicken, mashed potatoes and spinach salad, courtesy of Mary. Sit down, child. You look done in."

"Oh, good. I'm starved. Never did get time for lunch." She walked over to the sink to wash her hands. "Where's Cora Lee?"

Aunt Mary was taking Felicity's foil-wrapped dinner plate out of the warming oven but stopped, her back to the room. How much of this did Felicity know? Rather, how much had Noah told her?

"She's in Richmond." Noah didn't elaborate.

Felicity turned away from the sink, the dishtowel still in her hands. "What's she doing in Richmond?"

"Seeing an attorney." Mildred's voice was flat, almost devoid of interest. Almost.

"What attorney?" Felicity hung the dishtowel back on the hook and walked toward the table. Petal followed, but Felicity ignored her. She stopped in front of Noah, her eyes demanding an answer.

"Alan Baedeker."

Felicity didn't say anything, but her eyes widened and she shook her head. She grabbed the top of the chair next to Noah, pulled it back and lowered herself into it. "Damn. I'm exhausted."

"You know him?" Elizabeth seemed surprised and not a little displeased at the thought.

Felicity nodded. "He does wills, estates, probate, that kind of thing. My folks used him for theirs, and I've run into him a couple of times at the hospital. I had to witness a will one time. Why did she go to see him?"

"That's what we're wondering." There was something in Elizabeth's voice that made Aunt Mary pause before she slipped the food she'd been keeping warm in front of Felicity. Wariness? Disappointment? Certainly discouragement. It wasn't surprising.

It had been a terrible few months and things weren't getting any better. William's death, someone prowling the upstairs hallway, a crate pushed over, almost hitting her, then Monty murdered. Now Cora Lee, who she thought she could trust, might be trying to get Smithwood from her. Or, had she suspected that for some time? She'd told Aunt Mary she needed someone she could trust. Cora Lee might want Smithwood, but she wouldn't get it by maiming, or killing, Elizabeth. Neither would Noah or Mildred. They all had a vested interest in keeping Elizabeth alive and well. Who would? Calvin Campbell? No. He had a motive for killing Monty. Revenge. That didn't include Elizabeth. However, he kept showing up at odd moments. He'd worked here for years and probably knew every inch of the property. He could know how to get in and out of the house. Calvin bore looking into.

I pushed my plate away. The thought that any one of these people could have done such a thing ruined my appetite. Someone had, though. The questions was, who? Why?

"This is wonderful," Felicity effectively ended that train of thought. "Noah, do you think I could have a glass of that wine? Bring the bottle. There are some empty glasses here."

Noah jumped up to get the wine.

"I think Mildred needs to go home. She's looking tired and her head must be pounding." Aunt Mary held her glass out for him to pour a little in it also. "Why don't you and Felicity take her just as soon as she finishes?"

Felicity nodded and cut a slice off her chicken breast. Noah set a full glass in front of her. She smiled her thanks. "Are you sure Cora Lee went to see the lawyer? Robert Tucker is in that building. He's one of the best orthopedic surgeons in the state. I'd think she'd want a second opinion before she commits to anything. Of course, she could be updating her will before she goes into surgery. Although, a hip replacement doesn't—why are you all staring at me like that? Oh, oh. She hasn't told you."

"Hip replacement?" That got Elizabeth's attention. Her head jerked up and she stared at Felicity. "She hasn't said anything about a hip replacement."

Felicity sighed and laid her fork down on her plate. "I shouldn't have said anything, but I thought you all knew. You only have to watch her walk to tell she's in pain."

"I thought the cane was an affectation. A part of her statement. She's good at that kind of thing." Elizabeth's voice was faint.

That had been my assumption, too. Thinking back, the little winces, the leaning on the cane to take the weight off one side—how could I have missed it?

"We have to help her."

"Cora Lee doesn't want help. She doesn't even want us to know. She's a proud and stubborn woman." Aunt Mary was right.

But Elizabeth had suspected Cora Lee of doing something that would hurt her deeply. Now, in a fit of guilt, she'd try to make it up in an excess of sympathy. That wouldn't work.

Mildred nodded. "Cora Lee equates sympathy with pity and help with weakness. Felicity, why did she tell you?"

Felicity gave an embarrassed little laugh. "She didn't. I took a patient to X-ray a few weeks ago and there was a chart with her name on it. I picked it up and read it. I didn't realize she hadn't told any of you. I should have, though. She's so blasted proud. I'm really sorry." She pushed her plate away and leaned forward. "If you're going to start feeling sorry for Cora Lee, think again. This is a hip replacement. People have them all the time. She'll be fine. This is Cora Lee we're talking about. She looks fragile as glass, but she's as tough as a steel bayonet, and just as sharp. Quit worrying. She'll tell you when she's good and ready, probably the day before the surgery."

Elizabeth smiled broadly and leaned back. "I knew it all the time. Cora Lee wouldn't ever go behind my back."

Aunt Mary smiled also.

I didn't think she was nearly as convinced as Elizabeth, who had jumped to conclusions again. Cora Lee might be having surgery for her hip, but that didn't mean she wasn't trying to take back what she considered rightly hers. Cora Lee had gone into the attorney's *office*, not just the building. She might have intended to get her will in order, but perhaps not. I'd give a lot to know why Cora Lee really went to see that attorney.

Noah drained the last of his wine and pushed back his chair. "I'm sorry about Cora Lee, but Mom's fading fast."

Mildred looked as if she couldn't take much more. Her eyes were closing and the pain around them was evident.

Felicity took another look at her and nodded. "We probably shouldn't have brought her over. Although, it would have been a shame if she hadn't had some of this wonderful dinner." She took another quick bite, reached over, picked up Mildred's wrist and took her pulse. "Yep. It's time you went home. Noah, did they give her any pain pills?"

He nodded. "A few. Doc wrote out a prescription as well. He said not to give her anything but what he prescribed."

"Head wounds can be tricky." Felicity helped Mildred to her feet and looked around for her coat, which was draped over the rocking chair. Felicity thrust one of Mildred's arms in a sleeve then, carefully avoiding the bandage on Mildred's head, put the other in and pulled the coat up over her shoulders. "Your concussion was mild. That doesn't mean you don't need to rest." She gave Mildred a peck on the cheek. "You need sleep more than anything right now." She turned so she faced Noah and gently pushed her into his arms. "I'll be down directly. Noah, can you help her get into bed?"

"I don't need help." Mildred lifted her chin and glared at all of them. Or, she tried to. Pain and exhaustion made it a failed attempt. "It'll be a bad day when I can't get into my own nightgown." Starting for the door, she staggered and caught herself just in time.

"We're on our way." Noah had his hand under his mother's arm, ignoring her protests. "Thanks for dinner, and Flice, we'll see you soon?"

"Just let me finish this last bite and I'll be right behind you."

No one sat back down until the front door closed.

Then Felicity dropped into her chair and leaned her elbows on the table. "Okay. Just what's going on around here?"

"I wish to hell I knew." Elizabeth's jaw was set. She was angry and scared and had no problem showing it. "Mildred's getting attacked was the last straw."

"Did she say anything?" Felicity seemed as angry as Elizabeth. "She has fourteen stitches in her head and bruises on her shoulder and back. Whatever she was hit with wasn't too heavy, but whoever swung it whacked her pretty good."

"I think it was that shovel in the barn," I said. "I saw it lying just inside the door when they turned on the lights."

"I remember you talking about the shovel," Elizabeth said slowly. "Did the police take it?"

I shrugged. "I don't know. McMann knew about it. There was blood on it, probably Mildred's. They should be testing it for fingerprints."

"Fingerprints."

"Yes, Felicity. Fingerprints. I thought you might want to mention that to Noah, in case he doesn't know about it."

"You thought I might, huh?" Though still tense with anger, Felicity managed a smile. "Is there anything else I should mention to Noah?"

"As a matter of fact, there is," I persisted.

"There is? What?" No smile now. Felicity was on full alert.

"I heard a car engine while we were running toward the barn."

"A car engine. Where? Down by our house?"

"No. It sounded as if it was behind the barn someplace."

"Ellen's right," Elizabeth said. "I was so upset about Mildred, I didn't notice. Only, there aren't any roads there."

"There's that old farm road, but it doesn't go anywhere."

Elizabeth blinked. "What old farm road?"

"The one close to the river. Noah took me down it once, oh, ages ago. It's not much more than a track. They used it when the tobacco barges were running. There was a pier down there and an auction shed. Wagons loaded with bales of cured tobacco from several of the plantations would come, so would the buyers from the tobacco companies. Sometimes the buyers had already made a deal with the planters. Sometimes they had an auction. Then they loaded it on the barges and headed out. The pier's gone. So are the Smithwood drying sheds. The road's still there, barely. It doesn't go anywhere."

Elizabeth leaned forward. "That's right. This used to be an old tobacco plantation. William told me, but that was all gone before I came. We went down by the river once, but I didn't see any road. If one's there, that has to be how this person is getting on and off the property."

"One's there, all right. Probably overgrown by now, and it never did go up by the barns or the houses. Just ran from the highway down that hillside where the crops used to grow and stopped at the river. I remember the last auction." Felicity's smile was soft, dreamy. "My grandpa was an old tobacco man. He brought me out for that one. Said I needed to see a tobacco auction before they were gone. That's where I met Noah. Louis, Noah's dad, managed the sale for Smithwood. That was the only time I ever saw him, and Noah and I got in trouble for trying to climb on the tobacco bales. We were pretty little."

She paused but the smile still lingered.

It faded and her tone was brisk. "I think you're right, Elizabeth. That road has to be how this person is getting on the property. Noah will know and he'd better go take a look. I don't think he knows you heard a car."

Aunt Mary nodded. "What it doesn't tell us is who was driving."

I nodded. "Or how he's been getting in and out of the house."

We were all quiet for a moment.

"Well," Felicity sighed. "It's a start." She pushed her chair back, picked up her empty plate and walked over to the sink. "I want to check on Mildred before she goes to sleep and I have a whole lot to tell Noah." She rinsed her plate and slipped it into the dishwasher. Picking up her purse from the floor beside her chair, she added, "Elizabeth, don't you worry about Cora Lee. She loves Smithwood. She loved William and she loves you, too. She wouldn't do anything to hurt you. Or Mildred." She turned toward Aunt Mary and smiled. "Thank you for dinner. It was great. If I could cook, I'd ask you for the recipe."

The front door closed, a car engine started, gravel crunched and she was gone.

We returned to the gathering room, silent. I was absorbed in not very pleasant thoughts. Aunt Mary collected the remaining dinner dishes and carried them to the sink. Elizabeth collapsed into her chair, picked up a napkin and started rolling and unrolling it. Aunt Mary sighed, returned to her chair and looked at me. I nodded. It wasn't difficult to guess what her next question would be.

She leaned forward a little so that she faced Elizabeth. "Okay. Suppose you tell me, who is Louis?"

"I'll tell you." Cora Lee stood in the doorway, leaning heavily on her cane. Her eyes looked tired. The lines around her mouth were etched deep and her makeup was mussed. Clearly, she was not in a good mood. "He's Mildred's no-good thieving husband."

Chapter Eighteen

I WOKE WITH a start. What was that? I blinked, took a deep breath and tried to adjust to the darkness. I could just make out the bed hangings, canopy and feather quilt. What had woken me so abruptly? I listened. Nothing. Something had jerked me awake. I'd been dreaming. Was that it? A dream? I looked for the bedside clock. Four thirty.

I'd talked to Dan until after midnight and had tossed and turned for a while after that, so I hadn't been asleep very long. It must have been a dream. I pushed myself down in the bed and let my head fall back on the pillow. This whole thing was getting to be a bit much. Prowlers, muggers, murderers. We'd come east to help Aunt Mary's friend, thinking we'd be here a few uneventful days. I hadn't bargained on this.

There it was again. What was it? A banging noise. A door? And that creak, that was the stairs right outside my room. Someone was on the stairs. A dog barked. Just one bark. It sounded as if the dog was downstairs. Petal? Was Elizabeth going down to let her out? Or was the prowler back?

This time I threw the covers aside and swung my legs over the side of the bed. Slippers. Where were they? Light. I needed light. The bedside lamp was beside the clock radio. The lighted dial did nothing to help me find the knob but finally it turned. The light almost blinded me. A blink or so later I thrust my feet into the slippers while I struggled into my robe. Something was going on downstairs and I'd better get down there fast. Wait. I'd be an idiot if I charged downstairs without a weapon of some sort. Only, I didn't have one. My cellphone was beside the bed. I slipped it into the pocket of my robe but all it would do is allow me to call for help. What else could I use? There wasn't one thing. Muttering under my breath that this was a fool's errand, I walked over to the door and carefully pushed it open. Aunt Mary's door was ajar. So was Elizabeth's. Both rooms were dark and the hallway was empty. I stepped into it, pulling my door not quite shut behind me. A small sliver of light showed, but it didn't do much to chase away the shadows. I crept closer to the stairs. I could just make out a glow. Someone had turned on a light downstairs, something burglars seldom did. I started down the stairs, taking only a few at a time, stopping to listen, taking a couple more. The light came from the gathering room. Maybe it was Elizabeth waiting for Petal to come back in. I pushed the door from the hallway open a little and looked around. It was Elizabeth all right, Aunt Mary right behind her. Only, they weren't waiting for Petal. The door leading to the cellar stairs was wide open and Elizabeth stood in front of it, fireplace poker raised. Aunt Mary held the coalscuttle. They were both ready to strike.

"What are you doing?" The words came out almost before I realized I'd said them.

Elizabeth whirled around, poker over her head, poised to swing. "Oh, my God. You gave me such a scare. I almost hit you. What are you doing down here?"

"I heard noises. What's the matter? I thought I heard a dog bark." I looked around the room, but no dog appeared. "Where's Petal?" She had to be here. The French doors were securely locked.

"She went downstairs. I'm worried. She gave that one bark and ran through the door. She hasn't come back."

Aunt Mary lowered the coalscuttle. "Oh, I'm so glad it's you. I heard Elizabeth and came down to see what was wrong. The door was open."

I fumbled in my pocket for my phone. "Is someone down there?"

"I don't know." Elizabeth lowered her poker and leaned on it. "I woke up because the dog started to growl. She jumped off the bed and went into the hall. I followed her, not knowing what to think. I didn't hear anything so I thought maybe she wanted out." She paused and gestured toward the open cellar door. "When she came in here, I followed and turned on that light." She motioned toward the lamp on a table just inside the door. "The door to the cellar was open and Petal stood in front of it, growling."

Glancing once more at the open door, Elizabeth pulled a chair away from the table and almost fell into it. "Lord, I was so scared. I didn't know what to do. Then that damn dog gave a bark and disappeared through the doorway. I yelled and grabbed the poker. Then Mary came in and wanted to know what was wrong. She grabbed the coalscuttle. We thought we'd better just shut up and wait to see what would happen. Only, nothing did. Then you came in."

"You didn't hear anything more?"

"I didn't hear anything in the first place. Just the dog."

"The door was open."

Elizabeth nodded. So did Aunt Mary. I stared at the door, almost as if I expected someone or something to appear at any moment. I was about to say more when we heard a loud throat-clearing behind us. Aunt Mary's knees buckled, she gave a gasp and grabbed the table for support. I reached for her and we both did an about-face to confront the intruder.

It was Cora Lee. "What the hell do you think you're doing down here in the middle of the night?"

Aunt Mary sank into a chair beside Elizabeth. "You almost gave me a heart attack."

Cora Lee advanced into the room, gearing up for more complaining, then noticed the cellar door. "Why is that door open?"

"Someone's down there." Elizabeth's voice cracked a little, but she still held onto her poker.

"Not again." All the color drained from Cora Lee's face and she leaned even more heavily on her cane. She'd admitted to seeing the doctor, but just a routine visit. I didn't think so. She hadn't mentioned an attorney, but she sure hadn't been shopping, as she'd claimed. The circles under her eyes proclaimed she hadn't slept much since she'd gone to bed, either.

"Again." I pulled the cellphone out of my pocket and swiped the screen.

"What are you doing?" Elizabeth demanded. "Don't call the police."

"Call Noah," Cora Lee said. Arriving at the table, she, too, fell into a chair.

"No. Don't call him either," Elizabeth ordered. "We're going down there to find out who's been coming in and out of my house." Elizabeth pushed back her chair and got a firm grip on the poker. "We're going to find out what happened to my dog, too." She started toward the cellar door. "Are you coming?"

"Petal's down there?"

Elizabeth nodded.

"I'm not going down there armed only with this stupid coalscuttle." Aunt Mary hurried over to the wooden knife block. She pulled out a long thin knife and nodded. "Just the thing."

"You'd actually stick someone with that?" Cora Lee seemed torn between admiration and disbelief.

"I don't know, but it sure should give them pause." She tested the blade with her finger and nodded. "It would me."

I looked at the knife block, thought about the meat cleaver

and discarded the idea. I'd stick with the cellphone and hope I had reception down there.

"When you're ready." Elizabeth looked us over, shook her head slightly and started a slow, steady creep toward the open cellar door, poker out in front. Cora Lee crept right behind her, lifting her cane every few feet as if to make sure she could swing it if needed. Aunt Mary followed, knife out if front. This was ludicrous. Or it would have been if it weren't for the memory of Monty, lying dead in a pool of his own vomit. And Mildred, bloody in front of the barn. Someone wanted something in Smithwood, and they apparently didn't care what they had to do to get it. Going down there was dangerous, foolhardy, but I couldn't think of any way to stop them. I hitched my bathrobe up onto my shoulders, clutched my cellphone tighter and went through the cellar doorway.

It was dark in the cellar. I could barely make out Cora Lee halfway down the stairs. Aunt Mary was close behind her. I couldn't see Elizabeth. Why, oh why, hadn't I thought to bring Aunt Mary's flashlight? "Turn on the light."

Cora Lee was hanging onto the stair rail and making slow progress.

"Are you sure?"

"Yes." There was no doubt in Aunt Mary's voice.

Nor in mine. "If anyone's still down here, he knows we are, too. I have no desire to be jumped in the dark." I felt my way down another step and suddenly the lights came on. I stopped to let my eyes adjust. There was no one in sight. The pile of crates stood silently beside the staircase, with no evidence that one had been positioned to fall on us. Only, the stepstool was gone. There was no time to wonder about it now. I went down another couple steps. Cora Lee had reached the floor and was looking around. Aunt Mary stood on the bottom step, her hand holding the knife by her side. Where was Elizabeth? Keeping an eye on the crates, I descended the rest of the staircase.

"There's nobody here." Aunt Mary sounded almost disappointed.

"There doesn't seem to be," I said. "Where's Elizabeth? I can't see her anywhere." I looked around but she'd disappeared.

"Where's Petal?" Cora Lee pulled her flimsy robe a little closer around her and started forward across the brick floor.

The heels of her little satin mules caught on the uneven bricks. "For God's sake, be careful," Aunt Mary said. "You're going to trip and break your neck in those things."

Cora Lee turned and smiled. "Southern women learn how to maneuver in heels at a very early age. It's part of the culture. Like never having a bad hair day or mushy makeup." She immediately tripped and barely caught herself. "Damnation."

I smothered a laugh.

"Where are you?" Elizabeth called to us, "Hurry up. You aren't going to believe this. I've found … Petal. Stop that."

I took my eyes off the floor and Cora Lee's mules to stare straight ahead at what yesterday had been the end of the cellar. The cupboard that had contained nothing stood open and so did the back of it, revealing an open doorway.

Elizabeth stood in the opening, barely discernible, beckoning us to hurry. "This is how our prowler has been getting in and out. The back of this cupboard pulls away from the wall and just look at what's behind it."

We hurried forward, following Elizabeth into another large room. A long trestle table, thick with dust, sat in the middle. A fireplace very like the one in the Payton Randolph house and in Hattie's cottage was on the opposite wall. It contained nothing but ashes, cold and gray with age. The window was so dirt-encrusted there was no way to see what it opened onto. Even in the dimness of the room, it was evident that the door beside it had been opened recently. Marks on the dirt floor, hinges free of inhibiting dirt and a latch that was freshly oiled. This was how the cellar ghost came and went.

For a while nobody spoke. Aunt Mary was in the middle of

the room, slowly turning round. Elizabeth didn't seem to be able to take her eyes off the fireplace. Cora Lee walked over to the rickety plank table that stood on the dirt floor in the middle of the room. She stared at it then put out one finger, as if to see how sturdy it was. She got as far as the surface before she jerked it back.

"Ugh. There's two hundred years worth of dead bugs on that thing."

"As well as dirt." Aunt Mary walked over to join her. "I don't think there's a scrub brush in existence that could clean that." She stared down at the table as if trying to identify its original color but was distracted by a scratching sound. "Petal, what are you doing?"

The little dog was under the table, scratching at the earth while making growling, whining noises interspersed with an occasional sharp bark.

"What's she doing?" Cora Lee moved back in distaste. She brushed at the folds of her thin dressing gown, holding it closer around her.

Elizabeth glanced at them and then dropped her gaze down to the little dog. "There must be a bone of some kind buried down there. I'm amazed she can smell it after all these years."

"I thought dogs had a wonderful sense of smell." Cora Lee moved one step closer, shuddered and backed away again.

"She's a sight hound."

I didn't think that cleared things up very much, but I wasn't too interested in Petal's pursuit of ancient bones. Instead, I moved over to the only door.

"Where does this lead?"

"I don't know." Elizabeth joined me. "Cora Lee? Do you know?"

"This room is the old kitchen, so we're right under the passageway that leads from the main house to the east house."

Aunt Mary looked back at the doorway we had just come through, then at the cold fireplace. There was a little awe in her voice. "The old kitchen. That cupboard's back opens up onto the old kitchen? Oh, so the cook didn't have to go outside, around the side of the house, enter through that doorway over by Elizabeth's house and then go back outside carrying whatever they needed back here?" She turned to peer once more through the secret doorway. "Why? All the secrecy, I mean. Why not have a regular door?"

Cora Lee left the table to stand beside Mary. She looked back through the opening into the brightness of the cellar. "Because it was the slaves who did all the work down here and they weren't given free access to the foodstuffs stored in the cellar. That's where the wines were kept, where flour and corn meal were stored, where all of the apples, potatoes, barrels of salted pork and hams were kept. Lots of things. The colonists weren't dumb. They knew if they left all of the foodstuffs in easy reach of the slaves, they would rapidly disappear. Slaves didn't have ham or wine, or much of anything, so expecting them to resist helping themselves to a few apples wasn't realistic. The cellar would be kept locked, and when new supplies were needed, the master or mistress would open it and watch carefully how much was taken and log it in the housekeeping book. I'd bet dollars to donuts the first Smithwoods had no idea that cupboard opening existed. The slaves who knew about it, and used it, would be very careful to make sure they didn't take much, or too often. If the family discovered anything missing, they probably blamed it on mice."

Aunt Mary stared at the open cupboard doorway then back at Cora Lee. "Pretty well fed mice."

I had been staring at the back of the cupboard along with Aunt Mary but turned to look at the kitchen door directly across the room. It must open to the outside. So, the "ghost" could come in the kitchen, go through the cellar, up to Elizabeth's house then through the passageway into the main house. So much for ghosts.

It was Elizabeth who walked over and opened the kitchen

door. Aunt Mary and Cora Lee followed right behind, peering around, trying to figure out just where they were.

A grassy slope led down to the river.

"I thought you said we were under the passageway between the main house and the unused wing?"

Aunt Mary edged her way past Elizabeth.

It didn't look as if we were under anything. No, there, right above the kitchen. That wasn't a roof, it was bricks. The passageway. Right outside the kitchen door was a couple of wooden steps. A little rickety but usable, they ended on a packed earth path. I stepped past Elizabeth to stand on the top one.

"Look at all these tramped-down weeds." I pointed the other way, toward the unused east wing. "There are plenty of weeds down that way. This is the only place there aren't any." I went down the two steps to stand on the path and try to get my bearings. The kitchen was on the same level as the basement, so the houses and the passageways that connected them had to be above where I stood. I took a step farther away from the kitchen, careful to keep my eyes on the path. The ground seemed to fall away pretty fast here and the moon wasn't bright enough to illuminate much. The path continued on, but I couldn't see where it went. Why hadn't I brought a flashlight?

"I think there's a staircase going up here." My hand brushed up against something that wasn't part of a wall. I held onto it and felt around for a step. Yep. There was one. I could just make out what had to be the passageway above me, the one between the main house and the unused east wing. This staircase seemed to go right up to it. Of course. The kitchen servants carried all those platters of food up these stairs and down the passageway into the main house. I couldn't see much of the stairs. Should I go up? Absolutely not. I could barely make out the handrail and that was with the moon shining its brightest. There would be nothing but shadows in that covered passageway. All I'd accomplish would be a broken ankle. Or worse. I fleetingly thought of William's first wife Virginia lying on the cellar floor with a broken neck. The prospect didn't appeal to me. Besides, we had no idea where the person who was prowling around in Elizabeth's house might be. Gone, most likely, but you never knew. I thought about Mildred and quickly stepped back into the kitchen. At least there was a little light in there. The overhead lights from the basement could just be seen through the open cupboard. I headed inside and closed the door securely.

"I think we'd better go back upstairs," Cora Lee said. She had her dressing gown pulled tightly around her and was furtively glancing into dim corners as if she expected something dreadful to appear at any moment.

"I think that's a great idea." Aunt Mary walked over to Elizabeth, who was prowling around the kitchen, staring at the fireplace, the shelves, reaching out a hand to touch the iron bar embedded in the bricks. "We're going to call Noah first thing in the morning. Right now, let's go upstairs and lock up everything we can. I'm going to make us each a nice cup of cocoa before we go back to bed."

"I sure hope you're planning to put more into our cups than cocoa." Cora Lee shivered and headed for the still-open cupboard and the relative safety of the lit basement.

"Elizabeth, come on." Aunt Mary took her by the arm and pulled gently. "We can't do any more here tonight. We need more light than we're getting from the cellar."

The dog was still growling and scratching at the earth under the table.

"Petal, that means you, too. Let's go."

Elizabeth seemed to come slowly back from her mental journey to the eighteenth century. "I don't understand."

"You don't understand what?" I said. Probably none of this. I didn't either. At least Elizabeth had finally spoken. Now, if we could just get her back upstairs. That blasted dog as well.

"Let's go upstairs and see if we can make any sense of all this," I added.

Elizabeth didn't move. "Mary, why is someone doing this? Creeping through my house. Someone was in the house tonight. Attacking Mildred. Mildred! The nicest person I know. Killing Monty in my dining room. With my syllabub. Who is this person and what on earth do they want?"

The color gradually returned to Elizabeth's face. She was starting to get angry. Good. Scared out of your wits didn't help you fight back. Elizabeth seemed ready to do just that now. Aunt Mary had said she'd always been a fighter, that she'd never seen her quit, but this time had begun to look like the exception. This outburst was healthy.

"I don't know what they want, but one thing I'm sure of. Whoever is doing this believes what he or she wants is in your house. Now, let's go upstairs and get that cocoa. Petal, that means you, too."

Ignoring her, the little dog just kept digging and growling. Dirt flew.

"There's no point in trying to get her away right now." Elizabeth watched the dog for a second then headed for the cupboard doorway. "We'll leave this open and the basement door as well. She'll come up when she's satisfied there's no bone there."

We followed, but not before I paused to watch the dog again. I didn't care how long she kept on with her useless task, but I did care about not shutting everything back up. I pulled my robe closer around me and retied the rope sash. If the dog hadn't come up before we finished our cocoa, then she could just stay locked in the basement for what was left of the night. I, for one, had no intention of climbing back into bed without knowing the house was as prowler-proof as we could make it.

Chapter Nineteen

W E SAT AROUND the same square table, sipping hot chocolate liberally laced with a fortifying brandy. The door leading to the basement was open slightly, as Petal had not reappeared. The cellar lights were on, as was every light in the room. It didn't matter. The sky outside was no longer black. Streaks of pink were scattered across what was now the palest of blue. If I got up to look out the window, the blood red sun would soon be starting its daily progression across the sky. It gave every indication of being a beautiful day.

"It's five thirty." Cora Lee sounded personally affronted by that fact.

"Yes." Elizabeth nodded, took a sip of cocoa and set her mug back down on the table.

Finally I stated the obvious. "What could you possibly have in this house that would make someone so frantic to find it?"

Elizabeth sighed. "We've been through that. Nothing."

"There has to be something. Whoever is doing this is taking a terrible chance coming back here."

"Maybe it's something Monty left here." Cora Lee yawned broadly.

"Monty hasn't lived here in years. What could he possibly have left?" Elizabeth's tone was sharp.

"Monty knew how to get in and out of all these houses."

Maybe Cora Lee had a point worth considering. "Is it possible he hid something here, maybe while his mother was alive, and wanted it back?"

"What?" Elizabeth stared at me, her face white, her eyes red rimmed. "Why? If he were still alive, I'd suspect him of trying to find William's will, or deeds or something. But he isn't."

"Where is William's will?" Cora Lee looked into her mug as if she expected an answer to appear.

It took Elizabeth a minute. She seemed to see Cora Lee for the first time. Maybe it was the Rubik's Cube thing. Cora Lee showed a different pattern, one Elizabeth hadn't seen before.

"I have a copy with all my documents, and so does Mr. Glass. The original is at the courthouse. On file. So is the deed and everything else that pertains to Smithwood."

"How about your marriage license?"

"Cora Lee, Monty's dead. No one else is interested in my marriage license."

"I suppose not." Cora Lee kept her eyes on the contents of her mug. "I think I know where Monty might have hidden something."

Elizabeth and Aunt Mary gaped.

I was past that. "What are you talking about?"

Cora Lee smiled, that little "gotcha" smile she was so good at. "Ellen, I hope you don't mind."

"Mind what?" What I minded was Cora Lee's little games and, judging from that smile, Cora Lee hoped I minded a lot. I was tired, worried, hungry and about out of patience with Cora Lee. If she had one more bit of pertinent information, she'd better tell us, and fast.

"I helped Elizabeth decorate this house. I'm sure she told you."

Aunt Mary nodded.

"I took some of my favorite pieces from next door and moved them over here. That chest of drawers in your room? I took that piece from next door about the time Elizabeth and William came back."

I waited. There was a punch line coming, but I couldn't guess it. Yet.

"That was Monty's chest of drawers when he lived here."

A quick gasp of breath. It was me! My chest tightened as I held onto it. I let the air out slowly while I tried to sort out my thoughts. Did Cora Lee think there was something hidden in that chest? Did she think someone was searching the house, both houses, looking for the chest? Had someone come looking for it last night? Someone who might have come into my room if Petal hadn't barked? My stomach lurched.

"I didn't mean to frighten you." Cora Lee leaned over the table and patted my hand. She looked genuinely upset. "I don't think anybody but us knows it's there."

"Then why did you bring it up?" Elizabeth was about as exasperated as I'd seen her. "What difference does it make if a chest Monty used years ago ended up in Ellen's room? That thing is old. Lots of people have used it."

"That's not what I mean."

"What do you mean?"

"Monty could have hidden something *in* it."

"Didn't you go through all of the drawers before you had it moved?"

"Yes. The drawers were empty."

"For God's sake, Cora Lee. Stop being so obtuse and tell us what you're talking about."

"That chest dates back to the mid-eighteenth century. I think there's a secret compartment in it. Not having safe deposit boxes, they did that a lot."

"Where?" I tried to think where one could be. I'd opened all the drawers. I'd stored clothes in a few of them.

"Why?" Elizabeth shook her head as if to clear it. "What

would he have to hide when he was a kid that is so important someone would risk murder to get it back? It doesn't make any sense. I don't know why anyone is prowling around here, but I don't see how that old chest fits in."

"What if he had hid it more recently and then wanted it back? We know Monty knew how to get in and out through the old kitchen."

"Oh, I don't think so." Elizabeth paused. Petal stood in the slightly open door that led to the basement, something in her mouth.

"So you finally dug it up, did you? Well, you can't have it. I have enough problems without you dragging dirty old bones up here. Give it to me." Elizabeth got up and walked toward the little dog, her hand outstretched.

The dog took one look at her, charged through the room to the other side and jumped up onto the wing-backed chair.

"Oh, no, you don't. I'm not having any dirty old bones on my chair." Elizabeth followed her across the room.

The little dog hunkered down and growled.

"Elizabeth, watch out. She's going to bite you." Cora Lee pushed her chair back and took hold of her cane as if to protect Elizabeth.

"No, she's not. She can't bite me and hold onto that old thing at the same time. What is that? It looks like a glove. Oh, my God. It can't be. Come look at this."

All the color drained out of Elizabeth's face. She stood, frozen, staring at the softly growling dog. Whatever Petal had, she wasn't giving it up, and Elizabeth showed no more inclination to take it from her. I pushed back my chair and went over to where Elizabeth stood.

"What is that?" Elizabeth took a step closer, ignoring the warning noises Petal made. She moved a little to the side to get a closer look, stopped short, gasped and once more proclaimed, "It can't be."

"It can't be what?" Cora Lee was right behind me, Aunt Mary

next to Elizabeth. "What's that fool dog got?"

My jaw dropped. I took in a quick breath and snapped it shut. Could those really be? The dog dropped her treasure on the chair, straddled it with both front feet and growled again.

"It's a glove. An old leather glove."

"Look at what's in the glove."

"It's a finger." I tried to work through my shock. It couldn't possibly be. Only it was. The outline of a finger was clear under the thin fabric "What's left of a finger." The dog grabbed the glove and shook it. The badly decayed glove split apart. Bones flew out and landed on the floor. Petal seemed as startled as the rest of us. She stared at the floor instead of jumping down to guard her treasure. I squatted down and picked one up. Not a scrap of flesh remained. What had once been a hand lay on Elizabeth's floor. That was obvious, even in its scattered condition.

When I could take my eyes off the floor, I stood and spoke to the others. "I think this time we really had better call the police."

Chapter Twenty

"IT'S LOUIS." CORA Lee grasped Aunt Mary's arm, as if she'd collapse without support. "I'd know that ring anywhere. It belonged to Louis."

Petal sat in the wing chair, the now disintegrated glove in her teeth, still making low growling noises.

"Louis? What are you talking about? What ring? Oh. Oh, no." Elizabeth squatted down and looked more closely at the scattered bones littering her floor. A couple of the smaller ones had rolled under the table, but several still lay where they had fallen, right in front of the chair. One thick short one had a ring on it. A gold band with a small red stone in the middle. Elizabeth put her hand out as if to touch it.

"No. Don't touch anything. We need to get the police. Now."

"That ring. It looks just like the one Mildred wears."

"I told you. They had matching rings. His was just bigger. Oh, Lord. Those bones. They're Louis. Only where—"

"Is the rest of him?" Aunt Mary's tone was faint and I thought I detected a small tremor. Cora Lee was clutching Aunt Mary's hand. She patted the hand, removed it and eased her into the nearest chair. "I'd say odds are he's in the old kitchen, under that table."

"We've got to get Noah. He'll know what to do."

"Elizabeth, are you crazy? Louis was Noah's father!"

Aunt Mary took hold of Elizabeth as well, pulled her backward and helped her into the wing chair beside the dog. It grumbled but moved over. "We're going to have to tell Noah, and I think we need to prepare him before the police get here, but let's get them on the way before we do anything else." She looked around the room, I supposed for a phone. Mine was in the pocket of my robe. I handed it to her. To my surprise, her hands shook as she entered 9-1-1 and put the call on speaker so we could all hear. I listened as she tried to tell the operator what our emergency was. It took the woman a few tries, but finally she seemed to get it.

"You think the rest of the body is buried under the house? In a kitchen? How long did you say this person has been dead? I see."

It was obvious she didn't, but at least someone was on the way. Aunt Mary disconnected and returned the phone to me. She collected Elizabeth's empty mug, gestured at Cora Lee, who shook her head, and took hers and Elizabeth's over to the sink. She stared down into it for a minute, evidently trying to think what to do next. Make coffee. Cocoa, especially laced with brandy, was designed to relax, to help you sleep. There'd be no sleeping for quite some time and we needed clear heads. I'd never felt the need for a clear head as much as I did right then. This was murder. It couldn't be anything but that. How did this murder tie in with Monty's? It had to, of course. It was too much of a coincidence for it not to. Only, how? And, how were we going to tell Noah? Not Mildred. She'd been through enough. She didn't need to be told her missing husband was dead if he wasn't. Headache pain arrived. Was there any Tylenol or Excedrin down here? I wasn't sure I'd make it all the way up the stairs.

"I think we'd better get dressed." Cora Lee tugged her dressing gown back into place. Did she ever tire of fiddling with that thing?

"Good idea," I said. "You go first. I'll make the coffee. Would you bring down my Tylenol? The bottle is on top of the chest in the bathroom. Thanks."

Cora Lee nodded and pushed back her chair. She paused to take a good look at Elizabeth, who hadn't moved or spoken. She glanced back at Aunt Mary, shook her head a little and headed for the stairs.

Aunt Mary sat very still while I made coffee. She barely noticed when I took down fresh mugs, filled two of them, put one in front of her and set the other on the small table beside the chair where Elizabeth sat.

"Do you want cream, Elizabeth?"

"What?"

"Cream."

"For what?"

"For the coffee I just gave you."

Elizabeth looked over at the table, surprised to see the mug, steam lazily rising above it. "Oh. No. Yes, I would like some. Mary, what are we going to do?"

Aunt Mary already had the cream out of the refrigerator. She didn't bother with a pitcher. Those kinds of niceties weren't called for right now. She poured a large dose into Elizabeth's mug. She looked at the carton for a moment, then at her own mug, and set the cream on the table. I could practically read her mind. She was going to need every ounce of caffeine she could get and cream would only dilute it. "What are we going to do about what?"

"About Noah, for starters. We have to call him. He'll be up to feed soon. What time is it, anyway?"

"Not quite six." She dragged a chair over close to Elizabeth, where she could face her. "Elizabeth, you need to tell us about Louis. Cora Lee called him a thief. Why? What happened?"

Exactly the question I wanted answered. I filled another mug, pulled a chair beside Aunt Mary and sat down to hear the answer.

Elizabeth studied the light brown liquid in her coffee mug as if assessing how much cream was in it and if she needed more. Finally she looked up. "I never met Louis. It all happened long before I came on the scene, so I only know what William told me." She sighed, took a sip and set the coffee mug on the table. Aunt Mary looked at the hot mug, then at the magazine that should have been under it but, to her credit, didn't move.

"He disappeared one day. Noah was about three or four. I'm not sure. The Smithwood silver disappeared the same day."

Aunt Mary and I looked at each other, neither of us quite buying into that story.

"With no warning? He just up and left?" There was incredulity in Aunt Mary's voice. There was a lot in my mind, as well.

"Were he and Mildred having trouble? Did he have money problems? There must have been something—"

"No. They were happy. At least, that's what I was told. Mildred came to live here after she and Louis married. He'd always lived here, always loved Smithwood. He managed the tobacco fields. They still grew some cotton and had livestock. I'm not sure what, but it was a working farm. He seemed to love Mildred a lot, and he adored Noah. That's what made the whole thing so strange."

"He just disappeared." I found myself shaking my head.

"Because he stole the Smithwood silver tea and coffee service. At least, that's what everyone thought. It was one of Smithwood's most valuable possessions. It was made especially for Smithwood in the eighteenth century by someone in the Boston area, someone famous, and was evidently worth a lot of money. The set was complete. Most aren't. Pieces get lost or damaged over the years, so to have a whole set is rare." Pain filled Elizabeth's eyes. "William was furious. More than furious. He was hurt. He trusted Louis. He was in Wisconsin and he sure didn't trust Virginia to run anything. He came back here, had the sheriff out, had the whole county out looking for him. He didn't know what to do about Mildred, who was shattered. She kept telling them Louis would never steal anything. Something terrible must have happened to him, that they needed to search the woods. William didn't know what to think." She paused for a moment and sighed. Her voice was expressionless. "Leo McMann handled that case also. He was a young detective then, just getting his start, and he was convinced Louis stole the silver and skipped."

She twisted around toward the table, rummaged through the books and other things on it and picked up the napkin Cora Lee had used earlier. She dabbed at a drop of coffee that had spilled on the table then sat for a moment, saying nothing. Neither did we. Elizabeth needed some time to collect her thoughts, but we needed to know what else happened. Now. Aunt Mary reached over and took the napkin out of Elizabeth's hand. It was beautifully embroidered and obviously old. Too nice to be sopping up spilled coffee. Elizabeth didn't seem to notice, but she didn't object. Just used the sleeve of her robe to dab her eyes. Was she thinking of William?

I was sure thinking of Dan. Why had I told him not to come? I had never missed him as much as I did now. I needed him here, but he wasn't. "Go on," I told Elizabeth.

"Leo thought William should make Mildred leave. Said she couldn't be trusted and he was pretty sure she must have known what Louis was up to, maybe even knew where he was." She shook her head, as if she still couldn't believe anyone would think that of her friend. "William told me about it later, after we moved in together. I knew about his wife, of course, but not the Longos. He wanted to know what I thought. I told him he was right to go with his feelings. Just because Louis had deceived him didn't mean Mildred would, or had, and if he trusted her, he should let her stay. A good decision, even if Leo never quite forgave him for not taking his advice."

"Was his first wife, Virginia, still living here?"

"Yes. So was Monty. With Louis gone, William no longer had a manager. He wouldn't trust Virginia to manage her own checking account. That was when he asked Cora Lee if she wanted to come back here, not full-time, but often enough to manage the place. Having someone live here on the plantation, in this house, worked out. Well, for William and Cora Lee. Virginia wasn't too thrilled and Monty hated it. So, there they were. Cora Lee, when she was here, redoing this house. Virginia, alone in the main house, drinking herself to death. Mildred and Noah continued living down the hill."

"Drinking. Is that why she fell down the stairs? She'd been drinking?"

Elizabeth sighed. "The autopsy report said she was three sheets to the wind."

"So, that happened?"

"Nothing. They never found Louis. Not a trace of him. Never found the silver, either. The sheriff was positive it would show up in a pawnshop or some such place, but it didn't. That silver set was worth over one hundred thousand dollars. It belongs in a museum, one like the Metropolitan Museum of Art, or the museum here in Colonial Williamsburg. William had been thinking of working out something with Louis about the land before all that happened, but after that, well, he never mentioned it again. Neither did Mildred. At least, not until recently."

Elizabeth's expression hardened, and the lines around her mouth stood out. "Mildred's one of the bravest people I know. She already had her teacher credentials when this happened but she went back to school and got her master's. Now she's a principal. She stayed on here because Noah had a claim to the house and she never gave up hoping they could get legal title." She paused and took another deep breath. "She's become one of my very best friends. I don't know how she's going to take this. I know she's been in pain all these years, thinking her husband was a thief. Someone had to have murdered him and buried him in that kitchen. Don't you think? If someone did that, then he didn't steal the tea set."

"If he didn't steal it, where is it?"

I hadn't heard Cora Lee come back down, but there she was, dressed in a pair of dark gray wool slacks topped with a light gray long-sleeved silk blouse, every hair in place, a matching cardigan slung over her shoulders. Discreet makeup, as befit the solemnity of the moment, had been artfully applied. How she had accomplished that so quickly, I had no idea. I took the offered bottle of Tylenol and started to get a glass of water.

Cora Lee handed me one. "Take that fast and then get upstairs and get dressed. All of you. The cops are almost here. I heard sirens. Why they turned them on, I have no idea. Louis has been dead for years. There's not much need to rush." She took my glass and walked over to the sink. She kept her back to us and leaned both hands on the granite counter. "As to who killed him, my guess would be Monty. I always thought he stole things. We didn't pack all of the estate's things. Just enough to keep Mother from having that damn garage sale. I moved some furniture from the main house over here, but over the years there were things I could never find. Small things. Pictures, a blue and white rice bowl that came over from Japan toward the end of the eighteenth century, some serving spoons, beautiful silver but not engraved with the Smithwood 'S.' Things that could have easily been pawned or sold to antique dealers who didn't ask too many questions about provenance. Virginia used some, whatever she could find. She broke a lot of them when she was drinking. I was never sure if something was missing or if she'd swept up the pieces and wouldn't tell me. Anyway, I never could prove anything. Monty, of course, moved out when he finished college. Or got moved out. Then Virginia died."

"Did you notice anything else go missing? After Virginia died, I mean."

Cora Lee didn't hesitate. "No. I'll bet you anything Monty stole that tea set and somehow Louis found out and Monty killed him."

"Are you sure that ring belongs to Louis?" Elizabeth kept her eyes on the remains of what had once been a hand, scattered on the floor. The bone with the ring still on it was almost under her foot.

"I'm positive." The gravity in Cora Lee's voice was striking. After all the barbed quips, she had finally said something that rang true. For the first time, I wondered how much of that brittle, always amused, detached attitude of hers was a façade. Cora Lee might be a product of vast wealth, but it didn't seem as if her life had been very satisfactory.

"Mildred will confirm that soon enough," she added. "Right now, I think we'd better go upstairs and get ourselves dressed. You go next, Elizabeth. It's you they'll want to talk to."

And, of course, Noah and Mildred. Poor Mildred. Elizabeth pushed herself out of the chair and headed for the doorway. She walked like an old woman, stiff and stooped. Her braid hung limply down her back, hairs escaping, giving it the look of a rough rope. She didn't seem to notice that her bathrobe was partly unzipped and that her feet, encased in corduroy rubber-soled slippers, scuffed more than necessary. The anger that had flared up in the kitchen had once again been dampened by confusion and exhaustion. She had to be near collapse. She wasn't the only one.

Aunt Mary also found the energy to leave her chair. Anxiety had formed smudge marks under her blue eyes. "I might as well go up, too. I'll make sure Elizabeth gets back down."

"She'd better hurry. They'll be here any minute." Cora Lee paused. Uncertainty crossed her face. "I'm going to have to call Noah. I can't have the police charge down there, asking Mildred all kinds of questions without giving her some kind of warning. What am I going to tell him?"

There wasn't much she could tell him except that they

thought the body of his father lay buried under an old table in the Smithwoods' antique kitchen.

"Do you want me to do it?" I asked. It was an offer I didn't want to make, but the news might be easier on Noah if it came from me.

Something flickered in Cora Lee's eyes. Hope, maybe, but it passed quickly. "No. I'd better do it. I'll do it right now. I want Mildred to hear this from him, not McMann."

Aunt Mary nodded and headed for the stairs. I followed.

The shower ran in Elizabeth's bathroom. At least she'd been able to get that far. I stood in the middle of my room and slowly turned around, examining each piece of furniture. I wasn't sure what to do. I didn't want to get into the shower until Elizabeth and Aunt Mary finished and had no intention of going downstairs to meet the police. Instead, I sat on my bed. Could Cora Lee be right? Had Monty been stealing little things from Smithwood and selling them? Had Louis caught him? It was possible, but from what everyone said about Monty, he didn't seem the murdering type. Blackmail, petty thievery, yes, but cold-blooded murder, probably not. Of course, the most timid animal could be dangerous when cornered. What had it been like for a child growing up in this old house all by himself, his mother drinking herself to death and his stepfather never here, or ignoring him when he was? Couldn't have been pleasant. Hattie said Payton practically lived here when they were in high school. Had Monty stolen things to help pay for college? No. William paid. Who else? Calvin Campbell. He went to high school with both Monty and Payton and supposedly they'd been friends. Good enough friends that Calvin expected Monty to help him when he was in trouble. Calvin, keeper of the grounds, all of the grounds. Would he know about the old road? No doubt about it. Could he have found out about the secret door? Possibly. Monty had known. Maybe it hadn't been Monty stealing all those little things. Maybe it had been Calvin. He'd been around Smithwood then, with Payton and Monty.

They were all in their mid to late forties now. Louis must have been dead about thirty years. Elizabeth had said Noah was little, two or three? He was in his very early thirties now, I'd guess. Leo McMann would have been in his early thirties when Louis disappeared.

If Monty pilfered things, how had he sold them? Wouldn't he have needed help? Maybe that was where Calvin came in. No, that didn't quite fit. Would he know where to sell them? A picture of Lt. McMann appeared in my head. Why? He was a respected policeman. Not a particularly well-liked one, but that hardly made him a crook. So, why did he come to mind? Someone said something—right. He got in trouble with Mr. Smithwood when he worked here one summer and was fired, evidently unfairly. What if old Mr. Smithwood was right? What if the teenage McMann hadn't been above a little petty larceny? Even so, what did that prove? Exactly nothing. However, he knew about the road. The road down by the river that had to start somewhere up by the highway. Mildred said other plantation owners used to bring their tobacco here, to Smithwood, to ship to market. They had to get on that road somehow, and Lt. McMann would know the way. Could he have made a deal with Monty all those years later, helped him sell the things he'd stolen? Why kill him? Blackmail, of course.

I walked over to the door. The shower was quiet. Time to get out some clothes, but my mind wasn't on that. It was still on Lt. McMann. You shouldn't suspect someone of murder and robbery just because you thought he was a morose jerk. Dan wouldn't approve. Okay, not McMann. That brought me back to Monty. He had to sell what he took to someone. I walked over to the dresser, opened a bottom drawer and stared at the contents. The chest wasn't going to tell me if Monty was a thief or if it really was Louis buried downstairs or who put him there. However, Lt. McMann did seem to wander in and out of this story. It would be interesting to know a little more about him.

I backed up and sat on the bed. Had that crate been meant for Elizabeth? Had someone really meant to kill her or was it merely a distraction, providing time for the trespasser in the cellar to escape? If Elizabeth died, what would happen to Smithwood? Would it have been easier for Monty to lay claim? It wouldn't have helped any of the others. Calvin would be out of a job he evidently needed, Noah and his mother wouldn't stand a chance of getting their deed and—if what Mildred said about old Mr. Smithwood's will was true—Cora Lee wouldn't have been able to save a single teaspoon. Keeping Elizabeth alive, at least until they had what they wanted, was to everyone's advantage. Only Monty stood to gain, possibly, and Monty was dead. Maybe that hadn't been a deliberate attempt on her life. Then why had that person stood on a stepstool, behind the crate, ready to push?

I unwrapped my robe and tossed it on the bed. Where were the clothes I'd taken out of the chest? The drawer of the chest was still ajar. I hadn't taken them out. That's what preoccupation did to you. I walked back over to the high chest of drawers, started to look in the open drawer and stopped. What else was it Cora Lee said? Something about a hidden compartment. I let my fingers run over the drawer, but there was nothing suspicious. I dumped the contents on the bed, pulled it out and felt the bottom. No false bottom. At least, I couldn't feel one. I put it back, replaced my clothes and opened another one. Nothing. I tried them all, but they seemed fine. I stared at the chest, remembering something I'd seen recently on *Antiques Roadshow*. A chest of drawers, a lot like this one, and one of the appraisers had done … what? I let my fingers run slowly over the graceful carving across the top of the chest. What looked like crown molding circled a flat top with three small drawers directly below. Four other drawers, each a little deeper than the other, finished off the top piece which rested on a second piece, also with one long drawer and three small, shallow drawers that sat above the carved apron and graceful cabriole legs. I let my fingers trace the edges of the molding around the top, gently pushing on it as I went. My fingers lingered a little on the center. Something gave. I pushed on one side a little harder. The piece of wood at the bottom of the molding moved. I put my fingers under it and pulled. It slid out easily. Shocked, I stared at it then pulled again. The piece obligingly slid out a little more. I wasn't quite tall enough to see the top of the piece, but it felt as if this might be a shallow drawer, a hidden shallow drawer. Hadn't I seen a footstool up here? If so, it wasn't here now. My eyes rested on the Windsor chair. Should I? Yes. I pulled the chair over to the chest and, crossing my fingers I wouldn't land on the floor, hitched up my nightgown and knelt on it. I got one leg under me and, holding onto the chest and saying a little prayer it was heavy enough not to come crashing down, pulled myself up. I could look straight down into the drawer. It wasn't empty.

Just as my fingers touched the contents of the drawer, the door to my room flew open.

"Why aren't you in the shower?"

I almost fell off the chair.

"What are you doing?" Aunt Mary stood in the doorway, eyes wide, mouth slightly open, staring at me as if I'd gone crazy.

"Shush." I grabbed the contents, slid the drawer closed and knelt back down. "Close the door."

She stepped in and did as I asked. Her voice was hushed as she hurried over. "What have you found?"

"Cora Lee's secret drawer, for one thing. What else, I don't know yet. Come over here." I scrambled off the chair and headed for the desk. I spread the papers out and started to pore over them.

"What do they mean?" Aunt Mary picked one up and started to read. "I don't understand one word of this."

They were some kind of financial statements, but I didn't have time to figure out what they meant. I did know that

Chapter Twenty-One

THE PLACE WAS crawling with police. There was no other way to describe it. There were at least half a dozen assorted police vehicles parked outside. Through the windows beside the front hallway door, uniformed police, as well as people dressed in street clothes, milled around. There was even a squad of paramedics. It seemed a little late for them. Thirty years too late.

Noah and Mildred sat at the kitchen table talking to Lt. McMann. The bones were spread out on a piece of newspaper, but none of them were looking at them. That rather dubious privilege was accorded to a bald heavyset man. I watched him for a minute, fascinated. He placed each bone in a specific place. They were beginning to form a hand. Someone's hand. Probably someone named Louis. Who was married to Mildred. Who, in all likelihood, had been murdered and buried in that antique kitchen thirty years ago. That thought left me a little lightheaded. Coffee. That was what I needed. I headed for the cupboard where the mugs were kept, took one down and picked up the coffeepot. Enough left for one cup. I poured before I turned around to see what was happening at the table.

The ring, sans the bone it had encircled before, lay in front of Mildred. She didn't seem to be able to take her eyes off it, except when she touched her matching ring. Lt. McMann spoke to her in a low voice, but I wasn't sure Mildred heard him. She kept staring at the rings.

Noah heard him, though. His face was dark with fury and his eyes could have bored holes in the lieutenant. What was McMann saying? I sipped my coffee, trying to do so quietly. It didn't work. Lt. McMann glanced over at me and glowered. I set down my mug, picked up the now empty pot, rinsed it, filled it and reached for the filters. Unfortunately, the water drowned out most of what Lt. McMann said and all of Mildred's replies. Not, of course, that I was eavesdropping, but from the questions I heard and Mildred's demeanor, I had to conclude it was Louis buried in the kitchen. Lt. McMann suggested, somewhat strongly, that Mildred knew he was there. No wonder Noah was furious. I leaned against the counter and picked up my mug.

The man examining the bones pushed his chair back and got up. "Don't none of you touch these. Hear?"

Lt. McMann watched him leave. "Damned know-it-all." He seemed to take notice of me once more. "Anything we can do for you?"

I probably didn't belong here, but I also knew rudeness and sarcasm when I heard it. Dan would never treat someone like this, and I saw no reason to tolerate it from Lt. McMann. Police or not, rudeness wasn't necessary. "I'm waiting for the coffee to perk. Would you like some when it's done?"

Lt. McMann motioned toward his mug, which sat in front of him, steam curling lazily upward. "I have some."

"So you do." I continued to lean and sip. "Noah, do you have coffee? Mildred? Aunt Mary, would you like some?"

She stood across the room, looking outside through the French doors. She turned and walked back over to the table. "Coffee is just what I need."

Noah studied her for a minute, then smiled. "Actually, I'd love some, too. Can I help?"

"Oh, no. It'll be a minute anyway. Well, you can get the cream."

Noah pushed his chair back and headed for the refrigerator. "I see you dressed for cool weather. Forecast says rain. Great sweatshirt."

Aunt Mary looked at her shirt. For the first time, I did too. We'd been too preoccupied to take stock of what she had on. It was a chilly morning and evidently she'd grabbed the first warm thing she'd laid hands on. That happened to be her bright green sweatpants, the ones she got at St. Stephen's rummage sale, and her Santa Louisa Wine Festival sweatshirt. An image of a large bottle of bright red wine took up most of the front; the green grape vines with their ready-to-harvest grapes twining around it took up the rest. She got it because she helped my niece, Sabrina, in the Silver Springs winery booth at last year's Festival in the Park, and these sweatshirts didn't sell well. She said she'd chosen the extra-large size in case it shrank. It hadn't. She tried to roll up the sleeve cuffs. They didn't cooperate. She gave up and pushed the sleeves as far back as she could and reached for a clean mug. "Um. Where's Elizabeth?"

"Standing in the old kitchen, watching the police dig up my father."

Mildred shuddered.

The door opened and a uniformed policeman stuck his head in. "They need you out here, Lieutenant."

Lt. McMann grunted something, pushed back his chair and got up. He paused, glared over at Aunt Mary and then at me, picked up his mug and left.

"He's in a good mood this morning."

"About as good as it ever gets. He's not noted for his sunny disposition." Noah set the carton of cream down in the middle of the table and sat. He reached over and took his mother's hand.

She smiled weakly. "I'm all right. Just a little shaken. This is going to take some getting used to, but I'm all right."

I checked the coffee. It gurgled to a stop. I took down another mug, filled it, walked over to the table and set it in front of Mildred. "Of course you are. Cream?"

Mildred seemed to see me for the first time. She smiled then looked over at Aunt Mary. She blinked at the sight of her sweatshirt and smiled a little wider. "Yes, please."

Aunt Mary poured cream liberally into both their mugs and took Lt. McMann's chair. I leaned against the counter. "How old was Payton when he spent so much time out here?"

"What?"

"How old were the boys? High school? Had they started college?"

That was a question Mildred apparently hadn't been expecting. "All the way through high school."

"Was Calvin here also?"

"Calvin? Sometimes. He was a funny kid. He idolized Monty. Why, I can't imagine. Monty treated him like a pet dog. It was Payton who didn't like him." She stopped.

Aunt Mary motioned her to go on.

"Poor Calvin. He was a shy kid, didn't seem to be able to make friends. I don't think he realized Monty was playing with him. Not then, anyway."

"How old were the boys when Louis was—" this was difficult— "disappeared?"

Mildred didn't say anything for a moment, but the expression on her face registered a mixture of emotions. "Louis ... was killed the summer before the boys went away to college."

"I don't remember any of that." Noah frowned. He sounded as if these were facts he should have known or at least been told.

"Of course not. You were little more than a toddler. Those boys didn't even know you were alive. They went off to different colleges. I didn't see Calvin until he came back to take charge of the grounds. We didn't see much of Payton after that, either. Monty was in and out, but after he finished law school, he didn't come around much, and after Virginia died, not at all. Hattie, of course, was a different matter."

"Hattie. Was she out here a lot?"

Mildred nodded. "She and Virginia were friends, sort of. They both loved the 'lady of the manor' kind of thing. Except Virginia had no interest in how people lived years ago. Her only interest was in how she lived here and now. She loved getting out the silverware, the linens, the candles, all that kind of thing, and she'd serve tea. She couldn't cook a lick, but Hattie always brought more than enough, and they put on airs, just the two of them. Silliest thing I ever saw."

"She used the Smithwood things?"

Mildred's voice had a hard edge. "Everything Cora Lee and I hadn't either packed away or hidden. Luckily, she hadn't gotten to most of the antiques because she broke almost everything she touched. She touched some nice things. It really was a shame."

"Hattie quit coming after Virginia died?"

Mildred nodded. "There was no reason for her to come. Or Monty, either. William paid for law school for Monty, but as soon as he passed the bar, he was on his own. I don't think Monty ever quite forgave William for that. He was so sure he'd be able to come back here to live, bring his wife, manage the 'estate.' Poor boy. It was quite a shock when he had to go to work." It wasn't hard to figure out how Mildred felt about Monty.

"Why? Why are you asking all these questions?" Noah managed to pack a lot of suspicion into that sentence.

"Just trying to get some things straight in my mind." I ducked my head to take a sip of coffee and hide my face. So, I'd been right. Calvin had been a visitor to Smithwood long before he became its head gardener. How I'd find out if I was right about a few other things, I wasn't sure.

"Ellen, if you know something, you have to tell the police. Withholding evidence can be a prosecutable offense." Noah had on his policeman face, but underneath there was a layer of concern, as well as strain.

I was already guilty of that, but I wasn't about to share my discovery with Noah. Not when I hadn't had a chance to discuss it with Dan, first. For some reason he wasn't answering his cell. Maybe the battery was out. Or he'd forgotten to put it on the charger again. "All I've got are a whole lot of unconnected ideas." I smiled. "Don't worry. If any of them connect, I'll tell you immediately."

"Not Leo?" Noah's face softened and a hint of a smile appeared.

"Oh, I don't think so. You're so much closer." I smiled back. We'd just made a bargain. I was satisfied. I hoped Noah was also.

The door opened and Elizabeth walked in, followed by two dogs and a very elegant older man. The dogs plopped down in the middle of the room.

The man walked over to the table and held his hand out to Mildred. "Are you all right?"

"Good morning, Aaron. I guess so. Things have been coming at us so fast these past few days, I've lost track."

The man smiled, let go of Mildred's hand and nodded to Noah. "How are you doing?"

"Holding together. What are you doing here? Is it about Elizabeth again?"

"I'm afraid so." He seemed to see Aunt Mary and me for the first time, started to nod, took another look and smiled. "You must be Mary McGill. Elizabeth's been talking about you." He paused and looked at me inquiringly. "I don't believe I've had the pleasure."

"I'm Ellen McKenzie Dunham. I'm Mrs. McGill's niece." I smiled. Enlightenment had come. "You must be Mr. Glass. She's told us a lot about you as well."

He smiled and nodded.

So, this was the famous Mr. Glass on whom everyone seemed to rely. I could see why. He was dressed in a beautifully cut, expensive dark charcoal gray suit. His white shirt gleamed, and his black shoes gave off a shine that made Payton Culpepper's highly buffed ones look dull. It wasn't the clothes or the mane of meticulously styled, thick white hair that gave him his gravitas. It was the air of quiet confidence, of control without being overbearing. Old-world manners without the condescending manner that often went with them. This was a man who knew what he was doing, a man you immediately felt you could trust.

He examined us closely. He evidently liked what he saw because he smiled.

Aunt Mary smiled back, briefly. "Do we have a problem?"

"I'm afraid so."

"What kind of problem?"

"An English Yew problem." Elizabeth filled a mug with coffee and leaned back against the kitchen counter, next to me. "It seems Monty died of English Yew poisoning. It also seems my syllabub contained nothing I hadn't put in it, but that doesn't get me off the hook. There's a rather large amount of English Yew flourishing in my garden. So, according to Leo, I'm guilty."

Her tone was light, but the stress lines around her eyes and lips told another story. So did the hand that held her coffee mug. It shook so that she had to bring up her other hand to help hold it.

"Aaron, you can't let him arrest her. She isn't guilty, and we all know it." Mildred twisted around to confront him, equal parts alarm and anger in her voice and on her face.

"Don't worry. She's not going to jail. All they really have is suspicion."

"That and the fact that Monty was trying to blackmail me. That's motive. I had means and opportunity. Aren't they the three things the police look for?" Elizabeth sat, rigid from both anger and fear, her hands clasped together.

"Leo McMann is an idiot, and I just told him so. Arresting Elizabeth. I've never heard anything so stupid." Cora Lee pushed her way into the room, her cane making little staccato noises that kept time with the tap tap of her heels. "He needs to pay attention to what's going on down in that kitchen and find out who killed poor Louis. These two murders are connected, and not through Elizabeth." She patted Mildred on the shoulder and opened her mouth as if to say something then thought better of it. She tapped her way over to the cupboards, took down a mug, filled it and made her way back to the table.

"Is cream the strongest stuff we've got to put in this?"

"At this time in the morning? Yes." Elizabeth shook her head in disgust, whether at Cora Lee's suggestion or at the whole mess, I wasn't sure.

Cora Lee was using her cane a lot more this morning. Tired? Or was she hurting? Leaving her coffee where it was, she started around the table. "It's five o'clock somewhere, and after the night we've had, I need something to get me going."

"There's some Tylenol in the cupboard." Aunt Mary pushed her chair back. "I'll get it for you. Some water, also."

Cora Lee didn't say no. She stopped pacing long enough to swallow the pills Aunt Mary put in her hand. "Thanks." Handing the glass back, she turned her attention to Mr. Glass. "That idiot Leo is going to get a warrant, or whatever it is you get, and arrest Elizabeth. All because we have an English Yew in the garden. Half the gardens in Williamsburg have yews!"

Aaron Glass watched her patiently. "Cora Lee, will you sit down? Pacing around and calling Leo names isn't going to help. It isn't doing your hip any good, either."

If looks could kill, that statement would have been Aaron Glass' last, but she pulled up a chair. Instead of sitting, she tapped over to pick up her coffee mug.

"I would have gotten that for you." Elizabeth looked over

at Cora Lee as if she'd just noticed her juggling the cane and coffee mug.

Cora Lee set the mug on the table and lowered herself carefully onto her chair. She glowered at Elizabeth. "I'm quite capable of getting my own."

No one said a word.

Hip. The doctor visit in Richmond she'd finally admitted to but claimed was routine, the cane, the winces she tried so hard to hide, the even sharper remarks, they all added up to pain. Had she seen him before or after her appointment with the attorney? I wondered if the surgery was scheduled and how she expected to hide that. She was in her seventies. Just about the time people, especially women, started to have their parts replaced. Cataracts, arthritic hands, worn-out knees and hips, it was downright depressing, not to mention scary. Was Cora Lee not talking about it because she was scared or just irritated because she couldn't stop the ravages of aging? As with this old house, a coat of paint alone no longer did the trick.

"I assume Lieutenant McMann doesn't think Elizabeth is responsible for the death of the man in the kitchen," Aunt Mary said to Cora Lee.

It was Elizabeth who answered. "No." She sounded more tired than afraid. After all we'd been through this week, it was a wonder any of us was able to stay on our feet. "At least he hasn't accused me yet." A small smile appeared. "They seem to be sure the bones belong to Louis. As I've never met him, it'll be hard to get me for that one."

"They know it's Louis. They found his wallet." Cora Lee frowned. "Leo threw me out when they found it."

"What else have they found?" It was the first thing Mildred had said since she greeted Aaron.

"Are you referring to the silver tea set?"

Mildred nodded.

"Not a sign of it, but—" Aaron glanced over at Noah and stopped.

"Go ahead. We're going to hear it sooner or later."

"It looks as if Louis was shot." He paused, evidently trying to gauge how much Mildred could take.

She sat, hands clenched.

He sighed. "There's a bullet hole in the middle of his coat. Or, rather, what's left of his coat. It's pretty … Yes. Well. They also found a bullet. Only …"

"Only what?" Noah reached over and took his mother's hand.

Her fingers tightened around his, but her eyes stayed on Aaron.

"It's not a normal bullet. At least, it's not a modern one. It looks like—" he paused and took a deep breath—"it looks like one of those small round bullets that come from colonial era pistols."

Aaron Glass certainly had our full attention. Aunt Mary set her mug down and stared. Mildred quit pushing her husband's ring around with her middle finger and looked up sharply. Cora Lee, Noah, Elizabeth and I were all agape.

"A colonial pistol? How could that be? We don't have one. Do we?" Elizabeth turned toward Cora Lee, who said nothing.

Her hands tightened around her cane. Elizabeth waited. We all waited.

Cora Lee nodded once, as if she'd come to a decision. "We used to." She glanced over at Mildred.

"What do you mean, *used* to?" Aaron Glass didn't look any happier than Cora Lee.

"It was part of my father's precious antique gun collection."

"There were a lot of them." Mildred squinted a little, as if trying to picture something. "We packed them up when we moved your mother out." She paused. "I don't remember a small pistol, though."

"That's because we didn't pack it. I didn't pay much attention at the time. Everything was so hectic. So many details to take care of. I forgot about it. He kept it on a little stand on the mantle in the living room. All the other guns were in his study."

"What happened to it?" Aaron Glass didn't look, or sound, one bit happy.

"*I don't know*." Cora Lee stressed each word, as if straining to come up with the answer herself. "I didn't realize it was missing until after Virginia died. I stayed in the big house a lot while Monty was packing up all her personal belongings. After he left, there were a lot of things I couldn't find. The gun was one of them. William wouldn't let me confront him about any of it, and I'm afraid I forgot about it."

"We don't know that was the gun used," Aunt Mary offered tentatively.

None of us believed it.

"I'd be pretty darn surprised if it wasn't." Cora Lee, at least, put it into words.

Aaron Glass nodded. "It's not going to make much difference unless we find the gun. Maybe you can't do a ballistics test on one that old, but I know you need the gun before you can do anything." To Cora Lee, he said, "Do you have any idea when it disappeared?"

"No. I didn't go in that house much when Virginia lived there, and when I did, I never really thought about it. I don't know."

"What did you do with the guns you packed?"

"For heaven's sake, Aaron, I sold them. I hated those guns, but the antique dealer I took them to frothed at the mouth. Said it was the best collection of eighteenth-century guns he'd seen in years."

"So there are no guns around here now?"

"Not that I'm aware of."

"This isn't getting us any closer to finding out who killed my father." Noah's eyes were dark pools of anger. "All these years, my mother has gone through hell, thinking he was wrongly accused, that something dreadful had happened. She was right. We have to find out who was responsible."

"Hush." Mildred withdrew her hand and took a deep breath. She smiled at her son. "As terrible as this is, one thing makes me happy deep in my heart."

She didn't need to say it. She'd always known her husband wasn't a thief. Now, everyone else did, too. However, he had been murdered and the person who did it was out there, unpunished. Was it the same person who murdered Monty? Could it be? It could be and probably was. Although, if the papers I'd found in the highboy were what I thought they were, that changed things. I had to show them to somebody, but not Lt. McMann. I needed someone I trusted to help me decide what to do. Aaron Glass. Yes. I needed to have a private conversation with him. Only, I wasn't sure how to arrange it. I had time. The papers weren't going anywhere. I'd figure it out.

"Do you really think it was Monty wandering through the houses?"

"I thought it was him I saw in the hall upstairs that night."

"You thought he was searching for something?"

"Why else would he be out here, going through the houses? He'd long since pilfered all the small stuff he could carry out."

"Cora Lee, you don't know any such thing." Aaron Glass looked horrified. "You can't go around accusing someone with absolutely no proof."

Cora Lee smiled.

Mildred stayed on subject. "Do you think Monty killed Louis?"

Aaron Glass sputtered, but Cora Lee wasn't going to let him interrupt. "I don't know," she said. "He could have."

"Why?" Elizabeth's head was going back and forth, as if watching a tennis match.

"It had something to do with the tea set." Mildred's voice left no doubt in anyone's mind that she, at least, believed that.

Cora Lee nodded slightly, but her voice held doubt. "Maybe. Monty would have been in his late teens when Louis— disappeared. Why hasn't the silver shown up?"

I had been following all this as closely as any of them. I had an idea about that, but it wasn't nearly formed enough to say out loud. There was one question, however, they hadn't covered. "If Monty killed Louis," I said, "then who killed Monty and why?"

The conversation stopped while everyone seemed to consider that.

"We better find out soon before that idiot McMann arrests Elizabeth." Cora Lee pushed her chair back, walked over behind Elizabeth, put her hands on Elizabeth's shoulders and smiled. She gave her a gentle squeeze. "Not to worry, honey. If he arrests you, we'll feed the dog."

Chapter Twenty-Two

WE ALL SAT around a table in Shields Tavern in Colonial Williamsburg. No one wanted to think about ordering dinner. It seemed no one wanted to think about eating it, either. Noah had fumed the entire time Lt. McMann questioned Mildred and he hadn't quit. Mildred, on the other hand, sat stoically by—hands folded in her lap, expressionless—while Lt. McMann took her through the events of all those years ago. He stopped just short of accusing her of shooting Louis and burying him.

Now, at the tavern, Mildred's position and demeanor had not changed. Felicity sat quietly beside Noah. She'd given up trying to calm him down, contenting herself with keeping an eye on Mildred and listening to the rest of us.

"McMann is an idiot." Cora Lee's mouth was set in a rigid line. Her eyes blazed. She seemed to dare any of us to disagree with her. No one did. "Elizabeth isn't off the hook yet and McMann had better not try to put Mildred up there with her."

She took another sip of wine and glared at each of us in turn. No one commented. Much of Cora Lee's ranting seemed to be motivated by fear, but fear of what I wasn't sure. Fear of what might happen to her two best friends? Or was Cora Lee afraid of something else? I hoped not, but I couldn't be sure. Not yet.

Lt. McMann had poked and prodded Elizabeth almost all day, asking the same questions, getting the same answers. She didn't know what had happened in the kitchen all those years ago, but they'd gone over the role of syllabub in the equation a hundred times. When had she made it, who knew she'd made it, when had she left for the airport, when had Monty arrived. She responded to that one. How would she know? She hadn't seen him come. She only saw him after he was dead, lying on her carpet and not in any condition to explain why he was there. Lt. McMann left her alone for a while after that, transferring his attention to Mildred. He only stopped when Felicity told him in no uncertain terms that Mildred had just been released from the hospital and couldn't take any more of his badgering. If he didn't let up, she would be back in the hospital and it would be his fault. Lt. McMann had left, grumbling, and now we all sat in Shields Tavern, trying to figure out what to do next.

Aaron Glass threaded his way between tightly packed tables until he arrived at ours. He pulled out a chair and squeezed himself into it, barely missing the portly white-haired woman sitting behind him. She glanced back at him but declined to move her chair. Instead, she gave him a sour look. Aaron responded with a courteous nod of his head and moved his own chair a little to the right.

Cora Lee wasn't so courteous. She glared at the woman before turning her attention to Aaron. "What happened?"

"Nothing. Have you ordered yet?"

"Just wine. What do you mean nothing? You've been on the phone with Leo for almost an hour. What is this new evidence? That man's a menace."

Aaron smiled.

Noah leaned over the table, staring intently at Aaron. "What's he got?"

"Nothing. He said he had a new development he wanted to discuss. That's not the same thing as evidence."

"What was the new development?" I admired Aaron's deliberate approach, his calm manner and refusal to panic when the phone call from Lt. McMann came saying he had new information and wanted to question Elizabeth once again. Aaron told him Elizabeth was in no shape to come, but he'd be glad to listen. If it seemed Elizabeth needed to talk to him, well, they'd see. How he'd pulled that one off, I wasn't sure but was glad for Elizabeth's sake. However, now everyone needed to know. What, exactly, was Lt. McMann's new development and what was going to happen?

A waiter in brown cloth breeches, white stockings, soft black shoes with buckles and a full white shirt open at the neck appeared. "Red wine tonight?" He didn't wait for an answer but set a glass in front of Aaron. "I'll be right back with menus."

"You must come here often." Aaron hadn't bothered to glance at the menu or the wine list and the waiter had anticipated his choice of wine unerringly. "Often" was probably an understatement.

The waiter retreated into another room and reappeared just as quickly. He passed menus around the table and handed the wine list to Aaron. "Let me know when you're ready."

"I dine out quite a lot since my wife died. There are some excellent restaurants in town, but I love the historic district."

"The only reason we got a table is because of Aaron," Cora Lee explained. "So, quit acting so damn calm and tell us exactly what happened."

He picked up his glass, swirled it slightly and held it to his nose before taking a tentative sip. He nodded slightly and took another, somewhat larger one. "I'm going to miss Roger when he graduates."

"What? Who's Roger? Oh. The waiter. He goes to school here?"

Aaron nodded. "William and Mary. He graduates in a few

weeks. Already has an internship set up in DC. He's planning a career in politics. He'll be good at it."

"Aaron, forget Roger and his career," Cora Lee said. "We don't care, and if you don't tell us right now what Leo wanted, there'll be another murder and Leo won't have any trouble figuring out who did it. What happened?" Cora Lee's glare would have felled a lesser man, but Aaron Glass seemed impervious.

He simply smiled and turned his attention to Elizabeth. "Nothing. Nothing's going to happen. You aren't going to be arrested, and I told Leo that until he has something new and pertinent to ask, you won't be answering any more questions." He paused to take a small sip of wine and nodded approvingly. This time he addressed the whole table. "It seems they have identified the poison. It is English Yew. There is, as it happens, an English Yew tree in your garden, which is what set Leo off."

Cora Lee gave a most unladylike snort. "We knew that. Besides, there are English Yews in half the gardens in Williamsburg."

Cora Lee had said that before. She must know a lot about English Yews. Mildred gardened. She must, also. Elizabeth didn't. However, Calvin Campbell would. I let my mind wander for a moment, speculating, before I turned my attention back to the conversation

"Exactly. It also seems there's no way of identifying which bush, tree, whatever it is, this particular poison came from." Again he paused and smiled at Elizabeth, who immediately looked less tired.

"Then, he's not going to arrest me?

"No. He's not." He paused again, intently scrutinizing Elizabeth's face. "He wants to search your house."

Elizabeth blinked. "What for?"

"A mortar and pestle."

Never had I seen anyone look so blank. "A what?"

"A mortar and pestle. It's a bowl, usually made of marble or stone. The pestle is a round piece that fits in your hand and is used to grind up things in the mortar."

"What kind of things?"

I suspected they wouldn't find one in Elizabeth's kitchen.

"Garlic, silly." Aunt Mary didn't seem surprised at Elizabeth's lack of culinary knowledge. "Herbs. English Yew."

Elizabeth looked at Aunt Mary. "Oh." Then, as realization set it, she smiled broadly. "Oh!"

"I think we can let McMann search the house?" Aaron Glass smiled and took another sip.

"Fine with me."

"Someone had to grind up the yew leaves to put in Monty's drink." Mildred's tone was soft and speculative. She smiled.

Even Cora Lee smiled, but it immediately faded. "He's not to touch even one of our china cups."

"I'll make sure you're there when they search." Aaron sounded a little weary. Cora Lee could have that effect on you.

"Have you told Payton I don't need him or Harrison Silverstein?" Elizabeth leaned forward anxiously. She moved back as Roger set a fresh wineglass in front of her and proceeded round the table.

"We'll start with a white wine. Have you decided which one?"

No one had, but Aaron mentioned a label to Roger, who nodded in approval and went off to get the new wine.

"Yes, and I made sure Leo knows I—and no one else—represent you." He paused while Roger poured wine into everyone's glasses. "Ready to order? No? Let me know." He smiled and walked off.

"It seems Payton had been around, asking Leo all kinds of questions, intimating that he, or his firm, still represented you. Evidently, he got a little pushy. I told Leo, well … we got it all straightened out."

"I thought he went back to DC." Cora Lee frowned. I waited for a little barb, but none came.

"I don't understand. Why would Payton do that?" Elizabeth

didn't look particularly upset, but she did look confused. "I thought I made it clear you were taking care of everything. I was polite, of course. Thanked him and all that." She paused. "Maybe I was too polite. Why is he so insistent?"

I thought about the financial papers I'd found in the hidden drawer. I hadn't had time to do anything but thumb through them, but I had a pretty good idea of their importance. It was possible—maybe more than possible—they had something to do with Payton's behavior. I had to have that talk with Aaron soon. "I think he wants to keep track of how the case is building against Elizabeth," I said.

Aaron nodded as he raised his glass. "My thoughts as well."

"Why?"

"Because he killed Monty!" Cora Lee brought her point home with a thump of her cane on the wooden floor.

There was no trace of a smile on Aaron's face. "This afternoon you thought McMann was involved in all this, that he was a thief, maybe a fence and possibly a murderer as well. Now you've switched to Payton Culpepper. You don't have a shred of evidence against either man."

"Then why all the interest?" Cora Lee banged her cane once more.

The woman behind us turned and glared.

Cora Lee paid no attention. "Everything Payton does benefits him in some way."

"Don't forget, Monty and Payton were friends. Payton sent him overflow clients and he had Monty doing some lobbying work from time to time. It's entirely possible Payton is going to represent Monty's widow in some future capacity."

"Wrongful death." There was disgust in every syllable Cora Lee uttered.

Mildred's right eye twitched. Her hand shook a little as she set her wineglass on the table. I was sure Mildred was thinking about the deed and wondering if she and Noah truly were safe. Maybe we shouldn't have brought her. She and Elizabeth were both staying upright on nothing but adrenaline and must be about out of that. No. Bringing them had been a good idea. All either of them would do at home was sit and brood over things they had no control over.

Cora Lee opened her mouth as if to make another of her pronouncements, but Aaron got there first. "Shall we order? I, for one, am starved and we can continue this over dinner."

As if on cue, everyone picked up their menu. Although not extensive, Shields' menu was filled with hearty and delicious-sounding dishes. The kind, I supposed, people might have eaten in the eighteenth century. They also sounded like a lot of food.

Elizabeth turned to Mildred. "Want to split something?"

"Oh, my, yes. What do you want?"

"How about the chicken?"

"Sounds wonderful."

"Yes, it does." Aunt Mary put the menu down and looked at me.

"Of course."

"I'm having the crayfish and shrimp stew." Cora Lee shut her menu with a snap

A plate appeared in front of me. Salad. Had we ordered salad? The young waiter smiled at me. He put one in front of Mildred and handed one to Noah. He went around the table, placing a salad in front of everyone but Aaron, who got a cup of soup. He immediately scooped up a small amount, tasted it and smiled. "Peanut soup. Best stuff in the world."

Roger smiled as well, and walked into the middle of the room.

"Soup was very popular in the eighteenth century." His voice had the commanding ring of an actor determined to be heard in the third balcony. Or, a politician about to give a speech in the House of Representatives. "Eating it could be a challenge. Anyone know why? No? No spoons." He paused for dramatic effect and waited until the room quieted and everyone's attention was on him. No spoons? *Of course they had spoons.* I'd seen them. Hadn't I?

"In the eighteenth century, travelers, such as yourselves, wouldn't have a complete set of silverware put in front of you, as you have here. You would have brought your own. A poor man, or even one of the middle class, would have with him only a knife and perhaps a fork. The knife would have many uses—skinning a rabbit, fixing a piece of harness or cutting a rather tough piece of beef for dinner. It would have been wrapped in his napkin, which would bear little resemblance to the napkins you use tonight; they would look more like what they call 'bandanas' out west. They were used for many things, some of which we will not mention in deference to the delicate ears of the ladies." He made a small bow toward the table where we sat and followed it up with a wicked grin. "So," this was followed by a sweeping gesture, "if you wanted soup, or stew, or anything else we commonly eat today with the aid of a spoon, you had a problem. Rich men carried one with them, but spoons were hard to make; the castings they used were difficult to handle, and poor men couldn't afford them. What did they use? Anyone know?"

The crowd was grinning, chuckling, whispering among themselves, but no one offered an answer.

"A sippet, of course." It was Elizabeth.

"I beg your pardon, madam? A what?"

Elizabeth was actually smiling. "A sippet, sir. What else would a poor man use?"

Roger grinned, enjoying every minute of this little play. "Madam is correct. Of course, you'd use a sippet. But, good sir, you look confused." Roger stood in front of a smaller table, addressing an older man dressed in a suit and tie. His wife had on a pale green pantsuit and pearls. They looked as if they didn't know whether to be alarmed, insulted or to go along with the act. The man nodded his head and smiled a little.

Roger turned around, surveying the room. "Good people,

you all look confused. Am I to believe not one of you has brought your sippet with you?" Laughter broke out and the murmurs got louder.

"Then I must enlighten you, so you'll come properly prepared for your next journey. A sippet, good friends, is a piece of stale bread." He reached into his pocket and pulled out a rather misshapen, large and very hard piece of bread. "In the eighteenth century, bread had no preservatives, so it hardened quickly. Dinner was in the middle of the day, two o'clock to be precise, and supper was just that. Something to sup on before you retired for the night. If you were a poor man, you kept back a piece of bread. Then the next day you could use it to dip into your bowl, scooping up the liquid and—what did you do? You sipped it. Ergo, the sippet."

Spoons. Sippets. Silver. I began to see.

"I wonder. Do you suppose … and if that's the case, then … but how … It had to happen that way. Or at least, something like that. It's the only thing that makes sense."

All the people at our table were looking at me, and those at several of the adjoining ones. So was Roger, the storytelling waiter.

"Madam is correct. Sippets did make sense. On your next visit, I hope to see yours." He raised one eyebrow at me, made a small bow to the diners in the room, picked up a water pitcher and started making the rounds.

"You weren't talking about sippets, were you?" Cora Lee dove right in. "You know something. What?"

"I don't know anything, but I've got a pretty good idea where that silver tea set is and, if I'm right, who our thief and murderer is."

"Just one person?"

"If I'm right."

"Are you going to tell the police?"

"I'm telling one right now. I think I know how we can be certain."

"You're going to lay a trap." There was no question in Elizabeth's voice, just anticipation.

"*To catch a thief.* There was a movie with that name. Is that what we're going to do? Catch a thief?" Cora Lee's smile was bright.

"Maybe. Let's see if I'm right about the tea set first."

"You know where the tea set is?" Fear was on Mildred's face, but something else, too. Something I couldn't quite interpret.

Cora Lee broke my train of thought. "It's at Smithwood, isn't it?"

"I think so."

"Then let's go find it." The old Elizabeth was back, exhaustion forgotten, eyes bright, shoulders squared, ready for battle.

"You'll do no such thing." Aaron Glass couldn't have looked more upset. "You've had two murders at Smithwood. Practically the whole place is a crime scene. You can't go messing around, hunting for things. You shouldn't have gone down in the cellar to begin with."

"If we hadn't, we'd never have found Louis." Aunt Mary eyed me thoughtfully. I wondered if she'd made the same connection I just had.

"Aaron is right. The old kitchen is taped off, and that includes the basement." Noah paused and took a long look at his mother. "Keep your noses out of things. Ellen, if you have some ideas, tell me. I'll make sure we follow up."

"Not if Lieutenant McMann has anything to do with it. He didn't try very hard to find your father when he disappeared, and he doesn't seem too anxious to go hunting for murderers now."

Noah sighed. "That doesn't mean you get to go poking around looking for them, either."

Roger appeared with a round tray loaded with plates. He unerringly handed them around to the right diners and conversation ceased as we ate the delicious food.

It wasn't until plates were cleared that Noah spoke. "If you're finished, let's get out of here. There's a line of people waiting for tables."

"Good idea. I'll get the check." Aaron Glass raised his hand, put his other one out toward Noah, indicating the check was his, and handed Roger his credit card. "As soon as he gets back, we're gone." He turned to me. "Please don't do anything foolish. Leave that privilege to the police." He signed the slip Roger handed him and pushed back his chair. "I'll be in touch tomorrow, Elizabeth. Leo wants to do his search then. After he finishes and finds nothing, we should be able to bid all this nonsense goodbye. Which I will now wish all of you. Goodbye, everyone. Ladies, have a safe trip home."

Noah was on his feet, holding his mother's coat. "I have to drop Felicity off at the hospital and then I have some things I need to do at the station. I'll be home in a couple of hours. I'll try to be quiet as I expect all of you will be in bed by that time." This he addressed to his mother,

He gave each of us a piercing look, leaving no doubt that he expected *bed* to be the only place any of us would go as well. We looked at each other but no one said anything. Felicity, however, gave a snort of what might have been laughter.

Noah ignored her. "Cora Lee, are you all right to drive home?"

The look she gave him was scornful. "Are you suggesting a half glass of wine makes me incapable or that I'm too old to drive after dark?"

Noah sighed and turned toward Felicity, who struggled to keep a straight face. "If you laugh, I'll never forgive you." He took her by the arm. "I'll see the rest of you at home. Later."

We watched as Noah and Felicity threaded their way through tables and headed for the door.

"Ladies, are we ready to go?" Cora Lee picked up her cane, looped it over her arm and started to inch her way around her chair.

"I think so." Elizabeth laid down her napkin and pushed her

chair in as far as possible before she turned to the rest of us. "Can you get out? We have a lot to do and not much time to do it. Ellen, I assume you know where we're going to start?

Aunt Mary smiled. "Yes, Elizabeth, I think she does."

Chapter Twenty-Three

"It smells like mold in here." Cora Lee stopped and gave an disapproving sniff.

We were wandering the house that had been unoccupied for years—the east wing.

"It smells better than the last time we crept around an old house in the dark." Aunt Mary flashed her light on the walls. "Does this one have electricity?"

Elizabeth started patting the wall. "It must. They wouldn't put it in two houses and not the third."

"Don't count on it." Cora Lee felt the opposite wall with little success. "My father and grandfather weren't both nicknamed 'Scrooge' for nothing."

"Move over." Mildred eased by Cora Lee. "All the lights on this side are the old fashioned kind. You either pull an overhead string or there's a wall thing you push. Here it is."

Lights came on. We stood in what was beginning to feel like a normal kitchen. Only, in this room, the long plank table and the benches on either side seemed to be the focal point of the room. The fireplace was smaller and the hearth didn't extend into the room. There were no barrels beside it and no cooking pots or hanging utensils. There was, however, more furniture. What appeared to be a duplicate of Hattie's linen press sat on one wall with an open-shelved highboy beside it. One shelf was piled with white plates, mugs and serving bowls, now gray with dust. Another shelf was laden with pewter, equally filthy. A lovely gravy boat sat on a stack of plates; mugs and serving platters took up the rest of the space. The dust that covered them had turned each item almost black.

"Tell me again why we're here." Cora Lee leaned heavily on her cane, her mouth puckered in distaste. "The last time I was in this dreary little room was with Mother. We walked through this house deciding what to pack and what to just leave where it was. All we're going to find is dust and spiders."

"I think we might do better than that," I said.

"Why?" Cora Lee took a step across the wood floor. Dust blew up. Her sneeze wasn't gentle. "Damn. Does anyone have a tissue?"

Aunt Mary reached into her jacket pocket and handed her one.

"Why do you think the tea set is here?" Elizabeth hadn't moved since the lights went on. She stood beside Mildred, surveying the room, as reluctant as Cora Lee to start exploring. "It seems like a dumb place to hide something like that."

"I don't think the murderer had much choice." I started to move slowly around the room, looking at possible hiding places.

"What do you mean, not much choice?" Mildred followed my progress, mouth tight, eyes anxious. "What do you think happened?"

"I think whoever shot Louis hadn't planned to do it. I think Louis walked in on the murderer getting ready to leave with the tea set. They panicked and shot him. When they saw he was dead, they were afraid to carry the tea set out. I think they hid it, intending to come back later, when it was safe."

"You think they never came back?"

"I'm pretty sure they didn't, and I think I know why." I stopped my slow crawl and turned toward Cora Lee. "You and your mother did your walkthrough of this house before Virginia and Monty came to live here. After your father died and right before your mother moved out. Is that right? Over thirty years ago. Has anyone been in here since?"

Mildred answered. "Depends on what you mean by 'in here.' No one's lived here, but periodically we go through it, check for leaks, make sure no animals are setting up housekeeping. That's about all. The police supposedly searched through it when Louis went missing, but I don't think they tried very hard. They'd already decided he ran off with the Smithwood tea set. They put out an APB, alerted all the pawn shops and sat back and waited for him to show up." She walked around the room, stopping to look more closely at an iron candleholder. She rested her finger lightly on a Windsor chair and held it up to examine the dust. "He never did. Until yesterday."

Aunt Mary and I exchanged looks. It was going to take a long time for Mildred to get over her bitterness at how Louis, and she and Noah, had been treated. The easy assumption that Louis was a thief despite all appearances. Not only had he lived honorably, but he was an educated man with a degree in agricultural practices, known to be a loving family man and a loyal friend to the Smithwoods. None of that counted. He was a thief. Period. Mildred had lived with that injustice for thirty years, had tried to shield Noah from her bitterness, had raised him to be an educated man of high principles and made sure he thought highly of the father he barely remembered. In that, she had succeeded. The bile she'd swallowed all those years seemed not to want to stay swallowed any longer. Payton Culpepper had also had a father branded a thief, only his father had died in jail. What had Hattie taught Payton about his father other than that he carried an old and honorable name? Payton certainly was an educated man, but now rumors were flying that his principles had slipped. Was that true? I wondered. Hattie had her own set of values. Very different from Mildred's, but I was sure she clung to them with intensity. Whether they included "thou shalt not steal," I wasn't sure.

"What was this room used for?" Elizabeth turned in a circle, examining every corner. "It looks like a kitchen, but why would they need a second one?"

"They didn't." Cora Lee moved to the center of the room and stared down at the plank table. "This thing is filthy. Even worse than the one in the real kitchen."

"What did they use it for?" It reminded me of the room in Hattie's cottage, but hers had a cozy fire burning and was clean.

"This house was for the, well, lower class guests. Back then, roads were bad and guests often came unexpectedly. If it rained, they stayed."

"We know that. The house we live in was used that way."

Cora Lee nodded. "That wing housed the other plantation owners, people of wealth. Over here, well, over here were the river people. Oh, not the men who loaded the boats, or any of the laborers. Lots of them were black." Cora Lee took a quick glance at Mildred, but there was no expression on her face. "The people who stayed on this side were shopkeepers, small farmers, riverboat captains, people who traveled for a living, sometimes on the river, often by road. They expected to stay at the plantations and did. Only, not with the 'gentry.' They stayed in houses like this. They may have eaten the same food, but not in the dining room. They had beds, but not the best linens. In this case, the food came up from the kitchen downstairs. The plates for the dining room were filled, or the food was put on the best platters and then taken to the dining room; the rest was served to the people staying in this house. On those thick white ironstone plates, or the pewter ones. The only silverware was what they brought with them."

"No spoons?" Aunt Mary asked.

"No spoons. Except those used for serving. That's why the stairs lead from the pathway in front of the kitchen door up to the passageway between the main house and this one. It's the reason why, all these years, no one's ever bothered to come over here much. Nothing of value was in this house. Not trashy stuff, just not the good things. You won't find a silver spoon over here or a crystal wineglass. They drank out of glassware made on the plantation. Thick, blue, red or clear, with bubbles in it."

I stared at her for a moment. "I didn't know glass was made here."

"Oh, yes. It was made in town as well."

Aunt Mary had been examining each piece of furniture in the room, evidently assessing its potential as a hiding place for something as extensive as a tea set. She stopped and peered into a cupboard pushed up against the wall across from the fireplace. In the dark corner, it was barely visible. It was a fairly tall piece, with doors above and what appeared to be a deep drawer across the bottom. "This looks promising."

Cora Lee walked over beside her. They both scrutinized the cupboard. Elizabeth and I joined them.

"It couldn't be that easy, could it?" Cora Lee reached out as if to touch it, but pulled her hand back quickly and again leaned on her cane.

Aunt Mary shook her head. "Only one way to find out." She took hold of the leather pull on one of the doors and tugged. It came away in her hand. The look on her face was priceless.

"Leather." Cora Lee laughed. "Some of them had leather pulls instead of metal. Cheaper. Could be made from scraps of cowhide. You'd never find that in the main house, only over here. Let's see if I can open it." She pushed on the door a little then tried to get her finger into the space between the doors. "It's moving."

"For God's sake, be careful. You have no idea what's in that thing." Elizabeth stood behind Aunt Mary, Mildred next to her.

"Thanks." Cora Lee pulled her hand back and we all stared at the cupboard as if it might come alive at any moment.

"This is ridiculous. Cora Lee, move over." I wiggled the door, trying to get my finger into the space, but it wouldn't budge. "I think there's a catch in here of some sort. I need a knife or something to push it up. Wait a minute."

I wiggled it one more time and, with great reluctance, the door swung open.

"That's why it didn't want to open. Look how it sags. The hinges barely hold the door on. Oh, my god."

"What? What? Did you find something?" Cora Lee pushed past Aunt Mary to peer into the dark recess of the cupboard. "It's a bag. An old burlap bag." She reached out to touch it.

"Don't." Mildred hadn't moved forward but her face twisted with alarm.

"Why ever not? The tea set might be in there."

"Or mice."

Cora Lee's hand flew back as if singed. "Mice!" A shudder ran through her. One ran through me as well. Beatrice Potter notwithstanding, I'd never been fond of mice.

"We need something to poke that bag with before we pull it out. If there's anything alive in there, maybe they'll run out." Mildred looked around the room but her eyes kept coming back to the bag, which hadn't moved. "I hate mice."

"I don't see anything we can use." Aunt Mary looked around the room as well.

"I know." Cora Lee crept up a little closer to the cupboard and took hold of the door. She shook the cabinet. Nothing happened. She shook it a little harder. Still nothing.

"I don't think anything's in there." Elizabeth bent down a little to get a better look, still keeping her distance. "I think we can maybe pull that end …"

"We're going to scream."

"What?" Everyone stared at Cora Lee.

"Why?" I said. "Do you think that will make the mice run out?" This whole thing was just plain silly. "If we scream, all they're going to do is hunker down deeper in their nest and put their paws over their ears. Where are those dogs when they're needed?"

"Locked up in my house where we left them," Elizabeth told us as she stared at the burlap bag.

"We have the perfect thing right here." Aunt Mary pointed at Cora Lee. "Your cane. Go on. Give that thing a good poke."

Cora Lee leaned harder on her cane. "No. If they run out, I'll need it."

"To do what? Bash them? Here. Give it to me. You all go on the other side of the room."

No one moved, but Cora Lee handed the cane to Aunt Mary, who inched closer to the cabinet, pushed the crook of the cane into the interior and hooked the sack. She wiggled it gently at first, poised to flee at the first sign of movement, but nothing happened. She wiggled harder. Still nothing, so she pulled. The sack split apart, spilling its contents into the bottom of the cabinet and onto the floor.

A cream pitcher rolled out and stopped at Cora Lee's feet. She reached down and picked it up. Even black with tarnish, it was easy to identify. "We've found the tea set."

Chapter Twenty-Four

NOAH STOOD IN the doorway, ramrod straight. Anger, or maybe it was worry, made his words come out a little too loud. "What is going on? I thought I told you not to go prowling around, to go to bed."

Cora Lee gave a little scream and grabbed Aunt Mary's arm. Elizabeth grabbed the cane and whirled around, while Mildred, who evidently recognized her son's voice, sighed.

I wasn't surprised to see Noah. I thought he'd show up, but it was the other person who got my full attention. "Dan! What are you doing here?" I flew past Noah and into his arms. I got my ribs squeezed and a most satisfactory kiss.

"Surprised?"

I wasn't, very, but didn't think it was a good idea to say so. "I can't believe it. I'm so glad you're here." I hugged him back.

"We found the tea set." Cora Lee completely ignored Noah's scolding and Dan's and my reunion. There was jubilation in her voice as she held up the cream pitcher for them to see. "Now what do you think Leo McMann's going to say?"

"That you just disturbed a crime scene and if there are

fingerprints or DNA or any other kind of evidence on that creamer, you've ruined them."

Cora Lee let her hand drop. She stared down at the creamer, then at Noah. "Oh."

The expression on Dan's face plainly said he didn't think we'd ruined anything. Neither did I. Noah was simply having a stress attack. While I didn't blame him, I also had no intention of cowering before him and saw no reason any of the others should either. I didn't care a fig for Lt. McMann's crime scene. If, indeed, it extended to this old house, he should have taped it off and searched it. "Oh, for heaven's sake, Noah," I said. "If it's possible to get fingerprints off that thing, then all they have to do is take Cora Lee's and they can tell which are which. Surely your fingerprint people can do that."

Noah flushed. I could see it in his earlobes. "Of course they can. That's not the point. You had no business breaking in here."

"Breaking in!" Elizabeth had been studying Dan but now aimed all her fury at Noah. "This is *my* house and I have every right to go where I please. I'm sick and tired of playing these stupid games. People prowling my hallways at night, leaving dead bodies all over the place. It's going to stop and it's going to stop now." She wheeled around and confronted Dan. "Who are you and why are you here?"

"He's Dan Dunham, Ellen's husband and Santa Louisa's Chief of Police. I don't know why he's here." Aunt Mary walked up and hugged him. She got hugged back. "I'm so glad to see you, but why are you here?"

"Thought I'd give you folks a hand. Sounded like you might need one." He extended his hand to Elizabeth who, surprisingly, took it. "You must be Elizabeth Smithwood. I'm glad to finally meet you."

"How did you get here?" It finally dawned on me that we were a long way from the nearest airport.

"Noah picked me up. We've been talking and agreed my coming might be a good idea."

They had? Dan hadn't told me. I wasn't sure I liked that. However, I had other things to worry about. Mildred started to sway. "Oh, no, you don't." I grabbed her arm. Aunt Mary grabbed the other, and we turned her so she could sink down into the Windsor chair at the head of the table.

Hands on her hips, Aunt Mary said, "I knew we shouldn't have let you come. We've made you do too much."

"As if you could have stopped me. It's my husband lying there in that kitchen, or what's left of him, and this is what he's supposed to have stolen. You think a little head injury will stop me from helping to clear his name?" Mildred glared at Noah. "Why you're not helping, I don't know."

"Mom." That was as far as Noah got.

"And another thing." She swayed a little in her chair and put her hand up to touch the white bandage still plastered across the side of her dark head. "I'm going to need some Tylenol pretty quick, but first, there's something I don't understand."

"There's a whole lot I don't understand." Elizabeth shook her head and looked around. "I need to sit." She looked dubiously at one of the benches, but the need to get off her feet seemed greater than her reluctance to sit on so much dust. She pulled the bench out and blew on it. The dust didn't budge. She gave up and sank down on it anyway.

"What don't you understand?" I said.

"Why did they leave the tea set behind?"

"Oh, that's easy." I hadn't meant to say that, but I'd been trying to work all this out and that point seemed clear, even if a lot of the others didn't.

"Of course it is. I'm Cora Lee Whittingham, by the way." She dimpled at Dan, who smiled back, nodded and held me a little closer. "As for the tea set, Ellen will explain all that." Cora Lee sank down on the bench beside Elizabeth, but she went down slowly, mouth twisted in distaste. Evidently pain triumphed over concern for subjecting those lovely wool pants to the filth on the bench.

"Okay," Dan said to me. "Why do you think they didn't take the tea set?"

"They couldn't." I'd been working this out and spoke with some confidence. "I think shooting Louis wasn't in the plan. He must have surprised the thief, probably in the act of putting it into the sack, and got shot. When they realized he was dead, they had to figure out what to do, and quick. They could hardly leave him on the floor. He had to disappear, but they couldn't drag him out of the kitchen and up the stairs, so they buried him there and hid the tea set in this room. No one came in here anymore, and when they did, they didn't search in cabinets or anything. As long as the set didn't surface, everyone would think Louis stole it and it would be easy to come back when it was safe to get it."

"That cabinet isn't my idea of a hiding place."

"Elizabeth, think." Cora Lee had that jubilant look again. "What were they ... they?" She looked at me.

I shrugged. "Almost had to be. I don't think one person could have done all that."

Cora Lee nodded agreement. "Right. What were they going to do? They'd just shot a man. Someone else could show up at any moment. They must have been sweating bullets the whole time they dug that hole and buried him."

Aunt Mary put one hand on Mildred's shoulder and gave it a little squeeze. Mildred's hand flew up to clutch Aunt Mary's.

"I still don't know why they didn't take the tea set with them." Mildred's eyes went from one face to the next, anxiously demanding an answer.

Noah had been listening to all this with a passive face. His voice betrayed him. "The reason they didn't take it the day they killed my father was because they didn't want it on them if they got stopped. They were on private property, coming and going out a gate they had no business being near. They had already hung around a lot longer than they intended and were taking no chances. They may have planned to come back later to retrieve it or at least hide it better, but, Ellen, you're probably right. They no longer had access. Cora Lee and Mrs. Smithwood had locked up this house, and no one had any interest in unlocking it."

"I think Noah's right. As is my beautiful wife. All that's left for us to do is find out who 'they' are."

I smiled. It was nice Dan thought I was beautiful. I liked that he'd said "us" even better.

"Ellen will think of a way." Cora Lee's confidence might be misplaced.

"That's what had me worried enough to fly out here." Hm. Nice he was worried about me, however …

I frowned. He smiled. Aunt Mary grinned. I glared at her, too. However, Cora Lee was right. I had thought of a way.

"First thing we're going to do is inventory the tea set," I said. "Cora Lee, see if it's all here."

I didn't think Cora Lee was going to comply. She stared at me and then at the pieces spread over the wood floor, then at everyone else. No one offered to help. Finally, holding onto her cane, she knelt down, ignoring the accumulation of years of dust on the wooden floorboards. Lips pressed tightly together, she started to go through the pieces. She picked up the silver tray first, black with tarnish, and set it in front of her. The coffeepot was next, then another pot—smaller and more slender. Tea? Chocolate? I wasn't sure. A creamer came next, then a small bowl, used for lemon slices? I had no idea. Then the last piece. A shell-shaped spoon.

A sugar spoon, but no sugar bowl.

Cora Lee sat back on her heels, gave a little groan of pain and struggled to her feet. "The sugar bowl is missing."

Aunt Mary nodded. "Yes. It is." She looked at me speculatively, one eyebrow raised.

I shrugged.

She frowned.

Noah suddenly seemed to remember he was a policeman. "We shouldn't be doing this. It's police business. Murder, theft. I have to tell McMann."

"He did nothing to help when your father disappeared. He'll do nothing to help now. I say let's see what we can find out first." There was a little more color in Mildred's cheeks and a very different look in her eyes. They bored into Noah, willing him to do as she wanted. "Besides, Ellen already knows who it is, don't you?"

"No. At least, not exactly. It's just an idea. Mildred's right, though. Let's wait. I wouldn't be surprised if something happened pretty soon."

"What have you done?" There was wariness in Dan's voice as well as a little resignation.

"Hardly anything."

"What does that mean?"

"What's going to happen?" Cora Lee sounded apprehensive.

"I made a phone call."

"Who to?" Elizabeth was the only one who didn't sound apprehensive. She sounded confused. Understandably. She hadn't been privy to the small but key fact I'd discovered.

"I found some papers. I think they're Monty's." I stopped for a moment, listening. Was that a footstep? Soft, a scuffing sound, the kind a leather boot might make on a wooden stair. No. All was quiet.

The moment of stunned silence was broken by the voices of everyone in the room.

"Why didn't you tell me?" Dan demanded

"I tried but you didn't answer your phone. You were on an airplane. Remember?"

Dan grinned. "So I was."

"What papers?" Elizabeth sounded wary.

"Ones I found in Cora Lee's secret drawer."

"My secret drawer?" Cora Lee's eyes searched my face.

Elizabeth snorted in exasperation. "Ellen, for heaven's sake. This is starting to sound more like a Nancy Drew novel every minute. Hidden doors, secret drawers, ghosts who prowl the hallways. Would you mind explaining what's going on?"

"Where did you find these papers?" Noah's surprise had given way to a kind of wariness. His mouth was set in a straight line and tight little creases formed at the corners of his eyes as he narrowed them. He walked across the room, barely glancing at the silver set, and stood behind his mother, placing a hand on her shoulder.

"Where Monty hid them, in an eighteenth-century hiding place."

Noah stopped for a moment. It was as if he wanted to ask what that meant, but he didn't. "Did you read them?"

"I looked through them. Enough to get an idea of what they contained."

"Enough to tell you who the murderer is?"

"Oh, no." I tried to smile, not very successfully. "Although, they were certainly interesting."

A plainly exasperated Elizabeth blurted out, "Then what did?"

"Spoons."

Chapter Twenty-Five

"I'M DELIGHTED YOU found them interesting, even if they weren't informative."

The voice came from the open doorway that led into the passageway. The sight of the elegant gentleman, alpaca overcoat worn casually over a dark gray handmade suit, reduced us to stunned silence. That, and the look on his face. Last time I'd seen him, he'd looked confident, almost arrogant. Not tonight. His face was haggard, drawn. Stress lines showed around his eyes as he walked farther into the room and paused before me.

"However, I'm afraid I must ask you for them. They belong to me, you see."

"Who are you?" Dan pulled me a little closer to him but shifted his weight so that he was balanced on both feet. Why, I wondered but found myself doing the same.

"Payton Culpepper. And you are?"

"Daniel Dunham, Chief of Police of Santa Louisa California and Ellen's husband. Just what papers are you referring to? How do you know my wife has them, and why should we think they belong to you?"

"Too many questions, Mr. Chief of Police. They're mine, she

has them, and I want them back." Payton sounded forceful, almost arrogant, but there was a twitch in his right eye as he looked around at our little group that belied that impression.

"Good evening, Payton. I believe you know everyone else here." I sounded amazingly confident as I greeted him. But then, he wasn't the one I was worried about.

Glancing again at our group, Payton sucked in his breath as he caught sight of the tea set still lying on the dirt floor. He seemed to shudder a little as he tore his eyes away from it and addressed us as a group. "I had no idea you were having a party. You could have chosen a better spot for it. However, I would be obliged if you"—his eyes fixed on me and narrowed slightly—"would hand over the papers you found. I don't have much time."

"How do we know that?" There was grit in Dan's voice. I wasn't sure if his irritation was directed at Payton or me for getting us into this mess.

Payton's smile was cold and his hand dropped oh so casually into his right-hand coat pocket. A chill went through me as I saw that side of his coat sag a little. "I'd hoped your lovely wife would cooperate without a fuss." He looked around the room. The muscles around his mouth tightened more. "I wasn't expecting a party."

"How do we know these papers are yours?" Aunt Mary sounded a whole lot calmer than I felt as she repeated Dan's question.

She sat calmly on one filthy bench, Elizabeth and Cora Lee on the opposite one, immobile. Mildred was in the Windsor chair, Noah behind her, hand clutching her shoulder. Dan and I stood almost in the middle of the room, far too close to Payton. He kept his hand in his overcoat pocket, wiggling something in there as he continued to survey the room. He was making me nervous. Dan, however, did not flinch.

"Can you identify those papers, Mr.—Culpepper, isn't it? Tell us what's so important about them? I'd hate to have my wife give them to the wrong person."

"They have Montgomery Eslick's name on them, and my firm's as well. Is that enough for you?" He took a step closer to us. I stepped back, trying in vain to drag Dan with me. He seemed as rooted to the floor as a tree trunk.

"What's so important about those papers, Mr. Culpepper? There must be something to send you all the way out here to get them at this late hour."

Since when was nine o'clock late? The hour, however, wasn't important. The fact that Dan was prodding Payton was.

"Why was Monty blackmailing you? He *was* blackmailing you, wasn't he?" I gulped before I said that. Payton still had his hand in his pocket and I knew Dan was watching him closely. But we weren't getting anywhere with Payton and Dan trying to stare each other down.

"It seems you took the time to look through the documents." Payton's lips barely moved.

"All those deposits from your law firm into Monty's account were hard to miss. Only, they were labeled 'payments for lobbying.' Monty wasn't a lobbyist."

"He was an attorney. I hired him to work for my firm, at double the going rate, to keep his practice alive. Only, he never did the work. The little rat took my money and the clients' money and never did one damn thing."

"What do bank statements have to do with this?" Elizabeth had been following the conversation intently. Curiosity and a little trepidation were written all over her face.

"None of your business." Payton didn't bother to turn his head.

"Let me guess." I'd been thinking a lot about this and was pretty sure I knew what had happened. Or at least, a lot of it.

"I'd just as soon you didn't." Dan tightened his arm around my waist. "However, you're going to anyway, so go on."

Dan and I had discussed the possibility Monty had been blackmailing someone about something, but this was before

I'd discovered the papers. I hadn't had a chance to tell Dan about them and I could tell he was curious. More than curious. I decided to see if my theory was correct, hoping that the object in Payton's pocket was no more dangerous than a handkerchief. Dan still had his arm around me and he gave me a little squeeze. It gave me a little courage, so I let his arm stay where it was and actually leaned into it a little. "Monty had two sets of books. The ones he gave the auditors didn't show any payments from you. They showed on your books, though. Monty was supposed to account for that money, give you detailed accounts of how he spent every penny. You told the auditors for those clients bringing charges that you hired Monty. Unless you could come up with *this* set of papers, showing he received the deposits from your firm, you couldn't prove it. You weren't only on the hook for the money, you might end up in jail."

All eyes shifted from me to Payton, who said nothing. He continued to stare at me. His hand stayed in his pocket but his eye twitch intensified.

"Is that why you killed him?" asked Cora Lee.

"You have that part wrong. I didn't kill him." He glanced over at her for a moment, then his eyes shifted to Mildred, who sat rigid, staring at him as if he really was a ghost. "I didn't kill Louis, either. Please believe that, Mrs. Longo. I'm terribly sorry about what happened to Louis, but I had nothing to do with it."

"You know who did." Noah wasn't asking a question. "How? How do you know?"

Payton ignored him. "Mrs. Dunham, I don't have all night. I need those papers now, so shall we go get them?"

"If I say no?"

"Ellen," There was a warning in Dan's tone, but I chose to ignore it, at least for right now. Something else was going to happen, at least I hoped it was, and I wanted a little time.

Payton sucked in a deep breath, which he let out quickly. His eye twitched again. "Why would you not? I didn't kill Monty, although he asked for it often enough. I've never killed anyone and believe me, I don't want to start now." His hand was still jammed in his pocket. I abandoned hope that all he had in there was a handkerchief. I glanced up at Dan. He eyes were also on Payton's pocket and he didn't look happy. I could see the outline of Payton's fist tighten as he went on.

"Monty cheated me and I don't want to go to jail for something I didn't do. So, if you'll please get them for me …"

I glanced up once more at Dan. I didn't know what to do. There was no real reason for me not to get them, but the thought of walking back through the dark to Elizabeth's house, going upstairs followed by Payton gave me the creeps.

"I don't have much time, Mrs. Dunham. I want those bank statements and I want them now." Payton was losing patience, fast. His voice rose, and his gaze shifted around the room, stopped once more at the tea set before returning to me. Maybe I was imagining it, but this time I heard a threat in his voice. "*Now*, Mrs. Dunham. If you don't want to get them for me, perhaps Mrs. McGill will oblige. She seems to be familiar with their existence."

Aunt Mary gasped.

A woman's voice said, "For God's sake, is that the best you can do? You never could do anything right."

Payton swung around, his hand out of his pocket and carrying the object I had been afraid of. A not very big but very lethal looking gun. Acting as though by instinct, Dan released me and pushed me toward the table. I scrambled under it. Cora Lee got there ahead of me. I grabbed Aunt Mary's ankle and give a tug. She dropped off the bench and under the table in one move. Elizabeth scooted off the bench and wiggled feet first under the table. The bench went over with a crash, followed by the chair. Mildred and Noah joined us. I was pushed out the other side of the table, almost under the upturned bench, Cora Lee's cane entangled in my legs. I rolled over a little and peeked around the table leg. Hattie, mobcap slightly askew and still wearing her colonial dress and greasy apron, pointed a small colonial pistol at Dan. I gasped. Why Dan?

"Mother. What are you doing here?" Payton started to lower his gun and took a step forward. He stopped abruptly. Hattie changed direction and pointed her gun right at him.

I got to my knees, dragging Cora Lee's cane behind me, then squatted back on my heels, using the cane as a prop. Hattie looked way too comfortable with the gun and I wanted to be able to dive back under the table quickly. Even more, I wanted Dan under the table with me. In the meantime, I had a front row seat at an interesting little drama.

Mother and son faced each other, each holding a gun. Hattie looked ridiculous with the little silver pistol but Payton didn't.

"You were going to turn me in, is that right?" Hattie put her other hand up to steady the gun. It was pointed directly at Payton's chest.

"I wasn't. Now I'm not so sure." Payton looked at his mother as if he couldn't quite believe what he saw.

"After all these years. After all I've done for you."

"After all you've done for me?" Payton's voice, tight with anger, rose a little, and his gun dropped a little more. "I'm not the one who stole all those things. I'm not the one who fenced Smithwood silver for Monty, and I'm not the one who shot Louis."

There was a soft moan from under the table. Mildred. There was nothing any of us could do for her right now.

The quarrel between Hattie and Payton intensified. A flush rose up the back of Payton's neck and veins started to stand out.

Hattie only got cooler, calmer, almost icy. "I wouldn't have had to shoot Louis if you had helped me."

"Helped you! I covered up for you for years. You and Monty pilfering stuff from this place, trying to pass it off as Culpepper antiques. Culpepper. The family name. The real Culpeppers wouldn't know you, or me, and certainly not my father, if they fell over us in an alley. He wasn't one of them. He was a thief. He died in jail. Well, I'm not going to jail. Not for you and certainly not for a name that means nothing. You hear? Nothing." Payton's voice rose with each sentence. The last word came out as a shout. The veins in his neck throbbed. The twitch over his eye danced in double time.

Hattie became very still. Her eyes narrowed, her mouth pinched and a little tremor seemed to run through her. "Take it back. Take it all back. You're a Culpepper."

"So you've told me, for years. Over and over."

"Then start to act like one."

"I have no idea what that means. I've never met a real Culpepper. You're not one. You think you're 'gentry.' You're not even close." Payton's hand, the one with the gun, dropped down to his side and his other went up to his face. He rubbed his eyes.

That was when she shot him.

Payton dropped for what seemed an eternity. His white shirt front turned red. His soft overcoat billowed out around him and, as he sank to the floor, covered him like a shroud.

"My God! How could you?" Noah was beside me on his hands and knees, staring at Payton, then up at Hattie.

"Don't move, Noah, I wouldn't mind in the least shooting you, too."

"With what?" he said. "That little popgun only has one bullet and it's gone. Come on, Hattie. Hand it over. That's a good girl." His hand went under his jacket for his gun. Not quickly enough.

Instead of handing over the gun, Hattie threw it at Noah's head. It missed him by inches, but it kept him from reaching for his and gave Hattie just enough time to dive for the revolver Payton had dropped. Dan tackled her, but she'd already gotten the gun.

She lay on the wood floor beside her bleeding son, pointing the revolver at Noah.

"Get off my legs, you oaf. If you don't, I'll shoot Noah. Even if I miss, I'll get one of them."

Unfortunately, she just might. Everyone but Mildred was now on the wrong side of the overturned table, staring in disbelief at Hattie.

One look at her face made me a believer. Contorted with rage, eyes blazing, mob cap clinging to one side of her head, Hattie looked like the woodcuts I'd seen of the mad people in Bellevue. Moving wasn't an option. Only, neither was crouching there and giving Hattie a chance to shoot someone. Anyone. Dan. I inched the cane up a little, hoping Hattie wouldn't notice.

She raised the gun and pointed it directly at my head. It wobbled a little, maybe because of its weight. Not enough to give me hope. But hope had arrived, and just in the nick of time. Two men stood in the doorway.

"You were right for once, Calvin," Lt. McMann said. "Something *is* going on here. What the hell do you people think you're doing?" He stood next to Calvin Campbell.

It wasn't Lt. McMann's lucky day. Hattie got one leg free, kicked Dan with it and wheeled around, gun raised. She fired before she even knew who it was. He spun halfway around and hit the floor with a thud. Hattie didn't wait to see him fall. She twisted back, her gun aimed once more at its target, which was Dan. He tried to capture her flailing free foot, but it didn't matter. I was on my feet and charging, wielding Cora Lee's cane. The hook connected with Hattie's neck and I pulled for all I was worth. The gun went flying. So did Hattie, and Dan was there to catch them both.

Chapter Twenty-Six

"**A**LL PACKED?" AUNT Mary asked.

I stuffed the last pair of socks in my suitcase and tried to pull the zipper closed. "If I can get this blasted thing zipped, I will be."

Aunt Mary walked over to the bed and pulled the sides of the suitcase closer together. "Now try."

I tugged. The zipper resisted, but then suddenly gave up and made its way to the other end. "That did it. It wasn't that hard when I came."

"You're bringing home more than you brought."

That was true. Dan had brought practically nothing, certainly not enough for the week he'd been here, and he'd carried it all in the smallest overnight bag we owned. We'd gone shopping, both in Colonial Williamsburg and in the shops that adjoined the historic district. Actually, I'd gone shopping. Dan had spent the week helping Noah, who had been promoted to temporary head of the homicide division. It looked as if that position would soon be permanent. Lt. McMann was still in the hospital. He'd be out soon but would take that early retirement. I felt responsible for him getting shot, but Dan said

I shouldn't. Bursting into what was a potentially dangerous situation wasn't only stupid but poor police procedure. A mortal sin in Dan's eyes.

Cora Lee came into the room, leaning heavily on her cane, followed by Elizabeth and Petal. "Dan and Noah are on their way. Have you got everything?"

"I think so. How about you, Aunt Mary?"

She laughed. "If I forgot anything, donate it to a church rummage sale. Chances are it came from one of ours."

Cora Lee sat on the Windsor chair. "We're going to miss you two."

No little barb. No sarcasm. Aunt Mary gave her a huge smile. "We're going to miss you, too. However, this has been a little more excitement than I'm used to. I need to go home and do calm things, like organize St. Mark's summer rummage sale."

"Have you heard anything about Payton?" I'd been thinking about him a lot. He was out of the hospital, but I hadn't been able to pry out of Dan or Noah what would happen to him.

"He's out of the hospital, but he won't be going back to his office."

Elizabeth examined Cora Lee with narrowed eyes. "How do you know that?"

"I have my ways." Her little sarcastic smile was back.

"Hmm." Aunt Mary murmured. "I'm sure you do."

"What's going to happen to him?" I was certain her "ways" included that information.

"Nothing good. He's certain to be disbarred and probably will end up in jail, charged with accessory to murder and embezzlement. Using your firm's money to pay off your blackmailer isn't a good idea."

"Maybe they'll give him and Hattie adjoining cells." Elizabeth grinned.

"Judging from the last time I saw them together, they might not enjoy that." Aunt Mary smiled.

I laughed. Aunt Mary was right. Putting those two that close together would be punishment worse than jail.

"He must have some feelings for his mother. He paid blackmail all those years to protect her." Ever the optimist, Mildred refused to believe a son wouldn't have sincere affection for his mother. Hers certainly did. Hattie's didn't.

"He only did it to avoid being dragged into the whole thing." Cora Lee gave a small snort of disapproval. "He might not have cared about being a Culpepper, but he sure did about being a powerful attorney. It wouldn't have helped his reputation one bit to have his mother in jail for theft and murder."

"Which brings up another point." Mildred twisted so she looked directly at me. "How did you know it was Hattie?"

"Good question," Elizabeth said, pulling my closed suitcase off the bed, setting it on the floor and sitting in its place. "And what was all that about spoons?" Petal jumped into her lap.

"Tell them from the beginning, Ellen," Noah said. "Just like you explained it to me and Dan."

Dan hadn't been all that pleased, saying I could have gotten myself killed. Aunt Mary was more appreciative.

I smiled. "There were several things about Hattie that confused me."

"Hattie's had that effect on people for years." Cora Lee's little barbs were back. "Go on."

"She seemed to think Elizabeth was going to sell off a lot of Smithwood's antiques. She questioned you about it that day in the Randolph kitchen."

Cora Lee nodded.

"It wasn't until you told her about the school, how the plantation would be preserved and she could be a part of it that she got interested. It seemed to matter to her what happened here. I thought that strange. She had nothing to do with Smithwood. I didn't realize Monty had promised her she could live here and keep house for him, use all the things here, when he got possession. After she found out Elizabeth was going to do something a lot more interesting, from her point of view, and had no intention of letting Monty get his hands on Smithwood, she started to change her mind. I still hadn't made the right connections, though. It was that night at Shields, when Roger gave that little talk about sippets that it all came clear. Hattie's family was a no-spoon family. All those beautiful things she had, and didn't want us to see, would never have been in a home like hers and certainly weren't heirlooms from Jerome's side of the family. Monty stealing Smithwood treasures plus Hattie hoarding things she shouldn't have had equaled Monty selling them to her all those years.

"I still wasn't sure why she killed him until I remembered Noah saying Monty wanted to sell Smithwood off to developers. He wasn't keeping it a secret, either. That was the last thing Hattie wanted. If he ended up with Smithwood, it would have ruined her chances to come back and be the expert. He stood in her way, so she removed him, and with an eighteenth-century drink. There had to be some symbolism there, and after I understood the spoon thing, it all fit."

"Hattie had the sugar dish from the tea set." Aunt Mary said. "We saw it in that drawer in her house. As soon as you spread that set out and we saw the sugar dish was missing, we both knew it had to be Hattie. Ellen was ahead of me on that, but she wouldn't have had that sugar dish if she hadn't either killed Louis or helped someone else do it."

The front door slammed, male voices sounded then footsteps echoed on the staircase. Dan and Noah had arrived.

"I see you're ready to go." Dan nodded approvingly at our suitcase, which bulged alarmingly at the sides, and smiled.

"Aunt Mary's ready, as well. How did it go with Hattie?"

Noah sighed. "Her attorney is tearing his hair out. She can't seem to focus on anything but that she's a Culpepper and everything she did was for the family name. Pathetic."

"Ellen's been telling us how she figured out Hattie was the murderer and why she killed Monty, but I still don't understand why she did it in the dining room of my house." Elizabeth squeezed the dog so tight she yelped. "Oh, baby, I'm so sorry." Petal settled back down.

Dan smiled.

Noah leaned against the wall, glanced at his watch and gestured to Dan. "Tell them."

Dan sighed. "That woman's a mess. I suppose you know she thought she'd get to come live here if Monty got the place."

We all nodded.

"What Hattie didn't know was that Monty was blackmailing Payton, at least not until recently. When she realized Monty had some papers that might actually hurt Payton's career, she decided she needed to help. She wasn't about to let another Culpepper go to jail. She told Monty that if he gave her the papers he'd been using to blackmail Payton, she'd have Payton help him get clear title to Smithwood. I guess Monty thought that was a good deal, because he agreed. Only, he'd hidden them in that old chest. They decided he'd come in the old way, through the kitchen, but that he'd better disguise himself in case someone saw him. That was why he wore the Colonial outfit. Trouble was, Monty couldn't find the chest. He neglected to tell Hattie until the night he died. They'd arranged to meet here—again, Hattie's idea—and he'd hand them over. They'd have a little drink to celebrate. By that time, Hattie had decided he had to go. She was much happier with Elizabeth's plan, but she needed the papers for Payton.

"She'd already given Monty the syllabub and he'd finished it off before he told her he couldn't find the chest. She was furious when he died. Trouble was, she couldn't find it either. She searched after Monty died, but then Cora Lee came home. She was trapped. When the rest of you arrived and were trying to figure out what was going on, she hurried through the passageway, dropped her glass in the dishwasher and was through the cellar door before Elizabeth came back." He paused to nod at her. "Locking the passageway door was a good idea, and if you'd done it a few minutes earlier, she would have been trapped. She came back several times, trying to find that chest. She's the one who tipped the crate over and later hit Mildred with the shovel. She wasn't trying to kill either of you, just avoid being discovered. She was getting pretty frantic about those papers the last few days, so she jumped at the chance when my lovely but impulsive wife called her."

All eyes turned toward me.

"You did what?" Mildred's eyes grew large. "Why?"

"I couldn't think of any other way to make sure it was her. I called her and told her I'd found a tea set, but I wasn't sure it was the Smithwood one. Hadn't she and Virginia used it and, if so, could she identify it?"

"What did she say?"

"She claimed she didn't know a tea set was gone, but that, yes, she and Virginia used to have tea and had used the Smithwood set."

Cora Lee shifted her weight from one side to the other, leaning on her cane. "Then what?"

"I told her I wanted to pull it out and have another look. She didn't say anything at first. Finally she asked where I found it. I hadn't, so I crossed my fingers and said it was in the closed-up wing. I also told her I'd found some papers with the name of Payton's firm on them. Did she think they were important and did he want them back? Could she ask him for me?"

"Oh, boy." Cora Lee's eyes were bright and the chuckle full of satisfaction.

Dan wasn't as pleased. "I still don't understand why, if you thought she was involved in murder, you did something so foolish. You could have gotten killed. You almost did."

"I didn't think she'd have the nerve to kill me, or anyone. After all, she used poison on Monty. Besides, I was only fishing. It could have been Payton. For a while I even thought it might be Calvin." I smiled at Dan. "Is that why you came? To keep me from being killed? You must have set out before I made the connection."

"I knew you were hot on someone's trail and figured I'd better get out here before you ended up in a coffin. Besides, I didn't like the sound of Lieutenant McMann. So, I started talking to Noah, and we agreed I needed to be here. Good thing, too."

I wasn't sure I liked the idea of being rescued but knew I loved having him here. I'd sort all that out later. I smiled and nodded. "I hadn't entirely ruled out Lieutenant McMann, either. So, I called him."

Noah opened his mouth then closed it again with a snap. When he finally got words out, they sounded strangled. "You what?"

"Called Lieutenant McMann."

Dan groaned. He looked at Noah and shook his head. "Didn't I tell you?"

Mildred seemed caught between laughter and horror. "What did you say?"

"Nothing. I left a message that I'd found the tea set and was going to get it out of the old east wing and could prove Louis was murdered and who did it. Was he interested? I thought about telling him about the papers but didn't. If I had, he might have been more on his guard." I paused and gave a small sigh. "Anyway, he came. Calvin saw us go into the east wing and hung around, wondering what we were up to. Then he saw Payton and Hattie arrive and heard the shot. He was trying to call nine-one-one when McMann arrived."

"Oh, lord." Noah ran his hand over his short hair and studied Mary. "Leo must have just about had a stroke when he heard that one."

"Yes." I shook my head as if in disbelief. "I feel terrible he just burst in."

"Don't." Dan let his arm slide around me and pulled me close. I didn't even try to pull away.

"Why was Calvin here so late?" Cora Lee sounded anything but pleased. "He should have left ages before all that."

I'd wondered the same thing. "He said he was cleaning up

his equipment before he put it away." I didn't bother to hide my skepticism.

Cora Lee frowned. Calvin was in for a grilling.

"I'm still amazed you figured it out," Elizabeth said. "There were too many twists and turns in this for me." Elizabeth put her arm around Aunt Mary and gave her a squeeze. She got a squeeze back.

There was time for only one more question. "Mildred, how did your appointment with the contractor go?"

"Wonderful. I'm going to turn that neglected old house into something beautiful, and I'm really going to enjoy teaching in Elizabeth's history school."

"The best part is, you won't have to sleep on a rope bed or use a chamber pot." Aunt Mary smiled.

"The best part is I won't have to live with my son and daughter-in-law. They'll start their married life in their own home, with their own deed. Thanks to Elizabeth." Mildred smiled at Elizabeth. She got back a huge grin.

"The best part is, I'll have two of my best friends living right next to me." Elizabeth gave Aunt Mary another big hug. "Are you sure we can't talk you into staying a little longer? Maybe a lot longer?"

"No." Aunt Mary got to her feet and looked around at everyone.

Dan had already taken hold of the handle on our suitcase and was headed for the door. I picked up my purse and was right behind him.

"It's been wonderful," Aunt Mary said, "at least some parts of it, but I need to go home. I've got a rummage sale to put on."

"I've got a police department to run." Dan headed out the door, suitcase trailing.

I took Aunt Mary by the arm, looked back and smiled. "I've got a real estate career to get back on track." I looked back at Elizabeth, who stood, still holding Petal. I smiled. "And I've got a cat to feed." We went out the door.

KATHLEEN DELANEY HAS written four previous Ellen McKenzie Real Estate mysteries, but has never before transported her characters out of California. A number of years ago she visited Colonial Williamsburg and fell in love. Long fascinated with our country's history, especially the formation years, she knew she wanted to set a story there. Another trip with her brother and sister-in-law solidified the idea that had been rolling around in her head but she needed more information. A phone call to the nice people at Colonial Williamsburg provided her with appointments to visit the kitchen at the Payton Randolph house, where she got her first lesson in hearth cooking and a meeting with the people who manage the almost extinct animal breeds the foundation is working to preserve. A number of books purchased at the wonderful bookstore at the visitor's center gave her the additional information she needed and the story that was to become *Murder by Syllabub* came into being.

Kathleen lived most of her life in California but now resides in Georgia. She is close to many historical sites, which she has eagerly visited, not only as research for this book but